Mike ☑ **W9-APJ-455**

SELDOM HAS ANY NOVEL PRODUCED SUCH TREMENDOUS EXCITEMENT EVERYWHERE!

Overwhelming Praise for the

"Compulsively readable . . . As forcefully as any novel one can think of, this novel conveys the cynicism, the terror, and the appetite for new experiences that have marked recent years."
— *The New Yorker*

"A stunning exploration of what America has become in the 1970s . . . The ages-old chase plot is magic in Stone's hands."
— *Minneapolis Tribune*

"Powerful, literally chilling . . . The pusher, Ray Hicks, reminds one, all at once, of a Raymond Chandler private eye, Faulkner's Joe Christmas, and the movies' Billy Jack."
— *St. Louis Post Dispatch*

"A thriller I couldn't put down. I devoured chapter after chapter on a non-stop trip!"
— playwright and novelist Jack Gelber

Most Exciting Novel of the Year

Also by Robert Stone on the Ballantine Books list:

A HALL OF MIRRORS

available at your local bookstore

Robert Stone

DOG SOLDIERS

A Novel

BALLANTINE BOOKS • NEW YORK

BALLANTINE BOOKS
A Division of Random House, Inc.
201 East 50th Street, New York, N.Y. 10022
Simultaneously published by
Ballantine Books, Ltd., Toronto, Canada

TO THE
COMMITTEE OF RESPONSIBILITY

I've seen the devil of violence and the devil of greed and the devil of hot desire; but, by all the stars! these were strong, lusty, red-eyed devils that swayed and drove men — men, I tell you. But as I stood on that hillside, I foresaw that in the blinding sunshine of that land, I would become acquainted with a flabby, pretending weak-eyed devil of a rapacious and pitiless folly.

CONRAD, *Heart of Darkness*

DOG
SOLDIERS

THERE WAS ONLY ONE BENCH IN THE SHADE AND Converse went for it, although it was already occupied. He inspected the stone surface for unpleasant substances, found none, and sat down. Beside him he placed the over-sized briefcase he had been carrying; its handle shone with the sweat of his palm. He sat facing Tu Do Street, resting one hand across the case and raising the other to his forehead to check the progress of his fever. It was Converse's nature to worry about his health.

The other occupant of the bench was an American lady of middling age.

It was siesta hour and there was no one else in the park. The children who usually played soccer on the lawns were across the street, sleeping in the shade of their mothers' street stalls. The Tu Do hustlers had withdrawn into the arcade of Eden Passage where they lounged sleepy-eyed, rousing themselves now and then to hiss after the passing of a sweating American. It was three o'clock and the sky was almost cloudless. The rain was late. There was no wind and the palm crowns and poinciana blossoms of the park trees hung motionless.

Converse glanced secretly at the lady beside him. She was wearing a green print dress and a canvas hat with a sun visor. She had offered him a weary smile upon his sitting down; he wondered if there would be compatrial conversation. Her face was as smooth as a young girl's but gray and colorless so that it was difficult to tell whether she was youthfully preserved or prematurely aged. Her waxen coloring was like an opium smoker's but she did not seem at all the sort. She was reading *The Citadel* by A. J. Cronin.

The lady looked up suddenly from her book, surprising Converse in mid-appraisal. She was certainly not an opium smoker. Her eyes were clear and warm brown. Converse, whose tastes were eccentric, found her attractive.

"Well," he said in his hearty, imitation-Army accent, "we'll have some weather pretty soon."

Out of politeness, she looked at the sky.

"It's certainly going to rain," she assured him. "But not for a while."

"Guess not," Converse said thoughtfully. When he looked away, she returned to her book.

Converse had come to the park to catch the cool breeze that always came before the rain and to read his mail. He was killing time before his appointment, trying to steady his nerve. He did not wish to appear on the *terrasse* of the Continental at such an early hour.

He took a small stack of letters from his case and looked them over. There was one from a Dutch underground paper which published in English, asking him for a Saigon piece. There were two checks, one from his father-in-law and one from a newspaper in Ireland. There was also a letter from his wife in Berkeley. He took a handkerchief from his shirt pocket, wiped the sweat from his eyes, and began to read.

2

"Well, I went to New York after all," his wife had written, "spent nineteen days there. Took Janey with me and she wasn't really much trouble. I'm back at the theater now in time for a brand new beaver special which is the most depressing flick this place has put on yet. Everybody here says hello and take care of yourself.

"New York was pretty scary. Forty-second Street is incredible now. It makes Three Street feel nice and homely. You'll find it a lot less pleasant the next time you go buy a hot dog at that place on Broadway you used to go to. I went there out of spite anyway—shit like that doesn't bother me as much as it does you. Also I rode on the subway which I bet you wouldn't do.

"Took Janey up to Croton for a visit with Uncle Jay and his Hudson River Bolsheviks. We went to a National Guardian party and that really took me back, with all the folk singers and the tame spades. We ate somebody's idea of Mex food and there were mariachis from the Puerto Rican Alps and people telling stories about how Sequeiros was their buddy. No spicy stories for you this time because I didn't make it with anybody. If Gallagher was there I might have made it with him but he wasn't. Everybody's pissed at him up there."

Looking up, Converse saw a street photographer in a Hawaiian shirt advancing toward his bench. He put up his hand in a gesture of refusal and the man turned back toward Eden Passage. The Tu Do Street cowboys had come out from wherever they spent their siestas and were revving up their Hondas. There was still no breeze.

Converse read on:

"The heaviest thing that happened while we were in New York was we went to a parade which was for the War. Three of us—me, looking relatively straight, and Don and Cathy looking modified freaky. We weren't too well received. You had to see that

3

action to believe it. There were eight million flags and round little Polish priests goose-stepping around with their Boy Bugle Corps, Ukrainians with sabers and fur hats, German Veterans of the Warsaw Ghetto Battle, the Brotherhood of Former Concentration Camp Guards, the Sons of Mussolini, the Baboons Union. Incredible. My flash was that these people are freakier than we ever could be. One tends to think of them as straight but when you see them they're unreal. I had this snoutface meatyard accost me—'The rats are coming out of their holes,' he said. I told him, 'Listen mother, my husband is in Vietnam.' "

Converse looked up from the letter again and found himself staring vacantly at the lady beside him.

The lady smiled.

"Letter from home?"

"Yes," Converse said.

"When I was up in Croton, Jay asked me if I knew what was going on. With *everything*. He said he didn't understand anything that was going on at all. He said maybe he should take drugs. Sarcastically. I told him he was damn right he should. He said that drugs condition the intellect to fascism and came on about C. Manson and said he would rather die than surrender his intellect. He also said he didn't need dope which is a laugh because if there was ever one man who needed it *bad* its him. I told him that if he'd turned on he'd never have been a Stalinist. He brings out the sadist in me. Which is weird because he's really such a nice man. Our argument reminded me of when I was a kid me and Dodie were walking with him when we passed an integrated black and white couple. Jay dug the shit out of that naturally because it was so progressive, and he wants to show us kids. 'Isn't that nice?' he says. Dodie, who couldn't have been more than ten, says 'I think it's disgusting.' Dodie could always play him like a pinball machine."

Converse folded the letter and looked at his watch. The lady beside him had set down her A. J. Cronin.

4

"Everything fine with your folks?"

"Oh yes," Converse said, "fine. Family visits and things."

"It's easier for you fellas to do your jobs when you know everything's all right back home."

"I find that's true," Converse said.

"You're not with AID, are you?"

"No." He sought for a word. "Bao chi."

Bao chi was what the Vietnamese call journalists. Converse was a journalist of sorts.

"Oh yes," the lady said. "Been here long?"

"Eighteen months. And you. Have you been here long?"

"Fourteen years."

Converse was unable to conceal his horror.

There were faded freckles in the gray skin under the lady's eyes. She seemed to be laughing at him.

"Don't you like this country?"

"Yes," Converse answered truthfully. "I do."

"Where I make my home," she told Converse, "it's not nearly so hot as it is here. We've got pine trees. People say it's like northern California, but I've never been there."

"That must be up around Kontum."

"South of there. Ngoc Linh Province."

Converse had never been to Ngoc Linh Province; he knew very few people who had. He had flown over it, and from the air it looked thoroughly frightening, a deep green maze of iron-spine mountains. The clouds were full of rocks. No one went there, not even to bomb it, since the Green Berets had left.

"We call it God's country," the lady said. "It's sort of a joke."

"Aha." Converse wondered if all the flesh of her body were the same dingy gray as the skin of her face and if there were any more faded freckles in it. "What do you do up there?"

"Well," the lady said, "there are five different

5

languages spoken by tribespeople up around us. We've
been doing language studies."

Converse looked into her mild eyes.

Of course.

"You're a missionary."

"We don't call ourselves that way. I suppose some
people would."

He nodded in sympathy. They never like the term.
It suggested imperialism and being eaten.

"It must be . . ." Converse tried to think of what
it must be . . . "very satisfying."

"We're never satisfied," the lady said gaily. "We
always want to do more. I think our work's been
blessed though we've certainly had our trials."

"That's part of it, isn't it?"

"Yes," the lady said, "it's all part of it."

"I've been to northern California," Converse told
her, "but I've never been to Ngoc Linh."

"Some people don't like it there. We always loved
it. I've only been away for a day and I'm already
missing it so."

"Going to the States?"

"Yes," she said. "For only three weeks. It'll be
my first time back."

Her smile was mild but resolute.

"My husband was back last year, just before he
was taken from us. He said it was all so odd. He
said people wore wide colorful neckties."

"A lot of people do," Converse said. Taken?
"Especially in the big cities."

He had begun to sense a formidable strength in
the lady's bearing. She was quite literally keeping
her chin up. Softness in her eyes, but what depths?
What prairie fires?

"In what sense," he asked, "was your husband
taken?"

"In the sense that he's dead." Clear-voiced, clear-
eyed. "They'd left us pretty much alone. One night
they came into our village and took Bill and a fine

young fella named Jim Hatley and just tied their hands and took them away and killed them."

"God. I'm sorry."

Converse recalled a story he had been told about Ngoc Linh Province. They had come into a montagnard hootch one night and taken a missionary out and tied him up in a mountain shelter. To his head they fixed a cage in which a rat had been imprisoned. As the rat starved, it began to eat its way into the missionary's brains.

"He was a happy man all his life. No matter how great your loss is, you have to accept God's will with adoration."

"God in the whirlwind," Converse said.

She looked at him blankly for a moment, puzzled. Then her eyes came alight.

"Land, yes," she said. "God in the whirlwind. Job Thirty-seven. You know your Bible."

"Not really," Converse said.

"Time's short." The languor was leaving her voice and manner, but for all the rising animation no color came into her face. "We're in the last days now. If you do know your Bible, you'll realize that all the signs in Revelations have been fulfilled. The rise of Communism, the return of Israel . . ."

"I guess it looks like that sometimes." He felt eager to please her.

"It's now or never," she said. "That's why I hate to give up three weeks, even to Bill's parents. God's promised us deliverance from evil if we believe in His gospel. He wants us all to know His word."

Converse discovered that he had moved toward her on the bench. A small rush of admiration, desire, and apocalyptic religion was subverting his common sense. He felt at the point of inviting her . . . inviting her for what? A gin and tonic? A joint? It must be partly the fever too, he thought, raising a hand to his forehead.

"Deliverance from evil would be nice."

7

It seemed to Converse that she was leaning toward him.

"Yes," she said smiling, "it certainly would. And we have God's promise."

Converse took his handkerchief out and cleared his eyes again.

"What sort of religion do they have up in Ngoc Linh? The tribespeople, I mean."

She seemed angry.

"It's not a religion," she said. "They worship Satan."

Converse smiled and shook his head.

"You don't believe in Satan?" She did not seem surprised.

Converse, still eager to please, thought about it.

"No."

"It's always surprised me," she said softly, "things being what they are and all, that people find it so difficult to believe in Satan."

"I suppose," Converse said, "that people would rather not. I mean it's so awful. It's too spooky for people."

"People are in for an unpleasant surprise." She said it without spite as though she were really sorry.

A breeze came from the river carrying the smell of rain, stirring the fronds and blossoms and the dead air. Converse and the lady beside him relaxed and received the wind like a cooling drink. Monsoon clouds closed off the sky. Converse looked at his watch and stood up.

"I've enjoyed talking to you," he said. "I've got to move on now."

The lady looked up at him, holding him with her will.

"God has told us," she said evenly, "that if we believe in Him we can have life eternal."

He felt himself shiver. His fever was a bit alarming. He was also aware of a throbbing under his right rib. There was a lot of hepatitis around. Several of his friends had come down with it.

"I wonder," he said, clearing his throat, "if you'll be in town tomorrow would you care to join me for dinner?"

Her astonishment was a bit unsettling. It would have been better, he considered, if she had blushed. Probably she couldn't blush. Circulation.

"It's tonight I'm leaving. And I really don't think I'd be the sort of company you'd enjoy. I suppose you must be very lonely. But I think I'm really a lot older than you are."

Converse blinked. A spark from the Wrath.

"It would be interesting, don't you think?"

"We don't need interesting things," the lady said. "That's not what we need."

"Nice trip," Converse said, and turned toward the street. Two moneychangers came out of Eden Passage and moved toward him. The lady was standing up. He saw her gesture with her hand toward the moneychangers and the arcade and the *terrasse* of the Continental Hotel. It was a Vietnamese gesture.

"Satan," she called to him, "is very powerful here."

"Yes," Converse said. "He would be."

He walked past the moneychangers and on to the oily sidewalk of Tu Do Street. Afternoon swarms of Hondas crowded in the narrow roadway, manned by ARVNs in red berets, mascaraed bar girls, saffron-robed monks, priests in stiff black soutanes. The early apéritif crowd was arriving on the *terrasse;* an ancient refugee woman displayed her cretinous son across the potted shrubbery to a party of red-necked contractors at a table overlooking the street.

Across the square from the *terrasse* was a statue of two Vietnamese soldiers in combat stance which, from the positioning of the principal figures, was locally known as the National Buggery Monument. The Na-

9

tional Buggery Monument, as Converse passed it, was surrounded by gray-uniformed National Police- men who were setting up barricades on a line between the statue and the National Assembly building beside it. They were expecting a demonstration. They had been expecting one for weeks.

Converse walked the several blocks to Pasteur Street and hailed a taxi, taking care not to signal with the Offending Gesture. As he was compressing himself into the ovenlike space of the little Citroën, the rain broke.

"Nguyen Thong," he told the driver.

The monsoon battered them as they drove in the direction of Tansonhut; the rain darkened the ocher walls of the peeling villas and glistened on the bolls of barbed wire along the curbs. The Arvin sentries in front of the politicians' houses ducked into their tarpaulin shelters.

It was a drive of about fifteen minutes to Nguyen Thong, and by the time they pulled up to the end of the alley where Charmian lived, the potholes were filled to overflowing.

Blinded by rain, Converse waded through the ruts until he stood struggling with the latch on Charmian's gate. When he was inside he saw her sitting on the verandah watching him. The bleached white jellaba she wore, with her straight blond hair hanging back over the cowl, made her look like a figure of ceremony, as though she were there to be sacrificed or baptized. He was glad to see her smiling. When he came onto the porch, she stood up from her wicker chair and kissed him on the cheek. She had come from the shower; her body smelled of scented Chinese soap.

"Hi," Converse said. "The man been here?"

"Sure enough," she said. She led him into the enor- mous room where she slept and which she had filled with Buddhas and temple hangings and brass ani- mals bought in Phnom Penh. Her house was half of a villa which had been owned by a French brewer in colonial days. She was always finding old family photographs and novena cards in odd corners of the place.

"The man been," she said. She lit a joss stick, waved it about and set it down in an ashtray. They could hear her washing lady singing along with the radio in the wash house across the back garden.

"You're high," Converse said.

"Just had a little hash with Tho. Want some?"

Converse shook his head.

"Weird time to get high."

"John," Charmian said, "you're the world's most frightened man. I don't know how you live with yourself."

She had walked to a metal cabinet against one wall and was kneeling down to open a combination lock on the bottom drawer. When the drawer was open she took out a large square package wrapped in newspaper and held it out for him. The newspaper in which it was wrapped was the liberal Catholic one, identifiable by the strips of blank column which it carried to chafe the censors.

"How's this for terrifying?"

She set it down on a desk beside the smoldering joss stick and folded back the newspaper. There were two snow white cotton ditty bags inside with their tie strings done in dainty bows. Each was lined with several layers of black plastic U.S. Government burn bag and the plastic sealed with masking tape. Charmian peeled away the tape to show Converse that the bags were filled with heroin.

"Look at it down there," she said, "burning with an evil glow."

Converse looked at the heroin.

"It's all caked."

"So what? It's the dampness."

He gently put his finger into the powder and worked a tiny amount onto the nail.

11

"Now let's see if it's really shit," he said, sniffing at it.

She watched him amused.

"Don't think you won't get off on that. This is nearly pure scag. Can you imagine?"

She was standing on tiptoe with her hands tucked into the folds of her white jellaba. Converse rubbed his nose and looked at her.

"I hope you're not doing this crap."

"My opiate," Charmian said, "is opium. But I've been known to take a little Sunday sniff now and then same as anybody. Same as you."

"Not me," Converse said. "No more Sunday sniffs."

It seemed to him that he was able to feel a faint cold easing down from his sinuses, cooling the fever, numbing his fear. He sat down on a cushion and wiped the sweat from his eyes.

"Scag isn't me," Charmian said.

Charmian's daddy was a judge in north Florida. A few years earlier she had been secretary and dear friend to a one-man ant army named Irvine Vibert, who had come crashing out of the Louisiana canebrake one morning—young, smarter than hell, and insane with greed. The newspapers described him as an influence peddler, sometimes as a "wheeler-dealer." He had had many friends in government and all of his friends were nice to Charmian. They went on being nice to her after the inevitable scandal broke, and even after Vibert's death in a curious flying accident. The farther away she kept from Washington, the nicer they were. For a while Charmian had worked for the United States Information Agency, now she was the nominal correspondent of an Atlanta-based broadcasting syndicate. She liked Saigon. It was a bit like Washington. People were nice.

Converse was suddenly aware that he had stopped sweating. He swallowed, mastering a small spasm of nausea.

"Christ, it's merry little shit."

"Tho says it's fantastic."

"How the hell would he know?"

Charmian retaped the bags and wrapped them up. Struggling a bit, she lifted the package and handed it over to Converse. He took it, supporting its weight with his forearms. It felt absurdly heavy. Three kilos.

"You're gonna have to balance your weight right when you walk with that in the bag. Otherwise you're gonna look comical."

Converse put the package in the briefcase and zipped it up.

"You weigh it?"

She went into the kitchen and took a bottle of purified water out of the refrigerator.

" 'Course I weighed it. Anyway, you don't get burned with scag by getting short weight. You get it cut on you."

"And this isn't?"

"Uh-uh. No way. Like I know a lot more about scag than Tho does and he'd be scared to burn me first time out. I own a hydrometer."

Converse eased back on the cushion and rested his elbows on the tile floor, facing the whitewashed ceiling.

"Jesus," he said.

"That'll learn you, messing with the pure. Don't get sick on my cushion."

Converse sat up.

"Your friends can pick up from my wife on the twentieth in Berkeley. She'll be home all day. If she's not there, have them call the theater where she works. It's called the Odeon—in the city off Mission. She'll have a message for them."

"She better be around."

"We already talked about that."

"Maybe there's a side to her character you don't know about."

"In all modesty," Converse said, "there isn't."

"She must be a pretty good kid. You ought to spend more time with her."

Charmian sat down beside him on the cushion and rubbed at a mosquito bite over her Achilles' tendon.

"Maybe she's keeping bad company in your absence. Maybe she's hanging around with some far-out hippies or something who might encourage her to weirdness."

"If you don't trust us," Converse said, "pay me off and move it through somebody else."

She closed her eyes.

"I'm sorry, John. I can't stop doin' it."

"I understand. I think it's very professional of you. But stop anyway."

"Damn," she said, "I'd hate to make my living this way."

Charmian poured them out two glasses of the cold bottled water.

"How much do you think your friends in the States will make?" Converse asked her.

"Depends on how much they cut it. It's so good they can cut it down to ten percent. They could make a couple of hundred thou."

"Who are they? I mean what sort of people are they?"

"Not the sort you might think."

She stood up and shook the hood of her robe to free her hair.

"What they make is no concern of mine. I don't want their trouble."

"No," Converse said. She was watching him with country caution; her eyes held a measure of contempt, a measure of suspicion.

"What are you gonna do with your money, John? Such a dedicated nonswinger as you are."

"I don't know," Converse said.

She laughed at him. Her laughter was something soft and satisfying, good to hear.

14

"Shit, you *don't* know, do you? You know you want it though, don't you?"

"I desire to serve God," Converse said, laughing himself. "And to grow rich, like all men." His laughter felt a little too loose in the jaw to suit him.

"Who said that? Some great hustler of the past?"

"I'm not sure," Converse said. "I think it was Cortez. Maybe it was Pizarro."

"Sounds a little like Irvine," Charmian said.

She poured out more water and they went outside on the verandah to drink it. The rain slackened for a few moments, then came harder. It was a savage, not a sustaining rain. The bright fleshy plants in the garden folded to endure it.

"How's my Colonel Tho?" Converse asked.

"Pretty mellow today. He's got another big deal set up. He's dealing cinnamon now. Hey, you know a lot about tape recorders?"

"No," Converse said. "Why?"

"Tho wants me to tell him what the best kind of tape recorder is. That's his big thing now. He's gonna find out what all the best things in the world are and he wants one of each."

Two old women in *ao dais* ran delicately over the mud beyond the gate, sharing a single white umbrella.

"What do you think he wants to tape?" Converse asked.

"Who the hell knows? Me, I guess."

"I'm glad somebody around here knows what they want."

"Well, Tho knows all right. Then there's Victor Charles. Victor Charles knows."

"Maybe," Converse said.

"Absolutely," Charmian said firmly. She had a respect bordering on reverence for the Viet Cong and she did not like to hear their sense of purpose questioned. "Like even Tho is kind of an idealist. He used to be a very gung ho soldier at one time."

She leaned back in her chair and stretched out her long tanned legs to rest the backs of her ankles on the porch railing.

"He's always saying how all the graft and double-dealing pisses him off. He told me once that what this country needs is a Hitler."

"The Vietnamese have a terrific sense of humor," Converse said. "That's what keeps them going."

"He says that if somebody gave him a chance he'd like to serve his country like he was trained to do. He figures we corrupted him."

"Tho always says idiotic things when he talks to Americans. He's trying to make himself agreeable."

Charmian shrugged. "People can be corrupted."

Converse got out of his chair and went back inside the house. Charmian followed him in. He picked up the briefcase and measured its weight.

"Just don't get taken off," Charmian said.

He opened the case, took out his plastic anorak and got into it.

"I'm going. I'm having dinner with the Percys and I've got to get a flight down south for tomorrow."

"Tell them hello. And don't look so damn scared." She came up to him as he stood in the doorway and affected to smooth the wrinkles on his plastic raincoat. "When we get this cleared we'll get a bunch of us together and fly over to Phnom Penh and get stoned and have a massage."

"That'll be nice," Converse said. He had not been to bed with her for months. The last time had been after his return from Cambodia; bad things had happened there and he had not had it together.

He saw to it that she did not kiss him goodbye. Walking up the alley to Nguyen Thong, he flexed his free arm to keep his back straight against the weight of the briefcase. So as not to look comical.

Because of the rain, it was a long time before he found a taxi.

16

"Every day in this place," Sergeant Janeway said, "we entertain the weird, the strange, the unusual."

They were sitting in the refrigerated offices of JUSPAO, the public affairs office. The walls were government gray; there were no windows. The briefcase rested beside Converse's chair; rainwater ran from it onto the plastic tiles like an incriminating effusion. Like blood.

"If I had anything to say," the sergeant went on, "we'd really tighten up our accreditation procedure. We've got people around here with bao chi cards who are currency crooks, dope smugglers, God knows what. We've got hippies coming in from Katmandu who depend on Mac-V for their next meal. Sometimes I feel like a social worker."

Sergeant Janeway was the most articulate enlisted man in the American Armed Forces and was thus regarded locally as a sort of *idiot savant*. He enjoyed the familiarity and condescension of the international press corps's celebrities and was able to display toward them an ingratiating manner of extraordinary range. According to the taste of his interlocutor, he could project any manner of deference from the austere courtesy of a samurai to the prole-servility of an antique Cunard cabin steward. To the notables and the men of affairs, Sergeant Janeway was a picturesque menial at the vestibule of inside dope. Converse's relations with him were rather different. From Converse's point of view, Sergeant Janeway was in charge of the war.

"I don't understand what you want down in My Lat. Nothing's happening down there."

"I happen to think there's a story in the civilians," Converse said. "The merchant seamen and so forth."

Sergeant Janeway sat on a corner of his desk, drumming on a wicker basket with a rolled-up copy of *The Nation*. His haircut, Converse thought, appeared to be the work of a theatrical barber shop.

"Sounds pretty dull to me," the sergeant said. "But of course I'm not a journalist. Which one of your many employers do you think would go for that?"

"All of them, I hope," Converse said. "Anyway, it's none of your business. You're not a journalist and you're not a critic."

Sergeant Janeway smiled.

"Know how I think of you, Mr. Converse, sir? With all due respect? As a letterhead. Perhaps you're making a valuable contribution to an informed public, but I don't see any evidence of that."

"I had a piece in the *Irish Messenger* two weeks ago. If you want to find out what we're up to, get your clipping service on the stick."

He reached out and brought the briefcase a little closer to his chair.

"I'm accredited to this command. My card is as good as *Time*'s and I'm entitled to the same courtesy."

Sergeant Janeway picked up his telephone.

"I'm sorry you're not satisfied with us," the sergeant said. "Personally I'm not too satisfied with you. Since there's all this dissatisfaction, maybe you and I should talk to the colonel about your accreditation."

But the sergeant was not calling the colonel. He was calling Operations to get Converse on the morning run to My Lat. When he had booked the hop, he reminded Converse to renew his membership in the officers' club.

"They say the beach down there is very nice. I'm sure you'll have a terrific time. You better bring some malaria pills though."

"Christ," Converse said. He had forgotten to sign for them at Tansonhut. He looked at his watch; it was after four. The sick bays would be closed for the weekend and the duty corpsman would not issue pills without authorization from MACV.

Sergeant Janeway looked concerned. "I bet you went and forgot." Sergeant Janeway kept a supply of the pills in his office to dispense as a courtesy to his celebrated clients.

"You better get some somewhere," he told Converse. "They have all the nasty strains down there."

As it grew dark, there was a time of small rain, a sprinkle between the afternoon's and the night's downpour. Converse carried the briefcase through the hurrying evening crowds on Le Loi, walking as casually as he could. The weight of the case was causing him to sweat even more immoderately than usual and his shoulder ached from his effort to adjust his posture.

It was a city of close watchers. The hustlers sat in their open-fronted cafés checking him out, eyeing the briefcase. They did not bother to approach him now; his face had become familiar downtown. His cheap Japanese watch was known throughout the city and shoeshine boys unable to distinguish between round-eyed faces recognized him by its shiny tin band. It was Number Ten. Its lack of distinction sometimes caused him to be insulted in the street, but no one ever tried to grab it.

The watch was his talisman against street snatchers. In all the time he had been in Saigon he had been street-snatched only once, although he knew people who were street-snatched as often as twice a week. Almost a year before, he had lost a briefcase to a Korean in a passing jeep, and the Korean had thereby acquired the collected works of Saint-Exupéry and a Zap comic. In Converse's view, the idea of a Korean soldier reading a Zap comic was worth the loss of the case.

Opposite the flower market he stepped into the maniacal Le Loi traffic, attempting languor and unconcern. It was necessary to appear as though innate good fortune made one invulnerable. History had made the Saigonnais great believers in luck. Unlucky-looking people made them uneasy and even tempted some to assume the role of misfortune. It was as bad as looking comical.

On the far side of the street, a cyclo driver and an Army Spec One were engaged in some dispute. The Spec One was rubbing his thumb and forefinger together under the cyclo driver's nose and cursing in Italian. The driver, eyes rolling, was demonstrating *t'ai chi* strokes, weaving and dancing on the pavement. He was a great success with the crowd. People laughed and applauded. The ejercise he was performing in pantomime was the one called Repelling the Monkey.

The Hotel Coligny, where Converse lived, was just off the flower market, which enabled the more life-affirming of its guests to rush downstairs each morning and buy poinciana boughs and fresh roses to adorn their rooms. A Dutch correspondent in the room adjoining Converse's did so regularly. The Dutchman was a stoned head, and so fond of flowers that he had once taken to wearing marigold chains in his long golden hair. One day some street cowboys threw an uncharged hand grenade at him for a joke. The flowers had made him look unlucky.

As Converse entered the small dark lobby, Madame Colletti, the *patronesse,* who was a young and exquisitely beautiful Vietnamese lady, regarded him with suspicion and loathing. She regarded everyone that way.

Converse naturally preferred to deal with Monsieur, but he did not take Madame's attitude personally. Sauntering past the desk, he threw her a snappy *"Bon soir."* The Sisters had taught Madame Colletti to abhor those who abused the language of clarity. She stared at him with an incomprehension that bordered on horror.

"Bon soir," she said, as though his mouthings were human speech.

Converse rented a tin safe from the Collettis in which he kept his cheeks, notes, and such things as

Zap comics and the works of Saint-Exupéry. Acutely aware of the *patronesse's* close attention, he stuffed the briefcase inside. There were merchant adventurers in Saigon who paid the Indian currency sharks to hold their contraband in strongboxes that were as secure as anything there could be. But Converse was frightened of Indian currency sharks; he had decided to risk the tin safe. The briefcase was an awkward fit, but it went in.

When he turned round, Madame was staring at the closed door of the safe. He went past her into the small bar that adjoined the lobby; she followed to sell him a bottle of pilfered PX Sprite from the pilfered PX cooler.

"Beaucoup de travail demain," Converse said, attempting to convey zestful satisfaction in his profession.

Madame Colletti grimaced.

She never used the same expression twice, Converse thought. Conversation with her was a series of small unpleasant surprises.

Early in the spring, Converse had been away in the Delta, and Madame had rented Room Number Sixteen in his absence. The man who had taken it apparently had a thing about squashing lizards. Converse returned to find nearly a dozen of them mashed into the walls and the tiles of the floor. He had found it disturbing. Like most people he was rather fond of house lizards. They ate insects and were fun to watch when one was high.

The management had made a few gestures toward effacing the traces of carnage but there were still stains and remnants of tiny dinosaur skeleton. Murder haunted the room.

Whoever he was, he had spent hours stomping around his soiled gray hotel room wasting lizards with the framed tintype of Our Lady of Lourdes that stood on the night table.

Converse sat at his writing desk, drinking Sprite,

looking at the lizard smears. It was just as well not to wonder why. There was never any satisfaction in that. Perhaps the man had thought they would bite him. Or perhaps they had kept him awake nights, whispering together. The man had also diligently crushed all his used batteries so that the hotel flunkies couldn't recycle them through Thieves' Market.

An extrovert.

On the desk beside him was a thermos bottle filled with cold water. It was supposed to be bottled water, but Converse knew for a fact that the porter filled it from the tap. Every day he poured it into the shower drain. Every day the porter refilled it. From the tap. Every day Converse felt guiltier about not drinking it.

That was the liberal sensibility for you, he thought. It began to give in the face of such persistence. One day, perhaps, he would feel thoroughly obliged to drink it.

The thermos was somewhat original, an actual Vietnamese artifact, and Converse planned to take it with him when he left. Printed across it in bright colors was the picture of a wide-winged bat; on the bat's breast was the brand name—LUCKY.

He stood up and went across the cement air shaft to the bathroom, carrying the thermos with him. When he had locked the door, he turned on the cold shower and poured the contents of the thermos into the drain.

Fuck it, he thought, why me?

There were plenty of other Americans around.

CONVERSE WAS, BY PROFESSION, AN AUTHOR. TEN years before he had written a play about the Marine Corps which had been performed and admired. Since the production of his play, the only professional good fortune attending him had been the result of his marriage to the daughter of an editor and publisher.

Elmer Bender, Converse's father-in-law, edited and published imitations of other magazines. The name of each Bender publication was designed to give its preoccupied and overstimulated purchasers the impression that they were buying the more popular magazine it imitated. If there were, for example, a magazine called *Collier's,* Elmer would edit and publish a magazine called *Shmollier's.*

"Mine are better," Elmer would say. He was a veteran of *New Masses* and the Abraham Lincoln Brigade.

For seven years of his marriage to Marge, Elmer had employed Converse as principal writer on *Nightbeat,* which his lawyers described as A Weekly Tabloid With a Heavy Emphasis on Sex. He supervised a staff of two—Douglas Dalton, who was an elderly newspaper alcoholic with beautiful manners, and a Chinese Communist named Mike Woo, who had once attempted an explication of the theory of surplus value in the weekly horoscope. "Don't be afraid to ask for a raise, Sagittarius. Your boss always pays you *less* than your work is *actually worth!"*

Five days each week, Converse peopled the nation with spanking judges and Lesbian motorcyclists.

At the turning of the seventh year, he had written a memory lane story about the late Porfirio Rubirosa entitled "Rubirosa Was a Fizzle in My Bed," under the byline of Carmen Guittarez. In it, he had assumed the identity of a Sexy Latin Showgirl disappointed in the climax of her assignation with the World Famed Playboy and Bon Vivant. The story had led Converse to a Schizophrenic Episode.

For several days he had gone about imagining that a band of Bored and Corrupt Socialites might descend on his home in Berkeley, and in the name of their beloved Rubi, Wreak a Bizarre Revenge.

His difficulties with reality increased.

After a night of sinister racked sleep, he had gone to Elmer and enlisted his cooperation in securing press accreditation as a marginal correspondent in Saigon.

Bender had reluctantly agreed. It seemed to him that if Marge and Converse endured a period of separation, their union might regain some of its edge. Marge's mother had been a left-wing Irish vegetarian, a suicide with her lover during the McCarthy days. It was often observed that Marge was very like her.

Converse suggested that something worthwhile might emerge from such an expedition, that there might be a book or a play. The argument particularly moved Elmer, who was an author in his own right—one of his early stories had earned him a passionate letter of appreciation from Whittaker Chambers. Marge, who loved all that was fateful, had sullenly agreed.

He flew out of Oakland on the morning after their daughter's second birthday. In Saigon, Converse was able to extend his employment by taking over the positions of departing stringers and hustling a few of his own. And surely enough, the difficulties he had been experiencing with reality were in time obviated. One bright afternoon, near a place called Krek, Converse had watched with astonishment as the world of things transformed itself into a single overwhelming act of murder. In a manner of speaking, he had discovered himself. Himself was a soft shell-less quivering thing encased in a hundred and sixty pounds of pink

24

sweating meat. It was real enough. It tried to burrow into the earth. It wept.

After his exercise in reality, Converse had fallen in with Charmian and the dope people; he became one of the Constantly Stoned. Charmian was utterly without affect, cool and full of plans. She had taken leave of life in a way which he found irresistible.

When, after a little fencing, she had put the plan to him, he had found that between his own desperate emptiness and her fascination for him, he was unable to refuse. She had contacts in the States, a few thousand to invest, and access to Colonel Tho, whose heroin refinery was the fourth largest building in Saigon. He had fifteen thousand dollars in a Berkeley bank, the remnants of a sum he had received for an unproduced film version of his play. Ten thousand dollars, it developed, would buy him a three-quarters share on three kilos of the Colonel's Own Mixture and his share of the stateside sale would be forty thousand. There would be no risk of misunderstanding because everybody was friends. Marge, as he foresaw, had gone along. The thing had come together.

His own reasons changed, it seemed, by the hour. Money in large amounts had never been particularly important to him. But he had been in the country for eighteen months and for all the discoveries it had become apparent that there would be no book, no play. It seemed necessary that there be something.

Showered, under the ceiling fan in his room at the Coligny, Converse woke to the telephone. Jill Percy was on the line to say that she and her husband would meet him in the Crazy Horse, a girlie bar off Tu Do Street.

Jill was becoming an international social worker and she had conceived a professional interest in girlie bars. She was always trying to get people to take her to them.

Converse dressed, pulled on his plastic anorak and went down to the street. It had started to rain again.

As he walked toward Tu Do, he sifted through his pockets to find twenty piasters.

Halfway up the street, midway between the market and Tu Do, there was always a legless man squatting in a doorway. Each time Converse passed, he would drop twenty piasters in the man's upturned pith helmet. He had been doing so for more than a year, so that whenever the man saw Converse approach he would smile. It was as though they were friends. Often, Converse was tormented by an impulse to withhold the twenty piasters to see what sort of a reaction there would be, but he had never had the courage.

Having dropped the twenty P and exchanged smiles with his friend, Converse sauntered down Tu Do to the Crazy Horse. The Crazy Horse was one of the Tu Do bars in which, according to rumor, the knowledgeable patron might be served a bracing measure of heroin with—some even said in—his beer. As a result it was usually off limits, and on this evening Converse was the only customer. Facing him across the bar were fifteen uniformly beautiful Vietnamese girls in heavy makeup. He took a stool, smiled pleasantly, and ordered a Schlitz. The girl opposite him began to deal out a hand of cards.

Beer in the Crazy Horse cost 250 piasters without heroin, and Converse was not in the mood for cards. He glanced down at the poker hand on the chrome before him as though it were a small, conventionally amusing animal, and affected to look over the girls with a worldly expression. In spite of the glacial air conditioning and his recent bath, his face was covered with sweat. The fifteen girls across the bar turned their eyes on him with identical expressions of bland, fathomless contempt.

Converse drank his beer, his sinuses aching. He felt no resentment; he was a humanist and it was their country. They were war widows or refugee country girls or serving officers of the Viet Cong. And there he was, an American with a stupid expression and pockets stuffed with green money, and there was no way they could get it off him short of turning him upside down and shaking him. It must make them want to cry, he thought. He was sympathetic.

He was searching his Vietnamese repertory for an expression of sympathy when Jill and Ian Percy arrived. Jill looked at the girls behind the bar with a wide white smile and sat down beside Converse. Ian came behind her, stooped and weary.

"Well," Jill Percy said. "This looks like fun."

A girl down the bar blew her nose and looked into her handkerchief.

"That's what we're here for," Converse said.

The Percys ordered bottles of "33" beer; it was pronounced "bami-bam" and supposedly made with formaldehyde. Ian went over to the jukebox and played "Let It Be."

"Staying through the summer?" Jill asked Converse.

"I guess so. Till the elections. Maybe longer. You?"

"We'll be around forever. Right, Ian?"

"We'll be around all right," Ian said. Some "33" beer trickled from his mouth and into his sparse sandy beard. He wiped his chin with the back of his hand. "We're waiting around until we get an explanation."

Ian Percy was an Australian agronomist. He was also an *engagé,* one of the few—other than Quakers —one saw around. He had been in the country for fifteen years—with UNRRA, with WHO, with everyone who would hire him, ending with the Vietnamese government, which had him on loan from the Australian Ministry of Agriculture. A province chief up north had gotten him fired, and he had taken accreditation with an Australian daily which was actually more of a racing form than a newspaper. As an *engagé* he hated the Viet Cong. He also hated the South Vietnamese government and its armed forces, Americans and particularly the civilians, Buddhist monks, Catholics, the Cao Dai, the French and particularly Corsicans, the foreign press corps, the Australian government, and his employers past—and, most especially—present. He was said to be fond of children, but the Pércys had none of their own. They had met in Vietnam and it was not a place in which people felt encouraged to bear children.

"Bloody lot of people leaving," Jill said. "We're getting possessive about our friends."

"Nobody wants to be the last rat," Converse said.

Ian ordered another "33" beer. He drank "33" unceasingly from about four in the afternoon until after midnight.

"Poor old last rat," Ian said. "God help him."

Jill took her beer along the bar and started a conversation in Vietnamese with a bar girl opposite her. The other girls, softened by curiosity, leaned together to listen.

"What's she saying?" Converse asked.

"She's telling them her troubles." The girls across from Jill had turned toward Ian and Converse and were nodding sympathetically. "Later she'll come back and want them to tell her their troubles. She's writing a report on Saigon bar girls."

"What for?"

"Oh, for the information of the civilized world," Ian said. "Not that the civilized world gives fuck all."

They drank in silence for a while as Jill told her troubles to the bar girls.

"One thing," Converse said, "this war is going to be well-documented. There's more information available than there is shit loose to know about."

An image came to Converse's mind of the sheets of paper onto which the computers clacked out useful information for the conduct of the war. The prettiest were the ones which analyzed the loyalties and affiliations of country villages—these were known, with curious Shakespearean undertones, as Hamlet Evaluation Reports. The thought of Hamlet Evaluation Reports made Converse hungry. Each Friday the Vietnamese used them to wrap food in.

"Let's eat," he said. "Before it rains again."

They went outside and walked down Tu Do toward the river. On the first corner they came to, the MPs had a soldier in fatigues up against the wall and were searching his many khaki pockets while a crowd of silent Saigonnais looked on. Converse bought Jill a marigold necklace from a sleepy child flower-seller on the edge of the crowd. The marigolds when they were fresh smelled wonderfully on hot nights; they reminded Converse of Charmian.

"O.K.," Jill said. "The Guillaume Tell, the Tempura House or the floating restaurant?"

The floating restaurant would be too crowded, and Ian said that the chef at the Guillaume Tell had run away because someone had threatened to chop his hands off. They took the long way to the Tempura House, walking beside the lantern-lit barges on the riverfront. Mosquitoes hurried them on and reminded Converse of his fever. As they walked, they smoked Park Lane cigarettes, factory-packaged joints with glossy filters. "33" beer was supposed to be made with formaldehyde, Park Lane cigarettes were supposed to be rolled by lepers. The grass in them was not very good by Vietnamese standards, but if you smoked a whole one you got high. Little riverfront children ran up to them, fumbling at their arms to see their watches, calling after them—*Bao chi, bao chi.*

At the Tempura House they entered merrily, wafted on fumes of Park Lane, removed their shoes and settled down among the dapper Honda salesmen. Ian ordered more "33."

"Ever see Charmian?" he asked Converse.

"I just left her. She's the same."

"Somebody told me," Jill Percy said, "that Charmian had a habit."

Converse essayed a smile.

"Bullshit," he said.

"Or else that she was dealing. I can't remember which."

"You never know what Charmian's into. But if she had a habit, I'd know about it."

"You don't see her so much now, do you?" Jill asked.

Converse shook his head.

"Charmian," Ian said, "has a friend named Tho. He's an Air Force colonel. In the cinnamon business."

"You ought to look into Tho," Jill told her husband. "He must be looming large around here if Charmian's found him."

"I don't think Tho is coup material," Converse said. "He has a very satisfied look."

The waitress, who was partly Japanese, brought them a plate of red peppers. They rinsed their flushed faces with cool towels.

"Ever hear Charmian's Washington stories?" Jill Percy asked. "She tells super Washington stories."

"Charmian belongs to a vanished era in American history," Converse said. "Not many people can claim that condition at the age of twenty-five."

"Ghosts," Ian said. "The country's full of ghosts now."

Jill Percy whisked a pepper from the dish with her chopsticks and consumed it without flinching.

"You can hardly call Charmian a ghost. There are plenty of ghosts out here but they're real ones."

"Wherever you have a lot of unhappy people dying young," Converse said, wiping his hands on the cool towel, "you'll get a lot of ghosts."

"We had a right bastard of a ghost down in our village," Ian Percy said. "One of the sort they call *Ma*. He lived under a banyan tree and he came out during siesta to frighten the kiddies."

"After the war," Converse said, "they should fly over the Ia Drang valley dropping comic books and

30

French dip sandwiches for all the GI *Ma*. It must be really a drag for them."

Ian started another beer, ignoring the food before him.

"I'm not sure you've been around here long enough," he told Converse, "to talk like that."

Converse rested his chopsticks on the side of his plate.

"The way I see it, I get to say any fucking thing I want. I had my ass on the line. I been to war." He turned to Jill, who was frowning at Ian. "Ain't I, Jill? I appeared on the field of battle."

"I was there," she said. "I saw you, sport."

"We went to war, Jill and me," Converse announced to Ian. "And what did we do, Jill?"

"We cried," Jill said.

"We cried," Converse said, "that's what we did. We wept tears of outraged human sensibility and we get to say any fucking thing we want."

Both Jill and Converse had gone to see the invasion of Cambodia, and both had had experiences which had made them cry. But Converse's tears had not been those of outraged human sensibility.

"You're an entertaining fella," Ian said. "But in general I object to your being around."

Secure behind her porcelain smile, the waitress placed bowls of fish and rice before thcm. A party of American reporters came in, followed by four Filipino rock musicians with pachuco haircuts. The Honda salesmen and their Japanese girlfriends grew merrier as the *sake* flowed.

"I mean," Ian said, "I love this country. It's not the asshole of the world to me. I grew old here, man. Now when I leave, all I'll be able to think back on is bastards like you in places like this."

"Sometimes," Jill said, "you act like you invented the country."

"They're a pack of perves," Ian said. "You're a pack of perves. Why don't you go watch some other place die? They've got corpses by the river-full in Bangla Desh. Why not go there?"

"It's dry," Converse said.

A Vietnamese soldier with dark glasses and a white cane had been led in from the street by a little boy of about eight; they moved from table to table selling copies of the Saigon *Herald*. The American reporters reclining at the table behind Converse were watching them.

"Listen," one of the reporters was saying, "he can see as well as you can. The guy uses about six different kids. He rents them in the market."

"Yeah?" another reporter said. "I think he's blind."

"He's got fresh Arvin fatigues on every day," the first reporter insisted. "You know why he's got fresh Arvin fatigues? 'Cause he's in the Arvin. And even the Arvin don't take blind people."

When the Arvin and his boy came around, Converse and Ian bought Saigon *Herald*s and set them aside without looking at them.

"I met a lady today," Converse said, "who told me that Satan was very powerful here."

"Check it out," Ian said. "Don't dismiss anything you hear out of hand."

Jill was trying to watch the American reporters unobserved.

"They'd know," she said, nodding toward their table. "We could ask them."

Converse turned to look at the reporters; they were sunburned, they had impressive Mexican mustaches, they used their chopsticks well.

"They wouldn't go for it," he said. "Satan might be hot stuff to the montagnards, but he's just another coconut monk to those guys."

They finished off the fish and rice and called for more "33." The waitress brought them some peanuts which were inhabited by tiny spiderlike insects.

"Satan?" Jill said. "What do you think she meant?"

"She was a missionary," Converse said.

The Percys ate their peanuts one by one, patiently dislodging the insects. Converse did without.

"I wonder who Tho is," Jill said after a while. "I wonder what's in it for Charmian."

"Fancy fucking," Ian said.

Converse said nothing.

"An Arvin colonel." Jill thoughtfully sucked on a peanut. "What can that be like, I wonder?"

"Exquisite," Ian said.

"Do you really think so?"

"Best fucking east of Suez," Ian assured her. "I have it on good authority."

"I have it on good authority," Jill said, "that Kuwait has the best fucking east of Suez."

"If you like Arabs. Some do, some don't."

"There's an Arab blessing," Converse informed them, " 'May the poetry of your love never turn to prose.' "

"There you are," Jill said, "Kuwait for me."

"I know a Parsee in Karachi," Converse said, "who knows the Sultan of Kuwait very well. He's a caterer. When the Sultan goes falconing my friend the Parsee supplies his every need. He could fix you up."

"Crikey," Jill said. "We'd falcon under the merciless sky. And at night while I'm asleep—into my tent he'll creep."

"Exactly," Converse said, "and you'll tickle his prostate with an ostrich feather."

Jill affected to sigh. "With a peacock's wing."

Ian had turned to watch the waitress bend over her hibachi.

"This is sheer racism," he said.

"Well," Converse said, "that's fucking. East of Suez."

The shock came up at them from under the floor; Converse experienced a moment of dreadful recognition. When the noise ended, they looked, not at each other, but toward the street and saw that the glass window was gone and that they were looking directly on the metal grill that had stood in front of it. There was food in everyone's lap.

"Incoming," Jill Percy said. Someone in the kitchen cursed shrilly, scalded.

They knelt on the tea-stained mat, trying to find their shoes. The proprietor, who was a man of mild and scholarly appearance, was forcing his way toward the door in grim fury; people had begun to leave without paying. Through the space where the window had been, Converse could see a fine layer of dry white dust settling on the wet pavement.

The street outside was strangely quiet, as though the explosion had blown a pocket of silence in the din of the city, which was now only slowly drawing in the stricken cries and the police whistles.

Converse and the Percys walked toward the river; they could see the four American reporters at the corner ahead of them. Everyone seemed to know better than to run. Halfway to the corner they passed the Arvin newspaper seller and his rented little boy; the pair of them stood motionless on the sidewalk facing the street. The Arvin still had his glasses on; the boy watched them pass without expression, still holding the Arvin's hand. On the corner itself was an old woman who held her hands pressed to her ears in the position of hearing no evil.

"The tax office," Ian said. And when they turned the next corner they saw that it had indeed been the tax office. The street before it was in ruins; a whole section of the concrete pavement was blown away to show the black earth on which the city was built. Night-lights in the nearby buildings had been blown so it was a while before they could see anything clearly. By now there were plenty of sirens.

The tax office had been a Third Republic drollery,

Babar the Elephant Colonial, and the bomb had made toothpicks of its wrought-iron fence.

One of the balconies was lying smashed in the forecourt, surrounded by shredded personifications of Rectitude and Civic Virtue and the *Mission Civilatrice*. As they stood watching, a jeep with four Arvin MPs shot past them and pulled up on the sidewalk.

In the light of the MPs' torches, they could see that there were people sitting down in the street, trying to pick the concrete chips out of their flesh. It had been very crowded in the street because of the stalls. Families of refugees sold morsels of fish and noodles to the petitioners who stood all day outside the building, and at night they settled down to sleep among their wares. Since the building had been empty when the charge went, the street people had taken the casualties.

Converse and the Percys moved back against the metal shutters of a building across the way, as Arvin paratroopers arrived in canvas-covered trucks to seal off the street to traffic. The Arvins came picking their way through rubble, nervous as rats, poking people aside with the barrels of their M-16s.

After a few minutes, the barbed wire arrived. The emergency services in Vietnam always carried immense quantities of barbed wire for use in every conceivable situation. There was still no sign of an ambulance. They rolled the coils along the street to spread at each end of the block. Policemen were poking among the ruins by the fence, shining hurricane lamps. Now and then Converse could see marvelously bright gouts of blood.

When the ambulances came, fastidious men in white smocks got out and walked carefully toward the pile; when the wire caught their clothing they swatted at it with quick delicate gestures. Jill Percy followed them across the street and peered over their shoulders and over the shoulders of the National Policemen making a short patrol the length of their line. Converse tried to see her face in their lights.

From the way she recrossed the street, Converse and Ian could tell what she had seen. Her steps were slow and deliberate and she appeared confused. If one stayed in the country long enough one saw a great many people moving about in that manner.

"Crikey," she said. She made a small fluttering gesture with her hands. "Kids and . . . all."

Ian Percy had brought his beer bottle from the Tempura House; he let it fall from his hand to shatter on the street. The Vietnamese nearby turned quickly at the sound and stared at him without expression.

"Somebody ought to set a *plastique* at the London School of Economics," he said. "Or in Greenwich Village. All those bastards who think the Front are such sweet thunder—let them have their kids' guts blown out."

"It could be anybody," Converse said. "It could be an irate taxpayer. Anybody can make a *plastique*."

"Are you going to say it's the Front?" Jill asked her husband. "Because it probably wasn't, you know."

"No," Ian said. "I'll say it probably wasn't. It could have been anybody."

He began to curse in Vietnamese. People moved away from him.

Converse went across the street and watched the ambulance people lug body bags over the rubble. Dead people and people who appeared to be dead had been laid out on the exposed earth where the cement had been blown away, and the blood and tissue were draining into the black soil. There were chopsticks, shards of pottery and ladles lying about and on close inspection Converse saw that at least some of what had appeared to be human fragments might be chicken or fish. Some of the bodies had boiled noodles all over them.

As he went back to where the Percys were, four

men wearing rubber gauntlets came carrying large aluminum cans. When they reached the wreckage, they upturned the cans and scattered white powder over it.

"What is it?" Converse asked Ian.

"Chloride of lime."

Jill Percy stood with her shoulders hunched, arms folded.

"If you get run over in the street," she said, "they'll come and string barbed wire around you. If you don't get up fast enough they'll sprinkle you with chloride of lime."

They walked down the street a few yards until they stood before the glassless windows of a Toyota agency. In the glare of the lights, they could see the office inside with its charts and wall calendars and tiny electric fans on each desk. Reams of paper were scattered over the floor; because of the angle of the windows, the office had absorbed a great deal of the concussion. One of the interior walls was dappled with blood that looked as though it had been flung from a brush. Converse stopped for a moment to look at it.

"What?" Jill Percy asked.

"Nothing. I was trying to think of a moral."

He could not think of a moral. It reminded him of the lizards smashed on his hotel wall.

In his office just off the tiny lobby of the Hotel Coligny, Monsieur Colletti was watching "Bonanza" on the Armed Forces Television Network. Monsieur Colletti had taken eight pipes of opium during the afternoon; he had taken eight pipes of opium every afternoon for forty years. When Converse entered, he turned from the set with a welcoming smile. He was the most courteous of men. Converse and Monsieur Colletti watched "Bonanza" for a while.

On the screen, two cowboys were exchanging rifle fire at a distance of thirty meters or so. They were fighting among enormous rounded boulders, and as far as one could tell each was trying to move as close to the other as possible. One cowboy was handsome, the other ugly. There was music. At length, the handsome cowboy surprised the ugly one loading his weapon. The ugly cowboy threw his rifle down and attempted to draw a sidearm. The handsome one blew him away.

Monsieur Colletti, who spoke no English, brought his palms together silently.

"Hoopla," he said.

"It's the same in Saigon," Converse ventured. Monsieur Colletti always seemed to understand his French.

Monsieur Colletti shrugged.

"Here, sure. Everywhere it's the same now." Monsieur Colletti had been everywhere. "Everywhere it's Chicago."

He said it Sheeka-go.

"There was a bomb tonight," Converse said. "At the office of taxes. It's all ruined there."

Monsieur Colletti made his eyes grow larger in an expression of surprise that was purely formal. It was not easy to bring him news of Saigon.

"But no," he protested mildly. "Any dead?"

"Some, certainly. Outside."

"Ah," the *patron* said, "it's cruel. They're bastards."

"You think it was the Front?"

"These days," Colletti said, "it could be anybody."

When "Bonanza" was over, they shook hands and Converse went upstairs. Back inside his room, he turned on the overhead fan and the air conditioner. The air conditioner did not work very well but it provided a busy and, to the American ear, vaguely reassuring noise which drowned out the sounds from the street. The sounds from the street were not reassuring to anyone's ear.

He switched on the lamp on his writing desk to

provide his room with the most agreeable cast of light. Small tricks, picked up all over. He took a bottle of PX Johnnie Walker Black Label from a locked suitcase and drank two large swallows.

There it is, he said to himself. That was what everyone said—GIs, reporters, even Arvins and bar girls. There it is. It would have been good not to have had a bomb that night. To get stoned with the Percys and then sleep. Because of the bomb he felt numb and stupid, and although there were situations in which stupidity would do almost as well as anything else, he was not in one of them.

And getting drunk wouldn't do. Nor would smoking more grass. Better to have stayed downstairs and watched more Westerns with Monsieur Colletti.

In his own despite, he took another swallow of whiskey, lit a Park Lane, and began to walk up and down the length of the room. In the next room, the Dutch flower-lover was playing "Highway 61" on his tape recorder. After a few tokes, he decided that he was experiencing no more than a vague dissatisfaction.

Nothing serious. See them all the time. Side effect of low-grade fever.

After a while, he stopped pacing and went across the air shaft to the bathroom to squat over the hole. The hole had treaded foot grips beside it to put your feet on; it was a vestige of the Mission Civilatrice. Unlike some American guests, Converse did not object to using the hole. Often, especially if he was high, using it made him feel as though he were entering into communion with the tight-lipped *durs* of vanished France *Ultra-Mer*—the pilots of Saint-Exupéry, General Salan, Malraux. Sometimes he whistled "Non, J'ne regret rien" as he left the toilet.

Straining, trembling with the fever stirred in his intestines, Converse took his wife's letter from his trouser pocket and began to reread it.

"Re Cosa Nostra—why the hell not? I'm prepared

to take chances at this point and I don't respond to the moral objections. The way things are set up the people concerned have nothing good coming to them and we'll just be occupying a place that someone else will fill fast enough if they get the chance. I can't think of a way of us getting money where the money would be harder earned and I think that makes us entitled."

Perhaps, Converse thought, as he managed the business of the banknote-sized toilet paper and washed his hands, perhaps the vague dissatisfaction was a moral objection. Back across the air shaft, he secured the rusty double locks and took another swallow of Scotch. When Converse wrote thoughtful pieces for the small European publications which employed him, he was always careful to assume a standpoint from which moral objections could be inferred. He knew the sort of people he was addressing and he knew the sort of moral objections they found most satisfying. Since his journey to Cambodia, he had experienced a certain difficulty in responding to moral objections but it seemed to him that he knew a good deal about them.

There were moral objections to children being blown out of sleep to death on a filthy street. And to their being burned to death by jellied petroleum. There were moral objections to house lizards being senselessly butchered by madmen. And moral objections to people spending their lives shooting scag.

He stood facing the .wall where the lizard stains were, rubbing the back of his neck.

Everyone felt these things. Everyone must, or the value of human life would decline. It was important that the value of human life not decline.

Converse had once accompanied Ian Percy to a color film made by the U.N. soil conservation people about the eradication of termites. In a country that looked something like Nam, where there was elephant grass and red earth and palm trees, the local soldiery drove over the grasslands with bulldozers, destroying immense conical termite colonies. There was a reason, as he remembered; the mounds caused erosion or the termites ate crops or people's houses. The termites were doing something bad. When the colonial mounds were overturned, termites came burrowing up from the ruins in frantic tens of thousands, flourishing their pincers in futile motions of defense. Soldiers with flame throwers came behind the bulldozers scorching the earth and burning the termites and their eggs to black cinders. Watching the film, one felt something very like a moral objection. But the moral objection was overridden. People were more important than termites.

So moral objections were sometimes overridden by larger and more profound concerns. One had to take the long view. It was also true that at a certain point the view might become too long and moral objections appear irrelevant. To view things at such length was an error. The human reference point must be maintained.

Really, Converse thought, I know all about this. He pressed his thumb against the wall and removed a dry particle of reptile spine from its cool surface. It was an error to take the long view in the face of moral objections. And it was an error to insist on moral objections when they were overridden. If one is well grounded in youth, the object of love and sound toilet training, these things become second nature.

In the red field, when the fragmentation bombs were falling out of what appeared to be a perfectly empty blue sky, he had experienced no moral objections at all.

The last moral objection that Converse experienced in the traditional manner had been his reaction to the Great Elephant Zap of the previous year. That winter, the Military Advisory Command, Vietnam, had decided that elephants were enemy agents because the NVA used them to carry things, and there had ensued a scene worthy of the *Ramayana*. Many-armed, hundred-headed MACV had sent forth steel-bodied flying insects to destroy his enemies, the elephants. All over the country, whooping sweating gunners descended from the cloud cover to stampede the herds and mow them down with 7.62-millimeter machine guns.

The Great Elephant Zap had been too much and had disgusted everyone. Even the chopper crews who remembered the day as one of insane exhilaration had been somewhat appalled. There was a feeling that there were limits.

And as for dope, Converse thought, and addicts—if the world is going to contain elephants pursued by flying men, people are just naturally going to want to get high.

So there, Converse thought, that's the way it's done. He had confronted a moral objection and overridden it. He could deal with these matters as well as anyone.

But the vague dissatisfaction remained and it was not loneliness or a moral objection; it was, of course, fear. Fear was extremely important to Converse; morally speaking it was the basis of his life. It was the medium through which he perceived his own soul, the formula through which he could confirm his own existence. I am afraid, Converse reasoned, therefore I am.

I T WAS STILL DARK AT TANSONHUT WHEN CONVERSE arrived. Transport was an old Caribou with brown and green camouflage paint. As it fueled, he waited beside the strip with his briefcase in his hand, his anorak folded into a neat square and secure to his belt.

Waiting with him were three young men in madras shirts. They were Harvard lawyers from the Military Legal Defense Committee and from their conversation he surmised that they were on their way to My Lat to try the fragging court-martial of a black Marine. They were Movement people; they had Movement sideburns and Movement voices. Converse kept away from them although they did not seem at all unlucky.

The Caribou took off at first light. When it was airborne, Converse strapped his briefcase to the steel seat beside him and, through the hatch, watched the batteries deliver their morning rounds to the greening horizon. As the sky lightened, dark formations of bloated Dragon gunships spread out between the shells' illuminated arc and the morning star, coming home from Snuol and the Line.

There was too much noise for anyone to speak and be heard. Converse went to sleep.

When he awoke, the sun was hot in his eyes and he looked down through the after cargo door to see the plane's shadow running over pale green ocean. They were about two hundred yards offshore. There was a white sand beach lined with coconut palms and behind the beach tin roofs ablaze with the sky's reflected light.

My Lat was a cluster of warped metal; the scarlet flame trees rose among its rooftops like bright weeds among tin cans. Beside the harbor were the tiled buildings of the old French fort which served as the base headquarters. At the town center were two low church spires of oxidized copper surmounted by twin crosses.

On the port side, Converse could see the ships lying in the roadways—slate gray AKAs and AKs spiky with A-frames and winches. In the center of the line, guarded from amphibious sappers by two patrol boats, was the *Kora Sea*. The Skyhawks on its flight deck were fast under tarpaulin.

The Caribou came in abruptly, clanking down a

runway of perforated steel and halting among sandbags in a storm of white dust. Converse stepped out into a hot wind laced with stinging sand. There was no one to meet them. He and the lawyers made their way past the unmanned emplacements in the direction of some colorless plywood buildings with numbers stenciled on them.

The section of the base where they had landed was like a city of the dead; there was not a soul to be seen. The ground under their feet was gravel and crushed seashell, barren as if it had been sown with salt. Converse had brought no hat with him and by the time he found the public affairs office his hair felt like hot wire.

Inside he found a sleepy yeoman and a cooler dispensing Stateside water. He drank a good deal of it. The yeoman informed him that the public information officer was also the base first lieutenant and had important business elsewhere. He had not been seen for a week. The duty journalist was at luncheon.

Converse sat down on a runner's bench to read *Time* magazine. The office smelled of floor wax and stamp pads, odors of the American presence.

Within half an hour Journalist First Class Mac Lean arrived and introduced himself. Journalist First Class Mac Lean was a small round-bellied man wearing parts of a Seabee uniform with a forty-five holstered on his guard belt. His arms were freckled and thickly tattooed; he had a pink boozer's face adorned with a sinister goatee and wraparound sunglasses. It seemed to Converse that they had met before, in a bar near Santa Monica Beach. But then Mac Lean had been wearing sandals and carrying bongo drums.

"You wanna see the beach?" Mac Lean asked. "You gotta see the beach. It's the best in the country."

Converse had come to associate Vietnamese beaches with leprosy because of the beggars at Cap St. Jacques; he declined with grace. Instead of going to the beach, they went to sick bay, where Converse obtained his malaria pills and had his temperature taken. It was just over a hundred.

As the afternoon progressed, it became apparent to Converse that the PIO was utterly uninterested in his existence so that there would be no necessity for the tiresome business of pursuing a non-story for appearance's sake. However, it was difficult to detach from Mac Lean, who hungered for news of the Great World.

For what seemed to Converse a very long time, they chatted of Music, Literature, Film, and the pleasures of California. Mac Lean showed Converse current copies of the Gulf *Gazette,* of which he was the editor.

"I try to keep it hip," he explained.

He also showed Converse the file cabinet in which he kept his pornography collection and the movie film can that was loaded with Laotian Red. Converse promised to come back the next day and smoke it with him. As he went out, Mac Lean gave him the peace sign.

Heat lightning was breaking outside and there was a breeze from the ocean that was good for the soul. He walked past the helicopter pad and along a sandy road that led toward the church spires. Far off to his right were the low gray buildings of the wharf area, to his left thick stands of trees beyond the wire fencing. The ground within the compound was the color of ashes and looked as barren.

He walked wearily, shifting the briefcase from hand to hand. After a few minutes a jeep with two Marines MPs pulled up beside him.

"Come along, cousin."

Converse placed his bag inside the runner and climbed aboard. The driver asked him where he was from in the world. Converse said California and that made them laugh.

He asked them about the sappers.

"Oh wow," one of the marines said. "Fantastic. Unbelievable."

The other marine agreed.

"They got skin-divin' girl sappers, you know that? They swim over from the beach with charges in their teeth. They put adhesive mines on the hulls of those big AKs and blam!"

He opened his hands to signify an explosion.

The marines were deeply suntanned and under their green camouflage helmets they looked very much alike. They smiled constantly and had crazy doper's eyes.

"What I think about," one of them said, "is catchin' a sapper girl and fuckin' her to death. I'm a vicious freak."

"You know what else they got? They got porpoises out there. They got porpoises trained to kill gooks. Don't you wish you could get a picture of that action?"

Converse nodded. He was picturing the silent depths of the Bay, Navy-gray porpoises with spiked collars locked in combat with knife-wielding sloe-eyed sapper girls. The Battle of My Lat Bay, illustrated by Arthur Rackham.

"This is a very strange war," he told the marines.

"Yeah, it's weird, man. We're not supposed to talk about it."

Beyond the main gate was an open space from which the town of My Lat had been removed to a discreet distance from the wire. The base end of town had been mortared out of existence during Tet, 1968. What remained of it began with a fleet street of open-fronted stalls furnished with stolen Navy chairs and iceboxes full of "33" beer. The fleet street led to a larger artery, which in turn led to a square before the double-spired church. It was a pleasant square with tamarind trees, an ice cream parlor and a café framed with fancy ironwork. Long ago My Lat had been a resort.

Converse crossed the square and found a street market in the shade of the church. Across from the market was the bus depot and behind that a narrow street of Chinese noodle restaurants. Among them, a square cement building, was the Oscar Hotel.

The Oscar was a hotel in the neo-oriental manner—there were cubicles separated by bamboo partitions, mats on the floor, an iron teapot in one corner. Converse carried his own bag upstairs. In the next cubicle a card game was in progress; Converse could smell the players' cologne and the raw alcohol aroma of the local whiskey they were drinking.

He squatted down on a mat, the briefcase supporting his back, and found himself eye to eye with one of the sports next door. The man was a dark-skinned Asian of indeterminate nationality, perhaps, Converse thought, a Malayan seaman. He had come down on all fours to check Converse out, and they exchanged hostile stares until the man snorted with disgust and withdrew. It was said that Asians detected the presence of Westerners through the latter's exuding a scent like rancid butter; Converse wondered if the man had been able to smell him. He stood up and opened the shutters. As he did, the rain came down like a shell on the street below.

He had nearly dozed off when he looked up and saw a young girl standing in the doorway holding a cluster of cushions in her arms like an oversized bouquet. He stood up and watched her come in.

The girl dropped the cushions on the floor and looked at Converse as though he were in some way desirable. She was wearing Western clothes which she had probably made for herself and she looked perfectly marvelous. It was extraordinary how commonly one saw beautiful girls there.

"You know Ray?" Converse asked. It occurred to him that she might connect with Hicks in some way. She shook her head blankly, and advanced on him, cushions foremost.

The girl would not have been out of place around the Caravalle in Saigon; she wore the same eye makeup the Caravalle girls used to make their eyes rounder. Parisian chick was out at the Caravalle—in response to customer demand the Saigon girls had taken to imitating the style, and even the accents, of Delta Airline stewardesses.

"Fuck," the girl said.

Converse tried to appear amused. She came closer.

"Number one fuck."

He reached out and leaned a hand on her buttocks. It was always a kick; their faces made them look so ethereal and then you found that their asses were disproportionately full. She leaned a tit into the crook of his elbow. That was as high as her tits went. Looking past her, Converse found that he could see the upturned crepe sole of one of the card players squatting in the next apartment. The sole was new; it had a price tag pasted to it.

"Later," he told the girl.

She reached down and touched his belt.

"No," he said. "Not now. Later."

The expression on the girl's face looked like a smile, but wasn't.

"No fuck?"

"No fuck," Converse said.

She raised a finger to her nose and blew air through the free nostril. For a moment Converse thought that she would blow her nose on him. It was one of their gestures, he supposed. He had never seen it before. She bent down, picked up most of the cushions, and looked him in the eye. He took out his wallet and gave her two hundred piasters.

"More green," she said.

"No," Converse told her.

"Yes!" With the shrill Vietnamese inflection. Some people said it was a pretty language. Converse had never thought so. He jerked his head toward the open door.

She stooped for the rest of the cushions, fixing him with her non-smile. It was not pleasant to look at.

"You fuck little boy?"

Converse picked up the last cushion and handed it to her.

"*Diddy mao*," he told her. "Fuck off." He had never said *diddy mao* to a Vietnamese person before.

He stayed in the room for as long as he could bear it, waiting to see if Ray would come round. But after five-thirty, he had had enough. He picked up his bag and went downstairs to find the proprietor eating soup under a photograph of Chiang Kai-shek. The girl he had met earlier was standing by with a worried expression. As Converse came down the stairs she began to speak rapidly, pointing at him. The proprietor raised a hand to quiet her and continued eating.

"You get fucked?" he asked between mouthfuls.

"No," Converse said.

"You sure?"

"I'm sure," Converse said. "I always know."

"You know Ray?" the Chinese asked.

Converse nodded.

"Ray at seaman service geedunk. You know seaman service geedunk?"

"I'll find it."

He retraced his course through the wet streets; the base sentries passed him back inside on his press credentials. He set out wearily for the harbor area. The rain had stopped but the mosquitoes were out in alarming numbers and there was no jeep to ride in. At the perimeter of the base they were testing their searchlights for the oncoming night. Small patrol helicopters hovered over the treetops beyond the barbed wire.

The section of the base around the old fort was

49

more agreeable than the rest. There were royal palms and banyan trees and shell and gravel paths across the shaded lawns. There was an enlisted men's club, where marines and Seabees sat in the fading twilight drinking beer from pitchers and the jukebox inside played Johnny Cash at full volume. There was a movie theater playing *True Grit* and a plywood chapel with lawn sprinklers around it. The sprinklers had signs on them in English and Vietnamese that said DO NOT DRINK THE WATER.

The United Seaman's Service geedunk took up one wing of the old Legion barracks. Converse located the bar, which was large, pleasant, and nearly empty, and bought a gin and tonic with what remained of his military scrip. There was no sign of Hicks.

He waited at the bar until it was completely dark, then painfully took up the briefcase and went to check the outside tables in the back. His arm and shoulder were completely numb from the weight of the thing—he bore it through the heat like a festering limb, expecting that at any moment some passerby might protest at the smell of it or its unsightliness. He was almost too tired to be afraid.

J UST AFTER DARK, WHEN HE HAD FINISHED THE second beer, Hicks looked down and saw Converse in the small garden below him. When he switched on the reading light on his table, Converse looked up and saw him.

Converse came up the steps slowly, hauling a huge old-fashioned briefcase. He dropped the case on the floor and sat down heavily in a bamboo chair.

"I been carrying this forever," he said.

He reached over, picked up the Portable Nietzsche which Hicks had set on the chair beside his, and inspected the front and back covers. There was something slightly contemptuous about the way he looked at it.

"You still into this?"

"Sure," Hicks said.

Converse laughed. He looked wasted and flushed; there was pain in his eyes compounded of booze, fever, and fear.

"Jesus," he said. "That's really fucking piquant."

"I don't know what that means," Hicks said.

Converse raised a hand to his forehead. Hicks took the book back from him.

"I'm sorry I couldn't meet you on the beach. How'd you like the Oscar?"

"I been in worse."

"Did you get laid?"

"Everybody asks me that," Converse said. "No. I didn't feel like it."

"You were probably too scared."

"Probably."

Hicks lit a cigar.

"Too bad. You'd of liked it."

"I should have been taken off thirty times. It's a miracle I got that shit here."

Hicks looked down at the case and shook his head.

"That's about the sorriest piece of packaging I've ever seen. It looks like something out of *The House on Ninety-second Street*."

"I was hoping you could help me with that."

Hicks smiled. "O.K.," he said. "What you got?"

Converse looked over his shoulder.

"Don't do that," Hicks said.

"Three keys of scag."

Hicks had discovered that people disliked his looking at them directly and, out of courtesy, he often refrained. He looked into Converse's eyes, engaging the fear he saw there.

"I didn't know we were that way. I thought you'd have something else for me."

Converse stared straight back at him.

"We're that way."

Hicks was frowning down at the table.

"It's bad karma."

"Think of it in terms of money. You take it straight to Marge's in Berkeley. We'll pay you twenty-five hundred bills."

"You and Marge? Who's we?"

"That's a story in itself," Converse said. "If your stash is as good as you say, it'll be easier than carrying grass."

"It's unmakable. I got a whole aircraft carrier with practically no one on it."

"When do you get to Oakland?"

"Seventeen days, if we stop at Subic Bay."

"Then there's no problem. Deliver on the nineteenth. We'll have Marge home all day. If there's a hassle you can call the theater where she works after nine. It's called the Odeon. Third Street in Frisco."

"The thing is," Hicks said, "you're wasting your money. You ought to carry yourself."

Converse shook his head wearily.

"I'm on all the shit lists. Mac-V doesn't know whether I'm a Viet Cong spy or a poison toad. I wouldn't want to carry a joint through."

Hicks smiled and rested his cigar on the Portable Nietzsche.

"Tell me about *we*. I'll bet it's just you, you bastard."

"How could it be just me?" Converse asked. "How?" He was about to look over his shoulder again. Hicks restrained him with a hand.

"I have reason to believe," Converse said, "that this operation concerns the CIA."

Hicks laughed in his face. Politely, he joined in the laughter.

"That's folklore," Hicks said.

"Certain individuals."

Hicks tried to stare him down. It was not out of the question.

"Something else you better know," Converse continued. "They know about you. They know you carry. Your name came up right away."

"No," Hicks said, after a moment. "You're bullshitting me."

"O.K.," Converse said. "They know about you because I told them. In something like this, they have to know."

"Oh, sure," Hicks said. "I dig it." He looked out over the darkened bay, gnawing his lip. "Something like this they'd have to know." He looked back at Converse and found him feeling his forehead. "What are you doing to me?"

"Look," Converse said quickly, "they absolutely will not bother you. You're not supposed to know about them and they will not fuck with you if you deliver. Marge has twenty-five hundred bills for you. It's as simple as that."

Hicks was smiling again.

"If I deliver, right? But if I don't deliver—if I take you off because I happen to know you're an asshole—then the roof falls in, right? CIA time."

"Exactly," Converse said.

"If I were you and I wanted to keep a carrier honest, I might make up a bullshit story about the CIA. But I wouldn't try to lay it on a buddy."

Converse had begun to appear slightly upset.

"For God's sake, Ray, what would I be doing in a score like this on my own? Where would I get the money?"

It occurred to Hicks that there would be absolutely nothing dishonorable in ripping him off. He would have brought it on himself. Perhaps he would think it was piquant.

"You're terrific," he told Converse. "I really can't tell if you're lying or not."

"It doesn't matter whether I'm lying or not. That's the beauty of it. As it happens, I'm telling the truth."

Hicks fidgeted in his chair.

"It's a stupid expensive way to move weight. If the CIA needs the likes of you and me they're not what they're supposed to be."

"Who is, these days?" Converse leaned forward in his chair; he seemed guileless. "Look, Ray—it's certain people. Certain greedy people with CIA connections. They stand to make a tremendous profit and they can't use their regular channels. They can afford good security. But they have to know who's carrying for them beforehand."

"Are you supposed to be good security?"

"No, no," Converse said. "You. You are."

Hicks was silent for a while.

"I think this sucks," he said finally. "When I saw you last you were as skittish as a cooze, and now you're an operator from the CIA."

"You wanted to carry weight," Converse said. "I got you weight."

"I may just have to tell you no, buddy."

Converse was trembling, and Hicks watched him with concern.

"Then we both go," Converse said softly. "It's too late for that."

Hicks brushed aside the blue haze of his cigar and felt suddenly that he was trying to dispel more than cigar smoke. Converse's fear was almost palpable. Hicks was impressed.

"You deliver," Converse insisted, "and you split. You don't wait for a meet. You just take your money."

Hicks waited for him to go on.

"I'm a very timid person. I'm cautious. I'm a virtual paranoid. I've been around this place for a while and I know how this shit works. If it weren't a really cool number I wouldn't go near it."

"I didn't know you were such a money freak."

Converse shrugged.

"I suppose it's the way we're brought up."

"I thought you were a moralist. You and your old lady—I thought you were world-savers. How about all these teenyboppers OD-ing on the roof? Doesn't that bother you?"

"We've dealt with the moral objections," Converse said.

Hicks slumped down in his chair and leaned his chin on his fist, watching Converse.

"Let me tell you something funny," he said. "I met Mary Microgram in Frisco last year."

Mary Microgram was a girlfriend of Converse's. They had parted bitterly.

"You know what she told me? She told me you said I was a psychopath."

Converse looked chastened.

"It must have been some drunken piss-off. I really know better than that."

Hicks laughed.

"You bad-mouth me. You threaten me with the fucking CIA and claim you turned me. Then when you need honesty and self-discipline you come to me."

"When I was with Mary," Converse said, "I was very fucked up."

"It's outrageous," Hicks said. "I was hurt."

A burst of automatic-weapons fire sounded from across the bay. Searchlights played on the water, sweeping the line of palms on the far shore. Converse turned wearily in the direction of the noise.

"Sappers?"

"There ain't no sappers," Hicks said. "It's all a beautiful hoax."

Why not, he thought. There was nothing else going down. He felt the necessity of changing levels, a little adrenalin to clean the blood. It was interesting and kind of scary. Converse and his old lady would be a scene; he had never seen her.

"I'll carry your scag, John. But you better see I get treated right. Self-defense is an art I cultivate."

Converse was smiling.

"I didn't think there was ever much question about it."

"No," Hicks said.

Converse looked at the briefcase.

"You have anything you want in that case," Hicks said, "take it with you now. Otherwise just leave like it is."

"Just like that?"

"Like it is."

Converse went downstairs and brought up two cans of beer and two large gin and tonics. When he had taken a sip of the cold drink, he began to tremble again.

"You're mad," Hicks told him, "a great mind—warped—twisted."

It was an old movie line they had played with twelve years before in the Marine Corps.

Converse seemed particularly elated. He raised his glass.

"To Nietzsche."

They drank to Nietzsche. It was adolescence. A time trip.

Another burst of fire came from the opposite shore.

"I better get back to the Oscar," Converse said. "I'll miss curfew."

Hicks set his empty beer can down.

"What did you come here for? If I'm a psychopath, what are you?"

Converse was still smiling.

"I'm a writer. I wanted to see it." His eyes followed the searchlights on the bay. "I suppose there was an element of guilt."

"That's ironic."

"Yes," Converse said. "It's distinctly ironic."

They fell silent for a while.

"I'm tired of being bothered," Converse said. He rested his hand on the briefcase. "I feel like this is the first real thing I ever did in my life. I don't know what the other stuff was about."

"You mean you enjoy it?"

"No," Converse said. "I don't mean that at all."

"It's a funny place," Hicks said.

"Let smiles cease," Converse said. "Let laughter flee. This is the place where everybody finds out who they are."

Hicks shook his head.

"What a bummer for the gooks."

Converse looked at his watch and then rubbed his shoulders as if he were warming them.

"You can't blame us too much. We didn't know who we were till we got here. We thought we were something else." He took a large swallow of gin and tonic. "Hey, did you hear about the elephants?"

Hicks smiled. "Yeah," he said. "The poor elephants."

"The poor elephants," Converse said. They laughed together in the dark.

Converse's face was as wet as if he had been immersed. The drink was making him sweat.

"It's a Buddhist country. They must have a fantastic traffic in the transmigration of souls. Elephants and missionaries. Porpoises, sappers, lizards. Listen," he said suddenly, "I'm cold. Is it cold?"

"It's your fever. Go see the duty master-at-arms across the road. Maybe he can get you a ride to the gate."

Converse stood up and turned his back on the briefcase.

"You'd better be careful," Hicks told him. "It's gone funny in the states."

"It can't be funnier than here."

"Here everything's simple," Hicks said. "It's funnier there. I don't know who you're running with but I bet they got no sense of irony."

Converse stood over him, a bit unsteadily. He swung his arm in a broad gesture.

"As of now it can rain blood and shit," he said. "I got nowhere to go."

He walked down the wooden steps carefully. His sore right arm swung liberated; he felt gloriously free. As he reached the bottom step, it occurred to him that Hicks was probably a psychopath after all.

THE LAST MAN STOOD AT THE WINDOW, SQUINTING as though he saw his life's resolution off at a great distance, bathed in sunlight. When the ticket popped out, he spread his thick fingers over the smooth metal surface of the dispenser and groped for it unseeing.

A true groper, Marge thought. His fingers sought the pink ticket like blind predatory worms; finding it, they came moistly together, pressed it down, and slid it out of sight over the ledge. Marge identified with the ticket.

Every once in a while, Marge would steal a glance at the faces of her customers but for the most part she watched their fingerwork.

The last man paused for a moment at the rear of the booth to peer downward through the glass. He had transferred the ticket to his left hand; the talented right was already in his trouser pocket. Marge was not alarmed. She realized the man wanted to see her ass. But Marge had hung her sweater over the back of her chair so there was nothing to see. She had not done it out of spite but merely for convenience.

"C'mon, Jack," Holy-o told the last man. Holy-o stood beside the tin doors and took tickets. He took the last man's ticket, dropped the house stub in a wooden box, and closed the doors.

Holy-o had a truncheon in which he had carved designs—animal shapes and what he imagined to be the gods of his native Samoa. The truncheon hung by a leather thong from a screw eye in the oak ticket box. With the doors closed on the last man, Holy-o took his truncheon from its hook and stood out on the sidewalk in front of Marge's booth, cradling the club in his hands like a riot policeman.

Marge and Holy-o were waiting for the fellas to arrive.

The fellas arrived within two minutes of the last man. They double-parked their Thunderbird directly in front of the box office and climbed out briskly. They were well-groomed, clean-shaven young men with olive complexions. They both wore khaki half coats and one of them had a peaked waterproof cap with a belt that buckled in the back.

"Hiya, Holy-o." They came directly to the door of Marge's booth.

"Hiya, fellas," Holy-o said.

Marge opened up while the fellas looked the street over. Sometimes when they came, the fellas would see people whose appearance troubled them. If the troublesome-looking people were white, the fellas called them hard-ons. If they were black, they called them jigs. The fellas called the regular Third Street people and the customers of the theater mooches or mushes. Marge was never sure which.

"Hiya, sweetheart." It was the one with the hat who carried the bag.

Marge slipped her cash drawer out of its place and locked it.

"Hi," she said. She thought of him as Hat. Once when she had really been fucked up she had said, "Hi, Hat." She had been so fucked up that night she had been shortchanging herself instead of the mooches. Or mushes.

Hat had just looked at her. "Oh," he had said, "you like my hat?"

She followed Holy-o and the fellas into the darkened theater and they all went to Holy-o's office to unlock Rowena and the candy-stand money. Holy-o kept Rowena and the candy money locked in his office until the fellas arrived. Until a year or so before, he had locked the candy complex up in the ladies' room after the last film went on but ladies had started coming to the theater—things being what they were—and he had been compelled to leave the ladies' room open.

Rowena stood with the candy till at her feet, pulling her green poncho about her shoulders as though she were cold. In fact, it was not at all cold in Holy-o's office but it smelled strongly of the grass Rowena had been smoking.

"Hiya, sweetheart," Hat said to Rowena.

Rowena was biting her lip, peering bemusedly through her square spectacles.

"Hiya," she said and broke up. "Hiya, Hat."

Rowena was really fucked up and, of course, Marge had told the story of what had happened the other night. Marge shook her head. Silly Rowena.

They spread the day's gross on a sliding panel of Holy-o's desk and the other fella counted it.

"What is this?" Hat asked Holy-o. "Everybody likes my hat."

Holy-o shook his head in disapproval. Hat put the money in his bag.

"It's just a hat," he said. "It's my hat."

"Right on," Rowena said happily.

Hat looked up at Holy-o, blinked and stared at her. The smiling Rowena turned from the blank eyes of Hat to the stern gaze of Holy-o and back.

"Right on?" Hat asked. "What's right on? What do you mean, right on?"

"I mean right on," Rowena said. "Just right on." Her smile grew wider though less merry. "I don't mean anything."

"Right on," Hat sang in falsetto as he carried the

bag from the office. The other fella went with him. "Right on." He was mimicking Rowena.

"G'night, fellas," Holy-o said.

"G'night, Holy-o."

Holy-o was displeased.

"What are you," he demanded of Rowena, "dumb? "What are you, stupid?" He waved his arms about to disperse the odor of grass. "And looka this place."

"It's just smoke," Rowena said.

"You're gonna put your job in jeopardy," Holy-o told her.

For the last minutes of the film, Marge and Rowena stood behind the last row of seats. On the screen, long-haired young people were smoking grass and eating each other out between tokes. The night's house was mercifully well-behaved, silent except for its hoarse expirations and a certain rustle of cloth. When the lights came on, the girls retired toward the door of Holy-o's office; the mooches were filing up the middle aisle and the close presence of young women was sometimes difficult for them. Holy-o oversaw their going hence with his truncheon stuck in his breast pocket like a cigar.

When the room was clear, Holy-o checked out the ladies' room to see that no mooches had secreted themselves there and Marge and Rowena locked themselves inside. Rowena went to the toilet and lit a joint.

"An awful lot of them are Chinese," she said to Marge. "You notice that?"

The ethnic reference sounded a ghostly alarm from some dark place in the ruins of Marge's progressive conditioning.

"Sure," she said. "Chinese are just as horny as anybody else."

Rowena was thoughtful as she handed Marge the joint.

"I think the Chinese are into a different thing. I

think they dig the beauty of the bodies in a kind of aesthetic way."

"I think they're jerking off."

"They could do both," Rowena insisted. "I mean why should beauty be platonic? That's a western hang-up. They don't have the Judeo-Christian thing. You know?"

Marge was going through her black plastic carry bag, checking the contents. It had been locked in Holy-o's office with Rowena.

"Sure," she said. "The Judeo-Christian thing."

"Right," Rowena said. "Where sex is pejorative."

"I had a pack of cigarettes in here when I put this down," Marge said. "I'm absolutely sure of it."

"Oh, shit," Rowena said and gave Marge back her cigarettes.

"Ask," Marge said. "Please."

She took a comb from her bag and combed her hair, looking at herself in the mirror. Although she was only thirty, her dark hair was already streaked with gray. It looked good, she thought.

"It may happen," she told Rowena, "that you're short of money and you're in there with the stand money and you might be tempted. I advise you never, never to take any of it. Because if you do it even once these people will make you sorry you did."

Rowena regarded Marge with bewilderment.

"Just because I borrowed a cigarette." She sighed. "People are so uptight. It's weird."

"Bear that in mind," Marge said.

When they came out of the ladies', they saw Holy-o and Stanley Projectionist going over the vacant rows of seats for lost articles. Stanley took the left side of the auditorium and Holy-o the right. Holy-o had opened his nightly pint of Christian Brothers brandy and was holding it by the neck between his thumb and forefinger as he patrolled the rotten carpet. He moved part of the way on his knees and the heels of his hands. His inspections were always very thorough and he was clever about finding things; in the past week he had found two wallets with some money in them and a strange pair of black gloves. Stanley Projectionist was not nearly as good at finding things and Marge felt that he would really just as soon leave the whole room salvage to Holy-o. But Holy-o insisted. Marge had heard Stanley say that there was nothing on the floor after closing time except burned bottle caps and semen.

"How come he drinks?" Rowena whispered as they watched Holy-o proceed along the carpet. "I thought he was a stuffer."

Marge shrugged. "He's an old-timer. They're weird."

There was nothing nice for Holy-o that night. He walked Stanley to the door and stood looking into the street with a worried expression. He was worried about the danger of Indian attack.

For several weeks there had been a thing between Indians and Samoans in the cities around the Bay and Holy-o was afraid that the Indians would get him one night. He had stopped going by the Third Base Bar on the way to his hotel and instead waited until two Samoans who worked as janitors at the *Examiner* drove around to pick him up.

While Holy-o waited for the other Samoans and Rowena waited for her boyfriend, Marge found herself waiting as well. They sat in the office under *National Geographic* pictures of American Samoa and photographs of Holy-o in his Coast Guard uniform. On the wall over the door, Holy-o had hung a portrait shot of a cheerful red-headed woman with an Elvis Presley haircut—it was a photo of Miss Dowd, who had been the Odeon's cashier until the previous year. Miss Dowd had been murdered in her cage by a demented mooch and her picture held a dreadful fascination for Rowena.

"I wish I didn't know about it," she told Marge and Holy-o.

Holy-o closed his eyes. "Don't even think about it."

But Rowena continued to squint up at Miss Dowd's rosy features.

"Wow," she said, "there are sure some creeps around."

"A hippie," Holy-o said grimly.

"C'mon," Marge said. "Wasn't it just a guy with long hair?"

"It was a hippie," Holy-o said. "I was there, I oughta know. She died in my arms."

Holy-o's arms were short but powerful, encased in shiny blue Dacron. Marge looked at them and wondered what it would be like to die there.

"A hippie thrill killer," Holy-o said, running the brandy over his anger. "It wasn't even a ripoff. It was for laughs.

"Peace and love," he said. "The cocksuckers."

Rowena pouted. "It was just one person, Holy-o."

"One person shit," Holy-o said. "What about that bug up in Yellowstone Park? He had his pockets full of human finger bones. He ate his victims, the cocksucker."

"Like in Samoa," Marge said.

Holy-o flashed his wet hooded eyes. "That's bull-shit," he said. "Boy, just let one hippie show up in Samoa. Just let one show up. They'd fix his ass."

"You know, Holy-o," Rowena said, "just because the papers say something and J. Edgar Hoover says something doesn't make it true. Like this whole Charlie Manson number . . ."

As she spoke, Holy-o appeared to tremble. It was impolitic to provoke him further.

"We agreed," Marge said, "not to talk about him."

Rowena got up to go to the bathroom again. Holy-o looked after her with distaste.

"She goes to the toilet a lot," he said. "You think she's stuffin'?"

Marge shook her head.

"She don't know much," Holy-o said. "In the old days was the original bohemians. A lot of times the bohemian was really educated and a patron of art. Then you got the beatnik, maybe a lower class of person. Now you got fuckin' hippies everywhere."

"Holy-o," Marge said, "you know a writing doctor, don't you?"

Holy-o shook his head as though he were telling her no.

"So what?" he asked.

"If you can get dilaudid, I'd like some."

"What for? You got a pain?"

"Just wanted to try it."

"Try it?" He seemed to think it was a very strange notion. "You have a habit, Marge?"

"I just thought I'd like to get off," Marge said.

"Forget it," Holy-o said. "You ought to go out more. You don't need to tell your old man everything."

"I sort of like the idea of dilaudid," Marge said. "I can get some dolophine but I thought I'd dig dilaudid more."

"Dolophine is very bad," Holy-o said. "It's methadone. It'll kill you. You do better with scag."

"I don't want to know those people. Not on my own."

Holy-o smiled. "They're just fellas," he said.

When Rowena came back from the bathroom they watched her for popping signals.

"Hey," she said to Marge, "how was New York? I want to hear about it."

"I forget," Marge said. "I forgot I was there."

Someone was out in the lobby rapping on the tin doors; Holy-o went over and opened them slowly, holding the truncheon. It was Rowena's boyfriend;

he and Rowena shared an apartment on Noe Street and went to State. His name was Frodo.

"Jesus, it smells weird in here," Frodo told Holy-o.

Rowena went out to meet him.

"It really does," she said. "I notice it the first thing I come in."

Frodo giggled.

"It smells like the zoo. Like the monkey house."

The folds of brown flesh slid slowly across the surface of Holy-o's eyes.

"Next time," he told Rowena, "meet your boyfriend in the street."

"No reflection on you," Frodo said.

When Rowena and Frodo were gone, Marge started down the center aisle toward the back door and the parking lot. Holy-o called her back.

"I could give you a few hits," he said. He looked at her as though she were a child. "How do you want to do it?"

"I don't know. Just swallow it."

"O.K., Marge," he said kindly.

He had it in his pocket. He shook four tabs out of a plastic pillbox and into Marge's palm.

"Twenty bills. You pay me Friday."

He had overpriced it to put her in his debt.

"Dowd liked this," he said. "She liked it a lot."

His voice thickened as he spoke, his eyes shone. Marge smiled her gratitude and watched him. It was a seduction. The shit would seal some chaste clammy intimacy; there would be long loving talks while their noses ran and their light bulbs popped out silently in the skull's darkness.

"She liked girls too, didn't she, Holy-o?"

Holy-o smiled.

"Yeah, she liked girls but what she really liked was dilaudid."

Loneliness. He wanted it to be like Dowd again.

She thanked him and he told her not to take them all at once and not to take the first one yet since she had to drive. Then he walked her through the back door as he always did and stood by until she was in her car. Every night he performed the same gestures of vigilance—looking to the left and right, at the fire escape above the door and around the corner of the building.

When she was behind the wheel he scouted the alley for her and waved her on toward the street. As she came abreast of him he leaned down to the car window.

"You're gonna find this is good shit," he assured her. "People really like it and they're not just crazy. You see guys that are lazy bums and they turn into hustlers. They're out on the street first thing in the morning 'cause they wan' it."

"I guess that's the chance you take."

"Yeah," Holy-o said. "Absolutely."

"With me," Marge said, "it's a matter of principle."

Holy-o hastened to agree that it was. He nodded as she drove away and it was as if there were no Indians in all of San Francisco. She had never seen him so happy.

She took Mission to the bridge approaches. Her car was a yellow 1964 Ford and Marge was very fond of it because of the way she thought it suited her. Marge on wheels knew herself to be a thoroughly respectable sight—she and the car together projected an autumnal academic dash that might even evoke nostalgia if one had enjoyed 1964. Cops almost never stopped her.

Her house was directly up hill from the first Berkeley exit, on the first block of rising ground. Not very far away was the corner where the Oakland Police had stopped the Vietnam Day March and Marge had been there although she had not lived in Berkeley then. It had been eight years since Vietnam Day.

She let herself into the building and climbed up

two flights of fine redwood paneled stairway to the apartment. Before putting her key in the lock she rapped twice on the door.

"Margie?"

It was Mrs. Diaz, the baby-sitter.

"Hi," Marge said as she went in. "Everything O.K.?"

She walked past Mrs. Diaz and straight into the room where Janey was sleeping.

"Sure," Mrs. Diaz said. "Your father called."

Janey was huddled in her yellow blanket. Her mouth was open and her breathing thick and bronchial.

"Damn," Marge said. She found another blanket in the closet and placed it over the child.

"Did he want anything special?"

"He asked you to call him tomorrow."

In the kitchen, she put a pot of water on for instant coffee.

"So," Mrs. Diaz asked, "how's life on Third Street?"

"Oh, you know," Marge said. "Sordid."

The dilaudid tabs were in the pocket of her cardigan. She took one out and swallowed it.

"You take your life in your hands down there."

"It doesn't bother me," Marge said. "After working three years for UC I'd just as soon take my life in my hands."

She stood listening to the water beginning to boil and waiting for Mrs. Diaz to leave.

"Would you stay and have a cup of coffee?"

"No," Mrs. Diaz said, "I have to go."

As Mrs. Diaz put her cotton raincoat on, she asked Marge how her husband was doing in Vietnam. Marge said that it seemed as if he was O.K.

"You ought to get together with my niece," Mrs. Diaz said. "Her husband is over there too."

"Really?" Marge asked.

"Don't you worry? If it was my husband I'd worry."

"I do," Marge said. "But he's always been lucky."

Mrs. Diaz winced.

"You shouldn't say that. But I guess he's getting a lot to write about, huh?"

"He ought to be."

"You said he was writing a book about it?"

"Yeah, he wants to write about it. A book or a play or something. That's why he went."

"Boy, if that isn't crazy," Mrs. Diaz said. "I'm sorry but it's so crazy when he could be here. There's plenty here to write about."

"He's a funny guy," Marge said.

When Mrs. Diaz was gone, Marge went back to Janey's room and listened to the child's breathing for a while. Then she went back into the living room and sat in front of the television set without turning it on.

She lit a cigarette and dialed her father's number in Atherton.

Her father's friend Frances answered—Frances with the silicone tits.

"Six oh nine nine," Frances said. "And three A.M."

Marge had known that they would still be up, and she knew also that her father had picked up on the other extension.

"Hello, Frances, Hello, Elmer."

"Hi," Frances said and hung up.

"You're all right?" Elmer Bender inquired.

Marge put another dilaudid capsule in her mouth and washed it down with coffee.

"I just took a pill," she told her father.

"How nice for you."

She waited and in a moment he asked, "Are you suicidal?"

"No, I'm just fucking around. I feel kind of deranged."

"Come and see me tomorrow. I'd like to hear about New York."

"Is that why you called me?"

"I wanted to know how you are. Why don't you go see Lerner if you're deranged?"

"Lerner," Marge said, "is a senile Viennese asshole. And he's a lech."

"At least he's clean," Elmer Bender said.

"I'll come see you. If not tomorrow—soon."

"Are you still getting intimidation from that guy in Santa Rosa?"

"No," Marge said. "He went away."

"What's your situation?"

"How can I tell you? Your phone is tapped."

"Of course," Elmer said, "so what?"

"I'm off sex. Sex is just a room full of mooches jerking off in their pants."

Elmer Bender was silent for a moment. In the course of one of their conversations, Marge had discovered that he had a horror of lesbianism and that he worried that she might begin sleeping with women. It seemed that her mother had been known to.

"Don't you think it's time John came back?"

"That's gonna be strange," Marge said. "Really strange."

"I think the whole thing has gone on long enough. It was nuts, you know? What good is coming from it?"

Marge felt herself sinking into the chair she sat in. She felt as though she were sinking into its blue fabric in the most literal way. She held the phone to her ear with her left hand and stretched her right arm with the fingers extended toward the bar window that overlooked the street. It was satisfying to hold her arm that way. The shape the window viewed from her chair began to suggest a Larger World.

"How about a larger world?" she asked her father.

Elmer sighed.

"Marge, go to sleep, my baby. Be sure and see me tomorrow."

Some kind of wind had risen outside and was whisling through the rotten window casement and the ill-fitted panes. Marge sat facing the window, listening to the wind until it faded into a greater stillness. Her father's voice was still with her and she felt as though some essence of him remained in the room—a dry, abrasive, maddeningly reasonable essence. Points of light struck her eye as though reflected from his rimless spectacles.

"You would shit, wouldn't you?" she said to him.

She stayed in the chair surrounded by immensities of silent time. At the core of it, within her, a righteous satisfaction was rising. She sensed the outer world as an infinite series of windowed rooms and she felt a clear confidence that it contained nothing which she could not overcome to her satisfaction.

It was very unlike Marge to sit so long without fidgeting, even when she was alone. There was a noise in the street outside and although she could not identify it, she used it as a handle and made herself stand up. Upright, she was weary but unafraid. Not since she was much younger had she felt so satisfying a commitment as she felt to the caper and to the dope that would be on the water. High, she was party to it, in communion.

"All right," she said. It was all right.

When she saw herself in the mirror, she smiled and raised a hand to her mouth. She advanced on herself cautiously but with dignity, turning round before her turning image. When she examined her eyes she saw that the pupils were tiny and surrounded by what seemed enormous areas of gray.

Dilated. Dilaudid. Praise dilaudid.

"We are not afraid today," she said. Old song.

Us against them, she thought. Me against them. Not unlike sexual desire. The quickening of that sense brought her into other rooms and she flashed the mooches' fingers laboring over their damp half-erections, burrowing in the moldy subsoil of their trousers like arachnids on a decomposing log.

It made her laugh and shudder.

On the redwood table nearby there was a letter from him but she kept her hands away from it. He would be in Saigon, twelve hours removed—certainly alive somehow, probably afraid.

When she thought about him, she often wondered if there was a proper way to punish him for being there without her, or instead of her. But she felt at peace with him now.

She closed on the mirror and looked in her own eyes again.

Diluted.

When she felt herself leaning backward she turned and partly sat on the edge of the table where his letter was; she could see herself in profile now, her body bent at the buttocks which the last mooch had been so concerned to see.

"Your ass is on the line," Marge told herself aloud.

And it did seem to her that she looked vulnerable.

Deluded. Dilaudid.

She straightened up and walked from one light to another, turning them out. When the room was darkened she was aware of a glow from the street. It seemed the wind had stopped, and going to the window she saw that the street was hushed with fog and the street lights ringed with rainbows. It was all fine.

In the bedroom she passed Janey's crib and heard the troubled breathing. Vulnerable.

But it's righteous, she thought.

She straightened the child's blankets and undressed with pleasure. Lying in bed, she thought of him without wanting to hurt him at all. Us against them would be best.

And when she closed her eyes it was wonderful. She passed into a part of the sea where there was infinite space, where she could breathe and swim without effort through limitless vaults. She fancied that she could hear voices, and that the voices might belong to creatures like herself.

It WAS A NICE CROSSING, EXCEPT FOR THE AGENTS aboard. The trade winds were soft and the nights were starry and Hicks found time each morning, while the breakfast rolls and corn muffins were cooling, to do his exercises on the flight deck.

When they tied up at Subic and the liberty sections made for the lights of Olongapo, Hicks stayed aboard to observe the agents. There were three or four, disguised as hippies; they offered joints, giggled, and prowled the rows of disabled aircraft looking for stashes.

His own first stash had been in the mangled tail section of a Seasprite helicopter but he had moved it after a day, to lie under moldering naval heraldry in a disused flag locker. When they cleared Subic, he moved it again, stuffing the package in a flag bag and immersing it in a marked sack of cornmeal which he had set aside for the purpose. With it, he secreted two pairs of binoculars which he had stolen on the trip out and a Sunday Services pennant for a souvenir.

Each evening, he played chess with Gaylord X in the crew's lounge. The civilian crew of the *Kora Sea* observed strict social segregation, so Hicks and Gaylord played in nearly total silence. After each game Gaylord would say, "Ah, thenkew," and Hicks would reply, "My pleasure." His pleasure was quite genuine for, on this trip, he won every game. There had been one match during which Gaylord had rallied superbly in the end game—but at that point several of his fellow nationalists had sauntered by to kibitz and his counteroffensive collapsed under the strain of representing the race. Gaylord was the second cook, a Black Muslim and a secret Rosicrucian.

After the game, Hicks would brew a pot of verbena tea and turn in early.

He was trying to read Nietzsche again. To his annoyance, he found that he could not get with it at all.

"Whither does it move? Whither do we move?"

"Does not empty space whirl continually about us? Has it not grown colder?"

His copy was from the Seaman's Service library and the last reader had marked many passages with underlinings and exclamation marks. Hicks smiled when he came to them.

Some punk, he thought. Like I was.

He had read Nietzsche over twelve years before at the Marine Barracks in Yokasuka—Converse's book—and it had overwhelmed him. He had marked passages in pencil and underlined words that he did not understand so that he could look them up. Before his meeting with Converse in Yokasuka, the only books he had ever finished were *The Martian Chronicles* and *I, the Jury*.

Hicks knew very few people for whom he had ever felt anything like love, and Converse—whom he had not seen for twenty hours in the past ten years—was one of them. Seeing Converse again had made him feel good and young again in a simple-minded way; as though all the plans and adolescent fantasies they had shared in the service might take on some kind of renewed near-reality.

Effectively, their friendship had ended when Converse was discharged and Hicks became, as he thought, a lifer. Once while he was still married to his Yokasuka girl, Etsuko, Converse had come to Camp Pendleton without his wife, and the three of them had eaten *sushi* together. Very rarely they had met to go drinking in the city. But he was aware that Converse for the most part avoided him, and he was rather hurt by the fact.

He was hurt as well by what Mary Microgram had said that Converse had said. And he had been hurt further by Converse's sneering at his copy of Nietzsche and calling his reading of it piquant—presumably in the sense of appealingly provocative, pleasantly disturbing, rather than spicy, having a pungent odor.

At the same time that Hicks had come to know Converse, he had encountered Japan, and Japan—as he perceived it—had been immensely important to him. He had brought a Japanese woman home with him, and he had come, during his years as a professional marine, to think of himself as a kind of samurai. Although he had never approached satori, he was a student of Zen and he had once had a master, a German who could read the texts and was said to be a roshi. Even dealing, he endeavored to maintain a spiritual life.

In the course of his third hitch, after years of base and embassy duty, of shining shoes and saluting automobiles, he had gone ashore at Danang to face an armed enemy for the first time. His disciples had served him well.

He had been older than all of them—older than the teen-aged riflemen, older than the Princeton former football player who commanded his company. They expected that he be better and more professional at war than themselves, and he had been. He had never let himself question the necessity to be.

But it was not a war for a man who maintained a spiritual life, and who had taken an Asian wife. Many marines there were stronger against it than he; he declined to speak against war, any war. Yet people in the line who had come to hate the nature of the thing did not hesitate to talk to him about it. When one of the regimental communications companies in the grip of dope spirituality formed itself as a commune and declared for Joan Baez, the kids in it expected a certain sympathy from him.

One day, when the company was out of the line, he had, in a mood of vague disgruntlement, allowed a number of his people to walk into town and see Bob Hope, who was playing there. It was not, in the circumstances, a serious dereliction but it called for reprisal; reprisal came in the form of an undesirable patrol, which resulted in what Hicks had come to call the Battle of Bob Hope. Almost every man in his platoon who had seen Bob Hope died in it. He himself was shot and flown to Okinawa. At the end of the year his hitch expired and he walked.

It was a source of pride to Hicks that he was at home in the world of objects. He believed that his close and respectful study of Japanese culture had enabled him to manipulate matter in a simple disciplined manner, to move things correctly. He believed it was all in your head.

When, eighteen hours ahead of schedule, the *Kora Sea* tied up at Oakland, he did his exercises and meditated briefly on the righteous arrow and the inevitability of its union with the target.

Early in the afternoon, the yardbirds trucked Dempsey Dumpsters—huge mobile garbage cans—to the *Kora*'s after gangway. Hicks waited until the last Dumpster was almost full and then personally conveyed two cardboard barrels of bakery refuse to its maw. The package was inside in its cornmeal sack together with some yeast cartons, the binoculars and the souvenir flag. Attached to the sack was a length of pennant rigging, which he left adrift within reach of the opening chute. This much done, he returned aboard and took lunch. As he did so, the yardbirds responsible trucked the Dumpsters off to stand with their like in front of the A-dock welding shop. While the shore-bound sections changed into their shore clothes, Hicks busied himself with a scrupulous cleaning of the bakery.

Shortly after four o'clock, he went on the pier again and bought a bottle of Coke at a geedunk trailer at some distance from the welding shop. At four-fifteen the welders secured and washed their hands. At four-thirty the head cleaning crew signed in and their first stop was the men's room of the welding shop. They were silent somber blacks; one of them carried the tin refuse can from the toilet to a Dumpster and shoveled the contents into it—paper towels, empty half-pint bottles, cigarette wrappers. At this point, Hicks applied his only tool, which was a key to the welding shop toilet. He had an extensive collection of keys to various buildings and offices at the Army terminal, acquired over a number of years. When the head cleaning crew went round to the other side of the building, Hicks let himself into the toilet and waited until there was no one close at hand. As soon as things appeared suitable, he picked up the tin refuse can and carried it to the mouth of the Dumpster in which his bag was hidden. He held it up against the Dumpster's chute and with his right hand seized the flag line to pull the package up and shove it into the tin receptacle. He then carried it back to the welding shop toilet, where it would spend the night. There were very few functionaries, however mean, who would stoop to inquire into the maintenance of toilets. Only agents would do so—and although there were plenty of agents about, right thoughts and right actions enabled one to move discreetly. Blacks troubled him most because the sight of a white worker emptying shit cans engaged their attention.

Then Hicks changed clothes, packed his bag, and went to the terminal sick bay to make an early morning appointment for his mandatory chest x ray. He planned to return in the morning with his appointment slip, driving through the gate nearest the sick bay, pick up his package from the trash can before

77

the morning cleaners emptied it, and then drive out through the gate he had entered with the package concealed under a fender.

His normal procedure was to send his dope ashore in the plane parts and recover it from the railroad siding from which the parts were shipped to the repair facilities, but he had heard that the sidings were carefully watched now and the parts sniffed over by dogs. His present plan seemed to him audacious but sound.

The gate search he passed through on his way to the parking lot was thorough and businesslike, worse than he had ever seen it. When it was over, he started his car with difficulty and drove downtown to the Seaman's YMCA.

At the Y, he engaged a room and lay down on the bed for a while. When it grew dark he was able to discern the peephole in the door through which it was said the military police spied on the military personnel to see if they were buggering each other.

He was restless in the face of dead time. Hours of vacant unease had to be passed before he could return to cop his weight; self-discipline permitted, or required, light uncomplicated diversion.

When he went downstairs he saw that the lights above Oakland had come on, and the sky behind them was like deep blue marble. Even skid row smelled of eucalyptus. He was unmoved.

On a corner two blocks from the Y was a bar called the Golden Gateway. A sign over its side door read: LIQUOR BEER FOOD—Home of the Seafarers Club. Another sign made of cardboard, resting against the venetian blinds in the window, announced Seven Topless Dancers.

At one time the Golden Gateway had sold good cheap Italian food and there were pool tables in the back. The pool tables were gone now and the kitchen with them; in their place was a large cage with pink bars, inside of which girls of various colors and conditions frappéd themselves to music from the jukebox. Since the cage was installed, all manner of people fell by. Escaped lunatics up from Agnew came to engage the suburbanites who came to engage rough trade. There were agents representing every agency, and a contingent of neighborhood blacks who did their business there and never seemed to enjoy themselves. Finnish Alex, a bartender under the old regime, managed the place now, assisted by three shark-eyed barmaids.

Hicks went in, thinking he might bullshit with Alex for a while, but it was not much of a place to bullshit anymore. He was shortly drinking hard, following bourbon two-fers with nip bottles of Lucky Lager. The go-go girls were an affront to sex, and Hicks was mildly scandalized by the fact that one of them appeared to be Japanese. The false canine on the upper right side of his mouth began to ache.

Drunk now, he went to the gents', took the tooth out and ran cold water over it, and rubbed it with a clean handkerchief. It seemed like a good idea. He replaced his tooth, pissed, and went out, walking toward the bar in solemn processional step. A party of blacks watched him from their table like medical students regarding a charity patient with a curious low disease.

At the bar, he got to speak with Alex for the first time.

"I feel like a walking pair of teeth," he told him.

"That means you're drunk," Alex said. For Alex, almost everything meant that. "What kind of trip you have?"

"Good," Hicks said. "A good trip."

"They still got that good pussy over there?"

Hicks leaned his elbows on the bar and belched.

"Yeah," he said.

"When you gonna go back?"

"Soon as I can get out. I want to put some money

79

by and take a vacation. Go down to Mexico for a while."

"Mexico, that's a good place. They got that good pussy down there."

Hicks looked up at the girls in the cage.

"What a lot of shit this place is now," he told Alex. "Why do I have to look at those poor junkies? Christ, I just as soon look at you up there."

"I ain't got a costume," Alex said.

Hicks reached out and pushed him back against the booze locker.

"You got bigger tits, though."

Alex served him another nip.

"When you say you was goin' to Mexico?"

"I didn't say I was."

"Yes, you did. You just said you was."

"That's a dream," Hicks told him. "A dream."

"Ever see Coley?"

Coley was a dealer who had also worked for Sea Lift Command and had quit when paranoia overcame him. Hicks swallowed his beer and tapped on the upper tooth with his forefinger.

"Coley?"

"You know Coley," Alex said. "You used to drink with him here."

"Oh, yeah," Hicks said, watching Alex. "Sure. Him."

"I hear he went to Mexico."

"Yeah?"

"They say he went down there with a whole lot of money to buy something for somebody and he blew it all."

"Blew it all on the jai 'lai, huh?"

"Blew it all on good pussy. People are real pissed at him."

Hicks was about to say that he would be real pissed too if it was his money, but he let it pass. He had never heard Alex talk around dope before.

When the record on the box finished, the girls from

the cage climbed down and wrapped some sequined cloth around themselves. One of the girls was a mocha-colored East Indian with the features of a brahmin; she went to sit with a slightly frayed executive type at a back table.

"The guy's a bug," Alex said, looking at them. "He ties her up and beats on her. She loves it. They're both bugs."

Hicks stood up.

"I don't want to know all this shit, man," he said. "I don't want to know it."

He walked back toward the telephone booth through knots of drinking blacks.

Christ, there's a lot of them, he thought.

As he walked he tried to maneuver himself in such a way that he would not have to make anyone back up for him, or himself have to back up for anyone. He weaved skillfully among the black customers projecting a genial demeanor, but they seemed only to see the murder in his heart. They were funny folks.

Inside the booth, he secured the door with his foot and thumbed through the phone book. He could not remember deciding to call her. It was just happening.

Etsuko's second husband was named Eligio Robles, D.D.S. On deciding to leave Hicks she had enrolled in a dental technology course, financing herself by years of petty hoarding. Her English was good enough by then. Dr. Robles was a Filipino, her very first employer.

Humming to himself, he dialed Dr. Robles' number. And she answered.

"Konibanwa Etsuko? Shitsurayu Mrs. Robles-san."

"It's you," she said.

It seemed to him that he could picture her face exactly as she calmly attempted to determine what the call might mean.

"How's everything?"

"Fine. How's everything with you?"

81

"I just got back from Nam."

"How was that?" Not that she gave a shit, he thought.

"Fucked up."

She made no sound, but the line itself seemed to convey her impatience with his profanity.

"How's the good doc?"

"None of your business."

"I got some trouble with my teeth. You think he could fix me up?"

"Don't be stupid."

"He's a dentist, ain't he?"

He took the tooth out again and held it in his handkerchief.

"Ith orful."

"Why are you stupid?" she said. Cold, ivory anger. "You're drunk."

"Yeah."

"It's not a funny joke. Don't bother busy people who aren't bothering you."

He decided to ask a stupid question.

"Do you miss me, Etsuko? I miss you sometimes."

He could picture her again quite clearly; her mouth would be rippled with a small tremor of embarrassment and faint disgust.

"Give me a chance," she said. "Stop calling."

"Christ sakes, I haven't called you for a year. More than that."

"When I get calls from you," she said, "I think you're becoming a drunken bum. Too bad for a man of your intelligence."

"Why, you little shit," Hicks said.

She hung up.

"Interrigence the fuck indeed," Hicks said aloud. Her English had improved incredibly. "You little shit."

As he fumbled for another dime, a black girl in an imitation leather overcoat walked by the booth.

Hicks smiled at her absently, forgetting that his smile was missing its upper right corner. The girl stared at him and raised her eyes so that the whites were exposed and the irises fluttered under batting lids. Fuck off. As she went by, he blundered into eye contact with the other members of her party—three young men in black leatherette coats and pastel slouch hats. They were not amused.

"Asshole," he said to himself.

He kept looking back at them as he dialed. When June answered, he turned his back.

"Hello, June."

"Is that Ray?" She sounded ripped.

"Right," Hicks said. "I'm down here in Oakland. I'm fucked up and there ain't a white face in the joint. I want to make my will."

"Your will?"

"Forget it," he said. Laughs were hard to come by.

"Owen is here," June said.

"Owen is here! Terrific. Lemme talk to Owen. I'll call you tomorrow, O.K.?"

"Uh-uh," June said. "I don't want you to call me."

It was Dumb Question Night.

"Why not?"

"Owen is gonna kill you if he sees you. You know he's like armed, man. He's insane with rage."

Hicks shook his head. Someone tapped on the booth door with a coin.

"If he's insane with rage I won't trouble him. Can he hear you?"

"He's out in the garage working over the machine. Like I don't even want him to catch me on the phone."

"He wouldn't turn me, would he, June? He wouldn't narc me over?"

"I don't think so. Just don't be around."

"You asshole," Hicks said. "You told him. What did you tell him for?"

83

"Oh, man," June said. "Who knows why they do the shit they do?"

"The desires of the heart," Hicks said, "are as crooked as a corkscrew."

"That's about how it is," June said.

He held the receiver, hooked up with the general static. The bloods at the table were broadcasting cocaine vibrations. From his pocket he took a slip of United Seaman's Service stationery which had Marge's phone number written on it. When he had done that, he threw a snappy little hand signal to absolutely no one at a point beside the door. One of the bloods turned to check it out.

"Odeon," the voice said. Hicks smiled. A collegiate whine.

"Marge?"

"Yes?"

"This is Ray."

"Oh," she said. "Hi."

It was nice to be important.

"I'll fall by early tomorrow. Everything O.K.?"

"Yes. Yes, all right."

"See you then."

"See you then."

He left the phone booth and went quickly out to the street. For a while he walked away from the bay, toward the hills and the lights. In the first block he came to, there were two winos butting shoulders to see which of them could knock the other down. They stopped the game as he came up and approached as though they would panhandle him, but as he passed them they only stood panting and stared.

"I'm the one in the middle," Hicks told them.

In the next block a camperload of freaks sat eating white bread and bologna sandwiches on the sidewalk beside their vehicle. Hicks paused to watch them eat. One of the boys turned around to glare at him and he was offended.

"I'll fuck everyone of you," he declared.

"Oh wow," one of the girls said through a mouthful of bread and meat. They turned their backs on him.

"I was only kidding," Hicks said. "I wouldn't really."

In a third block was a bar with playing cards and wheels of fortune painted on the windows. The inside walls were dark blue and decorated with the same symbols but the customers were mainly old men. Whatever arcane scene once informed the place had moved on. Hicks sat down at the bar and continued with his party.

His head was going bad. The painted cards and dark walls oppressed him. Accumulated venom—from Etsuko, Owen, the blacks in the Gateway—was fouling his blood. He did not get drunk very often and sometimes then he did a gulf formed between his own place and the field of folk. His own place was represented by a tattoo he wore on his left arm. It was the Greek word 'Εσθλός; Hicks understood it to mean Those Who Are. When people asked him what it meant he often told them it meant that he was paranoid.

A familiar rage descended on him; it was like a binding in which he could hardly breathe and only blows could loosen it.

He sat drinking, trying to writhe free. For a while he tried to escape by pondering what things he might do with the money, but the money was in the hands of devious fuck-ups, and he became even angrier.

Just as he was attempting to summon sufficient self-interest to remove himself from the street, a rabbit-mouthed longhair came into the place, chewing on a toothpick, and settled himself a short distance up the bar. It occurred to Hicks that the youth might attach to the old action; he found the kid's presence and proximity disproportionately offensive.

The youth ordered a beer in a New York accent and drank it with a pill. He dropped his toothpick on the bar. When he saw that Hicks was looking at him, he said:

"What do you say, Cap?"

When Hicks did not reply, he flashed him a quick approving downward glance.

The kid was a pogue. It seemed to Hicks that if he got any drunker and his place any lonelier and more savage he might actually have some sort of a shot at him. The prospect, however remote, revolted him.

"You see the fight last night? What a fuckin' slaughter, right?" The kid advanced a step or so closer. "I tell you the only way you get a nigger to bleed is put a razor in your glove."

Hicks decided that he was crazy. He was not opposed, in principle, to beating up on crazy people.

"I'm from New York," the kid said. "You been there lately?"

Hicks finished his beer.

"Nobody asked you where you were from. Mind your fucking business."

"Far out," the kid said. He did not seem at all discouraged.

It was on rails now, Hicks thought. He became impatient for the thing to begin.

The kid studied him thoughtfully as though on the point of a decision.

"You're one mean motherfucker, right?"

Hicks shrugged and stood up, his right shoulder stooped.

"I'm what?"

The kid began talking fast New York.

"I said you were a bad motherfucker, man like you look like you could handle yourself. Like I wouldn't fuck with you." He held his hand out with the palm facing Hicks as if to intercept a blow.

"I thought you were."

"Jesus, Cap, I apologize. I'd buy you a beer and

a ball but I ain't got the bread. This is my last quarter I swear to God."

"I don't want your beer, pogue."

"C'mon. Don't call me that."

"I don't want your beer, pogue."

"O.K.," the boy said, "if you're gonna be like that."

Hicks had been counting on hitting him. But both he and the boy were aware of how drunk he was, and there was need for caution. The need for caution infuriated Hicks the more.

"I tell you what, Cap," the kid said after a moment, "you want to help me waste a dude?"

Hicks stared at him.

"I got a meet with this faggot. He's a really loaded dude, man, he's got like five-hundred-dollar suits. He's got this jewelry and a Rolex and shit and all these credit cards. You want to take him off?"

The boy moved closer.

"I could do it myself but this dude is like big. If there's two guys, one guy has a blade—no problem."

Hicks looked into his eyes. They were nearly sky blue with touches of amphetamine pink at the corners and long dark lashes. When he spoke, he rubbed his jaw with his thumb so that his fingers covered his mouth. He was one of the worst-smelling people Hicks had ever encountered.

"He's a Jew from television, a big faggot. We show him the blade, man, he'll shit his pants."

"You're putting me on," Hicks said.

It was almost funny. Maybe it *was* funny.

The kid took a cigarette from his shirt pocket without removing the pack. He was a museum of yard-bird reflexes.

"I swear to God," the kid said. "You want a piece of this?"

Hicks' anger was broken. He stared at the kid in wonder.

87

"With two guys, man—what do you say?"

"Have a beer," Hicks said.

The youth smiled. When he smiled his upper teeth settled on his lower lip, and he discharged air between them. If he had smiled a moment sooner Hicks would have cracked his skull. But Hicks had no desire to strike him now. The kid was a whole trip, the whole arcana. You couldn't just hit such people. They were holy.

"You the one with the blade?" Hicks asked.

The youth looked down at his own leg, and his eyes closed for a moment in sensuous anticipation.

Hicks kicked him in the shin. His foot struck a large object under the trouser cloth.

"What the fuck is that?"

The youth smiled modestly. "A bayonet."

Hicks laughed and struck the bar with the palm of his hand.

"You're not a self-respecting person."

"The fuck I ain't," the kid said. "That's why I got this man, because I'm a self-respecting person."

"You have a name?"

"Joey," the kid said. "This girl in Long Island used to call me Broadway Joe because I look a lot like Joe Namath."

"That's fine," Hicks said. "You can just call me Cap. I like it."

"Groovy," Joey said. "What it is, I gotta telephone him. He's set up in this motel over by the marina. I go up first, right? Then I let you in. See, the dude is a lush and we give him time to get mellow. Listen, you sure you're up for this?"

"Sure," Hicks said. "I hate the bastards. Give me his phone number. I'm gonna call him and I'll ask for you. Like I got a message or something for you. You tell me on the phone I should make it another time, but I won't hear of it. Tell him you're sorry I have to come up, but you'll get rid of me in a hurry. Play a role."

Broadway Joe appeared to think about it. "Yeah," he said. "O.K."

Hicks copied out the number on an envelope and had another drink while Joey telephoned.

"C'mon, Cap. Let's go to work."

"I wait here," Hicks said. "I call you from here. I got a car. I can be over there in a couple of minutes."

"No," Joey said. "Run me over there. You can call from some joint over there."

"I ain't using my car for this. You get yourself over there, we put the stuff in his car. Anyway, I don't want to hang around over there. I don't like it there."

"All right," the kid said. He gave Hicks another smile and poked a finger at his testicles. "I'll be seein' you. You ain't gonna let me down, right?"

"No way," Hicks said.

When Broadway Joe was gone, Hicks went to the men's room. In the process of returning to the bar, he was made to realize that it might be extremely difficult to make his way back to the Y. After a while, he got up again and dialed the number on the envelope. There was a firm businesslike hello.

"Hi, there," Hicks said.

"Who's this?"

"This is Cap, doll. Your boyfriend Broadway Joe has a bayonet. He's gonna do you some nastiness with it tonight He's on his way right now to fuck you over."

"Fuck me over?"

"It won't be as nice as it sounds," Hicks said.

After a thoughtful interval the man on the phone told Hicks that he was not exactly astonished.

"Then there's you," the man said. "What's your story?"

Hicks was outraged.

"I'm a nice fella," he said. "I'm a good citizen. That's my story."

"Tell me a little about yourself," the man said. "Are you big?"

Hicks sighed. He was thoroughly drunk.

"I'm enormous," he told the man. "I'm this huge motherfucker."

"I know what would be fun," the man said. "Turnabout is fair play. Why don't you come over and we'll put a little terror in Joey's young life?"

Hicks hung up and went back to the bar. There was a sign over it he had not noticed before that said:

Today is the First Day of the Rest of Your Life.

"That's pretty good," Hicks said to the bartender.

The bartender was a yellowing old man; he turned and looked at the sign with disapproval.

"I didn't put it up. It was here."

As Hicks went out, the old bartender reached up and took the sign down. There was no point in provoking people.

It was cold outside and the street was dimmed by fog.

"No place for me," Hicks said.

He walked looking over his shoulder. A few doors down from the bar he caught sight of a city bus coming his way and he forced himself to sprint for the corner. Stepping aboard, it seemed to him that somewhere in the course of his short run he had seen Broadway Joe, in an alley or doorway or up a sidestreet. He was too drunk to be certain.

He stood beside the nervous driver, fumbling for change; by the time he had the money in hand, he realized that the bus had carried him all the way back to Jack London Square, within a short walk of the Y. He put the change away, exchanged hostile stares with the driver, and climbed carefully down to the curb.

When he went upstairs in his room, he put a Band-Aid over the spy-hole and loaded his thirty-eight with the ammunition he had purchased for it. Before filling all the chambers, he put in a single cartridge and spun the cylinder. He did it three times, and each time the shell came up flush with the barrel. He could not determine whether this was a good or bad omen.

Waking the next morning, wretched and poisoned, he found the pistol lying on his table among a litter of bullets, cellophane, and pieces of the cartridge box. He was deeply ashamed. It was Uncontrolled Folly.

ALL THROUGH THE LAST HOURS BEFORE DAYlight, Marge dreamed. At the end of each dream, she would be shocked awake by a curious neutral explosion, stay conscious long enough to understand that her head ached, then slide again into sleep. But it was hardly like sleeping at all.

And the dreams, one after another, were bad stuff indeed. Janey teetering on a ledge with a storm-gray New York cityscape behind her, water towers, sooty brick. Something about a mad friar and fruit with blood on it. Something terrible among trees. Each dream incorporated her headache.

Afoot, she was edgy, cramped, accident prone. Coffee burned. A saucer broke. There were two caps of dilaudid left to her but she took some Percodan instead.

She drank the burned coffee as she waited for the Percodan to take. When she felt well enough she read some nursery rhymes to Janey. The nursery-rhyme book had a glossy colored picture of the Old Woman Who Lived in a Shoe; The Old Woman's many children balanced in the shoe's eyelets, swung on the laces, swarmed into the margins in bright dirndl skirts and lederhosen. There must have been fifty.

Fifty children. Janey wanted to know each one's name.

"That's Linda.

"That's Janey like you."

Fritz. Sam. Elizabeth.

Marge felt like weeping.

"I don't know *all* their names, sweetheart. How could I know *all* their names?"

"Oh," Janey said.

When the downstairs bell rang, Marge stood up suddenly and the rhyme book dropped to the floor.

"Oh my God," she said.

Janey stood looking up at her. She stared at the door for a moment and went to press the buzzer that opened the street door.

"Janey go ride your horsie for a while."

Janey's horsie stood in a fenced-off section of the backyard, a red plastic horse on springs. Sometimes when Janie rode it, she would pass into a kind of trance and bounce for over an hour in an unvarying rhythm with a blankness in her eyes which Marge found alarming. But Janey was not in the mood for horsie riding and she began to pout. Marge could hear a man's step on the hall stairs.

"Get," she screamed at Janey. "Get down there." Janey began to cry.

"Get, get," Marge shouted, shooing the child away. Janey ran to the top of the steps that led from her bedroom to the yard and stood just outside the door, tear-stained and obstinate. Marge closed the bedroom door. The man outside knocked.

"Yes?" Marge inquired. She stood motionless in the center of the room staring at the closed door.

"It's Ray," the man said.

Marge forced herself to open the door to him; he went quickly past her with a glance. He was suntanned and short-haired. He had cold eyes. Janey had insinuated herself back into the living room but when she saw the man she fled, through her bedroom and down the steps to the yard.

Ray set a dun-colored AWOL bag down on the living-room table and went to look out the window.

"I'm not ready for this," Marge told him.

He looked at her without sympathy.

"What do you mean you're not ready for this?"

"I haven't got the money," she said. Even in her own ears, the whine grated.

"Why, you dumb cooze," the man said softly.

She was trembling. That morning she had put on a dirty purple sweater and a pair of jeans out of the laundry bag. She felt soiled and contemptible.

"I mean I haven't got it here," she told the man.

He sat down in a wicker chair and rubbed his eyes.

"You got any coffee?"

Marge hastened to the kitchen. She poured the burned coffee she had been drinking into the sink and put on a fresh pot. Ray was pacing the living room.

"I called you, right? How come you don't have it?"

"I missed the bank. I went to the aquarium."

When she turned from the stove he was standing in the kitchen doorway with a slim smile.

"You didn't say anything on the phone about the aquarium. You said you'd be ready."

"I know," Marge said. "I really don't know why. I didn't want to on the phone. I was going to go to the bank today." The man was knitting his brows in mock concentration. "Somehow I thought you'd come at night."

"I hope you got off on the fish," he said. "You're not getting shit until I get paid."

"Any way you want to do it."

He looked her over and she hung back against the louvered kitchen doors, ashamed.

"When are your people coming to pick up?"

"Tomorrow, I think."

He turned his back on her and walked to the window.

"What do you mean tomorrow, you think? What is this shit?"

"Yes," she said quickly, "yes it is tomorrow. The twentieth."

"If I beat up on you and took off your smack I'd be within my rights," he told her. "You can't deal with people in this outrageous fucking manner."

"I'm sorry," Marge said.

"They get suspicious. They get mad."

"I understand," she said.

To her surprise, he smiled again.

"You're not trying to fuck me over, are you, Marge? You and some people?"

"Well, no," Marge said. "Honestly. It's just me and John."

"You and John," Ray said.

When the coffee boiled, he asked for whiskey to put in it but Marge had nothing in the house except cassis. He poured some over his black coffee.

"I got a hangover," he explained.

"Me too," Marge said.

He blew on the coffee.

"You a junkie, Marge?"

Marge tried to smile.

"Jesus," she said lightly. "Do I look like a junkie?"

"That's not always a factor."

"Well, I'm not," she said.

He stood by the window frowning, listening to the springs of Janey's horsie in the yard.

"What's that?"

"It's my daughter's toy horse."

He nodded and sat down on a cushion, clasping his hands between his knees.

"You've seen John?" she asked him.

"Yeah, I've seen John. If I hadn't seen John I wouldn't be here, right?"

94

"How is he?"

"Fucked up."

"Is he really in bad shape?"

"He ain't in no worse shape than you." He looked her over again, rather sourly. "You concerned or just curious?"

"Concerned," she said.

"Who are the people you're selling to?"

"Friends of friends."

"You mean you don't know them?"

"I don't know people like that," Marge said. "John set it up. He knows a lot of weird people over in Nam. He's good at that sort of thing."

"No, he's not."

"I thought he was," Marge said.

He stood up quickly and went to the window again.

"You're a mark, Stuff. The people you're dealing with are gonna know that right away. Unless they're as unconscious as you are."

For the first time, she realized that he was afraid.

"This sucks," he told her.

He had a hungry face; in it Marge detected a morphology she recognized. The bones were strong and the features spare but the lips were large and frequently in motion, twisting, pursed, compressing, being gnawed.

Deprivation—of love, of mother's milk, of calcium, of God knows what. This one was sunburned, usually they were pale. They always had cold eyes. They hated women.

"Well, what do you suggest?" She looked away from his eyes. "I mean, what do we do now?"

"You pay me," he said. "I give you the smack."

"Well, obviously," she said. "I'll have to go to the bank."

"Obviously."

She was aware that he had moved closer to her. He carried the hallucinatory circus scent of patchouli oil, the smell of dope and cold-eyed freakery. She shivered.

"You're a fuck-up."

She was almost too frightened of him to be angry.

"Listen," she said, "we'll just have to make the best of it."

"What do you think the best of it would be?"

He had reached out and placed his forearm across the back of her thighs; his arm slid upward until his palm was stretched across her buttocks. She was not facing him and he did not turn her toward him, but took one of her breasts in his hand and held it—not caressed but held it—an act of acquisition.

She could not make herself move. Her only act of resistance was to look at him, and what she saw repelled every instinct with which Marge associated her heart. His eyes seemed as flat as a snake's. There was such coldness, such cruelty in his face that she could not think of him as a man at all. His forward hand released her breast and slid along her belly, the one behind rose gently along the rear seam of her jeans to the small of her back; at first he made no move to kiss her.

When she felt his lips, his bitter greedy mouth against her face, it came to her clearly that it was what she wanted. Suddenly the whole terrifying enterprise had composed itself to incarnation—this man, this scented death's-head harlequin, with his fingers in her flesh, was embodiment to it all.

There was no power in her. She sought the stale mouth, warmed to the beak across her belly, curled herself in the fear, the danger, the death. The thing itself.

After a few minutes, he stepped back from her. Janey's horsie creaked relentlessly in the backyard.

"Hot pants," he said.

She shook her head.

He ran his hand over her rump again, and she shuddered.

"They are."

"Yes," she said.

"So you're what Converse is married to."

She shrugged.

"Far fucking out."

He began to seem more like a man to her; out of habit or duty she felt some tenderness.

"We could work this out a little," he said.

"Yeah," Marge said, "I'm for that."

"But we have problems, don't we?"

"I'm sorry about that. I'll go to the bank."

He stared at her for a moment and nodded. "Where is it?"

"A couple of blocks."

"I'll drive you," he said.

She went down to the yard to take Janey off the horse; it was not easily done. In the end she had to hold Janey's shoulders down to make her stop bouncing.

"We're going for a ride, Janey."

She had to say it several times before Janey was aware of her, and in the end she lifted the child from the red plastic saddle. Janey did not complain.

Washing Janey's face, she saw herself in the bathroom mirror, displaying a wan, fatuous smile. Madness.

She ran a damp towel across Janey's small face, pasting locks of wet brown hair to the temples. With every second, the thing that had passed between her and the cold-eyed man became more remote and impossible, a fantasy, a delusion. Dilaudid.

When Janey was presentable, they went into the living room; he was gone. She passed into Janey's bedroom, opened the back door, and saw that he was in the yard trying to look over the picket fence that separated her patch of lawn from the landlord's. As soon as she turned back toward the living room, she heard him running up the back steps—and turning again saw him charge through the door at her, straight from her last night's dreams. His eyes were empty.

Marge's first impulse was to run toward Janey, but before she could move she found herself flung backward through the living-room door and she did not realize how hard he had struck her until she collided with the living-room table and the warm coffee and cassis ran over her trouser leg.

He stood over her in an animal crouch, staring at the hall doorway. Someone was climbing the hallway steps—a heavy unhurried step.

"Tell them wait a minute," Hicks said. "Don't you open that door."

Still crouching, he ran back into Janey's bedroom. Just before the door closed behind him, Marge caught sight, over his bent shoulders, of a blond young man in the back doorway. The young man's arms opened as Hicks ran toward him.

Noises she could not understand came from the bedroom—soft scuffling, a few light thumps, what sounded like clothes hangers falling in the closet, finally a low groan.

There was a firm polite knock at the hallway door.

Marge clung to Janey and stared at the blank door in horror. The knock sounded again.

"Just a minute," Marge said.

The blond young man from the back door stepped into the living room; his nose was running grossly and copiously. Hicks was behind him lifting his shirt-tails, as though he were trying to undress him. The youth knelt down on the floor; Hicks was crouched above him, feeling him up. As if in a magic act, he produced a length of taped chain from the young man's person. Swinging the chain, he drew himself up—he was pointing at her, mouthing words.

Marge drew back, enfolding Janey in her arms and just as she was shaking her head to indicate her utter confusion, her incomprehension, her inability to cooperate in any manner, the hall door opened silently and a bearded man stood in the doorway. He looked down at Marge in mild surprise.

Instead of coming in, the bearded man took a quick step backward. A whirling gray shape rushed past Marge's face and something curled itself around the bearded man's head. Hicks dived for the doorway. He and the bearded man lurched into the apartment, panting.

"O.K., O.K.," a voice that was not Ray's was saying. "O.K., for Christ's sake."

It was the bearded man. Hicks was holding a pistol against his ear.

"I'll kill you quick," Hicks told the bearded man. He pulled the chain from around the man's shoulders and swung it so that it wrapped around his left forearm. The bearded man's mustache was bloody.

Marge stood up and carried Janey to the bedroom. They were both crying now.

"It's all right," Marge said. The terror in Janey's eyes was so total that Marge could not bear to look at it.

"It's all right, sweetie. You wait on the back steps. Will you? Please, Janey?"

Janey went to the back steps, sat on the topmost step and wept.

In the living room, Hicks was repeatedly kicking the blond young man. The bearded man, his hands apparently handcuffed behind him, watched with something like embarrassment.

"I don't blame you for doing that," he told Hicks after a while.

"I'm glad you understand," Hicks said. He left off kicking the youth and started going through the bearded man's pockets. The first thing he removed was a gold-colored badge set in a shiny plastic wallet. The badge was lettered "Special Investigator." Hicks looked at it and threw it on the floor.

"I'm a police buff," the man said.

Hicks regarded him in a way that was not altogether unfriendly.

"I gotta know," he said. "Was it you I talked to on the phone last night?"

"Let's not spoil it."

The blond man was standing up slowly. Hicks walked over to him and clapped him on the back.

"Say hello, Broadway Joe." He flicked the youth's hanging shirttail. "Blow your nose." Suddenly he kicked the youth in the shin. "Where's your blade today?"

"Fuck you," Broadway Joe said.

Hicks shrugged.

"You guys are something else. Did you really think I'd lay my good down and go queer-stomping?"

"It *has* happened," the bearded man said.

Hicks turned to Marge, who had backed up in the bedroom doorway.

"You know these guys?"

Marge shook her head.

"We're Federal Agents, lady," the blond kid said. "You're in plenty of trouble."

Marge looked at him for only a moment.

"Are they?" she asked Hicks.

"They're take-off artists," Hicks said. "That's who they are."

The bearded man carried a loaded Walther automatic with a spare clip; Walthers had become the counterculture's weapon of choice. His pockets contained a billfold with a dozen credit cards in different names, a key ring with a great many keys on it, a Mexican switchblade and chain manacle known to the police as a "come along." Hicks used it to secure Broadway Joe's hands to the drainage pipe of the kitchen sink. Broadway Joe's pockets had only his works—a dropper and a spike, still in its little box, straight from the doctor's sample bag.

The bearded man, his hands cuffed behind him,

was following Hicks about the apartment like a sales-man.

"You're not some asshole," he told Hicks. "Don't involve yourself in a disaster."

Hicks took him by the cuffs and began to pull him backward toward the bathroom. The man shifted his footing to keep his balance.

"Hicks, listen to me. There's no deal. It's just us. Always was."

Hicks propped him up against the bathroom door and let him talk. The man was smiling as though he were pleased with the elegant simplicity of what he had to say, but slightly impatient with his listener's obtuseness.

"It was just her and her husband."

Marge looked at him in wonder.

"Her and her husband, a couple of squares. A couple of idiots for Christ's sake. Nobody would pay them. Would you?"

Hicks pushed the man against the bathroom door so that it swung open behind him and he landed sprawled against the toilet.

"This is theft," the man said, standing upright. "You're gonna pay for this."

Broadway Joe began shouting from the kitchen.

"You're fucking A he's gonna pay for it, man. He's gonna burn for it."

Hicks called Marge into the bathroom, gave her the key to the fat man's handcuffs, and told her to unlock them. He stood in the doorway holding the thirty-eight in his right hand, with his left hand grasping his right wrist.

Marge knelt where she could not see the man's face and worked the key in the lock until the manacles uncoupled. Hicks sent the man sprawling against the toilet bowl again, slid his pistol across the bathroom tiles toward Marge, and went after him. He forced the man's arms downward behind the bowl and secured the handcuffs over his wrists below the porcelained pipe that joined it to the wall.

He picked up the handgun and then unbuckled the man's belt and lowered his trousers so that he appeared to be relieving himself.

"You're gonna end up in a bag, fool," the man said.

"If that's the case," Hicks said, "I better ice you fellas."

The man shook his head.

"That wouldn't help."

Hicks laughed.

"You think it wouldn't help, huh?"

"What did you get for this run, Hicks? A few grand? We'll double it. It's our smack, for Christ's sake."

"Maybe you ought to," Marge said.

Hicks did not look at her.

"Maybe you should let them have it," she said. "It's not worth it."

"This is an intelligent lady," the man on the toilet bowl said. He stared at Marge in a sort of passion; his brown eyes were moist. "Hicks, you hear what she says? She doesn't want to die."

Hicks walked out of the bathroom. In a moment, Marge followed.

"Listen," the man on the toilet called. "She wants to hand it over. He won't let her."

"You stupid cocksucker," Broadway Joe called from the kitchen. "You know what you're gonna get?"

Hicks walked into the kitchen, bent over Broadway Joe, and clubbed him twice across the face with the butt of the thirty-eight.

"You're not gettin' any cherry," Broadway Joe said softly, and fainted.

"I just can't leave him alone," Hicks said. "I love him."

They went into the bedroom and closed the door.

"Let's give it to them," Marge said tearfully. "I'll take the loss. I'll pay you anyway."

"Take all your letters," Hicks told her. "Take anything that can indicate where you might go. Don't forget anything." He touched her arm. "And make it quick."

"Let's give it to them." Marge said.

"They're not as reasonable as you. They'll kill us anyway."

He went back into the living room and stood by the window. "Hurry up, Marge."

Marge took up a leather portfolio and began shoving things into it.

Letters from Converse, lists of toll telephone calls, whatever came to mind and hand. She was not really concentrating well. Janey had come back up the back steps and was watching her through the glass doors.

When she had taken everything she could think of, she went into the living room for a quick last look and quite suddenly began to gag. It took her a moment and a few deep breaths to stop.

"I'm sorry," she told Hicks.

"You're not ready for this," Hicks said.

She went back to the bedroom, let Janey inside, and led her by the hand past the open bathroom door. She kept herself between Janey and the doorway but Janey peeked round her and saw the bearded man on the toilet.

"Kiss your ass goodbye, cunt," the bearded man said.

Marge did not look at him.

Hicks put the taped chain and the pistols he had acquired into his AWOL bag and led them into the hallway. They went down the two flights slowly, Marge pushing Janey before her. When Hicks opened the street door, the sunlight bathing the white and pastel buildings of the block made the world seem abnormally bright.

He stood for a moment peering outside.

"Where's your car?" he asked her.

"Beside the house. On the left."

"Get in it and start it up."

Marge led Janey to the car and turned the key. When the engine turned over, he came quickly down the front steps and climbed in beside them. They pulled out of the driveway and turned left toward the Bay.

"To the bank," Hicks said.

IT WAS A DIRT ROAD WINDING OVER BLACK CANYON. Above them were fields of blazing stars and on some of the curves Marge caught a glimpse of moonlight on rolling surf. The wind tasted of jasmine. On the far side of the canyon, at an uncertain distance, were colored lights which grew in number and brightness toward the horizon.

They climbed in low gear, Hicks driving, the Ford straining into each rise.

"O.K.?" Hicks asked her. She had been weeping quietly since nightfall.

"I should have brought her. She must be terrified."

"You did the right thing. June is really special with kids and she's a great hassler."

They had left Janey in Mountain View, at June and Owen's. The idea was that June would deliver her to Marge's father at the first discreet opportunity.

"I mean do you know what she's gone through today?"

"I was there."

On the next curve she strained to see the ocean, her hand covering her mouth.

"I was a kid once," Hicks said. "I had days like that."

She turned to him with a scornful smile. They could hardly see each other in the darkness.

"Not like *that*."

"Worse. Wait till I tell you the story of my life. You'll eat your heart out."

"How'd you turn out?" she asked after a while.

"Well, your husband says I'm a psychopath."

Marge shivered and said nothing.

"You think he's probably right?"

"It's a very imprecise term."

It seemed to her that he was laughing but she could not be sure. After another twisting mile, he pulled to the side of the dirt road and turned off his lights.

"There's somebody there."

"Where?"

"Where we're going."

She put her head out the window and when she had listened for a moment she imagined that she could hear voices and faint music.

He started the engine again and they climbed for several hundred yards without lights. When he pulled over he got out of the car and tapped on the door for Marge to follow.

The moon had come over the crest of the hills, a full hysterical shaman's moon that illuminated the canyon to half its depth. In its light, they slid down the dry scaly shoulder of the road, Hicks going before. There was a gate almost covered in brush at the end of a half-hidden fire trail; Hicks swung it open and they went carefully over an iron cattle grid and followed the trail downward. They could hear the music clearly now—"Credence Clearwater"—and the voices under it. When the side ended they heard the voices alone and it seemed to Marge that there was something wrong about the sound of them, some strangeness or absence of inflection, that did not suit the party music. Around the next hump of mesquite they came in sight of a building, its windows lit by firelight.

Hicks stopped her with a hand against her breast.

"I know who it is."

He stood watching the house as though he were trying to make up his mind.

"Hide," he said.

She looked into the shadowy brush.

"Hide where?"

Shadows moved against the lighted windows; Marge felt cold. She stayed where she was, waiting for him to direct her. But he kept looking down at the house.

"Belay that. Come on with me."

She followed him into a dirt yard littered with tire tubes and car parts. A number of vehicles were parked in the darkness behind the house but they could not see how many.

Hicks had a gun in his hand. As they neared the windows, she saw him slip it into his back pocket; the stock was visible against his belt. She pulled on his arm.

"It shows," she said.

Hicks only nodded. He moved into the shadow of the house and close alongside the window.

From where he stood, he could see most of the shack's single room. There was a hot fire in the potbellied stove and an oil lamp burning high on a table in the corner. Two blond girls in jeans and patches were kneeling on a mattress in the middle of the floor. They looked very much alike and neither of them appeared to be over sixteen.

Against the wall behind them sat two smiling young men in denim jackets. Their smiles were steady and vacant and they leaned against each other's shoulder. One of them Hicks knew as Shoshone; it was how he introduced himself. He was slight and copper-colored, an Indian or a pachuco who spoke unsullied L.A. The second man was a tall long-hair with pouchy eyes who was perhaps twenty years older than the two girls. From the play of shadows, Hicks reckoned that there were two more people inside who were beyond his scan. He felt they were female.

He found Marge hunkering in the darkness near the door and he pulled her to her feet.

"This is your house," he told her. "You better be stoned cool."

Now I'll see who I got with me, he thought. He knocked loudly on the door. He did not want to surprise them too much. Then he pushed it open and walked into the room.

The men in the denim jackets gaped. One of the teen-agers on the mat uttered a stifled scream. Across the room, a fat beetle-browed girl in a dirty serape stared at him in anger. There was a fourth girl too, a skinny redhead with prominent teeth and a corpselike complexion who was playing with a dark wig.

They watched him as he picked up the cassette tape recorder and shut it off. Trouble, as he suspected it would, came first from the lady with the eyebrows.

"What the fuck are you doin'? Who are you man?"

"If I weren't big and easy," Hicks said, "I'd ask you the same question."

The blondes on the mattress looked up at him with fearful, addled eyes. Shoshone climbed to his feet and came toward him.

"I didn't see who it was for a minute," he said. He was laughing, his voice slurred with reds.

The beetle-browed girl was beside herself with moronic indignation.

"What *is* this shit? Who is he?"

"He lives here," Shoshone said. He staggered backward and rested a lean brown hand on the top of his companion's head. "He lives here, right?"

Shoshone's friend watched Hicks with even, sleepy eyes.

"Well, I mean, where you been?" Shoshone asked. In the course of the sentence his emotional valence seemed to swing from chemical good nature to unnatural fury and at least part of the way back.

"At sea," Hicks said. He noticed that the people in the room were looking toward the door behind him where Marge stood. He glanced at her quickly and to his satisfaction saw her looking cool and arrogant. He had seen something of the same look about her when she was denying him his money. It had made him not trust her at first.

"You're a sailor. He's a sailor," Shoshone said to his friend. "I know this guy."

Shoshone's friend was looking at the pistol in Hicks' pocket.

"What kinda piece you got there?" he asked in a slow Okie drawl.

"Thirty-eight Special," Hicks said.

The Okie permitted himself a single weary guffaw.

"Like to look at some groovy weapons?"

Hicks shrugged.

"You might come see me before I split."

"Are you a sailor?" the redhead with the wig asked.

"That's right," Hicks said.

One of the teen-agers began to vomit quietly on the mattress. The fat girl was on her like a bacchante, folds of tie-dyed cloth billowing from under her serape.

"Lookitcha, you dumb cunt. Look watcha doin'." She had a willow switch in her hand and she whipped the girl across the shoulder with it. The blonde collapsed across her own watery vomit.

"Take us home," she wailed.

"Aren't they from around here?" Hicks heard Marge ask. She was still cool, half smiling. When she looked at him, he smiled back at her, trying to warn her off the issue. But he said nothing.

"I live," the second girl said, "at twenty-two thirty-one Sepulveda Boulevard."

The girl who had been hit moaned.

"Don't tell me where you live."

"Pick them up hitchhiking?" Marge asked.

"What's it to you?" the fat girl began to say, but she broke the sentence off with a shrug as if she were asking herself a question.

"They wanted a party," the Okie said.

"Yeah," Shoshone said. "We thought they were hip but you know they're uptight boojwa."

Hicks looked down at the mattress.

"They took a lot pills, huh?"

"They didn't have much choice," the redhead with the wig said.

"Lookatcha your mattress," the fat girl said. "Looka what those dumb cunts did."

Hicks grabbed a chair and sat down on it backward, facing his guests.

"I was gonna air it out anyway." He looked around the room and addressed himself to the Okie.

"I may have some heavy company pretty soon. I wish you'd take the party down the canyon."

The man nodded slowly. Everyone in the room watched him. He stood up lazily and shook himself in a little dance.

"I can dig it."

The fat girl stood over the teen-agers until they stood up.

"You probably ought to lose those two down in the park," Hicks said cheerfully. "They're jailbait for sure."

Shoshone patted one of the girls on the ass.

"We take care of 'em."

The fat girl whooped, covered her hand with her mouth, and shrugged.

When the others had filed outside, the Okie stood in the doorway looking at Marge, then at Hicks.

"I'll come back in a couple of days like you said. Got some things you might want to look at."

"Sure enough," Hicks said.

Hicks stayed in his chair as they listened to an

engine start up outside the house. Marge paced up and down. When Shoshone's truck was under way and the engine noise growing fainter, Hicks stood up and dragged the soiled mattress outside. He stood for a while watching the headlights coil down the canyon road. When he went in, he found Marge sitting in his chair with her head in her hands.

"What the hell was that?"

"Welcome to L.A." He touched her face as he walked past. He had taken a key from his pocket and opened a cabinet above a dry sink in the back of the cabin. In the cabinet were a bottle of blended whiskey and a car distributor; Hicks set them out beside the sink.

"That's just folks up here. This is where the canyon consciousness prevails."

"What happens to those kids?"

"You're thinking like a mother."

She stared at him; he saw her searching for the psychopath.

"Have a drink."

She looked doubtful. She had been fiddling through her carry bag for something and she seemed reluctant to let it go.

"O.K.," she said, setting the bag down.

He dusted out two fruit jars and poured whiskey into them.

"No water up here."

She drank, grimacing.

"You understand," Hicks said, "that we're not in a position to make a big thing over something like those kids. You walk around these canyons enough you'll come across a sleeping bag full of bones. I've seen a number, I'm not kidding. Fuck up a little bit once and the next bag of bones is you." He drank his whiskey. "We're everybody's meat. What's in that bag is what it all boils down to."

"What does?"

"Everything," Hicks said.

"How come you went for this?" he asked her. "Was it your idea?"

"He thought it up. My idea was to really do it."

He poured himself another shot. Marge declined.

"No. You were right this morning," she said. "It sucks. I'd like to give it back." She shivered. "To wherever the hell it emanates from."

"It doesn't emanate. People make it."

Marge moved closer to the stove.

"He'll be back before long. I wonder what he'll think."

Hicks laughed.

"I don't know what your scene is but I'd say he'll think you did him. He'll think that at first anyway. Until he's hassled."

Marge bit her nails.

"We should have let them have it. If I'd been there alone I would have."

"It isn't yours anymore," he said. He regretted it immediately. She was not without courage, capable certainly of spite and there was no point in asking for trouble.

She seemed more troubled than angry, as though the problem were a moral one.

"Whose is it?"

He felt that he would have to explain it philosophically or she would refuse to understand.

"It belongs to whoever controls it."

"So is it yours now?"

He went back to the sink for more whiskey.

"I been juicing ever since I hit this beach. I gotta stop tomorrow, you remind me."

"Why didn't you tell me in Berkeley about who controls it?"

"I had other things on my mind."

"What am I supposed to do," she asked with a thin smile, "go home and forget about it? Because it doesn't look like I can do that now."

On the drive down, he had given some thought

111

to using her as a decoy. Set in motion, she would soon be traced and while they ran her down he might sell out and get clear. But he could not simply turn her loose because there was a chance that she would crumble and go to law. He had devised false errands for her and rendezvous, all of them plausible.

"If you wanted to rip us off," she said, "you should have done it before. You should never have turned up with it."

He brought the bottle over to the stove and poured himself another shot.

"I can see where you could be a real pain in the ass," he told her.

It was pathetic, he thought, the satisfaction they took in being logical.

"I mean what are you saying? That you want your rights? Sue me."

She watched him in self-righteous silence. Arrogance.

"All right—it's your dope. You want it back? Take it and get on the road with it. Run it over to East L.A. and sell it to the pachucos. C'mon man, you fucked up—that's all. You can't do nothing with that shit."

"Why bring me all the way down here to tell me that?" she asked.

"Why'd you come down?"

"To tell the truth," Marge said, "I was just following you."

He stood up and walked over to the small single window and saw his own reflection in the lamplight.

"We ought to shitcan it and run."

"Now you're really scaring me," Marge said.

"That's the truth." He began to pace back and forth from the sink to the stove. "I got hardly any time. I never moved smack in my life. I can't move it without making myself known and when I do it's wide open city."

"What about our friends from this morning?" she

said after a minute. "Do you think we could sell to them after all? They offered you a deal. Maybe we could make one."

"Who's we?" he said. He sat down again beside her, laughing a little. "If I hadn't been so hung over and pissed off this morning this shit wouldn't ever have come about."

She moved away slightly, contentious.

"What about them?"

"Right. I thought about that. First thing, I don't know who they are."

"John must know. We could call him and maybe set something up."

Hicks shook his head.

"You gotta figure intangibles. They know what fuck-ups we are. They got their pride. I don't think we could pull it off."

"I think they're fuck-ups too," Marge said.

Hicks nodded. "They're animals. I wonder who the hell they are."

"John knows."

He smiled.

"You don't respect him very much, do you?"

"Sure," Hicks said.

"Why did you carry for him?"

"Why do you have to have it all figured out? I don't always have a reason for the shit I do." He picked up the jar she had been drinking from. "Drink with me."

She let him fill the jar. When she raised it to drink, he saw that she was clutching something in her other hand. He took the hand and spread the fingers and took a Percodan from her cold palm.

"How come you're taking Percodan?"

She sat stiffly back against the wall.

"Pain."

"Don't bullshit me. I asked you if you were a junkie. You can't fake it."

"I've been doing a lot of dilaudid. I wanted to quit. So I'm taking Percodan."

He gave her back the pill and she swallowed it with whiskey, gagging slightly.

"How much dilaudid?"

She turned away. He set his drink down and stretched out on the floor. He had taken the thirty-eight out of his pocket and set it down on the floor between them and as he lay beside her he became intensely aware of it. She was holding her hand out stiffly seeming to measure its steadiness. The hand hovered over his chest and he thought she must be about to touch him, but it was the pistol she took hold of. She turned it round in her hands, inspecting it. He watched her from the corners of his eyes until she set it down.

The wood stove was burning down, the oil in the lamp almost gone. Hicks moved closer to the stove, partly turning his back on her.

He had no rest there. When he turned toward her again, she was staring at him wide-eyed. Her stare made him lonely; it was utterly without warmth, without recognition—he might have been a snake.

"What are you doing?" he asked her, ashamed of the lame trivial question. Her gray eyes looked paler in the dim light. He wanted to ask her what it was she saw.

She laughed and he shivered, and at the same moment so did she.

The instant remained. He held his breath. Cold Zen.

He wondered if she had been aware of it.

As they undressed, their throats were close together, guarded. When she pressed herself against him, he held her away for a moment wanting to see her, the light on her breasts, the gray eyes, wanting to know the life under his hands that he could draw up from her mouth and breathe back inside her.

On the army blankets, she bent to his penis, a resolute harakiri, self-avenging; he could feel the abnegation, the death. He did not pull back or intimate any warning when he came. Withdrawn, he pulled her up to himself—she drew breath hard and he knew she must have paused between need and revulsion and the knowledge inflamed him again.

Because of his nature and circumstances, the most satisfying part of Hicks' sexual life had come to be masturbation—he preferred it to prostitutes because it was more sanitary and took less time. He did not take it lightly when, rarely, one woman pleased him, and his deepest pleasures were intellectual and emotional. He became a hoarder, careful and slow to the point of obsessiveness, a thinker.

He eased her toward the light, his strength in his tongue, stroking the sweet-sour depths and surfaces. When he was ready he went in, striking for the deepest darkest part of her the limits of himself could reach, then eased up, stirring, stroking from inside. She came and spoke to him; he thought she said, "Find thee."

And again—and he spent himself again—less thoughtfully, in lubricious happy chaos.

Lying beside her, he was at peace. He propped his head on his elbow, lights flashing in his brain, his spinal column denuded of sacred vital fluids, and inclined his head in gratitude. He was bound. He felt strong and in complicity with fortune.

When the lamp failed, he missed her eyes, although she clung to him.

He tried to make himself believe she had been with him in the shivering moment from which they had begun; there were no words to ask with. Not knowing caused him a stab of loneliness before he slept.

Much later, he woke up in darkness, thinking he heard footsteps outside. He rose quickly, stepped over her and prowled the windows. She was awake when he came back.

"What happens tomorrow?" she asked.

"Dig it." He put his finger against her belly and moved it downward until the tip pressed her labia. His lips were close against her ear. "We're dead."

SOMEONE HAD DRAWN A DEVIL ON THE WALL above Janey's crib. It had horns and bat wings and a huge erect phallus; there was enough characterization in the details of the face to make it distinctly frightening.

Converse sat in Janey's bedroom with his back to the thing. He had found the refrigerator working, but the meat in it had blackened and the milk soured. There had also been a bottle of cassis inside and Converse drank some with the idea that it might keep him awake while he decided what to do. He was nearly too tired to sit upright.

When she had not turned up at the airport and no one had answered the phone, he had taken a taxi from Oakland which had cost him over twenty-five dollars.

Through the back-door windows he could watch evening drawing over the hills. From time to time he would turn on the drawing, acting out the thought that it might disappear, a hallucination of his fatigue. But it did not disappear and before long he could not stop looking at it. Sometimes he thought he recognized people he had seen somewhere, and he searched the features for some sort of clue.

Things were funnier over here.

After sitting for an hour, Converse decided to have a word with Mr. Roche, his landlord. Mr. Roche was a tiny man who lived in a bungalow behind the apartment building. As Converse walked across Mr.

Roche's lawn, the unfamiliar wind, cold and sour, chilled him and added to his fear.

It took Converse several minutes to draw Mr. Roche from cover. Although Mr. Roche owned the building in which Converse lived, it pleased him to pretend to be the manager. In that capacity he could refer to himself reverentially as "The Boss." Mr. Roche stood slightly over five feet and had fine womanly Irish features. His face, like his apartment house, was his late mother's. Converse addressed him across two lengths of chain lock.

"Hi," Converse said, as though attempting to elicit a welcome of some sort. Mr. Roche seemed to dislike Converse and his family so intensely that Converse often wondered why he had rented to them in the first place.

Mr. Roche smiled a great deal; his life was not easy.

"I'm just back from overseas," Converse explained. "My wife's out now and I wondered if she left any messages for me."

"No," Mr. Roche said. His smile broadened and his eyes twinkled with whimsy.

Mr. Roche was a member of the parish Holy Name Society and of the American Party. He had once owned a dog named MacDuff. One evening while Mr. Roche was walking MacDuff on Ponderosa Street, a column of Gypsy Jokers had rounded the corner and the point rider's machine had struck MacDuff and crushed his spine. The rider was overthrown. When Mr. Roche, in his bereavement, had remonstrated with the group, the thrown Gypsy Joker had seized him and battered his small head against the curb until he was unconscious. It had been expensive, even with Blue Cross and Medi-Cal. The incident had made Mr. Roche, who was not adventurous, even more wary. When a representative of the American Party called on Mr. Roche to solicit contributions and discuss Americanism, Mr. Roche denied his membership and even pretended to be someone else altogether.

"Well," Converse asked, "do you know when she went out?"

"Days ago," Mr. Roche said. *"Days ago."* He shook his head in what appeared to be good-natured disapproval. "I understand there was some kind of trouble," he added softly.

"What kind of trouble? Where did you hear about trouble?"

"Oh, I don't know," Mr. Roche said. "I think it was one of the fellas that drives the trucks."

"Trucks?" Converse asked. He yawned convulsively.

"She didn't pay any rent for next month. The boss'll want you out."

"Look, I'll write you a check tomorrow. Don't worry about rent."

"He'll want you out. There's been people coming in."

Mr. Roche closed the door.

From the apartment, Converse telephoned the Odeon. A girl there told him that Marge had not turned up for a week or so. He drank another glass of cassis, looked at the devil picture for a while, and picked up the telephone to call Elmer.

But in the course of dialing he became uneasy about the security of his telephone. He replaced the receiver and decided to use the pay phone in the liquor store on the corner.

He went quickly along the block. It was nearly dark; the empty sidewalks and the ranks of huge headlighted American cars at the intersection frightened him. Passing under the dead eyes of the liquor store clerks, he dialed Elmer's special number at a phone beside the beer cooler. Elmer believed, with some reason, that Pacific Publications' phones were tapped and he had personally installed a separate

118

phone in one of the *Nightbeat* closets for the purpose of receiving private calls.

"Jesus Christ," Elmer said. "Where are you calling from?"

"A pay phone in Berkeley. Look—something weird is happening."

Elmer cut him off. "I know about it. Come and see me."

"Now?"

"Yes, now. Do you know who's following you?"

"Nobody," Converse said, realizing at the same moment that he must be wrong.

"That's impossible. Find out who it is and lose them on your way here. Do it right."

Converse's weary brain resisted instruction. He leaned his forehead on the cold metal surface of the freezer.

"I guess I'm in trouble."

"So it would seem," Elmer said.

As he walked out of the store a peculiar image thrust itself on his recall. The image was of steam rising from the shower room of the Yokasuka brig. For a moment, he experienced the image with intense clarity—the steam, the sound of the water needling the gray cement, the prisoners' voices. Converse had once stood by outside the showers while the CMPs, the prisoners, beat up a white rat. They had done it on Converse's watch because they knew he would not interfere. The recollection induced in Converse a sense of utter despair which he found soothing.

For a short time he stood in front of the store, studying the street with as much indifference as he could affect. The corner was empty and, as far as he could tell, so were the parked cars along the curb. He went back into the liquor store and called Yellow Cab.

It was fifteen minutes before the cab arrived. Converse purchased a pint of Gold Leaf Cognac to cultivate the management. When the cab pulled up, he slipped into the back seat and told the long-haired driver to take him to Macy's. As soon as they were out in traffic, Converse noticed that the headlights of a car parked across the street from the store went on. It was an ordinary-looking tan-colored car and Converse, who knew little about cars, could not tell what make it was without closer examination. It stayed several lengths behind them, all the way across the bridge and into downtown San Francisco. Converse drank his cognac without economy. He could hardly bring it into Macy's.

At the Grant Avenue doors, he eased the bottle onto the taxi floor, thrust a ten into the driver's hand, and hurried into Macy's without looking behind him. He hurried across the crowded street level with such haste and obvious alarm that shoppers turned to look after him. Macy's was number ten. It smelled of perfume and breath and there were horrible little bells.

Ascending on the escalator, Converse watched the door he had come in. To his horror, a dark-bearded man came quickly in from Grant and looked, rather angrily, among the crowd. Converse had almost cleared the second floor landing before the man looked upward toward him. He looked away from the man before their eyes met. The second floor was as crowded as the one below. Converse dashed round the posts to rise another story. The third floor was as high as he dared go; above it would be unpopulated wastes of furniture and carpeting in which he might be brought to bay. Stepping from the escalator he loped across the record department to find the other set of escalators. In the record department they were playing the "Age of Aquarius."

On the other escalator, he decided to ride all the way down. He was back on the street-level floor in seconds, making for the O'Farrell Street exit in prodigies of self-control. There would be another one outside, he realized, circling in the tan car.

The car was not in sight as Converse dodged through the Powell Street traffic. Rounding the corner of O'Farrell, he permitted himself a near run and he kept going until he reached a side door of the Mason Hotel. He crossed the lobby and walked upstairs to the mezzanine where he found a bar with a view of the doors. The bar was furnished in bamboo and its walls and hangings were designed to suggest the Orient. Converse ordered a Scotch and water, leaning forward in order to keep the length of the lobby in his scan. Sporting in the regency plush below were men with name cards on their lapels and a large number of blond children with crew cuts and bow ties. There were no bearded men.

He drank deeply of his weak drink; fatigue was undercutting the alcohol in his blood and he felt no closer to intoxication than tachycardia.

His choice of Macy's as a place in which to flee had not been an instant improvisation; he had been pursued through Macy's before and had escaped there. It had been Christmas time—the store had been more crowded and seasonally decorated. His pursuer at the time was a middle-aged man with a harelip whom Converse had rashly interrupted in the act of stroking ladies' privates on the Geary Street bus. The man had slunk off to the rear without a word, but he had followed Converse from the bus at Union Square. Cursing his own fatuous interference, Converse had dodged through the noontime crowds, but the harelipped man had been dogged and agile. At each intersection, Converse had cringed in anticipation of the bullet, the blade, the hatchet. At last he had darted into Macy's and escaped along a route very like the one just employed.

How peculiar and stupid everything was, he thought. In the short length of time during which he could force himself to reflect on the matter, he felt certain that it was preferable to be chased through Macy's as a scourge to the poor and a poisoner of children than as a hapless, cowardly concerned citizen. It was more chic, probably even in God's eyes. He ordered another drink.

If he had been just a bit less timid in Vietnam, he thought, he might be honorably dead—like those heroes who went everywhere on motorbikes and died of their own young energy and joie de vivre. Now it would be necessary to face death *here*—where things were funnier—and death would be as peculiar and stupid as everything else.

He paid for the drinks and went down to the Mason lobby. Returning to the side door, he stood just inside it for a while and then stepped out to the sidewalk. No beard, no tan car.

When he had crossed Mission, he turned in his tracks and looked around him, but he could see no trace of pursuit. He went all the way to Howard and followed it to Seventh and by the time he turned back toward Mission again, he was as concerned with the likelihood of being mugged as with whoever was following him. He was reasonably satisfied that he had, for the moment, broken free.

Elmer's office was above two stories of shirt factory on the corner of Seventh and Mission. Converse had a key to the elevator.

There was a bell beside the door that led to the offices from the darkened foul hallway. When he rang it, Frances called to him from inside.

"Yeah?"

"Converse."

He heard the sliding of a police lock and Frances stood before him in the office's fluorescent light, squinting with concern.

"Johnny! Jesus Christ, chum."

She had grown a bit soft under the eyes but her *poitrine* endured, firm as ever.

Pacific Publications was as he had left it. Over Mike Woo's desk was a photograph of Mao Tse-tung,

a written inscription across the buttoned pocket of
the Chairman's tunic:

> "To Mike Woo
> A real neat Marxist Leninist
> and a helluva nice guy
> Always a Pal
> Chairman Mao"

Converse had written it on the picture the day
before he left for Vietnam.

R. Douglas Dalton, the colorless odorless alcoholic,
sat late at his desk, typing the week's last story. He
was pale and natty as ever. When he saw Converse
he stood up slowly.

"Great Scott," he said, "young John fresh from
the steaming wartorn." His lips parted over a Draculan
smile. "Hip hip," he cried softly, "hurrah. Hip hip . . ."

"Douglas," Frances said, ". . . please." She watched
Converse with hyperthyroid curiosity. "Your father-
in-law would like very much to see you."

"Same here," Converse said.

Elmer Bender worked in a large gray room. Its
only furnishings, besides the desk, were a leatherette
armchair, an old-fashioned coatrack and an electric
percolator. Across the surface of the desk were spread
pictures of dead people which would be used to illus-
trate the stories in *Nightbeat*. Dead people could be
portrayed as anything—killer hermits, spanking
judges, teen-aged nymphomaniacs—they had no
recourse to law. Only in Utah could lawsuits be filed
on behalf of the deceased, so it was vital that the
dead people come from everywhere else.

Elmer sat primly behind the rows of photographs,
his hands folded beside a dummy of the current front
page. The headline was a ten-inch blue banner—MAD
DENTIST YANKS GIRL'S TONGUE.

"Sit down, dear boy," Elmer said. "Are you confused?"

Converse collapsed into the armchair.

"Yes, I am," he said. "There's weird shit all over our walls."

"I don't know about your walls. Marge is hiding somewhere. Janey is in Canada."

"In Canada? What the fuck is she doing in Canada?"

"She's with Phyllis and Jay. We got her out of California and off with them."

"Why?"

"Why? Because her parents are criminals. What the hell are you dealing in heroin for? Have you lost your mind?"

Converse closed his eyes. He saw the steaming shower room again.

"I take it," he said, "that we've been caught."

Elmer nodded briskly.

"Who was following me?"

"I'm not sure. Did you lose them?"

"Yes. In Macy's."

"What I don't understand is why they don't just arrest you."

"Then they're after me. Right now."

"After you? Dear boy—they got you. Do *you* know where Marge is?"

Converse shook his head.

"Maybe with the guy who brought it over."

"Maybe dead," Elmer stood up. "This time I'm resigned. She's my baby but I can't help her anymore. She's a big girl—I'm an old man." He stared at Converse, the ceiling lights glinting in his wire-framed glasses. "Who do you think you are? Some big hustler? Was it her idea?"

"Both of ours."

"I can understand Margie, she's disturbed. In you I'm disappointed."

"It was a crazy idea," Converse said. "You hear

stories over there. They say everybody does it. Being there fucks up your perspective."

"So we're led to believe," Elmer said. "Who are you in with?"

"These people. They're supposed to be friends of Irvine Vibert."

Elmer had a way of appearing to smile when people said things he found disagreeable.

"Irvine Vibert! The wheeler-dealer? Is it true?"

"I think so."

"Did you think you were a second Irvine Vibert, you schmuck? Do I have to explain to you the situation you're both in?"

He took a card from the corner of his desk blotter and handed it to Converse. "Benjamin Whiteson, Attorney at Law," it said on the card, with an address on Ellis Street.

"See him. He's a friend."

Converse put the card in his pocket and leaned his head on the back of the chair.

"I'm cracking up," he told Elmer. "I'm hallucinating. I just got off a plane."

Elmer pursed his lips and glanced upward.

"It's incredible," Converse insisted. "I can't believe I did it."

Elmer waved his hand as though he were dispersing an unpleasant odor.

"A sense of unreality is not a legal defense."

"I suppose not," Converse said.

"There was a man around here called Antheil, a Fed who talks like a lawyer. He asked me if I knew my daughter was mixed up in a narcotics ring. I said I couldn't believe such a thing—naturally as soon as he said it I knew it must be true. You know about my difficulties with the Feds?"

"Pretty much," Converse said. Elmer had had political difficulties.

"Well, this Antheil knew all about that. He accused me of hiding her, he threatened me in various ways.

Finally I think I convinced him I didn't know anything about it."

"Don't they watch this place?"

"They watch my house, not here. And they haven't been around the house much this week. Of course it's possible that since they lost you tonight they'll have a look over here."

Converse stood up, trying to shake off his fatigue.

"Are you sure they know about me? Maybe they infiltrated the people who were going to pick up. They might just be fishing following me."

Elmer made a sour face and shook his head.

"I don't understand what they're doing. Do you know a little bimbo called June? A nutty-looking little blonde?"

"I don't know any Junes," Converse said.

"Janey turned up with this June. Marge left her there. The only word I've had from Marge came through June and June's mind is so fried it's not easy to make out details. Apparently Marge still has your heroin and she's traveling with the guy who brought it. There was some kind of rough stuff with somebody."

"How's Janey?"

"She's unhappy and frightened—how else would she be? She's still salvageable, but she won't be much longer."

"I don't know what to do," Converse said. "I just don't."

"Judgment was never your strong point. You and Marge are quite a team. You better talk to Ben Whiteson before grand inspiration strikes you."

Converse stood unsteadily in the middle of the room and began to laugh.

"I've been waiting my whole life to fuck up like this."

"Well," Elmer said, "you made the big time. Congratulations."

"It's all true," Converse said. "Character is fate."

Elmer shrugged. He disliked words like "fate."

Converse was pacing again.

"If I could just get back over to Nam, I'd probably be all right. You can hole up forever over there."

"Hole up forever," Elmer said. "Sounds very nice."

"Better there than McNeil Island."

Elmer brought two cups from the bottom drawer of his desk and poured coffee from his percolator.

"It's up to you. But something very peculiar is going on. Whoever went after Marge in June's version doesn't sound like Feds. If there really is a tie-in with Irvine Vibert's friends this could all be very complicated. And Antheil." He sipped his coffee bemusedly. "Antheil has . . . a certain Bohemian flair, if you know what I mean. It's a quality I find very disturbing in policemen." For a moment he looked as though the coffee were making him sick. "I have a lot of experience with undercover types."

"You were a spy," Converse said. "That's different."

As he said it, Fran opened the door and came in with a basket of apples. She glared at him and he was not offered an apple. Elmer declined.

"Your father-in-law was not a spy," Fran told Converse sternly. "And anyway they were on our side." She gave Elmer a sympathetic look and went out.

Elmer sighed.

"Who says I was a spy?"

"Marge. She says your whole family were spies."

"Marge is an idiot."

They sat in silence for a while. Converse stared at the worn rug.

"I ought to know what I do next," he said. "But I don't."

Elmer took his empty coffeecup to the windowsill. His window commanded a view of the fire doors in the adjoining building.

"Stay away from your house. Sleep in the office tonight. Whiteson gets back about three o'clock, go

127

to him immediately." He looked at Converse for a moment and took out his checkbook. "You want your salary?"

Converse nodded.

Elmer wrote him a check for two hundred dollars.

In the outer office Frances was reading Douglas Dalton's latest *Nightbeat* story; the story was entitled "Mad Hermit Rapes Coed Campers." As Frances read, her lips moved.

"C'mon," she said, thrusting the piece back at Dalton, "put some pizzazz in it."

Dalton returned to his typewriter; Elmer watched his slow steps with resignation.

"He stinks," Elmer whispered. "He can size pictures—that's about it."

Frances was looking at the check which Converse still held in his hand.

"Hey, I've got an idea," she said pointedly. "How about Johnny-boy does some nice stories for us now he's back? Some spicy specials."

"He has too much on his mind," Elmer said.

"Does he? He couldn't even do a few headlines?"

Elmer smiled.

"It's a thought. Is it out of the question? In the worst of times we have to eat."

"In the worst of times especially," Frances said.

"You've been missed," Elmer told Conserve. "We've lacked imagination since you left us for the active life. We rely on gross obscenity now. We're so dirty we've been closed out in five states."

Converse put the check in his pocket.

"C'mon, Johnny," Frances said. "Gimme a headline."

Elmer clapped his hands softly. "A freak animal story—for five hundred words."

Converse shook his head.

"For Christ's sake." He walked to the window and back. "Birds . . ."

"Watch this!" Elmer told Frances. He leaned a

hand on Converse's shoulder like a track coach. "Birds what?"

Douglas Dalton came grimly forward with his revised version of "Mad Hermit Rapes Coed Campers." Frances read it with impatience. Elmer kept his hand on Converse's shoulder.

"C'mon, Douglas," Frances sighed. "Pizzazz."

"Yes," Douglas Dalton said. He took the story back to his typewriter.

"Birds what?" Elmer asked softly.

"Birds nothing!"

Elmer removed his hand. "Birds Starve to Death!"

Converse sat down on a desktop.

"Starving birds," he said. "All right!" He turned to Elmer in weary anger. "Skydiver Devoured by Starving Birds!"

Frances stared at him in astonishment.

"I'm going nuts," Converse said.

Elmer was already sketching it on a layout sheet.

"Excellent. I love it. Only you can write it. Now gimme another beauty. Gimme a rapist."

"Let's pack it in, Elmer."

"A rapist," Elmer said. "Please."

"Rapist," Converse said dully.

"Rapist Starves to Death."

"Pussy-Eating Rapist Starves to Death!"

Frances frowned. "That's not what *I* call pizzazz."

"Scuba-Diving Rapist?"

Elmer shook his head. "We already got a skydiver." He paused thoughtfully. "Skydiving Rapist?"

"Housewife Impaled by Skydiving Rapist," Converse said.

Frances shrugged. "Jesus! That almost makes it."

"Enough," Elmer declared. "He's gone cold. He has too much on his mind."

When Douglas Dalton came forward with the last rewrite of "Mad Hermit Rapes Coed Campers," Frances hardly troubled to read it.

"This is just filth," she told him.

When Elmer and Frances went home to Atherton, Converse and Douglas Dalton sat at Douglas' desk and drank bourbon from the bottle Douglas kept in the bottom compartment. It was his night to carry the completed layouts to the Greyhound Bus station, whence they would be conveyed to a non-union printer in San Rafael. He had finished with the mad hermit's excesses and was bracing himself for the walk along Mission and the longer one to his hotel on Sutter Street.

Douglas kept plastic cups to drink from. Converse had assembled a bunk from four chairs and across them had draped an ancient sleeping bag which Elmer Bender kept in a closet with his illegal telephone.

"All I need to know," Douglas kept telling Converse, "is that you're in trouble. That's enough for me."

Converse thanked him repeatedly.

"It's a long time since I've been able to help a pal. God's Blood, you look out of it. Am I keeping you awake?"

"I'll drink another one," Converse said.

Douglas nodded happily.

"Helping a pal was always very important to us. When I say us, I mean my crowd. That old gang of mine." He poured and consumed his third full cup of bourbon. Drinking seemed to make him grow paler.

"Who are they?"

"They're gone. Dead. Scattered. Reformed. All but yours truly—the last of a dirty old breed. I can't count Elmer. Elmer's a prince but he can't drink."

Converse allowed Douglas to pour him a measure.

" 'When like her O Saki,' " Douglas said, " 'you shall pass among the guests star-scattered on the grass, and in your joyous errand reach the spot where I made one—turn down an empty glass!' Do you know who wrote that?"

"Yes," Converse said.

"It wasn't Lawrence Ferlinghetti." He drained the cup and unsteadily poured another. Converse lay back on his row of chairs.

"Tell me what it was like," Douglas said suddenly. "What was it like?"

"Vietnam?"

Douglas nodded solemnly.

Converse sat up.

"You should really ask a grunt. For me it was expeditions. A lot of time I was in hotels. Sometimes I went out to the line. Not a lot. I was too scared. Once I was so scared I cried."

"Is that unusual?"

"I have the impression," Converse said, "that it's fairly unusual. I think it's usual to cry when you're hurt. But to cry before is uncool."

"But you went," Douglas said. "That's the important thing."

Converse did not see how it was the important thing, but nodded anyway. Douglas poured himself another drink. It was not pleasant to watch him drink.

"I too went," Douglas declared. "I was like you. But I was younger—you're twenty-five?"

"Thirty-five."

"Yes," Douglas said. "Well, I was twenty. My father tried to stop me, but I wouldn't hear of it. Do you know the Biltmore Hotel in New York?"

"I think so."

"You must know it. It's a block from the Roosevelt. Didn't you ever meet your date under the clock at the Biltmore?"

"No," Converse said.

'Well, my father met me in the Men's Bar of the Biltmore. It was the first time he and I drank together. As I recall, it was also the last time. He said to me—You're going to die in a ditch for Communism, and it'll serve you right. Do you know what I told him? I said—Father, if that should be my small place in the world's history, I am the proudest man in this place."

Converse watched Douglas' features compose themselves into a dyspeptic expression which he deduced was silent laughter.

"And the place, mind you—the place was the Men's Bar at the Biltmore Hotel!" He slapped Converse on the knee.

"The same night—the very same night—I went on board the *Carinthia* for Havre. Three days later I was in Spain." He seemed to hesitate for a moment and then poured himself another shot. "So I was just like you. I went."

"Douglas," Converse said, "the two things aren't the same. Fucking around in Saigon is not like volunteering for Spain. I mean, essentially we were on different sides."

"Who?" Douglas asked. "Different sides? You and me?" He laughed and waved a hand. "I suppose you're a Fascist."

"Objectively, I suppose so."

Douglas was delighted.

"Objectively! Objectively this and objectively that. Elmer used to talk like that. Did you know he was our political officer? He used to tell us that there was no difference between Mrs. Roosevelt and Hitler. Objectively! And that wasn't the line then—that was Elmer talking."

Converse pulled the sleeping bag over himself and leaned on an elbow.

"I had a friend at Amherst named Andy Stritch. I've always thought about Andy. He was killed at the Jarama. And there was a boy from the University of Indiana, his name was Peter Schultz. And there was a boy named Gelb who was only eighteen. He was straight from high school, can you imagine? They were all killed at the Jarama."

To Converse's astonishment he began to sing.

"There's a valley in Spain called Jarama." It went

to the tune of "Red River Valley." He stopped after the first line.

"Oh, don't sing it," he said to someone or other.

"The Moors! They were Moors. I thought—being very young—this is like the *Chanson de Roland*. Moors. They would come up to the wire and pretend to surrender. Some of them spoke English. And we poor little clots, we always wanted to believe them. Some of the fellas would let them come over and get a dagger in the gut for it."

"The gooks are like that," Converse said. "Objectively."

"You shouldn't call them gooks," Douglas said. "We didn't."

"They call us Thong Miao. It means gooks in Vietnamese."

"I had another Amherst friend—his name was Pollard. They shot him for cowardice. They wanted to shoot me. For cowardice. Not that I'd been all that cowardly, mind you. Elmer saved my life. But it hurt my feelings, do you see? It hurt my feelings very very badly. I wasn't in combat in the Second War."

Converse's elbow collapsed.

"If I'd been there, they'd have shot me. Somebody may shoot me yet."

"You can't be shot for cowardice in San Francisco, John."

"Yes, you can."

On the edge of sleep, something occurred to Converse that made him sit up again.

"It was Charmian," he told Douglas. "All this shit. It was because of Charmian."

"Lovely," Douglas said. "A lovely old Southern name."

"She's this girl. I'm in trouble because of her."

"So," Douglas said, "you're in love."

"No. Not at all. I was over there and there was this girl and I wanted to please her."

Douglas put the bottle away and stood up. He walked surprisingly well.

"That's all over for me," he said merrily. "Since the Jarama."

ON A FAULTLESS MORNING, MARGE AND HICKS drove down to the Strip for breakfast. It was clear and warm; a wind had insinuated itself from the outside world to disperse the smog and the sun shone agreeably on the polished automobiles and on the flesh of the young people in front of Ben Franklin's.

It was a nice day for bodies. There was a sensual anticipation about, an assurance of marvels shortly to be manifest. Marge, deluded, sniffed at it with everyone else.

"It must have been a paradise here once," she told Hicks as they finished their coffee. "If only they'd have left it."

Hicks said he had the L.A. blues.

They were going to see Eddie Peace. If anyone could move weight, Hicks said, Eddie Peace could.

His house was in a cul-de-sac up Laurel Canyon. There were three cars parked in the cobbled driveway in front of it—a Bentley limousine with fresh soldering on the chassis, a dusty Maserati, and a Volkswagen sedan. Hicks parked his car uphill from the Volkswagen and they walked to the Spanish double doors.

Hicks paused before ringing the bell; there was some disturbance of women inside. A lady was shouting in Spanish and a second in English. The Spanish-speaking lady was the more audible.

"Puta!" she shouted. *"Puta!" "Puta!"* And they heard a door slam inside. Hicks sounded the musical bells.

A small woman in large round sunglasses oberved them from behind a length of chain.

"Hello?" she asked, as though she were answering the phone.

"My name's Ray," Hicks said. "I'm an old friend of Eddie's. This is Marge." Marge had been smiling all the way up the canyon.

She looked at them both by turns.

"Puta!" someone cried from inside.

"Where do you know Eddie from?"

"From Malibu," Hicks said.

The lady removed her sunglasses; her eyes were dull with fear.

"C'mon, Lois," Hicks said, "for Christ's sake."

"I don't remember you," Lois said. But she opened the door.

They entered a large white room with a glass partition at one end which was open to a sundeck. From an unseen room came another explosion of shrill Hispanic rage.

"Shut up," Lois shouted—quite coarsely, Marge thought. "Shut up already!"

A baby began to cry. Marge turned quickly toward the sound.

"It's one of those days," Lois said. "I'm firing the cleaning woman."

Hicks nodded sympathetically.

"She speak English?"

Lois shrugged. "Sure."

A young Mexican girl came into the room, bared her teeth and gave them all the finger. She was wearing a pink imitation leather jacket with zippered pockets.

"Wow," she told them, "you some boss clique." She went out laughing unpleasantly. The baby, wherever it was, cried louder.

"Nuts," Lois said, "you know! A juvenile delinquent." She was looking about the room as though for solace. "She'll come back with her boyfriend and rip the place off."

They inspected an enormous painting above the fireplace. It was a portrait of a clown with a tragic

135

expression. Half-inch acrylic tears ran down the clown's rouged cheeks.

"Do you like it?" Lois asked faintly. "Some people don't like it." She began to seem alarmed. "But *I* like it. I think it's Eddie."

"Eddie all the way," Hicks said. He walked to the partition and looked out over the sundeck. "Is he around?"

"He's working." She watched Hicks without hope. "What did you say your name was? Like I don't remember you."

"Ray. From Malibu. Where's he working?"

"He's never in Malibu anymore," Lois said. "His Malibu period is over."

"Where can I get in touch with him?" From the sundeck one could see a hillside with growths of ponderosa and scores of sparkling amorphous swimming pools. No one was swimming.

"At Famous," Lois said. "He's working all day."

Hicks went to the phone and picked it up. "May I?"

Lois made a small feathering gesture with her hand and stamped her heel silently. He replaced the phone.

"He won't want to hear from you. He's had it with Malibu."

"This is not harassment," Hicks explained. "This is something of interest to him."

"No, it isn't," Lois said.

Hicks smiled and picked up the phone again.

"What's the matter with her?" Marge asked. She meant the baby. "Or him. Can I help you?"

Lois ignored her, watching Hicks dial information.

"He's not there."

Hicks stared at her.

"It's none of my business," he said, "but if I know Eddie he'll be really pissed off if we miss each other. We're passing through in sort of a rush."

Lois stood silent for a moment and then hurried out.

Marge sat down and leaned her head on her palm, hoping the baby would stop crying soon.

"Jesus, what an ugly room," she said. "What an ugly picture."

Hicks shrugged.

"We're making all the rooms," he said, sitting beside Marge. "Checking them out."

"Right," Marge said, closing her eyes and leaning on his shoulder. "We're passing through in sort of a rush."

When Lois came back the baby had stopped crying.

"Where is she?" Marge asked. "Didn't you pick her up?"

Lois looked at her in loathing.

"I'm sorry," Marge said. "I don't know what's the matter with me."

"I do," Lois said.

Hicks cleared his throat.

"About Eddie . . ."

"He's in Gardena." She sounded bitter and weary. "They're shooting at the Gardena Auditorium and that's where he is. You can wait down there till he's finished."

"One thing," Hicks said. "We'd like to use the shower, if that's all right."

"Oh, sure," Lois said disgustedly. "Anything you want."

Hicks brought some fresh clothes in from the car and they showered in turns. They were very careful to keep the turquoise-colored bathroom dry; they rinsed the shower stall when they were through and put their used towels in a hamper.

Lois was not to be seen as they left, and the baby was quiet.

Before they got into the car again, Hicks took out his knife and pried a Dizzy Gillespie for President sticker off their rear bumper. It had been there for years.

They rode the freeways to Gardena and cruised about to find the auditorium. The streets were dead straight, and the houses were not very large but most of them had little searchlights on their lawns for nightly illumination. There were a lot of poker joints on the business blocks.

Gardena Auditorium was a stucco building adjoining a park, built to resemble Union Station in miniature. Two huge generator trucks were parked in front of the ticket-holders' gate.

They had no difficulty getting inside. Wandering across the lobby, they came on a large tiled space surrounded by tiers of benches. In one of the tiers a glum crowd of sixty or so well-dressed people sat listening to a man with a megaphone.

"We want you to cheer, gang," the man with the megaphone was saying. "Please don't groan or scream. If you want to scream, do it outside in the street."

A boxing ring and its draped platform had been hauled to the wall opposite the occupied tier. People in bright casual clothes sauntered about and lounged on the empty benches. In the center of the space where the boxing ring should have been, there were two camera cranes with technicians standing beside them. At the far end of the place was a table with stacks of what appeared to be box lunches and, beside that, a partitioned area where there were lighted mirrors and barber chairs. Four or five tables were lined up beside the doors to the lobby.

"Stand by, gang," the man with the megaphone called.

Marge and Hicks walked closer to the crowd.

The man with the megaphone was watching a small sour-looking man who sat in a canvas chair behind him reading the *Daily Variety*. After a moment or so the small man looked up from his magazine, flung a hand toward the seated crowd, and returned his attention to the page.

"O.K., gang," the man with the megaphone cried. "Let's hear it!"

The crowd began to cheer for all they were worth. A camera boom descended on the third row and Hicks saw that Eddie Peace was sitting there. He was in an aisle seat beside two tough-looking men with vaguely familiar faces; Eddie and the two men beside him were the only people in the crowd who were not cheering. On the contrary, they glowered and sneered as though they found the spectacle of the camera, heartening as it was to everyone else, a loathsome provocation.

Amid the delirious cheering there sounded several distinct demented cries.

The man in the canvas chair threw his *Daily Variety* to the floor. He did not look at the crowd.

"All right," the man with the megaphone called through his megaphone. He waved the cheering down.

"You bastards who are screaming, please stop! There will be no more screaming!" A little flurry of giggles ran through the crowd.

"Is he there?" Marge asked.

"Yeah," Hicks said, "he's there."

When the cheering rose again, Eddie Peace and his companions once more registered their anger and disappointment. One of them turned to Eddie and whispered something in his ear. Eddie nodded in a purposeful and sinister fashion, stood up and made his way up the aisle, past the transported multitude. The camera boom tracked him. He had not gone very far when the screaming began again.

"Shit sake," the man with the megaphone cried. He turned his back on the crowd and conferred with the second man.

"All right," he announced. "Is there a union representative present?"

The crowd stopped cheering. Eddie Peace turned around and shook his head in good-humored frustration.

"We will take disciplinary action against you screamers. We'll take this up with the union."

After some further conversation, he raised his megaphone to announce a break. Hicks walked over to where Eddie Peace was sitting and waved. Eddie's bland eyes turned on him.

"Whaddya say?" He was wearing a blue blazer and a white polo shirt. He stood up smiling faintly, glanced quickly at the rows of seated extras above him and advanced warily. His hand slid under Hicks' arm.

"Whaddaya need?" he asked.

Eddie all the way. Marge came up to look at him.

"We thought we'd give you a buzz," Hicks said. "We fell into something."

Eddie laughed as though Hicks had told him a joke. "Oh, yeah?"

"This is Marge," Hicks said. "I was telling her about Malibu. About all those wild times out there. We thought we might do something like that again."

Eddie looked around again and fixed them with a smile of such singular radiance that he seemed to have obliterated any sensations which might distract him from their welcome presence. Hicks realized that Eddie did not recognize him.

"Lois said you'd be down here. I thought we could arrange a meet."

Eddie did not appear to have heard.

"How you been?" He kept right on smiling. "What you been doing?"

"We been traveling, Eddie. We wanted to say hello."

"Hello," Eddie said to Marge. "You stoned, maybe?"

Marge stepped back in surprise. He was looking at them in turn with his bright smile. Each examination was a fraction shorter than the last.

"Ray," he said suddenly, "you fucker. How come I didn't know you?"

"It's been a while. And I guess you're busy."

"I go to Quasi's now. You know Quasi's? I'll see you there."

"That's great, Eddie."

When they turned toward the door Eddie pursued them. He put a hand around Marge's shoulder and eased between them.

"Excuse the vulgarity," he said, "you want a blow job?"

Hicks smiled. "I don't want to take any favors."

Eddie looked insulted. He inclined his head toward the trailers. "There's a little Heinie for you. *Vos ist los?*" He rounded his lips. "Cute."

Hicks shook his head good-humoredly.

"Better not."

"You dirty rat," Eddie said—and scurried back toward the stands.

Marge and Hicks watched him go.

"He's a regular lonely hearts club," Hicks said. "He loves connecting."

They stayed to watch the extras cheer for a while. There was more screaming and more recriminating from the man with the megaphone. Presently a man in a tennis sweater came and stood beside them; he was carrying a pair of scissors in each hand.

"What kind of a fight crowd is that?" he asked them.

As they walked back to the car, Marge asked Hicks what Quasi's was.

"Quasi's is where we hang now. I guess it's a bar."

On the drive back to Hollywood, Marge remarked that Eddie Peace was an extraordinary fellow.

"You have something in common," Hicks told her. "You want to guess what it is?"

"I don't know. We're both friendly. And we can't do enough for you."

"You both do dilaudid. He does more than you."

"I better lay off, then. I wouldn't want to get like Eddie."

"Give it a shot."

"What is Eddie's scene? Is he an actor?"

"Not exactly. He's just around. All the warped shit that goes down—he's around it. He does favors. He's not stupid. But he's funny."

"Are people scared of him?"

"Some people are very scared of him."

"Are we scared of him?"

"We don't know the meaning of scared," Hicks said.

They ate lunch in Schwab's, and Hicks bought a pair of sunglasses for fifteen dollars. It was Converse's money.

The Strip was not as pleasant an experience as it had been in the early morning; the dew had dried on the potted shrubs, and everyone was settling into the day. Marge and Hicks wandered along. Whenever they encountered someone who looked as though he might know what Quasi's was, they inquired after it. As it turned out, quite a number of people knew and it was not difficult to obtain directions.

In Quasi's there were lighted alcoves with distorting mirrors and water sculpture with phosphorescent water. It was very dark and it seemed to be crowded—though they could make out little more than phantom shapes against the tinted lights. Each shape was encircled with a gray aura that was an after image of the sunlight outside. Uncle John's Band was on the box and there was a lot of laughing.

They groped their way to a plastic table and sat facing the swaying shadows at the bar. It seemed to Marge that their laughter was oddly cadenced, slow in the throat. Quaalude laughter.

Marge and Hicks waited a long time for the sight of Eddie Peace. They drank round after round of ice-cold beer and, after their eyes had adjusted to the light, they exchanged indifferent glances with the other patrons. The other patrons were youthful in manner and imaginatively dressed. After an hour had passed Marge went to her bag and fingered the plastic pill bottle there, but Hicks placed his hand over hers, warning her not to produce it. She managed to removed a Percodan and swallow it guiltily. At the end of a second hour, Hicks looked at his watch and said that if there was no Eddie within the next half hour they would drive back up to the canyon and come back after eleven.

Marge was tired and drunk—even with the Percodan she felt as though she might be catching cold. When Eddie Peace emerged from the darkness a few minutes later, she was genuinely glad to see him.

He came in like Escamillo, saluted by a chorus. People raised their glasses. There was a blond woman with him who wore heavy eye makeup and a dress made of leather. Eddie was introducing her around.

Hicks waited for a few minutes, then walked over and seized Eddie by the forearm. Eddie waved him off. Hicks shrugged and came back to the table to finish off the going beer.

"Let him do his number."

When the introductions and the double takes were done, Eddie whispered in the blond woman's ear and sauntered over to their table.

"What's happening?"

Hicks pulled a chair from the next table for Eddie to sit on.

"I got something for you if you want."

Eddie seated himself and called to the waitress for tomato juice and beer.

"How'd you know I was in Gardena?"

"Well," Hicks said, "we saw Lois."

"You saw Lois. What was that like?"

"She was kinda uptight. She told us to get lost."

Eddie looked pained.

"A dumb cunt. What you want to tell me?"

"I want to move some skezag. I can sell you a key for twenty. I'll give you a rate for three."

Eddie looked about the room as though he were looking for someone. He thrust two fingers under the turtle neck of his polo shirt in the manner of one suffering from the heat. "You know what I mean?"

"I don't foresee any trouble," Hicks said.

Eddie seemed reluctant to look at him.

"I gotta tell you this comes as a surprise to me, fella. It's not what I would expect from you personally."

"There's a different attitude about scag today," Hicks said. "With the situation over there, anyone who travels can run it."

"That's the fuckin' war for you," Eddie said. "It's stupid."

"I couldn't agree with you more. But there it is."

Eddie was shaking his head in stern disapproval.

"I'm not an expert," he said to Hicks. "Is that a good price?"

"My dear fucking man," Hicks said, "you better believe it."

Eddie drank thoughtfully for a while.

"Terry and the Pirates," he said. He was looking at Marge. "I bet you lead an interesting life." She shrugged and tried to smile.

"The big dealer and the woman of mystery," he said, looking her in the eye. "I love it."

Hicks leaned forward to engage Eddie's attention.

"I think we've both had enough of consorting with hoodlums, right? That's why I'm talking to you. Ideally, I'd like to approach a select circle of responsible people."

Eddie turned to him smiling.

"You'd like to sell scag to the film industry? Is that what you're saying?"

"Man," Hicks said, "I don't even go to the movies.

But I'm thinking, like, if there was a dude who had a personal clientele—then this would be perfect for him. Cheap—no risk—no hoodlums. It moves like coke—among friends."

"Attractive in theory," Eddie said.

"This is not a theory, Eddie."

Eddie was watching Marge in a way which made her particularly uncomfortable.

"She's stoned," he said to Hicks, "your Marge."

"This is not a theory, Eddie. It's pure shit, man, it can be cut to infinity."

Eddie seemed to glow with some inward laughter.

"What's life without a dream, hah Raymond?"

Hicks did not smile back.

"Raymond is a dreamer, isn't he, Marge?"

"That's a side of him I've never seen," Marge said.

Eddie was delighted.

"Jesus Christ," he said. He leaned over to inspect her more thoroughly. "You're a schoolteacher, aren't you? You give head?"

Marge stared at him blankly. She had never heard the expression "give head" before.

"Schoolteachers give head," Eddie declared. "That's what they say."

Hicks had moved his body back from the table. He sat upright with his hands folded.

"Isn't that changing the subject a little?"

"I'm thinking," Eddie said. "Lemme think." His happy eyes wandered about the room and settled on the blonde who had come in with him. She was in conversation with a gray-haired man in a paisley suit. Eddie nudged Hicks.

"What do you think of that, Raymond? Cute?"

Hicks shook his head impatiently.

"Does she give head?" Marge asked. She thought it an interesting turn of phrase.

"Not for you, she don't," Eddie said. He nudged Hicks again. "Her husband is a spastic. I'm not shitting you, he really is. He talks like duh duh duh. But you can't laugh, right?"

Hicks finished a beer and looked into his glass. Eddie watched the spastic's wife.

"So you got all this skezag under your mattress. Doesn't it make your heart go pitter-pat?"

"Not in the least," Hicks said.

"So. You're experienced now?"

"I'm just doing what everybody else is doing."

"Yeah but, Jesus, Ray," Eddie said in an earnest voice. "Here in the big town with all that shit. I'd be scared, man."

Watching Eddie, Marge began to think that she had seen him before. She thought it might have been at the Ulrich Studios in New York when she had studied there. He would have been fifteen years younger then—a young John Garfield. It seemed to her that she could remember him doing *Streetcar* for Ulrich.

She decided not to ask him about it.

"I can't waste time worrying, can I?" Hicks said.

"What I wonder, Raymond, is where you got it."

"I got it overseas. It's practically legal over there."

Eddie nodded and looked away again.

"I could tell you stories about that bitch," he said. He gestured toward the spastic's wife. "Things are getting so fucked up I don't believe it. Wild?" He raised his eyes. "You wouldn't believe half the shit that goes down in this town. It's a new world, man. I wish I was ten years younger."

"Tell me something, Eddie," Hicks said. "Am I making a mistake talking to you? Am I doing the wrong thing?"

Eddie shrugged.

"Am I God, Ray? How would I know?"

They sat in silence. "2001" came on the jukebox.

"These fuckin' people make me sick," Eddie said. "The Spock generation. Everything's a tit. I wannit, I wannit." He smiled at Marge and turned toward the people in the bar. "I sit still for every creep in town. Everybody's daddy—do me this, Eddie—do me that, Eddie. I could puke sometimes." He suddenly thrust a finger in Hicks' chest. Hicks looked down at it. "Even you, man. I'm sitting on all this shit, Eddie—please lay it off for me."

"If you want a piece, indicate by saying yes. If not, say no."

Eddie paid no attention.

"The people out here, man—they're so rotten they got this shit growing on them." It seemed to Marge that it was she whom he spoke to. "Fungus. You go into a room full of these people and you look around and some of them have it all over them. Every inch of skin, covered with this green fungus. Other people—maybe half their face has it. Other people —maybe one hand. Or they have spots of it growing on them."

He put his hand on her arm. She drew it away quickly.

"Grows on everybody in this place."

"How about you?" Marge asked.

Eddie's eyes were bright. Marge felt something in them which she recognized.

"Present company excepted."

Hicks looked at his watch.

"O.K., O.K." Eddie scratched his eyelids. "I can probably help you."

"Is that right?"

"I been associated with a guy. He's English, he used to be a masseur. He's got a bunch of goofs he works—swingers, whip freaks, far-out shit like that. He's got a lot of bread and he knows what everybody likes. He might be the guy to move it."

"Whatever you say, Eddie."

"The only trouble is," Eddie said, smiling, "I can't stand the guy."

Hicks shook his head.

"I don't need no trouble."

"What do you mean, you don't need no trouble?"

"I mean I don't want to play double-cross or fuck around. I don't want any part of burns or rip-offs or revenge. If you can connect me with a discreet civilized person, fine. No intrigues."

"Paranoia," Eddie told Marge.

"Why not?" Marge said.

"I don't have an enemy in the world," Eddie Peace said. "If you want, I'll put you in touch."

"How about tomorrow?"

"Tomorrow? You must be desperate."

"I don't see why we should procrastinate. Why not tomorrow?"

Eddie Peace stood up.

"Call my answering service—tell them you're Gerson Walter, that'll impress them. I'll have word for you."

He enjoined them to keep the faith and went back to the bar. When they were out in the parking lot, Hicks disappeared into the shadows to piss while Marge waited by the car. It was a street of small secretive houses with tiled roofs. No sound at all came from Quasi's; the music and the uneasy laughter were contained inside.

Hicks came back walking wearily and they got in.

"He's a snitch, I know he is. He'll burn me or turn me for sure. It's a circus."

"Actually," Marge said, "I think it's very clever of you to have come up with him."

"If I were really clever," Hicks said, as they pulled out, "I wouldn't even know Eddie Peace."

They rolled uphill to the Strip, past the Whiskey à Go-Go, the Chateau Marmont, the revolving moose. At a stop light, Marge found herself exchanging stares with a man in a Luftwaffe officer's hat.

"Why do you think he made me for a school-teacher?" Marge asked when the light had changed.

"Because that's what you look like," Hicks said.

CONVERSE WOKE IN THE MORNING ABOUT SEVEN. Sunlight lit the venetian blinds and glittered on plastic desk tops; for a moment he thought that he had awakened in the offices of MACV.

He took off his shirt and soaped himself in Elmer's washroom. He needed a shave. His Saigon khaki pants were clean. He had a long-sleeved blue shirt into which he had changed when arriving from the airport—and in which he had just slept—and a gray windbreaker. Relative invisibility, should it be required.

The machines in the factory floors were already turned on as he went downstairs and he passed hard-eyed black girls on their way to the stitching tables. Outside, the Bay wind, the California taste of the air, startled him again. Although the day was clear, it seemed very cold to him. He stopped when he reached the first corner and looked over his shoulder but he saw no tan car and no one on Mission Street seemed at all concerned with him. He walked in the direction of the Civic Center and stopped at the Foster's on the corner of Geary and Van Ness for Danish and coffee. The food, the briskness of the day, the availability of a lawyer led him toward optimism. It was possible that they had not connected him with anything directly. It was possible that all might yet be well. He strolled the Tenderloin streets for a while, almost enjoying the city and his return. When he was tired of walking, he went into a Catholic church on Taylor Street and sat before the plaster image of St. Anthony of Padua. He even considered lighting a candle.

It was the church and the proximity of St. Anthony that put Converse in mind of his mother. One of

St. Anthony's spiritual attributes was his willingness to assist in the recovery of lost articles, and in the declining years of her life, Mrs. Converse had conceived a particular devotion to him. More and more things were missing.

She had lived for seven years in a deteriorating hotel on Turk Street and Converse visited her about twice a year. At least once—usually around the time of her birthday—they dined out together. Converse had always taken particular pleasure in announcing that he was having dinner with her. It seemed to him to conjure up an image of deliciously respectable sophistication which, as Converse well knew, was quite different from the actuality of the event.

Sitting before St. Anthony, waiting to see his lawyer, Converse thought of her and it occurred to him that other young men on the wrong side of the law—perhaps other importers of heroin waiting to see their lawyers—might at the same moment be sitting at the feet of St. Anthony and thinking of their mothers. Since there was so much time to lose and he was in the neighborhood, Converse decided to take her to lunch. It would be kind and it would keep him busy until three o'clock.

His mother's hotel was called the Montalvo. The desk clerk was a black man with a Masonic tie clasp; when Converse asked for his mother the clerk pointed to a corner of the lobby where the television set was.

"That lady," the man said in stiff British colonial tones, "will be a problem to us all shortly."

The lobby smelled, very faintly, of garbage. They had taken most of the furniture out. Such of it as remained was arranged before a television set in a corner alcove where it decayed, splinter by thread, under the old parties who infested it.

Halfway across the stained floor, Converse caught sight of his mother, and stopped for a moment to watch her. She was absorbed in the entertainment on the box—something that sounded like a celebrity game show. Her false teeth were encompassed in a loose smile and her glasses were low on the bridge of her nose. There in the Montalvo lobby, Converse felt himself slide into some moment nearly thirty years vanished—he was beside her in a darkened movie theater, turning to look up at her as she watched the film on the screen. She was smiling over her glasses at the bitter wit of Dan Duryea or the suavity of Zachary Scott, unaware of the child beside her who was looking up at her in—in love, as Converse recalled. It seemed very strange to him as he watched her before the Montalvo's television set.

Suddenly her contented expression vanished. An old man had occupied the lipstick-red lounge chair beside her. He was quite well turned out, the sort of old boy, who, like Douglas Dalton, owned a couple of suits and a whisk broom. Converse's mother stared at him in hatred and terror. She began mouthing words in venomous silence; she clenched her fist in rage. The old man paid absolutely no attention to her.

Converse came around the set and stood above her trying to smile. It was several moments before she looked up at him and the smile she gave him was as joyless as his own.

"Is it you?" she asked. It was not a rhetorical question.

"Sure," Converse said. "Of course it's me."

He bent to kiss her on the cheek. The flesh his lips touched was swollen and bruised nearly black from her constant picking at it. She smelled of death.

"It isn't you," she told him with curious conviction. For a moment, he thought she was being coy in some infantile fashion but he shortly realized that she was probably hallucinating.

"Yes, it is," he said. "It's me. John."

She stared at him. The reptile faces of the other viewers turned toward them.

"Come on," Converse said. He managed to keep smiling. "We're going to lunch."

"Oh," his mother said. "Lunch?"

He helped her up and they walked slowly out of the lobby, past the stare of the clerk.

"You're in Vietnam," his mother said when they were out on the street.

"Not any more. I'm back now."

After a few uncertain steps, he got her to take his arm and he led her across Turk Street. He had thought that he would take her to Joe's Place where they had large martinis and good beef but it no longer seemed a very agreeable idea.

"How's everything?"

She answered him with a snarl of disgust. She had always been good at dramatizing herself; the sound conveyed genuine and profound bitterness.

". . . everything!" She shook her fist as she had at the old man in the lobby.

Joe's Place had a maître d'hôtel who seemed quite pleased to see them until he had a closer look at Converse's mother. He seated them at a small table in the rear room, in close proximity to two sunburned couples with Texas accents.

Converse drank his first martini quickly and hastened to order a second. It was, he reasoned, the only way through it. His mother drank her own drink greedily and although it did not make her a bit more presentable, it seemed to improve her mood.

"What do you think of my face?" she asked when she was three-quarters through the martini.

While trying to appear attentive, Converse had avoided looking at her face for very long.

"You look very well."

"I've got it back in place," she whispered happily. "I've been doing special exercises." She jerked at the folds of ruined tissue. In a moment, her expression darkened.

"They had it wrong. They had it all haywire." Suddenly she clenched her teeth and stared at him in a frenzy. "They were making me *black!*"

Converse glanced nervously about the restaurant.

"They talked to me through a tube. They said I had to marry Hodges!"

"Hodges!"

"Oh," she cried impatiently, "the clerk!"

She commenced an impersonation of Hodges, piping inaudible words in effete falsetto, rolling her eyes like a stage Othello.

Converse drank deeply of his martini. A freckled blonde among the party of Texans tapped her escort on his beefy forearm and nodded in their direction.

"Johnny," Converse's mother was saying, "they're after all your money! You mustn't give it to them!"

Converse watched her uncertainly.

"Who is?"

His mother flung her head in exasperation.

"The people in the hotel!" She lowered her voice and gripped his arm. "They're black but they pose as white! Except Hodges because he can't. That's why they want him to marry me. So they can have your money."

The money with which she was so obsessed was the money he had made from his play ten years before. Money had always been the overriding interest of her life and since the play she had come to see him as a guileless wastrel of limitless wealth.

"You mustn't let them have it!"

"Of course not," Converse said.

"Last night they came in and stretched my tights!"

Converse's eyes met those of the Texas blonde. She was eating chocolate and vanilla ice cream mixed together on her spoon; at the moment of eye contact she had removed the spoon from her mouth with some melting ice cream still on it and was dipping it into the dish for more.

"They came in and stole them and wore them all up and down the hall. Now they're all stretched and out of shape because it was some fat person. Fat!" She wrinkled her nose in disgust. "A big fat woman!"

She gulped down the rest of her martini and clenched her fist.

The Texans were awaiting their check in silence. At Converse's signal, a waiter rolled up a serving table and began to carve slices of roast beef. Converse's mother watched him divide portions with the closest attention. When the beef was served she called for horseradish and spooned an enormous amount of it out on her plate.

"Did you make a lot of money in Vietnam?" she asked, after a few mouthfuls.

Converse blinked.

"No," he said.

His mother looked alarmed.

"Why not?"

"It isn't a place where you make a lot of money."

"Yes," she insisted. "Yes it is!"

Converse addressed himself to the roast beef.

"Did the girl get it?"

She meant Marge.

"Did she? Oh," she wailed disconsolately, "the girl got it."

"Nonsense," Converse said quickly and looked at his watch.

"There *is* money in Vietnam," his mother said. "Did you know that Ho Chi Minh used to cook in the big hotels? Smart men very often like to cook."

The Texas tourists paid their bill and filed out, glancing sideways at Converse and his mother. The last out was a small pinch-faced man who had been sitting through lunch with his back to them. He had had a great deal to drink during lunch and he paused on his way to stare down at them with a mixture of bonhomie, curiosity, and suspicion. Converse's mother looked up at him in dread.

"Y'all havin' a nice time?" he asked.

"You!" Converse's mother cried. "Are you a friend of Johnny's?"

154

"No, ma'am. I just ast ye if y'ore havin' a nice time."

"Do you know a place I could stay? Somewhere they won't stretch my tights?"

"Thanks a lot," Converse said. "We're fine. You enjoy yourselves."

"Stretch your tights?" the Texan asked. His friends called for him and he went out with a puzzled expression.

The waiter brought coffee while their luncheon plates were still on the table. Converse hastened to call for the check but his mother lingered over her horseradish.

"They followed me to the Turkish bath," his mother told him. "They said I put dirt on the towels."

As Converse was shaking his head in sympathy, two long-haired youngish men came in and sat down where the tourists had been. One of them had a beard. He looked very much—very much—like the bearded man whose eyes Converse had fled in Macy's. He insisted to himself that it was not possible but the food went cold in his guts.

"As if I'd put dirt on the towels. They're devils, Johnny! They're devils!"

Converse glanced at the bearded man and the thrill of recognition rang loud and clear. The man was watching his mother eat in a way he found particularly unpleasant.

The second man was young and fair-haired. When Converse essayed a look at him he raised the point of his chin and bared his teeth in a kind of smile. It seemed to Converse that he heard someone speak the words "too old to fuck."

"The girl does bad things with Hodges," Converse's mother said. "I hear them through the tube."

The maître d'hôtel had come to the table where the two men sat. He was telling them that they could not sit there if they did not care to order lunch. They paid absolutely no attention to him.

Finally, Converse turned to face them. He tried at first to register indifference shading into disapproval. He and the two men looked at each other for a considerable time; when the exchange was over they rose and left as though they had come for no other purpose than to stare at him.

As he watched them leave Converse felt that he had failed to communicate indifference. It seemed to him that a surprising degree of intimacy had been established during the short time in which they had faced each other, that there would be things to talk about and that he would not enjoy it.

ONLY ANGELS HAVE WINGS WAS ON THE TELEVIsion set. Black and white. Converse had just had an injection; there were spots of blood on his forearm which were running into streaks. The blood tracks were familiar in some way. They had made him take his clothes off like doctors. The set was turned up to high volume.

"So nu," the bearded man named Danskin was saying, "where is it?"

"Where is what?"

"Where is what," the bearded man said mockingly. He pinched Converse on the cheek.

Smitty came in from the bathroom. The shower was on.

"What did he say?"

"He said 'where is what'."

"Ooh," Smitty said in an affected effeminate manner. He punched Converse across the face with a stiff girlish forearm. It was a joke but each of the punches hurt.

Converse was kneeling on the floor. He was extremely confused. His breath was labored and he felt very hot.

"I can't get no hot water out of that shower," Smitty said. Danskin shook his head.

"What kind of a place is this?"

Converse went into some kind of glide. It was the injection. When he came out he was looking at the television set. He knew what was happening there—he had seen the film. A mustachioed coward was attempting to bail out of his stricken aircraft with the only available parachute.

Danskin was watching television too.

"When in doubt," he told Converse, "bail out."

When Converse tried to stand up Danskin struck him on the side of the head and closed his right ear.

"Where is it, fucker?"

Converse shook his head. He was hot; he felt as though enormous quantities of sweat were straining against his pores unable to get through his skin. They had spread towels everywhere.

"What was in the needle?" he asked them. They watched him stand up. When he was upright, he tried to charge Smitty but his legs failed him. He was trying to bail out.

On the floor he looked up into Smitty's face. It was an undersea face; the eyes were only part of an inflated bag of venom behind it. If the bag were removed from the head, there would be eyes all over its surface. Protective coloration.

Smitty kicked him and he rolled over and retched into the towels. He had lost lunch some time before.

The television set was playing Rachmaninoff. "The world's finest melodies can be yours," it said.

"The world's finest melodies?" Converse asked. Danskin and Smitty laughed at him.

They had picked him up two blocks from the Montalvo in front of twenty citizens. He had ridden to the motel with a pistol pressed against his scrotum.

"Nobody out there but bloods, bubi," Danskin had told him. "They don't care."

"Where is it, fucker?"

"I don't know," Converse said. "What was in the needle?"

Danskin did accents. "Ve ask ze questions," he said.

They pulled him upright and walked him into a small kitchenette next to the Murphy bed. Smitty turned on one of the ring burners and they watched it until it glowed bright orange. They were both holding him from behind.

"Please," Converse said.

Smitty shoved the end of a towel in his mouth; Danskin was caressing the back of his neck.

They're going to do it, Converse thought. He strained backward and he was so frightened that they had a difficult time holding him. Somehow he burned his hand. And burned it. And burned it.

He screamed and they let him fall to the kitchenette floor. He rolled on the linoleum in the fetal position with the fried hand thrust between his thighs.

"I go nuts," someone on the television said.

Then they had him upright. The towel again. They were shoving his head forward and downward toward the burner. He was trying to jump up and down and the sweat broke through at last.

"When I say where is it," Jules asked, "what am I talking about?"

"The dope," Converse said, when Smitty took the towel from his mouth. Even fear could not keep him from another glide and he came out looking into Danskin's eyes. The phrase "fine eyes" crossed his mind.

Danskin embraced him.

"Hooray," Danskin cried. "Way to go."

Converse accepted Danskin's embrace. He was grateful. His hand hurt.

In a moment they had his face over the burner again. When he tried to turn away from it, they seized him by the hair.

"Here's the way it is," Danskin said. "I'm walking down the street. I come to a ladder up against a store window. I walk around it."

The skin on Converse's face began to hurt terribly. He struggled again and they pulled him back. Jules took his face between his two hands.

"Hurts?"

Converse nodded. Danskin pursed his lips as though he would kiss him.

"So I walk around the ladder. Suddenly this guy comes up to me. I see there's a camera on me. He says Good afternoon, sir, I see you walked around the ladder could you tell me, please why you did that? Then I realize—aha—it's Friday the thirteenth. It's a television show. It's the man in the street show. I'm on television!"

Converse nodded.

"So I say—Superstition!, heh heh—what a classy answer! What a clever dude -I am! And the little fucker with the mike says could you tell us about your superstitions. What do you think happened?"

Smitty began to giggle.

"What?" Converse asked.

"I couldn't think of a fuckin' thing to say. I froze. The little fucker looked at me like I was a dummy. I hated it."

He seemed enraged at the recollection and he forced Converse's face down toward the burner again.

Converse began to cry in his fear. "Please," he said.

They yanked his head back up by the hair.

"So I got home," Danskin said. "I turned on the set. What's on? Wise cocksuckers talking about their superstitions and there's me and I'm thinking of all the good funny shit I could say about my superstitions. I was so pissed."

"Please," Converse said. His tears fell on the burner.

"You say—the dope! Where is the dope?"

"I swear I'll tell you everything I know. I don't know where it is. Everyone was gone when I got here."

It seemed to him that he fainted then. They pulled him upright.

"That was his steak," a girl on the television said.

"What do you want me to do," Cary Grant said, "have it stuffed?"

"Give me nice simple answers," Danskin said.

"Anything."

"Your name is John Converse, am I right?"

"Right," Converse said.

"Your father was a waiter, am I right?"

"Right," Converse said.

"Was he a nice man?"

"He was a very nice man."

"Was he a good waiter?"

Converse swallowed.

"He was a head waiter during the war. He made a lot of money."

Suddenly they were shouting at him.

"Where do you think you are, fucker! Wake up!"

"I don't know where I am."

"Well you're here," Danskin said, "and I'm gonna burn your face! Tell me where the schmeck is!"

"I swear I don't know," Converse screamed. "My wife has it! She was gone when I got here!"

Danskin clapped him on the back.

"You're thirty-five years old. Your father was a waiter. Are you Catholic or Protestant?"

"Catholic."

"You go to church?"

"No," Converse said. "I don't believe in it anymore."

"You believe in telling the truth?"

"Yes," Converse said. "Yes."

"Are you scared?" Danskin was fondling his ass as though he were a woman.

"Of course," Converse said.

"Where's your wife?"

Converse turned to him in terror.

"I swear . . . I swear . . . I don't know. She's gone."
The tears were running down his cheeks.

Smitty seemed embarrassed

"We could fry your face all week, you cocksucker,"
he said.

Danskin appeared sympathetic.

"You're not lying, are you, John? You're not lying
to protect her ass?"

"Do you think I am? I'm not. I couldn't."

Danskin nodded.

"Of course you couldn't. And if we had a deal
for you—if you could help us, you would, wouldn't
you?"

"Yes," Converse said.

They let him go. He walked out of the kitchenette
and back to where the towels were.

Danskin shrugged. "Nothing there."

"You're not gonna make it, kid," the television
set said.

Converse was commencing another glide when
Smitty went berserk. Smitty punched him repeatedly
and he could not succeed in falling down. He found
himself in the bathroom slipping over vomit; Smitty
shoved him under the shower and began kicking him,
the bathtub, and the walls. Smitty was upset about
the lack of hot water.

But it was hot enough for Converse. It scalded
his burned hand. He scrambled out of the tub in
the face of Smitty's blows and collapsed on the fouled
tile floor.

After Smitty had gone out, Converse began to crawl
toward the bathroom door. It was open, and he
wanted to close it so that they would not notice him.

"Our land is your land," the television set said.

Danskin turned it off. Smitty was on the phone.
He handed the receiver to Jules.

"Antheil," he said.

J UST BEFORE SUNRISE, HICKS HELD HIMSELF A stand-to. Hunkering close against the shack in the last darkness, he saw blue police flashers playing on the rimrock of the canyon's far wall. He moved out of the shadows in a crouch so that he would not be visible against the lightening sky behind him. Dangling from a strap around his neck were a pair of binoculars he had stolen from the *Kora Sea*.

He settled himself beside a dwarf oak tree on a rise above the house, and poked at the ground around him to start snakes. Across the oak's dry roots he could see the length and breadth of the canyon. Its upper reaches were filling with pale daylight, but it was still night in the deep defiles where the police were.

At the canyon bottom, four cruisers were spinning blue light; there was an ambulance and four civilian cars, all balanced on the sloping shoulder of the lower canyon drive. A line of men with lights advanced across the bottom, their beams picking up beer cans and rusted fenders in the thorny brush. There was a handler with two dogs and a second line of men with rakes, hacking at the chaparral.

Hicks rolled over and sprinted back to the shack. He found Marge still sleeping on the pile of blankets near the stove; he knelt down and tried to gentle her awake. Faint sleep lay on the weary angles of her face like thin snow on stone. She woke at once.

"How's your need?"

She blinked and scratched herself; she had been scratching in her sleep most of the night.

"I don't know yet."

He held out two Ritalins and a sopor in the palm

of his hand. She took the sopor and closed his hand on the Ritalin.

"We got to run," he said. "The canyon's full of cops. They'll be up here any old time."

"Oy."

He grabbed a spade and a clean rag from under the deep sink and ran outside to dig up the stash. It was a cold morning, and his breath frosted on the air. He had no proper clothes for the weather, but the digging warmed him and by the time he had the airline bag above ground the sun was over the ridge.

He kept a Land-Rover, its distributor removed, parked under a tarpaulin in the brush behind the house. The airline bag went into the back of it, covered with a square of oilcloth. Security.

For a few moments he rested, shielding his eyes from the sun, then took the spade and began to dig in the dry earth along the rear wall of the shack. Buried there, contained within a metal footlocker and immersed in grease, he had the complete parts of an M-16 semiautomatic rifle, together within an M-70 launcher attachment. Clips for M-16 and the deadly little five-inch M-70 cartridges he kept in a sealed plastic envelope just under the locker.

He took the canvas seabag from the Land-Rover, wiped the weapon clean of grease, and dropped the lot into the seabag.

Marge came out of the house with a box of Kleenex. He waved her away from the canyon.

He went inside and secured. Whatever he thought they might need or might identify them, he stuffed into a backpack. There was no way to conceal recent occupation. When they came, they would know by the smell that the place had been inhabited. They would find the dug ground where he had buried his contraband, and the puke-stained mattress out back.

He loaded the Land-Rover and set about replacing its distributor. As he worked, he expected them to come up the road at any moment. Rat reflexes of flight. He struggled to keep his mind clear, his actions orderly.

The Land-Rover started nicely. Marge sat beside him, her arms folded across her chest, her head turned from the sun.

"Hang in, Marge."

He followed the road for a few hundred yards and then, gambling, turned down the first fire trail that wound down the seaward slope of the ridge.

"I saw them," Marge said. "What are they after?"

"Bodies." It was a pleasure to master the curves of the narrow fire trail. Four-wheel drive. "Sometimes they find a car off the road with nobody in it. They have to look for the driver."

Marge nodded.

"Some of these freaks up here love to strip wrecks. They'll see a drunk run his car into the canyon and they'll creep out at night to take the guy's wallet. They go for the credit cards."

"Christ."

"The big ones eat the little ones, up here," he said. He flung his free arm toward the hanging gardens of the canyon householders.

"All summer these people sweat fire, all winter they sweat the floods. Shit creeps out of the night under those sundecks, and they know it." He was shouting at her over the wind and the engine. "Fucking L.A., man—go out for a Sunday spin, you're a short hair from the dawn of creation."

"It's those girls," she said after a while. "That's who they're looking for."

"If it's not them," Hicks said, "it's some other creature."

He glanced at her; she looked limp and weepy, coasting on sopors and deprivation.

"Children," he thought she said.

"Yes. Children."

Less than a mile above Topanga Canyon Drive,

they passed a man riding a brush-chopping machine. The man never glanced at them as they spun the Land-Rover around him, but looking in the rearview mirror, Hicks saw him staring after the license plate.

The fire road led to a driveway connecting to Topanga Canyon Boulevard; the sign facing the highway read Official Vehicles Only. Hicks looked up and down for police cars and rammed the Land-Rover out into the westbound traffic. A helicopter shot across the ridges overhead and disappeared into the adjoining canyon.

They followed the coast road as far as Carillo State Park. Just beyond the park entrance Hicks stopped the Land-Rover before a hot dog stand that had a dachshund in a chef's cap over it. He bought three plain hot dogs and two cups of coffee. The young counterman thanked him and said Praise Jesus.

"Can you eat?"

She tried nibbling at the bulbous wad of meat and then at the toasted roll. She was holding the frankfurter near her eyes to blot out the morning sun; the ocean wind blew her tears across her cheekbones. She swallowed a little and took a breath.

"I can't eat it."

She thrust the hot dog away from her, an object of shame.

"No blame," Hicks said. He threw the thing in a litter basket. When he had swallowed his hot dogs and gulped the coffee, they were under way again.

The wind off the beach was so powerful it was difficult to hold the Land-Rover in lane. Hicks drove for almost an hour, until they saw a shopping center where the stores were built in the style of log cabins, with a length of hitching post in front of the parking spaces. Across the road from it, on the ocean side, was a cluster of pastel bungalows centering on a ranch house with a flagpole before it. He eased the Land-Rover off the road and up to the ranch house.

Marge stirred and shielded her eyes from the sun and wind.

"What's this?"

"This is Clark's."

They got out of the jeep and he looked her over.

"How are you?"

"Shitty," Marge said. "Like I have a cold but I guess it's not a cold. And . . ." she looked up at him and the very color of her eyes seemed faded; she looked as though she had been injured. " . . . my head is in a very bad place."

"Could be worse, right?"

She ran her chambray sleeve across her nose.

"I guess so."

The office was in a section of the ranch house. There was a tall, tanned man behind the desk who looked like a football player turned actor. He seemed to be deliberately not looking at them.

"Like an ocean view?"

"Certainly," Hicks said.

He gave them a key and Hicks gave him fifty dollars. They registered in the name of Powers with an address in Ojai and they carried their own bags. Marge opened the bungalow while Hicks parked the jeep in the appropriate space. When he went inside he found her huddled on the bed with the cotton spread wrapped around her.

The ocean view was available through a wall-wide greasy window that admitted the ocean wind as well. It was very beautiful outside. There was a surf running and the breakers were creased with white wind drifts that sparkled in the sun.

"It's cold," Marge said.

He found a heater switch beside the bathroom door and forced it up to high. It was difficult for him to keep from staring at the waves.

"My God," she said, "that goddamn wind."

He sat down on the bed near her and rubbed her shoulders but her body stayed tense. There was no

166

way for him to know how sick she really was. He had once smoked a great deal of opium but stopping had not been much of a problem to him. He knew nothing about dilaudid.

"Listen to it," she said. "It's just cruelty."

When he took his hands away she settled back on the sheets, still clutching the spread. The pain in her eyes gave him pleasure. If he could make the pain leave her, he thought, and bring her edge and her life back, that would give him pleasure too. The notion came to him that he had been waiting years and years for her to come under his power. He shivered.

"You got too much imagination for a dope fiend."

She turned her face away.

From the backpack he took a bottle of Wild Turkey he had bought with Converse's money and a bottle of sopors. He took two quick slugs of the bourbon and fed another sopor to Marge.

"Want some whiskey with it?"

"No."

"It helped me. I probably wasn't as strung out as you."

She was facing the wall and he thought she was crying.

"I can handle the rest of it," she said. "But what's in my head is really gruesome."

"It's just nerves. It'll stop."

"If there's one word I've always hated," Marge said, "it's the word nerves. Do you know the picture I get from it?"

"I think so."

"Do you?"

"Yeah, I know the picture."

Eventually, he thought, they would have to open the bag for her. He waited until the sopor dropped her into shallow sleep then opened the door as quietly as possible and went outside.

As soon as he felt the sun, the urge rose in his throat.

Go.

His jeep was ten feet away. He had the keys in his Windbreaker.

Go.

He walked to the jeep and circled it, inspecting the treads. The treads were just fine.

Hit the road, Jack. And don't you come back no more.

Dreams.

In the end there were not many things worth wanting—for the serious man, the samurai. But there were some. In the end, if the serious man is still bound to illusion, he selects the worthiest illusion and takes a stand. The illusion might be of waiting for one woman to come under his hands. Of being with her and shivering in the same moment.

If I walk away from this, he thought, I'll be an old man—all ghosts and hangovers and mellow recollections. Fuck it, he thought, follow the blood. This is the one. This is the one to ride till it crashes.

He watched the afternoon traffic, southbound.

Go anyway!

Thinking it made him smile. Good Zen. Zen was for old men.

There was a rust-colored slat fence connecting the walls of the bungalows, separating the patio from the beach. A stilted walkway led through a gate to the sand. Hicks walked toward the surf with his head down, to keep the blown grains from his eyes. For a while he stood on the soft sand, watching the waves break and the sandpipers scatter under them. He got cold very quickly.

To warm himself, he turned toward the ocean and began the motions of *t'ai chi*. His thrusts at the ocean wind felt feeble and uncertain. His body was slack, and as he grew colder and more tired, he felt the force of his will diminish.

Not a chance. There was not a chance.

She was some junkie's nod, a snare, a fool catcher.

It was folly. It was losing.

He planted a foot in the wind's teeth and shouted.

On our left, he thought, fucking L.A. On our right, the wind. The exercise is called riding it till it crashes.

As he passed over the walkway leading to the court, he saw some gliders being towed above Point Mugu, and he stopped to watch them for a while. He was sweating; the *t'ai chi* had made him feel better after all.

The choice was made, and there was nothing to be had from chickenshit speculation. The roshis were right: the mind is a monkey.

Marge woke up as soon as he closed the door. She had lodged herself in the space between the edge of the mattress and the wall.

"O.K.," Hicks said. "Let's get high."

She sat up with her hand shading her eyes.

"Is that a joke?"

He had taken the plastic-wrapped package from the airline bag and set it on a chair. "No, it ain't a joke."

He set a sheet of white writing paper across the telephone book and lifted a white dab from the package with a picture postcard of Marine World. She watched him raise the postcard and shake the powder onto the sheet, flicking it with his finger to dislodge the first flakes. White on white.

"We'll need some works for you if you're gonna be a righteous junkie. Maybe Eddie Peace bring us some."

He made a funnel from the back of a matchbook, took Marge by her damp and tremorous hand and led her to the desk.

He pared away a tiny mound of the stuff with the

cardboard funnel and eased it onto the postcard's glossy blue sky.

"I don't know much about dilaudid so I don't know what your tolerance is. Scoff it like coke and see if you get off."

He moved the bag from the chair; Marge sat down and looked at the postcard.

"It's scary," she said.

"Don't talk about it."

She crouched over the stuff like a child and drew it into her nostril. Afterward she straightened up so quickly he was afraid she would pass out. She shook her head and sniffed.

He made a second little mound for her.

"Go ahead. Hit the other one."

She hit the other one, and then sat stock-still; tears ran from her closed eyes. Slowly, she bent forward and rested her forehead against the desk. Hicks moved the phone book out of her way.

In a few minutes, she sat up again and turned to him. She was smiling. She put her arms around his waist; her tears and runny nose wet his shirt. He bent down to her; she rested her head on his shoulder. The tension drained from her in small sobs.

"Better than a week in the country, right?"

Holding to him, she stood up and he helped her to the bed. She lay across it, arching her back, stretching her arms and legs toward its four corners.

"It's a lot better than a week in the country," she said. She began to laugh. "It's better than dilaudid. It's good."

She rolled over and hugged herself.

"Right in the head!" She made her hand into a pistol and fired into her temple. "Right in the head."

He sat down on the bed with her. The glow had come back to her skin, the grace and suppleness of her body flowed again. The light came back, her eyes' fire. Hicks marveled. It made him happy.

"It does funny little things inside you. It floats inside you. It's incredible."

"People use it instead of sex."

"But it's just gross how nice it is," Marge said happily.

Hicks touched her breast.

"Walking with the King. Big H. If God made anything better he never let on. I know all those songs, my sweet."

Marge sat up in the bed looking in wonder at the sky outside the window, as blue and regular as the sky over Marine World.

"I see how it works. You have it or you don't. You have it—everything's O.K. You don't, everything's shit. It's yes or no. On or off. Stop or go."

"Write a poem about it," Hicks said.

She stood up and went back to the desk. She turned to him with a glance of quick mischief. "Please, sir—can I have some more?"

He made a gesture of abundance.

She set about separating another high from the dope on the sheet of paper.

"This one is for jollity," she said. "Purely recreational."

He checked the size of the dose and let her wail.

"It's its own poem" she said, when the lift came. "Very serious elegant poem."

"It's just like everything else," Hicks said.

She found one of his cigarettes by the backpack and lit it. He had never seen her smoke before. For a long time she stood looking out at the beach. Hicks watched her, wishing that she would speak to him again—but she was silent now, smiling, blowing smoke at the picture window.

"Remember the night we ran the freaks out?" Hicks asked her. "We made it after. You remember?"

She turned her lofty empty smile on him and he felt, again, a dart of loneliness.

"I remember everything. With absolute clarity.

Since you walked in on me." Her elbow slid from the windowsill where she had been resting it and she almost lost her balance. "Every twitch. Every bead of sweat. Every shiver. Believe me."

"What can I do," Hicks said. "I gotta believe you."

"I'm just a little slip of a thing," Marge said, "but I'm all primary process. I live the examined life. Not one funny little thing gets by me."

He got up and went to the desk where the leavings of Marge's measure lay across the Los Angeles telephone book.

"You would have come in handy. Where you been?"

"I've been maintaining an establishment. That's where I've been."

The matchbook cover Marge had used was wet. He ripped off another one.

"You talking about your old man? That's an establishment?"

Marge let herself slide down to the floor beneath the window.

"Don't you put my old man down," she said. "My old man is a subtle fella. He's a can of worms."

Hicks sniffed his dope and shook his head violently.

"The next fucking time he calls me a psychopath—I'm gonna tell him you said that."

He sat waiting to go off; in a moment he was in the bathroom vomiting bourbon residue from the bottom of his guts. When the vomiting stopped, he brushed his teeth.

Back in the bedroom, he surmised that he was high. The room was all easy lines and soft light, his steps were cushioned. He turned on the television set but he could not get it to work. There were some nice color bands, so he watched those for a while and then turned it off.

"Did you think I left you?" Marge asked him. "Is that why you did up?"

Hicks shrugged.

"Just for old times' sake."

He lay down on the bed beside her and watched dust columns spin before the window.

"Yes, it's easy," he said, laughing foolishly. "Yes, it's good."

"It is good, isn't it?" Marge said. "I mean high quality."

"So they tell me." He leaned into the pillows and breathed deeply.

"This is a different ball game," he said.

Marge was staring at the ceiling with an expression like reverence.

"It really had me there," she said. "I had cramps. My nose wouldn't stop running. I was genuinely sick."

"Maybe it was all in your head."

"Not all of it."

He moved closer to her and put his hand under the back of her neck.

"What a goof you are! Don't brag about it. It's not such a tough condition. It's not what you want."

"Maybe it is," she said. "It's simpler than life."

"Come on." He closed his eyes and laughed. "It's just like everything else. This is life."

"Where springs fail not," Marge said.

"Springs?"

She arched her back, letting her weight fall on the bed, making the frame creak.

"Springs fails not," she said. "It's a Polish toast. It means 'to life.' "

Hicks laughed weakly. "Jesus." He turned over on his stomach and folded his hands between her breasts. "It's a poem, you cooze. I read it. It's a poem."

She put her face close to his and laughed with her mouth open as if in surprise.

"Yes," she said, "it's a smack poem."

Looking into her eyes, he suddenly felt a perfect confidence. The payoff, whatever it was, would take care of itself. There was no stopping him.

He got up quickly and went to the telephone table. It was littered with dope and debris, the smack in its plastic bag lying beside the phone.

"This is ignorance," he said, and set about packing it away. "This is what they call in the trade 'plain view.' "

When the table was clear and the dope secured, he sat down by the phone with his forehead resting on his palm.

"I don't know what our chances are. I don't think they're too great. But I'm gonna call Eddie Peace."

"Whatever's right," Marge said.

CONVERSE HAD LITTLE SATISFACTION FROM THE lawyer.

A plantation of fine gray hair hung to shoulder length from the lawyer's bald crown, giving him the look of a mad pinko professor in a vintage Hearst cartoon. When Converse described his adventures in the motel kitchenette, the lawyer shrugged and smiled in an irritating manner. Converse had the impression that the lawyer did not like him and did not sympathize with his distress.

"This is common," the lawyer said. "This is the way they operate."

The lawyer said that if Converse wanted to approach the authorities with a statement he might indeed do so but that an attorney with better contacts in the district attorney's office might render more valuable assistance. He said that, obviously, Converse should be extremely careful—should not agree to private meetings with anyone unknown to him and should take whatever steps he was capable of to safeguard his residence and person. If arrested, the lawyer reminded him, he was entitled to a phone call.

Apparently, the lawyer remarked, Converse believed in rugged individualism, and this was just as well because it would require some very rugged individualism indeed to keep him afloat.

The lawyer used the term "afloat."

Converse had salved his ear in vaseline and bandaged it with cotton and gauze. He walked along Van Ness Street, avoiding eye contact. He had spent part of the night on the floor of the motel and the rest in Berkeley, asleep under the devil drawing in Janey's room. In the morning he had gone to the Pacific office and borrowed some of the Thorazine that Douglas Dalton kept handy for delirium tremens. He assumed it helped some.

Thus tranquil, Converse followed the street like a sleepwalker to Aquatic Park and sat on a bench among exercising bouncers and topless dancers with sun reflectors at their chins. Some of the girls aroused him and arousal made him think first of Charmian, then of Marge. The urgency of desire surprised him. After a while, he began to feel a peculiar kind of contempt for his own lust and for the women who inspired it—but anger eluded him. He had no anger to bring to bear. In time, he supposed he would lose even fear. He found fearlessness an extremely difficult state to conceive, like the hereafter.

When he had rested for an hour or so, he decided to go and have a talk with June.

The San Franciscan was a structure of pastel metal blocks built in the form of a wedge so that both grids of its minimal windows faced the harbor. The view from one angle was of Alcatraz, from the other of Coit Tower and the Bay Bridge. The attendants in the lobby were costumed as Santa Ana's hussars and many were actually Mexican.

June's room was at the end of an airless immaculate corridor; a closed circuit television camera surveyed the hall from a point just above her door.

For quite a while, she declined to open but after he had slid his red and yellow Vietnamese press card under the door she let him in.

"Why didn't you call up?" she asked him. She was fair-haired and freckled with a hardening baby face, wearing tight faded Levi's and a halter with anchors on it. Her voice reminded him of the voices of telephone operators who answered from Bismarck or Edmonton when he misdialed an area code.

"What else you got with your name on it?"

He showed her his passport. There was a color television set in the room tuned to the day's Giant game; the sound was off.

"How'd I ever get mixed up in this happy horseshit?" She took a cigarette from a pack on the television set and lit it. She seemed slightly drunk or fatigued.

"I understand you had my daughter for a while."

"Isn't she all right?"

"I hope so," Converse said. "I haven't seen her."

"Well, we took good care of her. You ask Bender."

Converse went to the blue tinted window and looked out at Treasure Island and the bridge.

"Do you know where Marge is?"

She widened her Scandian cornflower eyes in annoyance.

"Don't give me a hard time."

"Understand my position," Converse said.

June shook her head, and turned her back on him. He saw that there was another room with a second television set in it. A pale blue uniform suit with a flight pin at the breast pocket was spread on its hanger across a bed.

"What were you doing over there?" she asked him.

"Writing."

"So you're back and your old lady is doing something else. It's not unknown."

"It's awkward for me."

She gave him a brief, shrill laugh.

"Well don't be peasant about it, man. Learn to live with it because some things are more important than boy-girl."

"Boy-girl," Converse said, "isn't the trouble."

She looked at the bandage over his ear.

"No?"

"First there was the disappointment. Then yesterday somebody burned me over a stove."

She put her cigarette out and shook her head quickly with her eyes closed.

"It's not my problem, John. Don't give me a hard time."

"If this is your idea of a hard time, you haven't met the people I have."

"That's a threat," she said.

"No, it's not."

The walls were beige with silver bamboo leaves painted on them.

"Is this where you had Janey?" he asked her.

"I don't live here. Who burned you?"

"Two guys."

"Freaks?"

"More or less."

"I get it," she said. "I see."

He sat down carefully on the edge of a sofa that matched the walls.

"If you get it—where's Marge?"

Her eyelids fluttered. Her eyes looked slightly out of focus as though the effect of being casual was putting her to sleep.

"Marge is away, man. On vacation, Pee Vee. Guaymas. Rosarita, cha cha cha." She snapped her fingers twice. "They're hiding for Christ's sake. I don't know where they are."

"All right," Converse said.

She settled on to the far end of the sofa and looked at her watch.

"How did Janey end up with you?"

"I was doing a favor for a buddy."

"For Ray Hicks?"

"Yeah for Ray." She watched him drowsily and lit another cigarette. "They didn't screw you. I mean as far as I know they didn't. They got taken off."

Converse could not restrain a sigh.

"They still got the dope though. It's your dope, right?"

He shrugged without answering.

"Well, they still got it. Or as far as I know they still got it."

He was nodding thoughtfully as though the intelligence were of some value to him.

"Scared?"

"Yes, indeed," he said.

"You seem just like an ordinary guy. Why'd you try it?"

"We're all just ordinary guys."

June laughed.

"That's what you think. Do you know Those Who Are?"

"Those Who Are? Those who are what?"

"Forget it," June said. "It's a gag."

"It sounds really funny," he said. She looked at him with sympathy.

"Me, I'm getting loose of these people. I'm straight, I got a chance of my old job back. They won't see me around this town again."

"What's your old job? Are you a stew?"

"Used to be," June said. "Will be again for a while. See, when I knew Ray I was running shit from Bangkok. No scag—just Laotian Red and such. Then I started dealing myself and I met this guy Owen and then we were both dealing."

"I guess I ought to thank you," Converse said. "For having Janey."

"Sure," June said and looked at her watch.

"How was Marge?"

"Well, she wasn't hurt. She was pretty fucked up. You want to get back with her?"

"I don't know."

"I really hope everybody makes out," June said. "I been up against so many people's paranoia that I'm really turned around. When I get east, man, I'm gonna get some protection and nothing and nobody's gonna get to me." She watched the television set for a while; the camera was panning over the stands as the fans in Candlestick Park took their seventh-inning stretch. "That's what this country needs is protection."

"Tell me," Converse said, "who do you think it was that burned me?"

"Who do I think it was? Well, I guess it was the people who took off your wife. They were right there when Ray got in so they must have been expecting everybody. You can figure your troubles started over in Nam."

"Yes," Converse said. They sat watching the Atlanta pitcher warm up. "Do you know a cop named Antheil?"

"He's not a cop," June said. "He's a regulatory agent. I know him."

"He's been harassing my father-in-law. He seems to think Marge is mixed up in a dope ring."

"Well, you've got all my sympathy." She smiled and shuddered. "Is that what he said? A dope ring?"

"So I understand."

"That sounds like him."

"If you were dealing dope," Converse said, "How come you know what he sounds like?"

"Oh man," June said sadly, "I don't want your

paranoia. I know the dude, that's all. The guy I was with," she said, "he had dealings with Antheil. Antheil has lots of dealings."

"Why is he a regulatory agent instead of a cop?"

"Because he works for a regulatory agency. And that's what he calls himself."

"I see," Converse said.

"He knows everybody, right? He's got a lot of sources. He pays them. I don't know if he stands still for their dealing but I guess he'd have to.

"I made it with Ray, O.K.? Owen was very possessive, he found out about it. After they split Owen got loaded and called Antheil. He had a theory about where they were going." She watched a throw to first, an easy out. "I think he's wrong, I hope he's wrong."

"Where did he think they were going?"

June shook her head.

"You wouldn't find it by yourself. It's way out in the toolies. Anyway, it's not where they went."

"All right," Converse said.

They watched the game.

"Sorry to hear you got Antheil after you. He's very weird. He's not your ordinary nark."

"Why not?"

"He's a lawyer. He used to work for the civil service commission and for the internal revenue. Then some shit went down and he transferred. He knows a lot of heavy political people, Owen says."

A lock of Converse's hair had stuck to his bandage. He tried cautiously to disengage it.

"Do you have anything to drink?"

"I don't drink. I can give you a hit off a joint."

Converse declined.

"Did Owen ever mention Irvine Vibert?"

"Could be. I heard the name somewhere."

Her pale foxy face displayed a shadow of weary amusement.

"You look like you just figured out how and why."

"I just figured out how."

June had taken a joint from her pack of cigarettes. She lit it with seeming absentmindedness. When she passed it to him, he took it and smoked.

"You never should have tried it, friend. Why did you?"

"In the absence of anything else," Converse said.

The grass took him to Charmian. He had tried it in order to do something dangerous with her. The sex had been poorly because of his fear. When he spoke he could not make her listen; each time he had endeavored to engage her tripping Dixie fancy she had regarded him with such knowing calculation that he sometimes suspected she had the measure of his very soul. He had tried to extend, to surprise. As an act of communication.

"You mean you were broke?"

June had settled on the sofa with her legs tucked beneath her. Her head rested on the sofa back so that her torso was thrust forward and her breasts swelled under the halter. The rosy skin between the base of her breasts and her shorn armpit was firm and trim, without a wrinkle.

"No, I wasn't broke."

His belly warmed, his prick rose—it was beyond perversity. He sat desiring the girl—a speed-hardened straw-colored junkie stewardess, a spoiled Augustana Lutheran, compounded of airport Muzak and beauty parlor school. Her eyes were fouled with smog and propane spray.

What a feckless and disorderly person he was. How much at the mercy of events.

"It was just a kick," he explained. He was communicating again.

And what events. What mercy.

He reached over and took another toke of the joint she was smoking.

"I can dig it. And oh boy, is that a bad way to be."

She took the joint back gently.

"The way dealing is—scag for sure—you have to be ready to fuck people. You have to sort of like it. Somebody goes down on you, does you—you walk on their face." She set her feet back on the floor and leaned against the arm as though something had made her suddenly sad. "Owen used to say that if you haven't fought for your life for something you want, you don't know what life's all about."

"That must have been what I was after," Converse said.

"Well, I hope you're getting off."

When she passed him the joint, he eased beside her and she did not move away. She was warm, firm, comfortable. He felt in need of comfort. She observed his move without expression.

"You horny?"

"Just going with the flow," he said.

"Shit, man. Don't hurt your ear."

She uttered a little grunt and giggled wearily.

"You see," he communicated, "it's like the oriental proverb. There's a man hanging on the edge of a cliff. Above him there's a tiger. Underneath there's a raging river."

June seemed to be looking at the ceiling.

"And on the side of the cliff," she said, "there's some honey. And the man licks it."

"Owen do that one too?"

"Lemme tell you something," she said. "I've listened to every manner of shit."

He put his hands under her breasts and breathed into the dry coarse hair behind her ear. When he kissed her neck, she shifted to give him a wasted smile.

"You're a funny little fucker."

Converse was over five feet, ten and a half inches tall. He was at least three inches taller than June. No one had ever called him a funny little fucker before. The phrase rattled the shards of his vanity but it also found him out on a level he could not at first identify. He paused with his mouth against the terry cloth over her nipple, the strings of her halter between his fingers. He had been a funny little fucker in the Red Field.

He froze as he had then. He pressed against her as he had against the ground, stunned by the vividness of recall.

"We must read different manuals," she said.

He sat up and stared at her. She laughed softly.

"Lose the flow?"

"I don't know . . ." he began to say. He had wanted to take some comfort; he was tired of explanations.

"That was about as fucked up a come-on as I ever sat still for," she told him.

"No offense."

She shook her head amiably, tied her halter back on and looked at her watch.

"You don't know your mind, that's all. You don't know what you want."

"No," Converse said.

As he left he thanked her for having Janey and for talking with him. She did not care to be thanked.

"If you ever see Ray—tell him it was Owen that called Antheil. Tell him it wasn't me."

Converse assured her that he would pass the message.

"Take care," she told him as he stepped out into the corridor. "Take a whole lot."

When his hand touched the elevator signal it touched off the tiniest spark of static electricity. He drew it back and clenched it.

The Red Field was in Cambodia, near a place called Krek. It had been about two o'clock in the afternoon in early May, the hottest time of year. Since dawn, Converse, a veteran wire-service man, and a young photographer had been on patrol with a Cambodian infantry company. The Khmers held hands as they advanced and sometimes picked flowers. They stopped often and when they did Converse would hunt out some shade and sit reading a paperback copy of *Nicholas and Alexandra* which he had bought in Long Binh PX.

The Cambodians were impossible troops, they clustered and chattered and tried each other's helmets on. Walking in front of Converse was a little man called the Caporal who carried a Browning automatic rifle decorated with hibiscus. The white hot sun and the empty hours dulled all caution. It seemed that the very innocence of their passage could charm all menace.

When the silent jets streaked over the valley, they turned sweat-streaked faces toward the unbearable sky. They were surprised—but not alarmed. The aircraft were friendly. There was nothing else for them to be.

At the same moment in which they heard the engine roar the things began going off.

MACV called them Selective Ordnance; it made them sound like assorted salad or Selected Shorts.

They were Elephant Feet, the most dreaded, the most awful things in the world.

The Cambodians were still gawking skyward when bits of steel began to cut them up. Converse saw the wire-service man dive for the grass and did the same.

After the first detonations there was the sparest moment of silent astonishment. The screams were ground down by the second strike. Men rolled in the road calling on Buddha or wandered about weeping, holding themselves together as though embarrassed at their own destructibility—until the things or the concussions knocked them down.

A man was nailed Christlike to a tree beside the road, a shrine.

Converse lay clinging to earth and life, his mouth full of sweet grass. Around him the screams, the bombs, the whistling splinters swelled their sickening volume until they blotted out sanity and light. It was then that he cried, although he had not realized it at the time.

In the course of being fragmentation-bombed by the South Vietnamese Air Force, Converse experienced several insights; he did not welcome them although they came as no surprise.

One insight was that the ordinary physical world through which one shuffled heedless and half-assed toward nonentity was capable of composing itself, at any time and without notice, into a massive instrument of agonizing death. Existence was a trap; the testy patience of things as they are might be exhausted at any moment.

Another was that in the single moment when the breathing world had hurled itself screeching and murderous at his throat, he had recognized the absolute correctness of its move. In those seconds, it seemed absurd that he had ever been allowed to go his foolish way, pursuing notions and small joys. He was ashamed of the casual arrogance with which he had presumed to scurry about creation. From the bottom of his heart, he concurred in the moral necessity of his annihilation.

He had lain there—a funny little fucker—a stingless quiver on the earth. That was all there was of him, all there ever had been.

He walked from the Red Field into the lobby and there was no place to sit.

People passed him and he avoided their eyes. His desire to live was unendurable. It was impossible, not to be borne.

He was the celebrated living dog, preferred over dead lions.

Around him was the moronic lobby and outside the box-sided street where people hunted each other. Take it or leave it.

I'll take it, he thought. To take it was to begin again from nowhere, the funny little fucker would have to soldier on.

Living dogs lived. It was all they knew.

S HE WOKE TO MOONLIGHT, PHOSPHORESCENCE BE-hind her eyes dimming to sparkles. There was the slamming of a car door. At first she could make no sense of the place.

Hicks was asleep in a chair, his feet up on the writing desk. Moonlight lit half his face.

Standing, her knees trembled, a strange liquescence rippled under her skin. There was a tart chemical taste in her mouth. But it was not sickness, not unpleasant.

Another door slammed, footsteps sounded on the cement patio. She moved the hanging blind and saw Eddie Peace with a red bandana at his throat. It seemed to her that figures moved behind him—but she stepped back when his eyes swept the window where she stood.

Hicks was awake, rubbing his stiff legs.

"It's them," she said. "It's Eddie."

He went past her in shadow to crouch at the blind. There was a knock at the door. Over Hicks' shoulder she saw Eddie Peace before the bungalow door; a blond couple stood behind him. The couple looked very much alike and they were both a head taller than Eddie Peace. They did not, in the odd seconds before Hicks let the blind fall, appear to be the sort of people who knew everyone's weakness.

"Hello," Eddie Peace said.

Hicks sped across the room toward the moonlit picture window.

"Tell them wait."

"Just a minute," Marge called.

He peered into the moonlight, pressing his face against the glass.

"Can't see shit that way."

"Hey," Eddie Peace said.

"Don't let them in yet."

"Coming," Marge said.

He seized the backpack from beside the bed, shook it, and disappeared into the bathroom.

"O.K.," she heard him say through the bathroom door.

She opened to Eddie Peace's thick-lipped smile.

"Hello 'dere."

Eddie led his friends inside. The blonds nodded soberly as they passed.

"Jesus Christ," Eddie said, "could we have some light?"

When she turned the lights on, Eddie looked around the room.

"So where is he?"

Marge had no answer. The blond couple watched Eddie Peace.

"What'd he do? Take off on you?"

When Hicks came out of the bathroom he held a pistol in either hand; he bore the weapons before his shoulders with the barrels raised like a movie-poster cowboy.

Eddie drew himself and displayed empty hands.

"Jesus, Mary and Joseph," Eddie said. "Look at this!"

The woman looked at Hicks with a sensitive frown. Her companion moved in front of her.

"Buffalo Bill," Eddie said.

Hicks stared at him and glanced about the room. He was looking for a place to put the pistols down.

"You asshole," Eddie said. "If I was the narks your asshole would be dead."

"So would yours," Hicks said.

Marge went into the bathroom and brought the

backpack out. Hicks put the pistols inside it and slung it around his shoulder by one strap. Then he went to the door and looked outside.

"Don't you love the guy?" Eddie asked his friends.

The man nodded sadly as though Hicks represented a mode of behavior with which he was wearily familiar. He was a big soft man. He had steel-rimmed spectacles and dim blue priestly eyes. The woman was very like him, as bland to look at but perhaps a shade meaner. They were both wearing light-colored leather jackets and bell-bottom pants. The clothes appeared brand new.

Hicks came back from the door and sat on the bed beside Marge. He set the backpack between them.

"If these people are buying weight," he told her softly, "things are really getting fucked up."

Eddie Peace had linked arms with the couple; he hauled them before Hicks' blank stare.

"These folks, Raymond, are the nicest folks you could ever want to meet. Gerald and Jody—this is Raymond."

Jody stooped to shake Hicks' hand as though he were an Indian or a lettuce picker. Gerald saluted briskly.

"Sit," Hicks said.

Jody spread herself cross-legged on the carpet. Gerald and Eddie Peace took the only chairs.

"Gerry is a writer," Eddie Peace explained, "and he's one hell of a writer too. He wants to see the scene."

"What scene?"

"Oh man, like the old Malibu scene. You know."

"Man," Hicks said, "I don't have a notion."

"He wants to look at some scag," Eddie said. "For atmosphere." He turned toward Gerry in coy apology. "I'm sorry, Gerry—I'm just teasing you. Why don't you explain yourself to the man."

"That may not be easy," Gerald said modestly. He did not like to be called Gerry. Everyone watched him.

"I'm a writer," he said.

Eddie Peace joined the tips of his thumb and index finger like a billboard chef and blew him a kiss.

"Now scag is a problem . . . or a phenomenon . . . that's important. It's a subject which has a lot of significance, particularly right now."

"Particularly right now," said Eddie.

"I mean," Gerald told them, "I've done dope, like a lot of people have. I've blown acres of pot in my time and I've had some beautiful things with acid. But in all honesty I've never been in a scag environment because it just wasn't my scene."

"But now," Marge suggested, "it's your scene."

Gerald blushed slightly.

"Not exactly. But it's something I feel I should address. As a writer. Because of the significance it has."

"Particularly now," Marge said.

Eddie looked at her goodhumoredly, avoiding Hicks' eyes.

"Why don't you shut up?" he asked.

Gerald was looking thoughtfully at Hicks' bottle of Wild Turkey which stood on the floor beneath the picture window.

"My next project concerns . . ." he paused for the appropriate word . . . "drugs. I want to do something honest and real about the heroin scene."

Eddie Peace nodded approvingly.

"I see it," Gerald told them, "as a chain. People linked to each other through this incredible almost superhuman need. A chain of victims."

"Like our whole society," Jody said.

Eddie Peace sat straight up in his chair.

"That would be a great title for a flick, right, Jody? Chain of Victims!" He winked at Hicks very quickly.

"But somehow I don't feel as though I have a *right*

to it." His hands orchestrated a moral balance. "I don't think I can approach it as a project if I haven't paid my dues."

"He wants to cop," Eddie explained. "He wants you to turn him on. He'll pay for it."

"It must strike you as weird," Gerald said. "It strikes *me* as weird—but it's a way of connecting with the project. I mean whatever the risk is I'm prepared to take it. Experience is what makes work valid." He fixed his earnest eyes on Hicks. "I hope I'm not making you paranoid."

Hicks stood up.

"Excuse me," he said. "I want a word with your friend."

Eddie Peace rose slowly as though there were water at his feet.

"Ain't you gonna hear him out, Raymond?"

Hicks went out the bungalow door and held it open.

"He wants a little schmoozing," Eddie Peace explained to his friends.

Alone with Marge, Gerald and Jody looked at each other in silence.

"Would you like a drink?" Marge asked them. The way in which she asked it set them slightly more at ease. She supposed that she had meant it to.

"Please," Gerald said quickly.

Jody looked uncertain.

"I don't know. Would it go?"

"I think we should have a drink," Gerald said.

Marge moved the backpack with the pistols in it to the far edge of the bed and brought Gerald the bottle of Wild Turkey.

"I'm afraid there aren't any glasses."

"That's all right," Gerald said. He held the bottle toward the light, examining the texture of the whiskey. "Very fine stuff."

He took three large swallows and passed the bottle to his wife. Jody drank from it grimly.

"Do you?" she asked Marge inclining the bottle.

Marge took it and drank. For some reason it tasted sweet to her, like sherry.

"Are you an addict?" Jody asked.

"Certainly," Marge said.

Jody smiled intelligently.

"No. Really."

"I don't know if I am or not."

"Doesn't that usually mean you are?"

Marge shrugged.

"How about him," Gerald asked. "Is he?"

"No."

"Aren't there some funny moral areas there?" Jody asked.

"I guess it depends on your sense of humor," Marge said.

Gerald had another drink.

"We're not here to judge," he said. "There's such a thing as personal necessity. Maybe it's beyond moral areas."

Marge found that the liquor made her eyes ache. She closed them against the light, and leaned back on the pillows. She had already been told to shut up.

"You must be a terrific writer," she said.

Hicks and Eddie Peace huddled against the dark wall of the last bungalow. Eddie hugged his shoulders, his back to the wind.

"Ridiculous," Hicks said. "Ridiculous bullshit."

"I thought you'd be amused for Christ's sake."

"Amused?" Hicks shivered. "You got a lot of nerve. What happened to the Englishman?"

"I got news for you," Eddie said, "your shit has a bad rap."

"Then there's a misunderstanding."

"I don't think so," Eddie said.

Hicks ran a hand over his hair.

"Then get those assholes out of here." Eddie shook his head in impatience.

"*You* don't understand, Raymond, that's the misunderstanding. You don't know how things work here. This guy has just been paid an absurd figure. His wife is an heiress. I tell you these people have no conception of money."

"You're the con man," Hicks said, "not me. I've got quality shit to sell—why do I want this insanity?"

"Raymond," Eddie said, "Raymond, try to learn something. I deliver this goof into your hands." He reached out, took Hicks' right hand and squeezed it. "He's a nice fella. He's very polite."

"I don't know what you're talking about."

"Then you're stupid, Raymond. I tell you your shit is a no-no around here. I'll give you six thousand for what you can give me. And with a little imagination you can screw Gerald for a lot more. Listen, it would wipe out what I've got working with those two. The guy is scared shitless—even if he doesn't know it yet. He's *gotta* be discreet."

"You'll give me what?" Hicks said. "What's that figure again?" He put his hand on Eddie's shoulder.

"You just take it easy," Eddie said.

"Man, I'll burn it before I take a fucking like this."

Eddie twisted slightly to dislodge Hicks' hand from his person. Hicks seized the leather and held him.

"You'll take a fucking like you wouldn't believe if you don't get hip, Raymond. I'm warning you."

"You're doing me," Hicks said. He pulled Eddie toward him.

"Take your hand off me, Raymond."

"You're doing me."

His teeth clenched, Eddie Peace struck Hicks in the stomach with the points of his fingers. Hicks released him surprised.

"Take your hands off me, cocksucker."

To Hicks' utter astonishment, Eddie slapped him twice across the face.

"You nickel and dime asshole—don't you dare threaten me with violence." Eddie thrust his chin upward and pushed Hicks backward. "You're way out of your league, Jack. You're not selling grass to college girls down here. You and that bitch can get offed on account of that shit. For Christ's sake, you big creep I'm doing you a favor."

A one-man Mutt and Jeff routine, Hicks thought, stepping back to let him work. He had balls and audacity, without question.

"I can lay this off for you, stupid. Nobody else can."

Eddie had balls and audacity and he was not basically rash. He was operating in midair—but he held the superior position and it was not unreasonable that he dare to assert it. His trouble, Hicks thought, was that he was too much of an optimist, like all hustlers. And for all his imagination, he was not a good judge of character on limited acquaintance.

He rubbed his cheek where Eddie's first blow had fallen. The sound of it rang in his soul like a mantra.

"You're too vain, Eddie," Hicks said.

A faint caution troubled Eddie's eyes—only for a moment.

"You think so, huh?"

"You don't have the bread."

Eddie smiled.

"Sure I got it. When we're finished here we'll take a ride and do some business."

"Finished what, for Christ's sake?"

Eddie shrugged in mock despair.

"We're turning Gerald on, Raymond. We're showing him how it is. And he's gonna do us a few favors because he's a nice cat and we're gonna make him scared."

"How?"

"How? We're gonna put you in his life. Then he's gonna want everything back like it was when he didn't know nothing." He patted Hicks' arm in a friendly fashion. "You'll make out fine. Look at the bright side."

Hicks began to laugh.

Eddie grinned happily.

"You're smiling. You like it."

"Sure," Hicks said. "Anything you want."

Eddie and Hicks returned while Jody was explaining to Marge that she, Jody, was fundamentally a revolutionary and that if Gerald was not fundamentally a revolutionary at the moment, she considered it likely that he soon would be. Hicks was so tense that Marge was aware of his body's rigidity when he sat down on the bed beside her. His right hand rested on his knee; the discolored palm opened and closed as he stretched his corpse-white fingers. When she looked at his face, it struck her that in some curious way he had come to resemble Eddie Peace and after a moment she realized that it was his smile. He was wearing Eddie's smile in some private mockery. When he turned it on her, she took it for a signal the significance of which she could not understand.

"Everybody makes out," Eddie told them.

Jody studied him for a moment and giggled, a hand to her mouth.

"Ed is my absolute picture of an operator. Look at him."

Everyone looked at Eddie Peace.

"Mine too," Hicks said.

"Raymond is the operator," Eddie said softly, "not me. He's the original hip guy. The whole world is goofs to him."

"What's that like?" Gerald asked. He had begun to enjoy himself.

Hicks walked over and took the bottle from his hand without looking at him.

Eddie Peace watched him.

"What's it like, Raymond?"

Hicks closed his eyes for a moment, drank some bourbon, and gave Eddie Peace his own smile.

"I don't know what it's like, Eddie."

Marge leaned against him and felt him trembling.

"What are we doing here?" she asked. "Are we going to do up or what?"

Eddie came over to pat her on the head.

"Mar-gee wants her smack-ee."

"Please," Marge said. "Really."

Eddie laughed.

"I already asked ya if you was a schoolteacher, didn't I?"

"Yes, you did," she said.

Eddie clapped his hands.

"C'mon c'mon, Raymond. It's all you. Where's this famous shit?"

The bleached fingers shook slightly as he opened the bag. His Eddie Peace smile was an uninhabited rictus. Marge grew frightened of him.

When the dope was out everyone regarded it with silent respect. Gerald and Jody stood to see it.

"Well, O.K., there, Mr. Hicks," Eddie said. "Let's try it on."

Since their arrival, Marge had been trying to decide whether she would do up with them. The fact that there seemed to be a decision involved encouraged her to pass; with the stuff laid out before her like a midnight picnic, her faint resolve wavered.

So far as she could tell, she felt all right. Perhaps it had been just nerves the last time, nerves and the lack of dilaudid. If she declined, Eddie Peace would be irritated and confused and that made it almost worthwhile. On the other hand, it was all such a drag, so scary and depressing and the high was so righteous and serene. She never thought about Janey when she was high.

"You want to go first?" Eddie asked her gently. She glanced at Hicks and it seemed to her that he shook his head almost imperceptibly. It was probably imagination, she thought, she could not read him at all that night.

"You go ahead. I'll think about it."

Eddie smiled.

"Yeah, you do that, Margie." He looked about the room. "I'll go first. Because it's my party."

Hicks bowed his head in deference, the terrible smile still in place.

"Your works or mine, Eddie?"

"Mine," Eddie said. "They're new."

His works were new, a regulation syringe, without improvisations. He had cotton and a jar of surgical alcohol. Hollywood.

"Now that's what I call narcotics paraphernalia," Hicks said.

"I got better than that," Eddie said. "I got coke to run with it. I don't go for that nowhere noddy feeling."

"I do," Marge said.

"Sure you do. You're a broad."

He assembled the needle and admired its luster. Jody watched him.

"But is Ed an addict?" she asked her husband. "I ddn't know Ed was an addict."

Gerald looked puzzled.

"Ed's an addict," Hicks said. "Ain't you, Ed?"

Nothing could spoil Eddie's mood.

"None of your fucking business," he said good-naturedly.

Hicks took the cap from his Wild Turkey bottle, rinsed it out in the sink—and with his baker's measuring spoon—poured in what he judged to be the fifth part—a nickel bag. Eddie followed him about, watching over his shoulder.

"That's enough?"

"You'll find out."

"It's that good?" He took the cap and looked into it. "And we do it aged in oak."

There was a pool of water in the bottom of the sink. Hicks drew up enough to fill the dropper and transferred it to the cap in three measures.

"Gerald," Eddie said. "C'mon Gerald, social significance time. We're gonna cook up here."

He held the cap with an alligator roach clip, they cooked up with his propane lighter. When the heroin began to melt, he produced a tiny make-up box and spooned an edge of his cocaine from it into the mix.

"Aged in oak and cut with coke, Gerald."

Gerald nodded as a man will who has spent much time being shown things.

"Aged in oak and cut with coke and bless my soul," Eddie said.

He took the works from Hicks' hand and loaded his shot.

"Cheers," he told them.

He tied up with the red bandana and went into the big vein. When he shot, a burst of bright color rose in the valve and a liquor of blood and melted heroin spread across the pure glass surface in delicate butterfly patterns. When he took the needle out he ran a swab across his arm and over the point of the spike.

"Aw shit," he said tenderly, moved to emotion.

After a minute or so, he stamped his feet.

"Ai yai!" He grinned furiously at the people in the room. "Ai chihuahua."

Jody watched him with an expression of incredulity and delight.

"Is it Mexican?" she asked.

"Is it Mexican?" Eddie cried. "Bless your heart!"

Everyone laughed except Gerald. Hicks' laughter was his Eddie Peace smile expanded in a spasm.

"She asks me if it's Mexican!" Eddie roared. His hilarity was boundless. "Outasight!"

Jody was nearly beside herself.

"Who's next."

"Who's next, Marge?" Eddie asked.

Marge shrugged.

"I don't care. I'm still thinking about it."

"What about me?" Jody demanded.

"Gotta be you," Eddie said. There was a little bit of spittle on his lip and he wiped it away. "Gotta be you. Stone the gash."

"Did you want to go first?" Jody asked her husband.

"Maybe I ought to," Gerald said.

"I don't see why. But you can if you want to."

"No," Gerald said. "No. There's no reason you shouldn't."

"Stone the gash," Eddie Peace said.

Jody offered her arm manfully. Eddie held it and turned to Hicks.

"I gotta say, Raymond. . . . I gotta say . . ."

"Glad you like it, Eddie."

He looked down at Jody's arm and shoved it away.

"I don't want that," he declared. "Gimme some leg."

"Some leg?" Jody asked.

"He wants to put it in your leg," Gerald explained, "instead of the vein."

"Somewhere nice," Eddie said. "C'mon Gerald, tell her take her pants down."

Gerald stood up uncertainly, as though he thought he might be useful.

Jody unbuckled her brand new leather belt and peeled the fawn colored cloth down her left hip to expose an area of skin below the margin of her panties. She blushed charmingly and held her trousers up with her right hand. She looked at her husband while Eddie shot her, and did not flinch.

"O.K., Jody," Eddie said, patting her on the rump. "You're fixed." She walked away looking thoughtful and sat down on the floor beside her husband. For a moment they held hands and looked at each other.

"Raymond," Eddie said, "take care of Gerald. I want to goof." He began walking up and down in the middle of the room, silently mouthing a song of his imagining. Goofing.

Hicks measured and cooked up again.

Gerald took the chair where Jody had been sitting; he sat erect and grim, with the air of a man about to do something valorous in a good cause. When he looked at Hicks, his eyes held humility and trust.

"Shall I take my pants down," he asked.

"You don't have to," Hicks said.

Hicks drew up the liquor, pink with blood and lined up the spike with Gerald's bare arm.

Eddie stopped goofing for a moment to watch.

"Hey, Raymond, don't hit him in the vein, man."

"No," Hicks said.

Jody tried to stand up.

"Oh my God," she said softly.

"Isn't that the vein?" Gerald asked. At the last moment, he tried to pull his arm away. Hicks held his wrist and pushed the shot home.

"What are you doing?" Eddie asked. He was still smiling. "What the fuck are you doing?"

Gerald's eyes opened in astonishment. His feet made a quick convulsive shuffle. When he fell sideways, the needle went with his arm.

Marge stood up in terror.

"No," Eddie said. "You crazy cocksucker . . . !"

Jody took a step toward the bathroom and vomited on the tile. She was trying to scream.

Eddie Peace stared down at Gerald and then at Hicks. The smile had not completely disappeared even then and it seemed that at the core of his amazed stare there was some grain of admiration. Eddie was a true joker.

Slumped in the bathroom doorway, Jody was trying to make sense of what she saw.

"Please," she said to Eddie Peace.

Marge sprang forward and bent over Gerald. She could not tell if he was alive or not. It would be shock at the very least. She remembered something about salt.

"Salt," she said. "What about salt?"

She looked up and saw that Hicks had thrown Eddie against the window. That had been the signal, the meaning of the smile.

"Hustle now, creep," Hicks told Eddie. "Let me see you hustle now."

Jody kept saying "please," and retching.

"What have you done?" Eddie asked sadly. "What have you done?"

Marge started for the door with an idea of obtaining salt. Borrowing it from a neighbor. A cup of salt for an OD.

Hicks grabbed her. He was holding the backpack.

"There ain't no salt," he said. "Get your gear."

She could not get past him.

"Why?" she asked him in a whisper. "Why in the name of God?"

"Get your gear," he told her and stepped around her. He was pointing the gun at Eddie Peace.

"Look what you done to him," Eddie said. "Look at him."

Jody, deathly pale, knelt over her husband, rocking on her knees.

"You're too vain, Eddie," Hicks said. "You're too small to take a joke."

"No" Eddie said, "you're wrong. I can dig it."

"I liked the look on your face when I hit him."

"I liked the look on his face," Eddie said.

"What are you gonna do, hustler?"

Eddie shook his head, vexedly.

"I don't know, Raymond."

"You understand, don't you, buddy? It was unacceptable."

Eddie smiled faintly and shrugged.

"What can I say, Raymond?"

Marge stopped gathering her things and looked down at Gerald. There was foam or mucus around his mouth.

"Isn't anybody going to try . . ."

"C'mon," Hicks said. "Hurry it up."

Jody still knelt, gagging, beside her husband. She looked up at them in stoned terror and tried to stand.

"Is there salt?" she asked.

"Not today," Eddie said.

She made an ineffectual lunge toward the door; Eddie caught her easily and pulled her to him.

Hicks looked straight ahead as they walked to the Land-Rover. Marge trailed behind him with an armful of hastily gathered clothing. The football player was at his desk in the motel office and it seemed to Marge that he must have heard their carrying on—but as they passed he never turned his head or looked up from whatever he was reading. The house had been paid in advance.

As they climbed into the Land-Rover, the door of the bungalow opened and Jody's struggling silhouette appeared for a moment in the doorway. Eddie pulled her back inside.

"It's gonna be a long night for Eddie Peace," he said, when they were on the road. His face looked as bloodless as his hands. As he drove, his cold gray eyes roamed the night outside, their scanning was like some process from the ocean floor.

Marge was crying again.

"I can't hack it," she explained. "It's too much."

"You're doing fine."

They followed the coast highway south past Santa Monica and the arcades of Venice.

"So why Gerald?"

"Because he's a Martian. They're all Martians."

"What are you?"

"I'm a Christian American who fought for my flag. I don't take shit from Martians."

"My God," Marge said, trying to keep the tears out of her voice, "you killed the man."

"Maybe."

"He was just a jerk with a dumb idea." She stared

at the merciless eyes, trying to see him again, trying to make him be there. "The same as us."

"Peace was fucking me. He was fucking me bad."

"Last week we were ready to throw the shit away."

"He hit me," Hicks said.

Marge wiped away her tears and touched her forehead.

"He hit you?" Her voice rose to an incredulous whine she could not control. "Are you three years old?"

"I was drunk. It seemed like a good idea."

Marge tried to experience Gerald's overdose as a good idea. It was not the way she was used to looking at things.

"So fuck Gerald?"

"That's right," Hicks said. "Fuck Gerald."

"For all the obvious reasons."

"Fuck all the obvious reasons."

Feeling indifferent to Gerald made Marge cold. She put her sweater on.

"I should have done up when I had the chance," she said. "I bet I get sick now."

"Hue City," Hicks said. "We had guys who were dead the day they hit that place. In the morning they were in Hawaii, in the afternoon they were dead. I had six buddies shot to shit in Hue City in one morning."

"I quit," Marge said. "Fuck Gerald."

They did the freeways and Marge tried to map-read in the haphazard light. Near Ontario, a highway patrol car tailgated them for several miles. Sometimes people they could not see followed them from lane to lane, flicking brights.

Twice Marge routed them into wrong turns; they had to stop and reverse in an empty shopping center, in a weed-grown cul-de-sac between two illuminated lengths of wire fencing. Hicks said: "I want to get out of this city." They drove east toward San Bernardino.

"Now what I do that for?" he asked after a while.

"Revenge?" she suggested. "Honor?"

He said nothing.

"Manhood? Justice? Christianity? Hue?"

"I knocked the fucker loose of his hold."

Marge turned up the knitted collar of her sweater.

"He didn't like his hold," she said. "He felt guilty about it . . . It's a political thing. Maybe you don't know about that."

Hicks laughed silently.

"What I do know . . . we're fucked now."

"Well," Marge said, "you know me. I wouldn't have it any other way."

"O.K.," he said.

"Maybe we should split up?"

"No," he told her, "we ain't gonna split up."

She did not look at him when he said it and she did not answer. It seemed to her that if she thought about pulling out even for a minute, she would be done for.

Please, can I go home now? Craven, chickenshit, and bourgeoise.

Better stay. If you can't hack it straight up—be a shadow.

Somewhere on 15, in the desert, she had him pull up. He held her for a while; he was exhausted.

"Want me to drive?"

He took a canteen from the back seat and poured water over his hand and slapped it on his face.

"You don't want to drive, you want to do up. Anyway I know where we're going now. I know where we can stop."

It was grossly uncool doing up. Warm canteen water in the canteen cap, the bag open on the floor, a propane lighter too hot to hold. Marge was being a shadow.

"What we need," she said, popping in her thigh, "is some commitment."

When she was stoned it was all terrific. The sun came up over the desert—there was tumbleweed and silence.

"You are what you eat," she said.

C ONVERSE FOUND THE BUS TRIP BACK TO BERKE- ley wearing. On the way to his house he paused on Telegraph Avenue to look over the machines in a used-car lot. Whatever became of him, he reasoned, it was after all California and everything from suicide to civil insurrection required a car to be done properly. Inspecting the price cards, he recalled that he had only what remained of Elmer's two hundred dollars. In order to cadge more he would be morally bound to write some *Nightbeat* stories—in order to produce the stories he would have to spend several hours sitting around smoking dope. He decided it was out of the question.

When he arrived at his house and started up the front steps, Mr. Roche came out on the sidewalk and called to him.

"The lock's been changed," he said roguishly. "You won't get in with your key."

Confronted with Mr. Roche's happy smile, Converse considered how stimulating it must have been to smash his head against the pavement. In happier times, he might have found a *Nightbeat* headline in the reflection.

"I paid your rent, for Christ's sake. What do you want from me?"

"I'll tell you what," Mr. Roche said. "I'll let you in myself."

He sprang up the steps ahead of Converse and led him toward the front door.

"What about a new key?"

"It's being taken care of," Mr. Roche crooned.

They went up to the second floor. Mr. Roche opened the apartment and stood at the door with such deference that Converse might have been the Cardinal Archbishop of Los Angeles. There was someone waiting inside.

"Here he is, captain," Mr. Roche said. Laughing gaily, he closed the door behind Converse.

It was a tall broad-shouldered man, slightly balding.

"What the fuck!" Converse exclaimed. Quite involuntarily.

"Actually," the man said, "I'm not a captain at all." He pulled Converse toward him. Spun partly around, Converse saw that there were two other men in the room. When he had his balance he saw that they were the men with whom he had watched television on the previous evening. The discovery alarmed him so thoroughly that he tried to force his way back to the door. The tall man pinned him neatly and led him to the center of the room.

"Don't try that again, creep."

They sat together at the end of his redwood picnic table. They appeared somehow embarrassed, and did not look at him.

The tall man released Converse and produced a badge. Converse, in spite of his alarm, took the trouble to examine it closely.

"Come on," the agent said.

Converse followed him into Janey's bedroom. Antheil closed the door and sat in an armchair under the devil drawing. He wore a tweed jacket over a dark blue turtle-necked jersey, and he had a robust mod mustache. He looked rather like a sympathetic young dean at an eastern liberal arts college. He looked like a friend of Charmian's.

"What's the matter with you? What are you so scared of?"

"What have you got?" Converse said.

At that moment, it was not fear he was experiencing. The sight of Antheil brought Charmian back to him with particular clarity. Something of her honeyed aura clung to the man's tweed.

Converse was not ready for anger. What he felt was awe.

The agent smiled at him.

"You know what I was just reading? I was just reading your play."

They were agreeable to look at, Converse thought. Antheil and Charmian. Big and elegant and expensive.

"I thought it was out of print."

"Sure, but we have it. I liked a lot of it. I didn't like the main character though. I didn't think he was much of a marine."

"No," Converse agreed.

"I mean it doesn't have to be the halls of Montezuma. But the guy was a real jellyfish, wasn't he?"

He seemed to be waiting for an answer.

"I mean I couldn't sympathize with a character like that."

"Not everyone did."

"I guess you were supposed to like him because he was against the Marine Corps. But if he was against the Marine Corps why didn't he do something about it? Like refuse an order. Or go over the hill. You'd respect him more if he did something like that."

"That would be a different play," Converse said.

Antheil shook his head thoughtfully. He looked, not unkindly, into Converse's eyes.

"That character—is that what you're like? Is that you in the play?"

"No," Converse said.

"Maybe a little?"

Converse shrugged.

"My questions are crude, huh? I don't read as much drama as I should."

He touched Converse lightly on the arm.

"Hey, little June's a cookie, right?"

"What?"

"I said," he enunciated slowly, "little June is a cookie."

"She's all right."

"What did she have to say?"

Converse thought about it.

"To me—nothing. I thought she was sort of crazy."

"She's got some very bad friends in this town. Did you know that?"

"On some level."

Antheil chuckled.

"You're one wise cocksucker, aren't you?"

Converse tried to brace. There was nothing to brace on.

"You know what I think on some level? I think you smuggled a shitload of heroin into this country."

He did not try to answer.

"I think you're the kind of smart cocksucker who writes a tear-jerk play against the Marine Corps and then turns around and smuggles heroin."

"I deny that," Converse said. "No more literary conversation until I call my lawyer."

"You're a classy one," Antheil said with a disgusted smile. "Who's your lawyer?"

"Benjamin Whiteson. Thirty-five Columbus Avenue."

"Whiteson? Whiteson's a Communist, you asshole. He can't help you. What—seriously—do you think you're going to do?"

"I haven't made any plans."

"I have a plan for you," Antheil said. "I think I'll just let you run loose. I guarantee you'll be picked off the street within twenty-four hours." He leaned forward confidentially. "Did you think about who you were cutting in on, running scag? The bike clubs. The black dudes in Oakland. The syndicate. I think I'll feed them your ass."

"Tell me this," Converse said, "who are those guys out there?"

"Do you know those men?"

Converse did not answer. Antheil was delighted; he laughed.

"That's all right, baby. I know you know them. Jesus, they really put the fear of God into you, didn't they? Well they're tame rats, Jim. They're nothing compared to what you've got coming on the street."

"Who are they?"

"They're my witnesses. They're cooperating in the investigation."

"I see," Converse said.

"You know the customs they have around here for dealing with clowns who try to take a piece of the trade?"

"It doesn't concern me."

"They'll shoot you full of STP and put a blowtorch to your balls."

"I've heard the stories," Converse said.

"See, that's all they do is deal dope and fuck people over. They spend a lot of time thinking up new wrinkles. I can see to it they get you."

Through the bedroom window, Converse could see Mr. Roche hosing down the lawn behind his bungalow. Mr. Roche appeared to be singing.

"What do you think of your wife and Hicks?"

"I feel left out."

Antheil looked at him as though a part of his face were missing.

"I'd say you took a fucking."

"Look," Converse said. "We have nothing to talk about."

"You must be stupid. You're not left out where I'm concerned."

"What does that get me?"

"Maybe it gets you put to sleep. Or maybe you get to live your crummy little life."

Converse laughed.

"What's the matter with you? You think I'm being funny."

"No," Converse said. "I know what you're being. You've got my number."

Antheil watched him in silence for a moment.

"You better believe it," he said.

"Oh I do," Converse told him. "I do."

"You're an educated man. You turned yourself into an animal for dirty payoff."

"I don't admit that," Converse said.

"You turned yourself into an animal for a dirty payoff. Where's your daughter? Don't you care about her?"

"Sure I care about her. She's wherever Marge left her. I don't know where."

"Terrific for the kid."

Antheil stood up with an expression of indignation.

"Listen, Converse," he said earnestly, "no Commie lawyer is going to save you. None of your lame maneuvers are going to save you. But I can—I can keep you alive. If I want to."

"I see," Converse said.

"I want to hear about your wife. What can you tell me about her?"

Converse thought about Marge and what there was to tell Antheil about her.

"She worked for a theater in the city. Before that she worked in the Anthropology Department at U.C. She studied acting in New York a long time ago."

Antheil sat down again. He shook his head in controlled impatience.

"I know all that shit, man. I know about her whole funny family. I want you to tell me what you *want* to tell me."

Therapy, Converse thought. He had once been to a session of encounter therapy; the other participants had informed him that he was cold and remote. Someone had applied to him the term "automaton-like" and they had tried to force him under a mattress.

So the last seventy-two hours were only the California sensibility continued by other means. Lots of confrontation between liberated psyches, lots of free associating.

He tried, wanting to tell Antheil something about Marge and then discovering what it might be. Esalen style.

"She's half Irish and half Jewish," he said. That usually went over—it had social content and an element of popular humor. Marge was driven to fury whenever he mentioned it in company.

"I'm trying to treat you like a human being," Antheil said, "but you're a fucking animal. Wait till you're up to your neck in sand and the Bay's coming in on your face—then get clever."

Converse hastened to apologize.

"I mean," Antheil said, "I want to know how to deal with her. Is she the kind of bitch who'd burn her own husband and split with a boyfriend and love every minute of it. Or is she a victim of circumstances? You know what she's like."

Something of the concerned public servant had crept into his manner. Converse felt that he was being offered a choice of responses. If he wanted her back, Antheil would offer to preserve her from the blowtorch. If he wanted revenge, there would be some of that.

"I think," Converse said, "that she's pretty moral basically."

Antheil looked thoughtful for a moment, then his wholesome features expanded in a grin.

"Yeah?"

"She's been under a psychiatrist's care."

Antheil put a hand over his face and laughed heartily.

"Oh Jesus," he cried. His good humor was nearly infectious. "What a couple of yo-yos you are. You must have been out of your minds, the two of you.

A psychiatrist's care!" It took him a moment to regain his composure. "Well listen—if you show me it's worth it to me, I can take care of both of you. But you better do what you're told."

"If I'm in trouble, I'd like to square it."

"You're in plenty of trouble, my friend, and so's your crazy old lady. If you act in good faith you might get out of this with your skin on. If you bullshit me, I'll see you die."

"What do you want me to do?"

"I want you to help us get in touch with her."

"I wish I could," Converse said. "But as I explained to your witnesses out there, I don't know where she is."

"So I gather," Antheil said sympathetically, "but we think we do."

"Then why not get in touch with her yourselves?"

"The people she's with are as bad as it gets. When we go in there, there won't be much conversation. If you could get to her—persuade her to help us out—things might go a lot better for both of you."

"Who are the people she's with? I thought it was Ray Hicks."

"Do you know Those Who Are?"

"No," Converse said.

"They're very nasty people. They're friends of Hicks'."

"I don't want to be facetious," Converse said, "but what is it they are?"

"Everything," Antheil said. "Dealers, faggots, extremists. Scum of the earth."

"What do they mean, Those Who Are?"

"I don't know," Antheil said, "and I don't give a shit. You want to help us out or you want to take your chances on the street?"

"I'll talk to my lawyer."

"No, you won't, friend. You won't talk to anyone—I won't take the chance. If you want to square it, we'll keep you where we can save you from yourself. And you'll keep your mouth shut."

"Suppose I walk out? Right now."

"I told you what'll happen to you."

"Suppose I walk out anyway."

"You can't," Antheil said. He seemed genuinely angry for the first time during the interview.

Converse elected to preserve what remained of the fiction of volition.

"Where do you want me to go?"

"Out of town. Not too far."

"This can't be legal."

"You let me worry about that. I'm pretty good in court."

"O.K.," Converse said.

Antheil relaxed visibly.

"You've just done something smart for a change. Maybe you're getting smarter."

"I hope so," Converse said.

"I don't want you to panic," Antheil said playfully. "I'm going to ask Mr. Danskin and Mr. Smith to come in now."

He opened the door that led to the living room.

"Mr. Danskin," he called. "Mr. Smith."

Mr. Danskin and Mr. Smith entered with the air of men performing a mildly disagreeable obligation. Antheil turned to Converse.

"I think you all know each other."

"It's great to see a real loser really lose," the bearded man told Converse. He was Mr. Danskin.

"I just told him he was getting smarter," Antheil said.

Mr. Danskin shrugged.

"Who said he wasn't smart?"

"You're going on the road, fellas," the agent said. "You know all about it."

"That's right," Mr. Danskin said.

Antheil clapped his hands.

"O.K. So do it."

"How long will we be away for?" Converse asked. "Should I bring some stuff?"

He had hesitated to ask, fearing that the question might produce silence or even levity.

A brief silence did in fact ensue.

"Sure," Antheil said. "Bring whatever you want."

Mr. Smith came into the other bedroom with him to watch him pack. Mr. Smith was the younger, blond one. He picked out some shirts and a sweater. Everything was still in his suitcase; he put the clothes in a cardboard shirt box. When they went back to Janey's room, Antheil was admiring the drawing on the wall.

"That's your counterculture right there," he said.

No one disagreed with him.

"Converse," he declared, "I've enjoyed talking to you. You just confirmed a whole lot of ideas I've had about the way things are going. I'm really glad to have met you."

"You're not coming?"

Antheil shook his head.

"You got nothing to worry about. You'll be in good hands." A thought seemed to strike him on the way out.

"You know I have a kid," he told Danskin, "he's twelve now. He lives with my lately wife. Last summer I sent him to survival school. Toughen him up for the big shit storm."

"What do they do there?" Mr. Smith asked.

"What do they do there? They survive."

Everyone smiled politely.

Mr. Danskin was looking at Converse.

"You never went to survival school."

"No," Converse admitted. "I don't think they had them."

Hicks drove on speed. His fatigue hung the desert grass with hallucinatory blossoms, filled ravines with luminous coral and phantoms. The land was flat and the roads dead straight; at night, headlights swung for hours in space, steady as a landfall—and then rushed past in streaks of color, explosions of engine roar and hot wind. Every passing truck left in its screaming wake the specter of a desert head-on—mammoth tires spinning in the air, dead truck drivers burning in ditches until dawn.

Marge nodded in the back seat. Now and then she spoke and Hicks could not understand her. She scratched in her sleep.

The state did not seem like sleep to Marge. She had turned inward from the chaos of motion outside. Her head was filled with freakery—that she was turning to rubber, that her mind had been replaced by a cassette.

Security was fled. Sometimes she simply set the bag on the seat beside her. There was so much that she was profligate; the seat was sitcky with it, grains of it glistened on the rubber matting of the floor. After doing up, she would sit beside him in the front for a while, but they did not speak very much, there was nothing that would bear exchange.

They stopped at night—so that Hicks could sleep for three hours or so, drop more speed, and put them on the road again. They avoided the Interstates, the military reserves, the Indian reservations, trying for roads that were obscure but not deserted.

Late in the second day, they passed miles and miles of spinach fields watered with sprinklers. Roads met at perfect right angles; the white farmhouses had groves of pale aspen surrounding them. A town called

Moroni had a plaster angel in its dusty main square and they stopped there for gas and bought lunch meat and whole-wheat bread at a Japanese grocery.

By the time night fell, their road led upward over the slopes of half-fallen mountains where broken boulders were piled on each other's backs. In the twilight, the great rocks came to look like statues and the scrub pine growing from the crevices beneath them like offering flowers.

They drove all night to climb the ridge. A few hours before dawn, Hicks pulled over to sleep.

"Who's up here?" she asked him.

"My alma mater's up here," he said with his eyes closed. "My freaked-out old roshi. They have writing doctors—this guy is a writing roshi."

"You mean he deals?"

"Deals isn't the word."

While he slept, Marge listened to owls.

Late the next morning, Hicks was laughing to himself as he drove. The sky was obscene in its brightness, the crimson rocks a bad joke. Then, gradually the route wound downward, switchback after switchback. Trees were thicker, there were wildflowers beside the road. Abruptly they were driving between clapboard buildings on a street of sorts, in a kind of town at the base of a sheer cliff that kept half the place in welcome shadow.

As they followed the road, Marge became aware that there were people among the unpainted buildings. The first group she saw were children—little girls in frilly white blouses with patent leather shoes. Then, before the next shack, a group of men in beige suits and dark ties. Some of the men carried books under their arms. Farther along, a young black haired woman in a pink blouse nursed a baby in the shade.

The road ended with a curving flourish over a sandy pit in which lay a few car skeletons and the rotting remnants of a tepee. To one side of the pit was a cluster of orange and blue tents; beside the tents fifteen or so International Harvester trucks were lined up. The trucks were painted in bright colors, Mexican pastels. They were open in the back; each truck had benches across its van with lengths of knotted rope along the sides for hand grips. They were the sort of trucks which one saw carrying braceros in Mexico and southern California.

A group of silent people gathered slowly near the place where they stopped the Land-Rover. They were Mexicans, Marge saw, dressed with a curious formality. All the men wore the same cut of beige suit with wide lapels and thick stitching. Their dark ties were held in place with cheap tin tie clasps. Waves of lacquer black hair curved above their brown faces. There were little boys among them, small replicas of the men down to the tin tie clasps. Instead of shoes, they wore plastic sandals over socks; their feet were covered with dust. Marge stared at them through the insect-spattered windshield. They returned her stare without hostility and without greeting.

"Are those people really out there?" she asked Hicks.

Hicks turned over the engine and looked at her.

"I don't know what's really out there."

He sat rubbing his temples, laughing at something. Marge climbed out and faced the group. Hicks came around from the other side of the car.

"Oh you mean these folks," he said. "Yeah, these folks are really out here."

"Hello, brothers," he told them. *"Hola, muchachos."*

They stepped aside for them. Hicks put his arm over Marge's shoulder.

"Caballeros," he said clasping her tightly, *"caballeros, muy formal."*

More people in the roadway between the shacks, all watching them as they walked holding each other.

"Do they like us?" Marge asked. "Do they want us to go away?"

"As long as we're not the cops," Hicks said. "Or the ASPCA, they couldn't care less."

He stopped for a moment, looked up and down the street and then moved her toward the largest of the several buildings. There were people huddled in the doorway, facing the interior. Hicks moved her between two low broad backs and into a large white-washed room.

The room was crowded with men; there were no women among them, although a line of small boys sat with black books in their hands along one wall. Some of the men had chairs to sit in, others stood or squatted on the floor. Everyone was facing a raised platform at the far end of the room where a small brown-skinned man in a dark rayon suit read aloud from a book he held in his right hand. Beside him on the platform was a banner strung on a brass flag-pole. The banner showed a curled shepherd's staff and beneath it a haloed lamb, hoof raised. A sancti-fied aura of gold cloth surrounded the lamb's white body.

The man read in a voice which started low in his throat and rose almost to falsetto and then fell again at the conclusion of each phrase. What he read was like verse or the words of a song and he seemed to begin every stanza at a slightly different pitch so that the sound built a tension which coiled farther and farther back on itself without breaking. His voice did not suit him at all.

The men in the room listened with closed eyes.

Next to the platform, closest to the reader of anyone in the room, was a fair-haired boy of about twelve, the only person there besides themselves who was not Mexican. The boy looked up at the speaker with a wide smile, but it was a spectator's smile, not a communicant's.

As Marge watched, the boy turned to them, smiled wider in surprise, and rose to pick his way toward them among the crowd.

The attention of the people in the room followed him as he came up to them. Marge imagined that the people there could see the drug on her or sense it.

The boy led them outside into the sun. He was carrying a faded cowboy hat in his hand and when they were outside he jammed it on the back of his head.

"How are you, you little shit?" Hicks asked him.

"Last time I saw you," the boy said, "you were fishing for steelheads."

"I was too," Hicks told Marge. "Where's your old man?"

"Up the hill."

Hicks looked around him.

"I see the folks are here."

"That's right," the boy said. "You'll be in time for the fiesta."

They walked to the jeep and Hicks took out the pack and the bag in which he had put his machine gun. He strapped the pack on his back and slung the seabag over his shoulder.

"This is K-jell," he told Marge. "K-jell, this is Marge."

She was tired of the boy's smile; it had something of the formal beatitude of hippie greeting, mindless acceptance soul to soul. It annoyed her to see those things on a child's face.

"Let's go see the old man," Hicks said.

They walked along the dirt road toward the foot of the mountain, past the car skeletons and the tepee to a patch of soil where rows of blackened vegetable leaf withered in the company of thorny weeds and broom. The patch was enclosed with chicken wire.

"Christ," Hicks said, "Sally's garden."

"Yes, sir," Kjell said.

"They strung that wire underneath the whole bed," Hicks told Marge. "To keep the gophers out."

Marge nodded wearily.

"Most people poison gophers. But it was the time of peace and love and all that lives is holy." He turned to the boy. "You remember that time?"

"I don't know," Kjell said.

"In the end somebody got drunk—I don't remember who—and came down here with a shotgun and blasted all the gophers they could find."

"That was a reaction," Kjell said. "Because it was so much work putting in the chicken wire."

A narrow trail led along the foot of the mountain, turning at length into a narrow windless passage between walls of red rock that widened into a pine glade. The deep shade and the smell of the pines in the heat gave promise of rest. They could hear fast water not far away. Beyond the glade was a grassy field with a stand of cottonwood trees beside a stream. The stream had been dammed with blocks of concrete to form a pool, where bubbles rose from an unseen bottom marring the reflected image of the sheer mountain over them.

"You want a bath?" the boy asked. "The creek's nice and warm right here."

Hicks was looking at the rock face.

"Where the hell's the cable lift?"

"He dismantled it," Kjell said. "Tore it up just the other day."

"All the way here I been waiting to ride that cable. What the hell possessed him?"

A small black and white quarter horse was nibbling grass among the trees. The boy walked up to it and pulled its head up with the bridle, leading it out of the trees. A length of red cotton cloth trailed from one of his hind feet.

"What have you got on him?" Hicks asked.

The boy swung into the saddle and brushed the horse's neck.

"I was trying to make a gypsy hobble. He didn't go for it."

"You'll get your teeth kicked out. How come he took the lift down?"

"Well, Gibbs was here last week. He took it down when Gibbs split."

The good humor drained from Hicks' face.

"Oh my God," he said. "Gibbs was here?"

"Yeah," the boy said, "he was here. Sorry I can't take you up behind me but the track's too steep for anybody riding behind."

"We'll walk," Hicks told him.

Kjell kicked the horse's flank and trotted off up the stream.

Hicks took the canteen from Marge's carry bag and stooped at the waterside to fill it.

"Gibbs was here," he told her, "and I missed him."

"Is that pretty bad?"

"Well, it's cruel, that's what it is. It's ironical."

It was a three-hour climb to the top and shade was the only comfort. At every rounding turn they sprawled against the rock to take some water and some salt from a zuzu-stand shaker bag. Step over step, Marge followed his tracks upward; by the time they were under the crest she was cramped and weeping.

Around the last bend was another stand of forest, cedar and pine. Under the sound of wind in the trees were strange soft noises—tinklings and faint bells. Whenever Marge turned after a sound, she caught a small flash of unnatural color, a glint of bright metal or glass. As they walked she saw that some of the branches hid wind chimes and mirrors, bells of Sarna, painted dolls.

"He's got all the woods around here done this way," Hicks told her. "He's got speakers out here too. And lights."

"Doesn't he like trees?"

"Not him. He's a pioneer."

The forest ended at a wall made from the mountain's

stone. They followed it up the slope for about a quarter mile until they came to an arched doorway, large enough for a crouching man to walk through. Above the doorway were inscribed the letters A.M.D.G.

A paved stone path led up from the gate, rising to a clearing that was bordered on two sides by the top of the forest. It seemed at first to be the crest of the mountain—but there was higher ground above, a scrub-grown bluff from which a narrow stream descended. The fourth side of the clearing was sheer cliff drop, attended by a barrier of split rails. From the cliff edge one could see the narrow valley below and the lower ridge across it, beyond that another ridge and another beyond that. At a great distance, the ghostly frost of a snow peak seemed suspended from the clear sky.

At the edge of the clearing farthest from the cliff was a corral from which Kjell's pony, unhobbled, watched them come up. Near it, within the trees, was a cabin with wires leading in several directions from its roof. A low business-like hum sounded from inside it.

The purpose of the place was a vaulted whitewashed building with a tall bell tower. It was a severe building of simple construction—except for the decorated façade around its entryway, approached by three low worn steps. The façade was small but ingeniously worked; scrolls and biblical scenes appeared beside swastikas and rain patterns. A figure in soutane and biretta looked down on martyrs who carried their own heads in one hand and ceremonial gourds in the other. The serpent tempting Eve bore a set of carefully rendered rattles. The uppermost figure was Christ in Judgment, wearing the feathered headdress of a cacique.

Marge looked up from the façade to the bell tower and saw that it supported a set of loudspeakers on either side. She shaded her eyes and shivered in the bright sunlight.

A balding red-faced man walked down the steps from the doorway. The first thing about his face that Marge noticed was the mouth. He was bearded and the dark brown hair of his whiskers and mustache outlined the thickness and pinkness of his lips. A breeze stirred the short hairs on his rosy scalp.

"Look," the man said, "we've found you again."

Hicks nodded to him with a smile that was affectionate and contemptuous.

"I wasn't sure you'd be here. Just took a flyer."

"We stayed," the balding man said, "in case everything might begin all over." He had a very slight accent, Dutch or German.

"The last time I was here," Hicks said to him, "I was fishing for steelheads. K-jell just reminded me." He let the seabag fall.

"You should have stayed with us," the man said.

Holding the same ironic smile, Hicks bent and touched the top of the man's Mexican sandal. The man had stooped to intercept his gesture.

"What's the matter, Dieter? Can't a man loose your sandal these days?"

"These days a man can do what he likes."

He turned to look at Marge.

"You're tired?"

She nodded. His smile, she thought, was the same as his son's, a bit too serene for her liking.

"Is there something we can get you?"

"Who, me? Not a thing."

"C'mon," Hicks said, "we just climbed your goddamn mountain. Give us a beer at least."

They followed Dieter through the ornate entrance and into a large cool room with an enormous stone fireplace facing the door. There was a single narrow window opening on a shaded garden and when the door was closed it was difficult to see. She made out the letters A.M.D.G. over the lintel.

Near the fireplace was a refrigerator; Dieter opened it to shelves piled with Mexican beer and several pitchers of tea-colored liquid. He opened them each a beer and filled his own glass from one of the pitchers.

Hicks took Dieter's glass from his hand and sniffed the contents.

"What kind of piss is that?"

"Rose-hip wine," Dieter said.

"Is that a more enlightening drink?"

"Yes," Dieter said. "The taste of Zen and the taste of rose-hip wine are the same."

Across from the straight-backed refectory chair in which Marge sat was an altar on which stood a crucifix hung with Christmas balls and gift-wrapping paper. Behind it was a large reproduction of Ilya Repin's portrait of the dying Moussorgsky.

"So he drinks about twenty pitchers a day of it," someone said. It was Kjell, sprawled on a mattress in a confusion of electronic equipment—microphones, headphones, speaker tubes, and a labyrinth of insulated wires. A copy of *Treasure Island* lay face down across them.

"I make it myself," Dieter said, "it's stronger than beer. I'm sure the Jesuits did better but they had more organization." He turned to Marge, who was fidgeting. "What would you like to do? Freshen up?"

"I guess so," Marge said.

"It's a long climb without the lift." He stood hospitably. "It's outside. I'll show you."

Marge was going through her bag nervously.

"I know where it is," Hicks said. "I'll show her."

He picked up the bag and led her through a curtained doorway at the rear of the altar and down a sunlit passageway that opened to an overgrown garden beside the stream.

"You want the john or this?" he asked, showing her the pack.

"I thought I might as well."

"You're going right from dilaudid on to the purest

shit in America. I can see you passing the time on a ride but you better use some moderation."

"What the hell," Marge said, "I've already missed my modern dance class." She took the pack from him. "It's the kid, I guess. It bothers me."

He took the works inside out of the wind and loaded the spike for her.

"Someday," she said, "I'll get what Gerald got."

She held the needle point upward and looked at the sky.

"This might be a good place for it."

"Now, now," Hicks said to her.

With her tongue in the corner of her mouth, she jabbed her thigh, lay back, and handed him the needle.

He sat watching her until she smiled.

"Feel better?"

"Are you kidding?" she asked him.

He left her nodding over the stream, dragged the seabag with the gun in it to a corner of the corridor, and went back to his beer.

"To suffering sentience," Dieter said, raising his glass. "May it endure."

"I think you're loaded, Dieter."

Dieter looked at the bag which he had set by his feet.

"More in the bag, is there?"

"There's a lot more in the bag," Hicks said. "I want to move it."

"Is that why you came out here?"

"We're hot. We've got to get loose of it."

"I thought you might have come to stay awhile."

"How about it, man?"

Dieter shook his head.

"Not here. Not me."

Hicks let his eyes settle on Dieter's.

"No? But Gibbs was just here. K-jell told me."

Kjell looked up from *Treasure Island*.

"Gibbs brought mushrooms for the fiesta. That's the only dope we have around here now."

"Nobody asked you," Dieter told his son. "Go tune your guitar."

Kjell tossed his book aside and went out the front door.

"Gibbs brought mushrooms for the fiesta. That's the only dope we have around here now."

"Dieter, man, all you have to do is call some people."

"I don't call people anymore."

"Look," Hicks said, "I have to take care of it. I really went for this one."

He told Dieter about Converse and Marge and the things that had happened. Dieter went to the refrigerator and took out another pitcher of wine.

"I envy your energy," he said.

"It was there," Hicks said. "I went for it. Maybe next year I'll do it all over again."

"And then next year, it'll be the same. Lots of scurrying around and no payoff. You should have stayed with us."

"Well, the fishing was good," Hicks said, "no question about that. I could put myself to sleep fishing that stream in my head. Pool by pool. Like Hemingway." He rubbed his face and stood up. "I'm dead, man. I've got to crash."

"Yes, crash," Dieter said. "You know where it is."

In the pool beside which Marge sat, the fish were nearly tame. They nibbled wrists and sailed confidently into cupped hands below the surface, but they could vanish in an instant at the slightest capturing gesture, leaving a tiny sunlit ripple. Marge sat and played with them beneath the vaults of time and silence to which she was becoming accustomed.

At some point, she decided to put herself in the water. She left her sour-smelling clothes on the bank and eased in. The bottom was pebbles, the water was sun-warmed; she ducked her head under and came up feeling faintly sick. The wind smelled of pines.

Kjell was sitting on a rock a few yards downstream. She turned around and waved to him mechanically.

"Want some soap?" he called to her.

"Sure."

He ran inside and came out with a square of lye-smelling homemade soap.

"Look," he said pointing to the edge of the building, "there's a shower over there. You use that and the soap won't hurt the fish."

He watched her soberly as she climbed out of the stream and walked to the shower. The water was cold, much colder than the stream. She soaped herself as the boy looked on, rinsed, and wrapped herself sarongwise in the towel.

"O.K.?" she asked him.

"Sure."

He walked across the creek from rock to rock and sat down on the bank opposite her.

"Nice place," she said.

"Pretty nice. Nothing like it was though."

"How was it?"

"Oh, it was full of people all the time."

"It's better like this, don't you think?"

"I don't know. The fishing's better."

"How can you fish," she asked him, "if you're worried about soap hurting them? Doesn't the hook hurt them?"

"I don't think it's the same," Kjell said. "Some people around here used to say fishing was cruel. Dieter says the people who objected to it most are all murderers now."

"You mean they've killed people?"

"Well, it could be symbolic. Or it could be they've killed people."

"I see," she said. "Have you lived here all your life?"

"Most of it. I was born in Paris though."

He was quite perfect, an exquisite artifact of the scene like the Indian bells in the trees. He was a child of Advance as she herself was—born to the Solution at the dawn of the New Age.

It was impossible for her not to think of Janey but the drug dulled her panic nicely.

"Where's your mother?"

"Back east in the hospital. She left here a long time ago."

"She get tired of the crowds?"

"She thought he was God."

"Well," Marge said, "that was silly of her."

"No," Kjell said, "she thought he really was God. Some people used to. Once some regular church people came up here to ask him about it."

"What did he tell them?"

"He kind of let on that he was."

"Did he think he was?"

"He sort of did. Now he says he wasn't any more God than anybody else but other people didn't know they were God and he did."

"Do you think he was God?"

"I don't know. Maybe he is. I mean, how could you tell?"

"Now when I was a kid," Marge said, "there was an organization called the League of the Militant Godless."

"Goddess?"

"God-less," Marge said. "They did without."

"And they were pissed off?"

"Everybody was pissed off when I was a kid. I was pretty pissed off myself." She stood up and shivered inside the towel. "Hey, it's nice up here. What is this place?"

"That's a story," Kjell said. "It's called El Incarnación del Verbo. It was a Jesuit house in the mission times—then the Mexicans passed a law against Jesuits so the priests buried all their gold and left. Then it got to be part of the Martinson ranch. We go out—me and Dieter—we go out with the metal detector sometimes to look for the gold. We found a whole lot of great stuff. But no gold."

"How'd Dieter get it?"

"I guess Mom gave it to him. Her name used to be Martinson."

"Well," Marge said. "How nice for him."

She dressed, and sauntered into the front room looking for Hicks.

"He's asleep," Dieter said. He offered her a beer and she took it. "Couple of hours he'll be up and hustling and you'll be on your way."

"I thought we were on our way here."

"I'm afraid I can't help you with the heroin."

"I must have it wrong then. I thought you were somehow in the business."

"You have it wrong." He sipped his wine and watched her in what she considered to be a rather proprietary way. "How much are you shooting?"

"I don't really know," she said. "There's so much of it."

"If it's Vietnamese and you keep shooting it, you'll end up with a hell of a habit. You may have a habit already."

"We think it may be all in my head."

"How long has it been?"

"Not so long."

"Good," Dieter said. "Then you can quit if you want to. I can help you."

"Can you really?"

"Don't be scornful," he said. "It's ugly."

Marge stretched. She bore him no ill will.

"Please don't give me hippie sermons, Mr. Natural. I'm not part of your parish."

He fixed his small gray eyes on her.

"How important is the money to you? Do you really want him doing this?"

"I don't give a shit about the money."

"Good. Throw it over the drop and we'll go fish-ing."

"Talk to him about that."

He fell silent, sitting with his wine on the bottom step of the altar as though he were trying to gather strength.

"I like you," he said after a while. "I'm glad you're here."

"How nice of you to say so."

"Has he told you about what we did here?"

"He said you were a roshi who freaked out. I don't really know what that means."

Dieter took a deep drink of his wine.

"Years ago," he said gravely, "something very special was happening up here."

"Was it something profound?"

"As a matter of fact, it was something profound. But rather difficult to verbalize."

"I knew it would be. Did it have to do with your being God?"

Dieter sighed.

"I am not now—nor have I ever been—God. In any ordinary meaning of the word. I made certain state-ments for political reasons. In my opinion they were what the times demanded. If things had worked out everything would have been clear in the end."

Marge laughed.

"You're like my father—he's a Communist." She wiped the mellow smack tears from her eyes and shook her head. "So many people have it all figured out and they're all full of shit. It's sad."

"Listen," Dieter announced, "a hippie sermon —When the soul leaves the body it approaches the void and there it is assailed by temptations. In its first temptation it encounters two people fuck-ing—naturally what remains of its prurient interest is aroused. It draws closer and closer until it's drawn in. It has been visualizing its own conception. It goes back the way it came and that's the end of liberation.

229

Well, that's what happened to us," Dieter said. "I suppose it was the dope that stopped us. We were drawn in because it was so much fun. As a junkie, you should understand that."

"Absolutely," Marge said. She closed her eyes. "It's too bad, really it is. It's too bad we can't get out of this shit into something better. If there was a way to do it, I'd say—I'd say—let's do it."

"Let's do it," Dieter said. "Get him to stay."

Content within the vaults of the drug, Marge laughed.

"If I could pray," she said smiling, "I would pray that God would cause the bomb to fall on all of us—on us and on our children and wipe the whole lot of us out. So we could stop needing this and needing that. Needing dope and needing love and needing each other's dirty asses and each other's stupid fucked-up riffs.

"That's the answer," she said placidly. "The final solution."

Dieter drew himself up in a magisterial fashion.

"Foolish girl," he said softly. "That's the problem, it can't be the answer. When you say that, it's cheap junkie pessimism. If you spend time making holes in yourself and tripping on the cracks on the walls—how else can you think?

"You begin from there," he shouted at her—"life belongs to the strong!"

"The strong?" Marge asked incredulously. "The strong? Who the hell is that supposed to be? Superman? Socialist man?" She stood up wearily and leaned against the wall. "You're an asshole," she said to Dieter. "You're a Fascist. Where were you during the Second World War?"

Laughing to herself, she staggered out of the room and went down the corridor to the cell where Hicks was sleeping. The bag was beside him; she pulled it out and opened it and spent a long time staring at it in wonder. Her hand absently caressed the outer covering in a ridiculous manner and the notion came to her that it was like a child but less trouble. It was a stupid thought and she was not amused. She got up and went out again to the garden where the stream was and sat beside it with her head in her hands. When she looked up she saw Dieter standing in the doorway.

"It doesn't get better," he said.

"You don't know what you're talking about," she told him. "Mind your business."

When she looked up again he was still there.

"If I didn't have it now, I'd be out of my mind. Things are crazy and it's been horrible. It's like I haven't slept for a week."

He smiled with his thick hairy lips in a way that she thought at first was extremely cruel but when she had stared at him for a few moments she was no longer sure that it was cruelty she saw there.

"But you're all right," he said. "You have it."

Converse AND HIS COMPANIONS SPENT THE FIRST evening of the journey at a hotel called the Fremont. It was in the mountains, across the road from a yellow slope on which Herefords grazed.

As soon as Converse determined that it was not the last day of his life, he began to drink in celebration. He drank Bacardi because that was what Danskin liked.

Danskin and Smitty sat on the bed playing chess with a portable set that had tiny plastic pins for pieces. In play, Danskin was imperturbable; he slumped motionless over his own belly, his shoulders hunched, his feet on the floor. His breathing was always audible; for all his size and apparent strength, he did not seem to be very healthy.

Smitty hummed and tapped his foot and licked his lips frequently.

"Check . . ." Danskin said wearily. "And mate."

Smitty's eyes narrowed in panic. He removed his king from its fatal position and surveyed the board.

"Where the fuck did that come from? I never seen it."

"Checkmate," Danskin said.

He watched Smitty move the king from one square to another, and finally replace it in the trap.

"You got me," Smitty said.

Danskin sighed.

When they stood up, he struck Smitty across the mouth with his fist—a lightning right cross from nowhere that had the whole weight of his trunk behind it. Smitty caught it flat-footed; he had not even tried to duck. The blow stood him on tiptoes and he staggered backward and caught himself against the wall. He felt his lip, spat blood, and walked into the bathroom. Danskin followed him stolidly.

"You stupid little bastard, I'm tired of your jailbird chess. You better learn to play."

He turned to Converse, who was pouring another Bacardi.

"I hate jailbird chess," he explained. "I hate the style. No foresight, no reasoning. Just like a little kid." He pursed his lips and spoke mincingly, raising his voice for Smitty to hear. "Just like a little tweety bird! Oooh, here's a move. Oooh, there's a move. It's fucking degrading."

Smitty came out of the bathroom holding a face towel to his lip, and sat down on the bed.

"You hit my fucking bridge, man."

"Tough tit. Why don't you read a chess book once in your life?"

"Plenty of guys will belt you when they lose," Smitty said thickly. "Fuckin' Danskin—he wins and he hits you."

Danskin shrugged and lay down beside Smitty with a book of road maps of the national parks.

"Where do you think I learned the game, man?" Smitty demanded. "I learned it in the slams, I can't help that." He looked at his bloody face towel. "Fuck you, man, I ain't playin' no more chess with you."

Danskin looked up at Converse.

"Play chess?"

"I'm very weak," Converse said.

Danskin laughed.

"He's very weak," he told Smitty.

"I don't think I have the cast of mind for it."

"That's odd," Danskin said. "It can't be that you're stupid, can it?"

"No," Converse said.

He went to sleep in his chair.

When he woke up, he had the sense that some hours had passed. It seemed to him that there had been sunlight on the drapes before and there was none now. His head ached, and he was thirsty; he was on the floor.

When he tried to stand, his legs would not respond. He twisted round and saw that there were handcuffs on his ankles.

One of the small table lamps was lit. Smitty sat beside it in a blond wood armchair giggling at him silently. Danskin was in bed with a pillow over his head.

"Where you going?" Smitty asked merrily.

"I'd like to get some water."

"Go ahead," Smitty said.

"For Christ's sake," Converse said. "I agreed to come out here. I don't see the necessity for this kind of thing."

"If you want water, get it. I'm not stopping you."

He drew himself up and hopped to the bathroom.

"I'll wake up the whole damn place this way," he told Smitty.

"Fuck the whole damn place."

Converse drank and washed his face under the tap. He held to the sink to keep from falling over. When he had finished, he hopped back into a chair across the room from Smitty.

There was a red binding mark around Smitty's spindly arm; the skin in the crook of his elbow was black and blue. His undersea eyes were at peace.

"You from New York?" Smitty asked.

"Yes," Converse said.

"You know Yorkville?"

"Yes."

"You know Klavan's?"

Converse knew Klavan's well. It was a bar on Second Avenue in which he had drunk illegally when he was under the required age. On St. Patrick's Day, 1955, he had been beaten up there and it was there he had attempted the seduction of Agnes Comerford, a nursing student at Lenox Hill Hospital. He had invested a considerable amount of his life's energy in transporting himself as far from Klavan's, in every respect, as he was capable.

"No," he said.

The idea of being held prisoner in a California motel by a denizen of Klavan's was profoundly distasteful to him.

"You know, I was in Vietnam too," Smitty said. "I got fucked up there."

"What happened?"

"I stepped on a pungi stick. Hurt? Jesus! It got me the fuck out of there, though."

"Good," Converse said.

Smitty glanced over his shoulder at the bed, and listened with satisfaction to Danskin's asthmatic breathing.

"Some nut, huh?"

Converse grunted.

"You know what his I.Q. is? One hundred and seventy. A rating of genius."

"I'm not surprised," Converse said.

"You're riding with the guy and some classical music comes on the pipe—he says that's Mozart. That's Beethoven. What good does it do him?"

"How do you know each other?"

"Through Antheil. He introduced us."

"Antheil's quite a fella."

"He's the coolest," Smitty said. "Fuckin' guy's got bread stashed away, a beautiful home, chicks coming and going. They say the system don't work, man—don't tell that to Antheil."

"Does he pay you?"

"You think I'm out here for nothing? You think I'm a buff?" He tossed his head with self-satisfaction. "I got a crack at a job with the agency after this."

"Don't you have a record?"

"That don't mean shit. If Antheil says you're in, you're in. And I could really go for that, man."

"You could be a second Antheil."

"You're not kidding," Smitty said.

"How about Danskin? Does he want to work for the agency too?"

Smitty looked over his shoulder again and lowered his voice.

"He's a brute, man, a psycho. A dude like that couldn't deal with the public."

Converse nodded thoughtfully and slid back onto the floor to sleep. After a few moments, he heard Smitty approach softly. He opened his eyes and turned over on his side.

"I was married," Smitty said.

"Is that right?"

"I had enough of that, though. It's stupid."

"I suppose it's a matter of personnel," Converse said.

"Look at you," Smitty told him. "Look at the grief you got."

"It's a funny situation."

"You're lucky we came along, man. We'll give you some peace of mind."

235

Converse turned his back on Smitty and leaned on his elbow.

"I seen your old lady," Smitty said. "She's big."

"Big?" Converse said. "She's not big."

"Yeah, she is. I seen her."

"You're mistaken."

"Maybe so," Smitty said.

Converse eased away from him. He had been drawing closer and he smelled.

"My wife's in Staten Island," he told Converse. "She got hot pants for this guy twice her age. A guy that owned a restaurant out there."

"Maybe," Converse suggested, "you shouldn't talk about it."

"When I was in the can," Smitty said, "we did this thing. We'd talk about our old lady—like where they were, what they were doing."

Converse pretended sleep.

"What they looked like. How they like to fuck. Whether they were fucking somebody." He put his hand on Converse's shoulder and shook him. "Right?"

"Right," Converse said.

"Some guys couldn't take it, they went batshit. It would drive you nuts."

His hand slid from Converse's shoulder, along his side, to the inside of his thigh. Converse rolled over convulsively and faced him.

"Keep your hands off me."

Smitty was not discouraged.

"Your wife is fucking that guy, you know that."

"Just keep your hands off me," Converse said.

"Keep your hands off him," Danskin said.

Smitty jumped as though he had been struck. Danskin was sitting up in bed staring at them with an expression of deep melancholy.

"Get in bed," he told Smitty.

Smitty stood up quickly, brushing his hair.

"You didn't take a shower," Danskin said. "When you gonna take one?"

"In the morning."

"Take one now."

Smitty went into the bathroom to take a shower. Converse huddled against the wall, with the feeling that Danskin was watching him from the bed.

In a few minutes, Smitty came out of the bathroom, turned out the table lamp, and climbed into bed with Danskin. It shortly became apparent to Converse, as he lay in the darkness, that Smitty and Danskin were having sex together. As they went at it, he eased silently across the carpet to where the Bacardi was and very carefully brought it down to the floor with him.

Only fear kept him from retching when he had taken a long drink. When Danskin and Smitty were silent, he crawled to the cot which the management provided for third guests, climbed in it, and pulled the spread over him.

He dreamed of Charmian.

The following morning they started early and drove almost until dusk without stopping. It was superhighway driving through the desert; Danskin and Smitty took turns behind the wheel and they became more tense as the day passed. There were dried apricots and candy to eat and more Bacardi. Converse drank the better part of the rum. They did not make him wear cuffs in the car.

About seven, they left the Interstate and drove with the declining sun on their right through fields of green crops and small farming towns. High brown mountains rose ahead of them.

Once Converse woke to conversation.

"You told him you were in Vietnam. I heard you."

"I was," Smitty said.

Danskin looked over his shoulder and saw that Converse was awake.

"He was never in Vietnam. He was never anywhere except Haight-Ashbury and the slammer."

Smitty sat and sulked.

"But when he gets going," Danskin said, "he tells stories like you could never forget. Ears cut off. Balls cut off. Little kiddies on bayonets. The most awful shit you ever heard." He turned to smile at Smitty and wiped sweat from his forehead. "And the kicker is—he was never there."

"How do you know I was never there?" Smitty said.

"That's his way of making out, you know what I mean? He meets a chick and right away she's hearing about the atrocities. 'And then I machine-gunned all the kids. And then I strangled all their grannies. And then we set the mayor on fire.' He goes on and on—and you know what?"

"They love it," Converse said.

Danskin laughed with satisfaction.

"Your fuckin' A. They love it. The more ghastly, the more horrible, the more they love it."

"Jesus," Smitty said, "you're embarrassing."

"Then he gives them the switcheroo. He tells them how he was punished for disobeying orders. The general says, 'Smitty, take these nuns out and bury them alive in shit.' Smitty says, 'Fuck you, general.' He punches the general in the mouth and they put him in the joint. That's what he did time for, he tells them."

"I don't know," Converse said.

"What don't you know? Did they do all that shit over there? Is it all true?"

"Some of it isn't, obviously. Some of it is."

"Man," Smitty said, "if I was a writer I'd be rich. I ought to do that with you, Converse. I tell you stuff and you write it down."

"You stupid fuck," Danskin said, "people always say that to writers. Now he thinks you're an asshole."

"Not necessarily," Converse said. "Some people tell me things and I write it."

"Then you get the bread," Smitty said, "and they get shit."

"Not anymore," Converse said. As they drove through fields he told them about the stories he had written for *Nightbeat*. He told them about the Skydiver and the Mad Dentist. He told them Exploding Cigar Kills Nine, Hoarder Crushed by Small Change, and Wedding Night Trick Breaks Bride's Back. They were amused and it passed the driving time agreeably.

Smitty was a bit shocked.

"How can they put stuff in the papers if it's not true? Isn't it against the law?"

Danskin whooped in scorn.

"Not at all," Converse said.

"You should talk," Danskin said to Smitty. "Not a true word comes out of your mouth." He sat thoughtfully for a few minutes and then exploded with laughter.

"You and your pungi stick," he cried. "One time you're gonna tell that story one time too many, man. Then you know what I'm gonna do? I'm gonna make one of those things and put it right through your foot." He leaned into the back seat and slapped Converse on the shoulder. "Right through his fuckin' foot I'll put it. Then he could talk about how it hurts."

They drove through long shadows in golden light; the road followed a ridge overlooking the valley, then turned south in hairpin curves over high treeless passes through the mountains. In one of the passes they pulled off the paved highway and parked out of sight of it, among limestone boulders. Below, the ground sloped to a brown depression with a pool of slow-moving muddy water at its bottom.

"Let's take a rest," Danskin said.

They climbed out of the car and made their way

down the slope. Danskin carried the rum and a plastic gallon can.

"It's a hole," Danskin said, looking up to the hills around them. "It's a literal hole." He threw the plastic can to Smitty. "Fill it up for the radiator. It's all dry from here."

He took a sip of rum and passed the bottle to Converse.

"How you doing, Mr. Converse?"

"O.K.," Converse said.

"You're pretty cool, considering."

"Well, I decided to come. I might as well live with it."

"You decided? What do you mean you decided? You think you could have walked away?"

Converse looked at the sky. Far above, beyond hearing, the tiny silver body of an airplane inched across the cloudless blue. It occurred to him that he had spent a great deal of time on the ground wishing he were in the air, and rather a lot of time in aircraft wishing he were on the ground.

"Well, it doesn't matter now, does it?" It was a perfect place to kill someone, he thought. A shot would probably be heard for miles—but there was no one within miles to hear. From the top of the pass they had not seen a single sign of human habitation, not a fence, not a wire. Only the plane, six miles up.

"You're indifferent?"

"I'm trying."

Danskin reached inside his gray cardigan and removed a pistol. He sat down on a rock and leaned the gun on his knee so that the barrel was pointed a few inches to the left of Converse's leg.

"See this thing?"

Looking at the gun made Converse sleepy. His eyelids grew heavy.

"Sure I see it."

"Looks like a regular thirty-eight?"

"I don't know anything about handguns. I had

a forty-five once. I could take it apart and clean it."
He shrugged. "That was a while ago."

"This is what it shoots." Danskin took a small
canvas roll from his breast pocket and held it out
for Converse's inspection. "That's the slug. It doesn't
penetrate. It flattens out on contact and mashes the
shit out of anything it hits. Makes a wide shallow
hole."

Converse yawned.

"That's what the air marshals carry," Danskin said.
"Remember that if you feel like hijacking a plane."

Smitty was carrying the plastic can up the side
of a rock where wildflowers grew. The climb was
steep and he went slowly.

"Work for it," Danskin called to him. "Work for
it, mother." He shook his head. "He's gonna do up,"
he told Converse.

"Has he a habit?"

Danskin shrugged.

"Sometimes he shoots a bag by himself. Sometimes
he doesn't. I think it's the spike he likes."

They watched him climb until he disappeared
behind the top of the rock.

"He's shy," Danskin said primly.

"He tells me he's looking for a job in the agency."

"Who, Smitty? Smitty doesn't have the intelligence
of an Airedale. He can't tell the difference between
a nickel and a quarter. How's he gonna be in the
agency?"

"He says Antheil'll get him in."

"Sure. He can be whatever he wants. He can be
governor, he can fly. That's what Antheil tells him."

"What does he tell you?"

Danskin shook his head slowly. "Don't, man."

"Just curiosity," Converse said. "I know why Smitty
works for him. I couldn't help wondering why you
did."

"I like it. I'm a student of the passing parade."

Smitty appeared at the top of the rock; his arms

flapped loosely at his sides as he scampered down the face of it. He waddled in a contracting circle beside the water and sprawled on the ground.

"Hey, man," Smitty called happily.

Danskin smiled indulgently down at him.

"Hey, Smitty."

"You know what, Danskin? It's too bad we can't have a fire."

"It's too bad we can't toast marshmallows. It's too bad we can't have a sing-a-ling." Asthmatic laughter shook him, he wrinkled the folds of flesh around his eyes. "You're a child."

Danskin walked over to where Smitty lay and stood over him.

"You want me to tell you scary stories?"

Giggling, Smitty covered up and crawled away from Danskin's feet.

"No, man."

"All right for you. No stories." He turned to Converse and his stare hardened.

"Why don't you tell us about Vietnam? What did you do there besides cop scag?"

"I hung around."

"That's all?"

"Once I went up the Mekong on a patrol craft with the Navy. And I went into Cambodia with the First Division."

Smitty was looking up at him with a loose smile.

"You kill anybody?"

"I wasn't a combatant. I didn't carry a weapon."

"Man, I would have," Smitty said. "I woulda carried every fuckin' weapon."

"For most people in the line it was firing at leaves or points of light. There isn't a lot of personal combat."

He turned to Danskin and saw in the man's face a sudden hatred which surprised him, and frightened him as the gun had not.

"You disapprove of that shit, right?" Dumb unreasoning fury welled in Danskin's eyes. Converse looked away quickly. "You're against violence and killing. You're above it."

"I've always . . ." Converse began. "Yes," he said, "I'm against it. I don't know about being above it."

"You have contempt for it, right?"

He looked into Danskin's mad eyes and felt anger. It was an unfamiliar sensation.

"I've seen people kill," he told Danskin. "It's not all that terrific. A snake can do it. So can a mosquito or a few thousand ants."

"You're O.K., Converse," Danskin said. "First you bring people Vietnam scag, then you tell them how it is. So they shouldn't do the wrong thing and bring you down." He reached out and gently took the tab of Converse's collar between his fingers. "Don't shit me," he told Converse softly. "You're a vindictive nasty little prick—I can tell that by looking at your face. But you're a coward. It's as simple as that."

"Maybe," Converse said.

"Maybe, hah? Listen, man, you think I don't know what you bastards are like? You think I don't know how you have fantasies—the guy kicks sand in your face you're gonna kill him? You karate the walls, you talk tough to the mirror. You eat shit all your life and you hate every fucking minute of it and you'd like to fuck over half the country but you have to swallow it because you got no guts. I don't know about that, huh Converse? You think I'm stupid?"

"No," Converse said.

"You think I'm sick?"

"No."

"What am I then?"

"Ah, man," Smitty said. "Don't get twisted. Take it easy."

"I could beat you to death, you know that?"

Smitty stood up and dusted himself off.

"Sure he knows it, man. What are you trying to prove?"

"He thinks he's superior," Danskin said. "The guy's a heroin hustler and not even a good one."

Biting his lip, he walked away from Converse and started up the slope to the road.

"Let's get going. We'll drive tonight."

Smitty gave Converse an apologetic smile.

"Don't argue with him, Converse. Let him wail when he's pissed off."

It was nearly dark, the brown hills melding into shadow, the stars out.

Danskin looked up and down the darkened road and climbed behind the wheel.

"Sit up here," he told Converse.

Smitty climbed in the back and slammed the door.

"You think it's a good idea to drive at night like this?" he asked Danskin. "The border patrol rides around up here."

Danskin switched on the car lights and started up.

"They have enough to look for. They don't have our plates on their list, they shouldn't bother us."

"Antheil should have cooled them."

"If we get stopped and rousted," Danskin said, "we take the fall and keep quiet. Antheil can take care of it after. That means you too," he told Converse.

They rounded curve after curve in the darkness. There were mule deer in the hills and several times Danskin had to halt the car and kill the lights to let them cross the road. Smitty went to sleep in the back.

Converse was dozing when he felt Danskin nudge his elbow.

"Talk," Danskin said.

"What do you mean?"

"I mean I'm going to sleep here. Say something and piss me off."

Converse looked at him for a moment and then leaned his head back on the seat and closed his eyes.

"Converse."

"Yeah?"

"I was locked up for nine years, you know that? In the madhouse. For a violent act."

"Maybe," Converse suggested, "you'd rather not talk about it."

"You don't want to hear?"

Converse hesitated.

"No," he said.

Having said it, he turned an anxious glance. He could see Danskin's face dimly in the panel lights; he seemed to be smiling but one could never be sure. Converse shivered.

"You've already impressed me," he told Danskin. "Save it for the next guy."

"You ever locked up, Converse?"

"Never."

"Then you're a fucking virgin. You don't know what anything's about."

"Yes, I do," Converse said.

"Nineteen sixty to nineteen sixty-nine, I was inside."

"You missed a lot."

"You think so?" Danskin snorted with contempt. "I missed nothing. Anything was going on outside, man it was going on in there. Sometimes stuff started in there and hit the streets later."

"That I can believe."

"When I got there, Converse, I was in a dungeon. There was a guy there—anything they put in with him, he'd eat it. A mattress. Your arm."

Converse nodded.

"I learned to be a pussycat in there. They'd take me down to the shrink and he'd try to piss me off so the goons could bounce me off the wall. I'd smile.

"Finally I got out into population and that was O.K. Nurses, all kinds of dope. I saw it all, Converse—everything you think I missed. We had civil rights assholes come in there. We had a guy who checked into a hotel in Mobile and lived on canned tortillas and tried to radiate love energy all over Alabama until the cops took him out and tied him up. We had a beatnik poet who wore salami patches on his tweed sport coat. The real Mr. Clean—he was there, he was gonna sue Procter and Gamble. A guy who said he was Fred Waring. Another guy, he took a shotgun and blasted four secretaries at Adelphi College. If I hadn't been there I wouldn't be talking to you because it was dope and politics in that place, just like outside. But man, they *did not* want me out of there. I didn't ever think I'd make it. It was kind of a famous case."

"All right," Converse said. "What did you do?"

Danskin nodded with satisfaction.

"You know Brooklyn?"

"Sure."

"Saturday night," Danskin said. "The Loew's Lido, East Flatbush. *The Searchers* is playing. John Wayne.

"I was seventeen years old, I was a freshman at Brooklyn College. I was a virgin. I had never had a girlfriend. So, it's Saturday night and I'm going to the movies by myself.

"Just as I'm about to buy the ticket, I see the ticket-taker walk into the john. So I ask the cashier for change of a bill and then—very nonchalant—I walk past the doors and into the movie house. I skip my usual bag of popcorn and I go and find my favorite seat. On the left side toward the front.

"Very soon there's a little commotion at the back and I figure—Fuck, man, I'm discovered. Down comes the usher with his light. Now the usher is a kid I know and his name is Bruce. Bruce and I were at Midwood together. We have a strong mutual contempt. Bruce stands there shining his light in my face and I become extremely upset.

"Because Bruce is really very intelligent. Bruce has always had girlfriends and now he has a girlfriend, the sister of a guy I know, the most beautiful girl you could imagine. Bruce is a superb athlete. Bruce has a scholarship to Cornell.

"So Bruce shines the light and he says—in his cultivated about-to-go-to-Cornell voice—'O.K., Danskin, wise guy, where's your stub?' "

Danskin shrugged as he drove, and mocked himself in falsetto.

" 'I don't have a stub, Brucie. I lost it.'

"So he laughs at me. He says, 'You were with another guy, there's two of you, where's the other guy?' So me—quick thinker—I say, 'No, Bruce it was just me.'

"The manager is there now, they're both standing over me with the light, they're both laughing. 'Danskin,' Bruce says, 'come with me, please.' They escort me up the aisle, past maybe twenty people I know or who know me and outside to the cashier's box.

" 'This is where you buy the tickets,' Bruce says. And just before he went inside he gave me a look, a little expression, a little twinkle of the eyes which says, 'Danskin, what a schmuck you are, what a contemptible idiot, what a fucking fool.' "

Danskin sighed.

"Needless to say, I no longer felt like the movies. I walked home and all I could think about was how after the show Bruce is going to meet his girlfriend and he'll tell her. They'll laugh about the moron, the funny animal. She'll tell Bruce how clever he is.

"I got home and for a couple of hours I worked on my stamp collection. That almost always calmed me down. Only this time, it didn't. I couldn't get it out of my head, you understand. I realized . . ." He turned to Converse ferociously. Converse looked nervously at the road.

"I realized this was it! There was nothing else for me to do. I had absolutely no choice.

"First I took my whole stamp collection—I started it when I was about six—I took the whole thing to Prospect Park Lake and threw it in. I could have been mugged. A cop could have grabbed me. But they didn't. Then I went in my father's truck and I got a tire iron. I called up Bruce's mother and she told me he was on a date. He wouldn't be home until late.

"New Utrecht Avenue, there's a playground between the subway stop and where Bruce's house was. I waited in the playground, I sat on a bench holding the tire iron in my lap. Must be four in the morning—out of the subway—here comes Bruce. He didn't see me until I was right on top of him. I was careful because he knew karate. He would, right?

"When he saw me, man, he knew! He knew then and there.

"The first one is right across the face and he's down. No karate. Not a sound. I just stood over him and bam! Bam, that's for your girlfriend. Bam, that's for your scholarship to Cornell. Bam, that's for the little twinkle. Bam bam bam bam bam. Lots and lots of times and Bruce's little twinkle and his scholarship to Cornell is just a lot of mucus on the asphalt. Every light in every building on the street is turned on, three hundred cops are there, and I'm still pounding crud into the street and the playground looks like a meat market."

"So they locked you up."

"So they locked me up," Danskin said. "I feigned madness. I babbled, I recited Heine. Nine years. Here I am."

They rode in silence for a while.

"But you're still pissed off."

"Now more than ever."

"Are you sorry?"

"I'm sorry I got put away. I'm not sorry I wasted Brucie. The fucking guy would remember me all his life. He'd be a rich doctor or the Secretary of Interior and he'd have this picture in his mind of me being thrown out of Loew's. I'd rather have done the time."

He seemed to be growing angry again. His jaw trembled.

"He'd be married to Claire. She'd say, remember the great fuck we had the night you threw that schmuck whatshisname out of the movies?"

Danskin released an asthmatic sigh and relaxed.

"That's not the way I want to be remembered."

"When I went to school," Converse said, "they used to tell us to offer our humiliations to the Holy Ghost."

"That's sick," Danskin said. He shuddered with revulsion. "That's fucking repulsive. Why the Holy Ghost?"

"I guess He likes to see people fuck up."

"He must get a kick out of you, huh?"

"I think the idea was to make something balance."

Danskin shook his head.

"People are so stupid," he said, "it makes you cry."

"So what happened," Converse asked, "after you got out?"

"I came out of there with a Jones, that's what happened. I was dicking this wiggy nurse and she turned me on. On grass. On acid. On screwing for that matter. She was queer for madmen.

"We'd go down to the swimming pool and shoot dilaudid tabs, then morphine. It was really nice. The shrinks would try to get to me so I'd chew the rug and I'd just smile, man. Just—hello sunshine! They'd look me up and down, going hmmmm—you know what I mean? And I'm standing there so fucking loaded I think I'm in Rockaway. They wouldn't go for that now, but in those days it never occurred to them.

"Finally I hit the street and I know shit from nothing. I got a habit the size of Manhattan Island and no dealer will touch me. I appear and they run, right, because I'm incredibly naive and uncool—I grew up in the fucking madhouse. I run after them on the street—Please, please—they say Get Lost, Lemme alone, Help—I get one guy who's so far gone he'll sell to me, and the fourth or fifth time out—slam! We're both busted by a spade in an army coat and sneakers.

"So my status was weird because I'm just out of the hatch. I got passed around from one guy to another and I end up in the Federal Building having a long talk with this Irishman. I can have a break if I'll go out to this college on Long Island and hang with the radicals there. They have me by the balls. On account of the bust they can put me back in the mad-house for life. If I bitch anywhere I'm crazy. If I do what they want, I'll get maintenance and stay out.

"Well, I went out there, man, and after a while I really got interested. I played a couple of colleges in the East—the Feds passed me from one handler to another and I worked up some far-out shit. Chicks want to rob banks with me. I say Let's go to Nyack and kill all the cops there, they say Great! I say Let's blow up Orange Julius—they say Right On."

"I knew some people in the movement," Converse said. "I don't think they would have gone for you."

"You can say that," Danskin said, "but you never saw me work. I got their scene figured. You're an American college kid—that means you get anything you want. You get the best of everything that's in—think it up, you got it. So revolution is in—boots and cartridge belts and Chinese shit. All the rich suburban kids—their parents never bought them cap pistols, now they want to kick ass. Revolution—they gotta have that too.

"The richest fuckin' people in the richest country in the world—you gonna tell them some little guy in a hole in South America can have something they can't? Like shit, man. If the little guy in the hole can be a revolutionary, they can be revolutionaries too."

"Did you get a lot of convictions?"

"I did O.K. I was better in the field than in court,

though. I turned some guns, some explosives. What I mostly got them was dope busts—that's how I got to Antheil."

"Don't you think sometimes," Converse ventured . . . "don't you think there ought to be more to life than that?"

"You should talk," Danskin said. "What have I got to learn from you about what there should be?"

Converse was silent.

"Anyway, it's interesting. I'm like the Holy Ghost, man. I like to see shit heads fall on their ass."

"Tell me something," Converse said after a while. "Did you put that drawing on my wall?"

Danskin laughed, incredulous.

"What do you think I am, a moron? Smitty did that. Did it scare you?"

"Yes," Converse said. "It did."

Danskin laughed and pounded on the wheel.

"Why, you simple asshole!" he said. "Good for Smitty."

A NTHEIL WAS WAITING FOR THEM BESIDE A PICKUP truck at a turn in the road. He had parked at the edge of a pine forest; there was a Mexican with him, a somber squab-nosed man in a khaki shirt with a broad-brimmed beige fedora.

Danskin eased the station wagon over the pine needles and parked it beside the truck.

"He's pissed off," Smitty said.

Antheil was dressed for an afternoon of outdoorsmanship. In his Roos-Atkins collapsible hat and safari jacket, he might have stepped from the pages of *Field and Stream*. But he did appear anxious and depressed, red-eyed, pissed off.

He had spent the previous evening on the south

side of the border with his lone Mexican companion, whose name was Angel.

When they pulled up, he walked over to their station wagon and looked in at Converse with resigned disgust, as one might inspect a consignment of spoiled meat. Danskin and Smitty got out and stood by apologetically; they seemed to despair of pleasing him.

"What's the matter with the radios?" he asked them sharply. "I had no idea where you were."

"They're not much use," Danskin said. "The hills are in the way."

Driving in, they had been trying to make contact on a battery transmitter over the citizen's band; an elaborate code had been prepared to disguise the substance of their conversations. But there had been no contact, the hills had been in the way.

"Well, I hope you'll be able to use them going in," Antheil said. "Otherwise things may get pretty fucked up."

Angel looked at Danskin and Smitty as though they aroused some dreadful appetite. He bent to the car window to look at Converse. Converse nodded to him.

Angel was a policeman in the adjoining Mexican state, and in the past he and Antheil had collaborated in matters relating to law enforcement. In the spirit of *alianza para progreso,* they had gone drinking and Antheil, who prided himself on the knowledgeable finesse with which he handled Latins, had found the evening trying and even dangerous. Sober, Angel was a public man of massive, somewhat grim, dignity. In liquor he became sullen and contentious. Simpatico as he was, Antheil's Spanish was uneven. Several times in the course of their revels he had inadvertently given offense to Angel in matters which, to his own understanding, were trivial in the extreme. There had been a period during which it appeared that Angel—whom he was after all engaging as a body-guard—might shoot him. Angel had recounted many stories illustrating his own prowess and cunning as a police officer, and Antheil had been compelled to simulate intense admiration.

Angel was sober once again, but it had been ill preparation for the day's business. When they arrived to find truckloads of people encamped at the derelict village, Antheil became even more uneasy.

He paced up and down beside the cars, holding a Geological Survey map in one hand and fingering the corners of his mustache with the other.

"You're about two miles from the ranch property. There are two trails going up to the house, and you'll find them marked on here." He handed Danskin the map. "Can you read it?"

Danskin looked at the map in sullen silence.

Antheil cleared his throat and glanced at Angel.

"There's some kind of lettuce-pickers' convention going on down the road where the trails start. There are a lot of Mexican people there. My friend here has indicated to me that they are members of a pentecostal church and that they come here every year. The houses they're in are outside the ranch property, and so far as we know there's no connection between them and Dieter Bechstein."

"Wait a minute," Danskin said. "That changes things a lot, right?"

"It doesn't change anything. If I understand the cultural pattern correctly, they should be more hostile to the people up the hill than to us. Angel and I just drove through. There are no phone wires on any of the houses, and nobody looked twice at us." He stopped pacing and placed his hands on his hips. "In fact," he said, "you might attempt to determine if these people are actively hostile to the creeps up there. You may be able to utilize their assistance. They may have specialized knowledge about access routes."

"You know," Danskin said with a faint smile, "this is different from what we figured."

"That's correct," Antheil said. "And let me make

one thing clear. By tomorrow afternoon we are going to act officially. There will be local police involvement. There will be regulation procedure and there will be arrests. There will be confiscations."

"So," Danskin said. "We have until tomorrow afternoon to get it off them. Are you going in with us?"

"To some extent."

"What the hell do you mean, *to some extent?*"

"We'll be here to back you up. We don't want to get smeared all over this thing, you know."

Danskin moved closer to Antheil and fixed mad sorrowful eyes on him.

"I thought you had this place cased, man. You said you had maps and shit." He looked with distaste at the surrounding hills. "We don't know what the fuck we're doing down here. We don't know how many people they got up there, for Christ's sake."

Antheil met his eyes resolutely.

"We're almost sure there are no more than two or three." He looked at Converse in the station wagon. "His wife, Hicks and Bechstein."

Danskin nodded sulkily.

Antheil strolled over to the station wagon and leaned his arm on the window.

"Hi there, fella. Gonna help us out?"

"Sure thing," Converse said.

"How?" Danskin asked. "How's he gonna help us out?"

"He's gonna have a word with his old lady. You're going to arrange a reunion."

"She'll tell him to fuck off," Smitty said.

"I don't think so. You send him ahead of you—keep him where you can see him, and see what it gets you. Personally, I think it should have some psychological effect."

"I don't see it myself," Danskin said.

"Do it anyway," Antheil said. "What could we do, leave him up in the city pissing his pants? I want the principals in one place."

He glanced in at Converse again and smiled at him.

"He's fun, huh?"

Danskin looked sour.

"Sure. Let's get going."

When they started the car and pulled out, Antheil walked after them.

"Any mishaps—get out of it by first light. I'm not kidding—we'll be all over cops."

Antheil and Angel watched sadly as they pulled back onto the road.

"He's not pissed off," Converse said, when they were on their way. "He's scared."

Danskin stopped the car at the side of the road.

"You just shut the fuck up," he told Converse.

"From now on, keep your mouth shut." He was turned around in the driver's seat, in a rage. "You don't say a word, not one word. When you're supposed to talk, I'll tell you."

"O.K.," Converse said.

In a few minutes they were driving by the houses which Antheil had described. People looked up scowling from their Bibles. The men stood together without speaking.

"I don't see no lettuce," Smitty said.

They parked near the pit where the ruined tepee stood. A few yards away was a dusty Land-Rover with California plates. Smitty and Danskin got out of the car and walked over to it.

"That's gotta be theirs," Smitty said.

They looked inside, peering under the seats and into the back.

Danskin laughed bitterly.

"Look at it. It's all over the place."

The chatter of playing children drifted over from the tent village beside the rows of parked trucks. People were singing in one of the clapboard houses. Five men in brown suits sat beside each other on a bench in front of the largest structure. Smitty sauntered toward them, nodding his head to the junkie beat, projecting deranged menace at anyone within sight of him.

"They're all dressed up," he told Danskin.

"Maybe it's a wedding."

"Christ," Smitty said. "I thought we'd have a bunch of twisted wetbacks over here."

A small Willys jeep pulled up on the road behind them, and they turned toward the sound. Behind the wheel, a Mexican in a Stetson sat watching them. There was a rifle in a gun rack in the seat behind him.

When they walked toward him, he put the jeep in gear.

"Wait a minute, *señor*," Danskin said.

The Mexican turned his engine off and waited for them to come up. He was looking at their car, and at Converse, who had stayed in the rear seat.

"You live here?" Danskin asked.

Smitty took the rifle from the rack and inspected it.

The man nodded.

"Up the hill there—there's some freaks living up there, am I right?

"Freaks," Danskin insisted when the man was silent. "Hippies. Long-hairs."

The man stared as though he had never heard of such ones.

"Hey man, there's a house up there. There's people living in it, right?"

"A house," the Mexican said. "Somebody lives there—I don't know."

"You don't know? You don't know whose vehicle that is?"

The Mexican shrugged.

"Hippies," he said.

"This fuckin' guy," Smitty began.

Danskin silenced him with a gesture.

"How can we get up there?"

The man looked up the hill as though he were pondering it.

"We don't go there," he said.

"But you know the way, don't you, *señor?*"

"I don't go there."

"Look," Danskin said, "there are these hippies up there. They have dope. Drugs."

"You police?"

"They have something of ours. They stole it."

The Mexican nodded. Danskin opened the jeep door and put a hand on the man's shoulder.

"You help us get up there and we'll take care of you."

The Mexican climbed out. Danskin took twenty dollars from his wallet and put it in the man's hand. The Mexican looked at it for a moment and put it in his pocket. They got into the station wagon, Danskin and the Mexican in the front seat and Smitty in the back with Converse.

"Other guys here," the Mexican said. "In a truck."

"They're our friends. They're gonna wait for us while we get our stuff back. They want to see we get back all right, because the hippies up there are very bad, you know what I mean?"

"O.K.," the Mexican said.

"O.K. is right."

They drove round the edge of the pit and up an ascending track that ran through groves of aspen. The Mexican stared straight ahead. Before long the woods were so thick that they could no longer see the houses or the hills around them.

When the road ended in underbrush, Danskin turned to the Mexican with a patient sigh.

"This must be where we get out, huh?"

He climbed from behind the wheel and leaned against the door. Smitty opened the trunk and took out a Mossberg rifle. The Mexican watched him load it, expressionless. Danskin looked up the steep hillside with a dyspeptic grin.

"We ought to tell him to shove it," he said.

Smitty opened the rear door and pulled Converse out on his feet.

"Who," he asked, "Antheil? How we gonna tell Antheil to shove it?"

"I don't know how," Danskin said. "I'll think about it."

Moving through the trees they came to a limestone bridge over a whitewater stream. On the far side of it the foot trail rose very steeply into birches.

The Mexican walked in front, then Danskin, then Converse with Smitty behind.

From the moment they began to climb, Converse began to experience a curious elation. As they struggled up through the birches, he felt it more and more strongly.

The wind was cool. The birch leaves were delicately pale, almost lemon-colored. When he looked up, the perfect patterns of leaf and branch calmed, yet excited him in a way he could not understand at all. A mindless optimism rose in him like adrenalin—perhaps, he thought, it was adrenalin—no more than that. Utterly without designs, equipment, opportunities, he felt incapable of despair. It occurred to him that his inability to despair might be just another accommodation.

When they rose above the birches, Converse missed them overhead. There were pines now, the ground was rocky and without cover except for the resinous stalk trunks. The trail was steep as ever, with slippery planes of dark rock that slowed them. Ferns grew beside it.

They were all sweating hard. Danskin's tortured breathing marked time. Converse grew increasingly excited.

Within fifteen minutes, Danskin had them stop for a rest. They sprawled panting on the ground, resting their weight against the rocks. The grassy valley was spread out before their feet; the slope on which they rested seemed so perpendicular that one might drop a stone and hit the hamlet below.

Converse watched Danskin close his eyes and breathe carefully. He felt a certain indulgence; in a few hours, he would be either dead or away from them.

His thoughts raced. Within the same second, he was immersed in speculations of the hereafter and the efficacy of contrition—and the question of whether they had brought another pair of handcuffs up the hill. Marge was supposed to be somewhere on the same mountain, but he could not bring himself to believe it, and the thought merely confused him. He felt intensely aware and alive, the way he had felt in the moment when he decided to buy the dope for Charmian.

When they started up again he was thinking of Ken Grimes. Ken Grimes was a medic with the 101st. Jill Percy had discovered him in her obsessive pursuit of moral reference points, and Converse had looked him up in Danang.

Grimes had fled to Canada and then returned to be inducted as a noncombatant. He carried candy to give people when his morphine ran out.

They had spent an afternoon drinking beer in an EM club and, when drunk, Grimes had several times amused Converse by remarking that man must endure his going hence even as his coming hither. He said it was his motto. Converse said it was a hell of a motto for somebody who was twenty years old.

Sometime later, Converse learned from Jill that Ken Grimes had died in the Ia Drang Valley, reading *Steppenwolf*. His death was one of the things Jill cried about. She regretted meeting him, she said. It made her tired of living, and that was a dangerous way to feel.

Converse felt differently. Grimes had provided him

a solitary link with an attitude which he publicly pretended to share—but which he had not experienced for years and never thoroughly understood. It was the attitude in which people acted on coherent ethical apprehensions that seemed real to them. He had observed that people in the grip of this attitude did things which were quite as confused and ultimately ineffectual as the things other people did; nevertheless he held them in a certain—perhaps merely superstitious—esteem.

After the fact, he had written a feature story about Grimes in which he had conveyed grief and rage at the waste of a life. The grief and rage conveyed were entirely professional, assumed. At the core of Converse's reaction to Grimes' life and death were a series of emotions which were not grief or rage and did not make him tired of living—they were compounded of love, self-pity, even pride in humanity. But his story as written was false, facile, a vulgarization—that was, after all, his business. He had considered destroying the story as an act of homage, but he had filed it in the end, spent it as moral coin, so that Grimes' moral explorations in the face of mass murder and young oblivion had served him for a moment's satisfying warmth, like a hot towel in a barbershop.

As he followed Danskin's faltering heels, the notion struck him that it was the writing of that story he was paying for. The idea of such justice both comforted him and terrified him.

Man must endure his going hence even as his coming hither; the words were repeated in his mind until their meaning faded. The manic exhilaration he was feeling made him wonder if a victim frozen before the predator's eyes did not experience some profound dumb animal illumination just before the strike. He moved like a sleepwalker, almost beyond fear, invoking Grimes' memory.

Further up, they came on hardwood forest and

the angle of the slope grew gentler. Danskin called for a rest and lumbered past the Mexican to occupy the highest ground. Angry-eyed, he waved his air marshal's thirty-eight, sportively sighting it at Converse.

"Put those manacles on him."

The Mexican did not seem surprised to see his weapon.

"The cuffs?" Smitty said. "I left them down there."

Danskin shrugged expansively, with a tragic smile.

"Don't give it another thought. What the fuck? Happy-go-lucky, that's us. We don't give a shit."

"Oh, man," Smitty said. "I'm sorry."

"Just keep fucking up. See what it gets you."

Smitty pouted.

"You know," he said, "I'm thinking maybe you're right, you know. About we tell him to shove it."

It would be soon, Converse thought; he felt the diver's fascination for the deeper down. He was glad to be alive.

Danskin stared moodily down at his own boots.

"How far, *señor?* To the house."

The Mexican indicated the ridge just above them.

"What, just up there?"

"A mile," the Mexican said.

"How many people up there?"

The man pursed his lips and showed his palms.

Danskin took the thirty-eight, held it in both hands, and pointed it in the Mexican's face.

"I'm sorry. I have no time for fucking around. Answer the question."

"Always different," the man said. "Maybe not so many."

"They have weapons?"

"I think some of them."

"Hicks is a gun freak," Smitty said. "He'll have heat."

"You like it?" Danskin asked. "I don't like it."

Smitty shook his head.

Danskin stood and looked up the slope.

"I ain't going in just us. I want at least that big motherfucker up here." He waved them to their feet with the pistol. "We'll go up and have a look."

Converse and the Mexican went in front. At the top of the ridge was a barbed-wire fence with a metal swing gate leading through it. They went through the gate across a meadow of yellow grass. As they cleared the rise, they came in sight of a rock pinnacle looming over the trees on the far side of the field. Smitty looked up at it through his binoculars and shrugged.

They went two abreast across the meadow and stopped at the edge of the wood on the far side. Danskin tried his radio.

"Max one," he said into the speaker. "Max one, over."

They got what sounded like Wolfman Jack, extremely faint.

"Maybe we ought to try it from lower down," Smitty said.

Danskin slapped the antenna down into the box.

"He must buy this stuff on Times Square. If he used government equipment it might work for a change." He turned to the Mexican and did an impression of cheerful briskness. "Where's the house, *señor?*"

The man pointed into the woods with his chin. His legs were trembling. Danskin looked at him with suspicion, took the glasses from Smitty, and surveyed everything within view.

"Anybody see us from here?"

"It's down," the Mexican said. "We go down now."

They followed him into the woods, Smitty cradling his rifle across a forearm, Danskin carrying the handgun pointed at the ground.

At a turn in the trail, Smitty froze and crouched. Danskin went down with him.

"There's some fuckin' thing in the tree, man. Look at it."

"It's a mirror," Converse said. He walked up to the tree and looked up at it. The next tree was garlanded with angel's hair, a third with black rosary beads.

"There's another one," Danskin said. He and Smitty stood up. The Mexican stood stock-still. Converse saw him swallow.

"What's all this jive in the trees?" Smitty demanded. "What is that about?"

"Decorations," the Mexican said.

Danskin was standing under a tree on which a small speaker was mounted; its wires trailed down the trunk and led off into deeper wood.

"For Christ's sake," he said.

Smitty looked up apprehensively.

"You think they can see us with that stuff? Or hear us?"

"Don't be an idiot," Danskin said.

They walked warily under the decorations; lengths of insulated wire from the tree-mounted speakers ran beside the trail and snaked over an outcropping of rock which the trail dipped to circumvent. As they walked in the rock's shadow, Converse heard the Mexican draw breath and saw him spring into the bushes just ahead of them. Danskin swung at him with the pistol, then shoved Converse aside in pursuit. There was a furious beating of the brush.

Cursing, Smitty swung his rifle up and peered down into the thick green. In a moment, they could see the Mexican run across a rocky clearing. He ran in a comic manner, lifting his knees high, his elbows pumping furiously. Smitty fired at him, deafening them both. The bullet rang against rock. The man was gone.

"There's a trail down here," Danskin called to

them. "He took off on it." They climbed down the slope to where Danskin stood and saw that there was indeed another trail, much narrower and oppressed with undergrowth.

"How come you couldn't shoot him?" Danskin asked.

"I don't know," Smitty said sadly. "First I didn't want to make the noise, and then I couldn't see him."

"Goddamn it," Danskin said, "I knew he wanted to run. I didn't think he'd get it on."

"Maybe he didn't go to the house," Smitty said. "He didn't follow the wires. They go the other way."

"Let's see where he went," Danskin said. "We know the way out. We're not gonna get lost."

The brush was much thicker and it was difficult to see ahead. Smitty went first, forcing his way through the branches that closed in on the trail. At the first turn he shouldered his way through a brake shielding his eyes with his elbow, and abruptly disappeared from sight. They heard him call out in fright.

Suddenly there was a ledge before them, a deadfall. Smitty was rolling down a grassy slope just below where they stood; the slope ended in a drop to the canyon below. Across perhaps five hundred yards of space, on another edge of what might be the same mountain, was a stone building like a church. There was a corral beside it, in which a horse grazed.

Smitty stopped rolling about five feet short of the edge. He stood on his hands and knees, his face blanched, staring down into space.

"Jesus Christ," he said. "Did you see that? Did you see it?"

"Yeah," Danskin said. He nudged Converse down onto the slope and climbed down himself.

They were on the edge of the mountain. The cliff with the slope above it ran along it as far as they could see in both directions.

"So where the fuck did he go?" Smitty asked. "There's no trail."

They spent a few minutes trying to find a track which the Mexican might have taken, but they found nothing except sheer drop.

"That's it," Danskin said, looking across at the stone building. "Let's get off of here before we get shot at."

They climbed up into the brush and lay down in a spot where they could look across the canyon.

"Well, we're fucked," Smitty said. "We can't do anything from here."

"What do you think of that?" Danskin asked Converse.

"I don't know," Converse said.

Danskin smiled at him.

"Looks like we might not need you, friend. Looks like maybe the play's over."

"I hope not," Converse said.

"Ask the man," Smitty said. "See if you can get him."

Danskin set the radio in front of him and pulled up the antenna.

"Max one. Max one, over."

"Hello, Max one," Antheil's voice replied. "You know I can see you?"

"No shit," Smitty said, astonished.

"We need a hand, if you have a minute," Danskin said.

"It's getting late," Antheil said. "How the hell did you get up there?"

"You follow the trail and climb."

"Hang on," Antheil said. "We'll do what we can for you."

Danskin replaced the antenna and turned over on his back.

"Lost in Space," he told them.

MARGE LAY DOWN BESIDE HICKS, ON THE FLOOR between his mattress and the bag. When she woke up it was still light. Kjell was playing with his horse in the meadow across the warm stream; she sat on the bank and watched him for a while. She walked in the woods at the edge of the meadow and looked at the trinkets in the boughs.

Coming back to the house, the space and the distances began to oppress her. The space was comfortless, the time empty and without any promise of peace; she was at their intersection, and it was not a place she could occupy. It was desperation, nowhere.

She went back into the room and cleaned the spike with alcohol and cooked up in a stained silver tablespoon, making for the timeless vaults. The shot nearly knocked her cold; she went out and vomited beside the shower.

When it was all right, she went into the main room to lie down. Dieter was at his console, working with wires. Beside him, in a Mexican ceramic dish, were clusters of small gray mushrooms, flecked here and there with a curious chemical blue.

She eased herself on a Navaho rug in front of the empty fireplace.

"You want to get high?" Dieter asked her.

"I am."

He turned from his work to look at her and took a delicate bite from one of the mushrooms.

"That's not high—what you are."

He brought the bowl to where she lay and held the mushrooms before her face.

"I used to go down for these myself during the season. It's a fantastic scene. Kids sell them." He

266

nibbled another portion. "The better they are, the more blue. Sometimes the kids who sell them take blue dye and color them."

She shook her head.

"I've been sick."

Dieter took the bowl away and went back to his console while she coasted among the ceiling rafters.

"What are you doing?" she asked him suddenly. "How can you concentrate if you're stoned?"

"I can play polo stoned," Dieter said.

From somewhere in the valley, a trumpet sounded four wavering notes. The striking of colors, an alarm.

Marge smiled when she heard it.

"It's the trumpet of the Mexican infantry," Dieter told her. "A very tragic sound. It calls huge numbers of Mexican soldiers into battle against tiny determined bands. The tiny bands hold them off for three months and kill half of them."

"Does it mean someone's coming?"

He put the wires aside, picked up a pitcher of wine from the stone floor, and sat down at the edge of her blanket.

"I don't know what it means. It has something to do with the fiesta."

"What's the fiesta like? Is it nice?"

"They take a lamb up on the pinnacle and sacrifice it."

She looked into his saintly long-lashed eyes. They were naked, comically blue. She laughed.

"To you?"

"Obviously," Dieter said, "you insist on misunderstanding. They sacrifice it to its heavenly father. They crucify it."

"Really?"

"Sure," Dieter said.

"And they do psilocybin?"

"The psilocybin they got from me." He turned his gaze toward the ceiling beams. "They get high

267

and crucify it, and they ask, Little Lamb Who Made Thee?"

"And what does the lamb say?"

"The lamb says baaa."

Marge shook her head.

"They got a lot of nerve," she said. "So do you."

She stretched out across the floor and thrust her clasped hands between her knees. Dieter's red swollen face hovered above her.

"You're a Jew," she heard him say.

She stiffened and stared up at him.

"Am I? Does that make us buddies?"

Dieter eased down beside her, still holding his wine.

"I detect a certain astringency in your manner. I thought it might be Jewish."

"Because Jews dislike bullshit?"

"That's not my experience. They're just fussy."

His flowing red face was close to hers; she could smell the wine on his breath. She thought he was going to kiss her, but she did not move.

He pulled back and removed himself from her space, crawling off the blanket.

"I was not always as you see me now," he said.

"Me neither."

"I know what you want from him," she said a little later, "but what does he want from you?"

"He wants me to sell three kilos of heroin. That's all he wants."

"No," she said, "he has some hit on you."

"I suppose it's that I'm part of his history. That's the way his life has been—he takes his history seriously. He take people seriously." Dieter began to laugh. "He takes everything seriously. He's a serious man, like your President—*un homme sérieux*. He's a total American."

"You're being snotty."

"Not at all. I know him very well. I was his first master."

"That's a funny thing to hear somebody say," Marge said. She saw that Dieter was not listening to her. He was staring past her with a smile still on his face.

"He was beautiful. He was your natural man of Zen. You could have done anything with that guy."

"What does that mean?" Marge asked. "What do you mean, you could have done anything with him?"

"He was open. He was there. He was. When I called it Those Who Are, it was him I thought of."

"Those Who Are what?"

Dieter discovered her in front of him.

"He was incredible. He acted everything out. There was absolutely no difference between thought and action for him." He clapped his hands and held them together in a grip that whitened his fingers. "It was exactly the same. An enormous self-respect. Whatever he believed in he had to embody absolutely."

Marge put a hand to her face and laughed.

"Wow."

"Wow," Dieter said. "Wow is right."

He looked about his chamber fondly.

"You have to know what it was like here then. We didn't drink—we didn't do up. We washed our dishes in the stream and listened to the birds. Just . . . clarity." He held out his hand and formed a circle with his thumb and forefinger to indicate clarity. "It was before Christine flipped. She was very happy then."

"I didn't know happy was part of it. I thought you weren't supposed to think in those terms."

"Let's face it," Dieter said, "we were happy."

He took a sip of wine from the pitcher and fixed Marge with his Himalayan stare. She had no idea how many mushrooms he might have eaten. They seemed to have no effect on him.

"I went down all the rivers," Dieter told her. "Like a prospector. I knew all the gurus and poseurs. Fuji. Mount Athos." He numbered Fuji and Mount Athos off on his fingers. "But I succumbed to the American dream."

Marge laughed.

"You don't seem to me," she said, "like someone who succumbed to the American dream. You seem more the opposite of that."

"Not at all," Dieter said. "When I came I was naive. I believed all the old bullshit. Innocence. Energy. I believed it so much that for a while it came true for me. Christine and I moved up here—others came. Ray and others. Marvelous things happened to us. We were levitating, we were delirious."

He farted loudly and without embarrassment.

"Then it occurred to me that if I applied the American style—which I didn't really understand—if I pushed a little, speeded things up a little, we might break into something really cosmic. The secular world was falling apart. Nobody knew what they were doing or what they wanted. There was a great ear open. Waiting for something."

Dieter closed his eyes and put clasped hands over the top of his head.

"I was sitting up here hearing it! What they wanted"—with a thrust of his chin he indicated the world below—"I had. I knew! So I thought, a little push, a little shove, a little something extra to shake it loose. And I ended up as Doctor Dope."

He opened his eyes and shrugged.

"It's a fucked-up world. One's a weak vessel."

"Everybody came down."

"Nobody came down," Dieter shouted at her. "We disappeared without a trace. We haven't been seen since."

"Look at Ray," Dieter said. "He's trapped in a samurai fantasy—an American one. He has to be the Lone Ranger, the great desperado—he has to win all the epic battles single-handed." He stood up wearily. "It may not be a very original conception, but he's quite good at it."

Kjell came in from outside carrying an armload of kindling and set it down next to the fireplace.

"We gonna play Go tonight?" he asked his father.

"We'll see. Why don't you go and wake Ray up."

"He's awake," Kjell said. "He's washing." He turned to Marge.

"Play Go?"

"I'm sorry," Marge said, "I've forgotten how."

"Myths," Dieter was saying. "Phantasmagoria. Projections."

Hicks came in, drying his face with a towel.

"It was all shit," he declared. "Wasn't it, Kjell?"

"Shit as opposed to what?" Dieter asked. "If it was shit, what was good stuff?"

"It was a flash."

"It was our responsibility. We should have stayed with that flash forever."

"Whatever it was, we never put it all together. A miss is as good as a mile with that shit."

"We used to have a little song," Dieter said to Marge. "Allow me to recite it for you.

Of offering more, than what I can deliver,
    I have a bad habit it is true
But I have to offer more than what I can deliver,
    to be able to deliver what I do."

"We had a few laughs," Hicks said. He was not laughing. He reached into the bowl, took out one of the mushrooms and nibbled at its blue surfaces.

Dieter spread his palms face up and shook them in the gesture of not comprehending.

"Why is it too late?" he demanded. "Maybe it's not. Look, you don't want that filth you're carrying. It takes you nowhere."

He walked up to Hicks and raised his elbows as though he were about to put his hands on Hicks' shoulders, but he kept his hands away in the end.

"Stay," he said commandingly. "Stay, both of you. We'll give it another shot."

Hicks looked away from him, and took another bite of the mushroom.

"Look," Dieter said, "here we are, yes? The last crumbling fortress of the spirit. The world is breaking down into degeneracy and murder. We have to make islands for ourselves like the ninth-century monks. We're in the dark ages."

He looked over his shoulder and saw Kjell watching him from beside the fireplace. In a moment the boy went outside again.

"We have to get it down before it goes forever. It may never come together again."

"Forget it, man," Hicks said.

"Forget?" Dieter asked in amazement. "You're joking. Who can forget?"

"I'd like to help you get it down, Dieter, but I got some shit to move."

Dieter seized Marge by the arm.

"Tell him."

She shook her head.

"Nobody bought me no mountain, Dieter. I got to live, damnit."

"Nonsense! Bullshit! You don't have to make your living that way."

"Sorry, man," Hicks said.

In the hills outside, a rifle shot echoed over and over, diminishing from rim to rim.

They looked at each other.

"That part of the fiesta?"

"No," Dieter said.

Kjell came in carrying a single log and stood just out of the sunlight that streamed in behind him, with his head cocked toward the open door.

"Sounded like a great big deer rifle," he said.

Hicks went to the other side of the door and looked out at the stone plaza.

"Hunters?"

Dieter shrugged.

"We've never had any before."

"Wouldn't be somebody shooting at us, would it?"

"Maybe somebody's sending us a message," Dieter said.

There was a brick chamber behind Dieter's altar where a ladder was pitched against the platform of the bell tower above them. Hicks climbed it, with Kjell following him up.

A whitewashed wooden rail ran around the tower platform's protecting wall, and between the rail and the brick surface of the wall was an indented space through which a man could look out from concealment.

Hicks walked the rail's length peering through the space; Kjell handed him a pair of glasses. He went round again with the glasses pressed against the rail, studying what he could see of the surrounding hill.

"I think you can still smell the cordite," Kjell said. "Unless it's my imagination." He stood still for a moment with his arm out before him. "Wind's south, I think."

Hicks went to the south side of the tower and searched out the opposite hill. Of all the nearby hills, its pinnacle was closest to their mountain, and it was the most thickly wooded.

He scanned its high points over and over, but the only movement he could make out was the slow stirring of Dieter's bright ornaments on the lazy wind.

"They ought to be over there," he said, "if it's blowing down on us."

He made another round of the tower, standing on tiptoe to tilt the angle of the glasses downward toward the valley. Among the trees on the road far below, he made out a yellow pickup truck. He handed the glasses to Kjell.

"Who's that?"

"Don't know them," Kjell said, when he had looked

through the glasses. "Could be . . . well, I don't know who it could be. People camping maybe."

"They'd have to be pretty fucking dedicated to camp around here."

He called down the ladder to Dieter and brought him up, blinking and unsteady in the sunlight.

"Whose pickup is that?"

Dieter took the glasses and Hicks guided their angle to the road.

"Never saw it before. He's blocking the road out to the flats, though. And he can see the house from there."

"That's good enough for me," Hicks said. "Look," he told Kjell, "hang up here. Let us know if that thing moves or something happens."

They went below to the main room; Hicks gathered up the wet shirts he had been preparing to hang and pitched them on the stone floor.

"How about walking?" he asked Dieter. "How far was it across the flats?"

"Twenty miles to the highway," Dieter said. "But whoever is in that car will see you start out."

"What are flats like?" Marge asked.

"Well, they're flat," Hicks said. "And they're dry and windy and hot. On the other side of them is a highway that runs a couple of miles from the Mexican border."

"Surely you're not going to carry it over there?" Dieter said. "That would be madness. You'd just have to get it back in again."

"I wouldn't take it over the line. But I might have a shot at the highway if I thought I could walk twenty miles."

"The wetbacks do it," Dieter said. "They follow the ore tracks right into this valley."

"What about the border patrol?"

"They fly over it a couple of times a week. Not every day."

"Maybe that's the border patrol in that pickup, Dieter. Maybe they're cruising your fiesta."

"Those people are American citizens," Dieter said. "The border patrol knows that."

"They're setting us up, damnit. They're setting us up for a bust. That shot was some nark tripping over his cock."

"One thing I assure you," Dieter said, "we cannot be surprised up here. Besieged, surrounded, but never surprised. And if they were going to bust us they'd have helicopters and dogs—it's a carnival the way they do it."

"Maybe they're waiting for dark." Hicks walked to the open door that led to the plaza and slammed it shut.

"We've been turned, Marge. We're gonna have to sprint."

"Hey," Kjell called from the tower. "Galindez is coming up."

Dieter opened the door and looked out into the slanting afternoon sun. After a minute or so, a man in a bleached white shirt came up the steps, walking cautiously, and came inside. He looked at the people in the room and at the empty wine jar in Dieter's hand. When he recovered his breath, he spoke quietly in Spanish to Dieter.

"There are three men on the hill across from us," Dieter said when Galindez was done. "They have guns, and one of them has a rifle. There are two more down by the pickup. Galindez says one is a Mexican cop."

Marge sat down at the altar steps and tucked her knees under her chin.

"What were they shooting at?" Hicks asked.

"At me," Galindez said.

"Would you get the boy off the roof?" Marge said. "Before somebody shoots him?"

"You were followed," Dieter said to Hicks.

"We weren't followed. We were turned."

"By whom?" Marge asked. "June?"

Hicks shrugged.

"Maybe they made a lucky guess. I'm sorry," he told Dieter. "We brought you trouble."

"They're always out there," Dieter said. He made a gesture of philosophic resignation; his hand shook.

"If June turned us in," Marge said slowly, "maybe she didn't get Janey to my father."

"June is a stand-up chick," Hicks said. "Don't worry about it." He turned to Galindez and then to Dieter. "Are they coming up? What are they gonna do?"

"At the moment," Dieter said, with a faint smile, "they're lost. Elpidio took them up and left them."

"What the hell kind of cops are they? Ask him what they look like."

"One has a beard," Dieter said when he had spoken with Galindez. "One has bleached hair like a *maricon*. One is ordinary."

Hicks examined the portrait of Moussorgsky.

"You know what?" he said. "They may not be cops at all."

THEY WAITED IN A GRASSY HOLLOW CONCEALED from the house across the canyon by an outcropping of blue-black rock. Smitty was leaning over the ledge spitting, watching his spittle whip on the wind and sail into the treetops below.

"Lost in Space is right," he said. "Weird stuff in the woods. Walkin' everywhere."

Converse watched him spit with fascination. His thick lips puckered as he sought secretions to disgorge. The pink point of his tongue slid between his lips conveying gathered saliva, a homely little entity in the cosmos.

On the climb, Converse had fallen back on the Long View. It came to him that Smitty, in some respects, bore a physical resemblance to Ken Grimes. What a ruffianly sense of humor things had, he reflected, to compose themselves now into a Grimes, then into a Smitty.

He glanced at Danskin and saw that he too was watching Smitty spit. There was a fond possessive smile on his face.

Danskin extended a leg and kicked Smitty on the elbow, causing him to lose his balance for a moment.

"Whoa," Smitty cried, and seized firm ground.

"What are you thinking about, dipstick?"

Smitty pulled himself away from the ledge.

"A dream," he said.

Danskin nudged Converse covertly.

"I know all about that shit," he told Smitty. "Tell me, I'll interpret."

Smitty blushed and bared his gums.

"I got this guy," Smitty told them, "it's like him." He pointed to Converse. "I kidnapped him, right? But suddenly he's gone. I want the bread from his folks. But I don't have him. I'm gonna be like the dudes up in Canada, I'm gonna cut off his ear like and send it to them. Pay up or I slice more. But he's gone. I got to cut my own ear off and mail it."

Danskin slapped his hands in delight.

"Wait, wait," Smitty said. "It doesn't work. I got to cut more of myself off. They still don't pay up. I got to cut myself all into strips and mail it all to his folks."

Danskin rolled over on his back, his belly heaving.

He waved his hands, fingers splayed, like a salvationist.

"You wonder," he asked Converse, "why he's my buddy? Who else could have such a dream?"

When he had finished laughing, he stared at Converse.

"How about you? What were you thinking?"

"I was thinking, 'Why me?' " Converse said.

"Ha!" Danskin said.

"You did wrong," Smitty informed him, licking the spittle from his lips. "You gotta admit it. You're a crook."

"I'm not a crook at heart," Converse said.

Smitty was staring into the brush above them. They turned suddenly and saw Antheil climbing down to their cover.

"I surprised you completely," he said. "I could have been anybody." He looked down at them peevishly. "What are you doing lying around up here?"

"We had a guy bringing us up," Danskin told him, "but he cut out on us. I don't know where he went or how he did it."

"You shot at him?"

"Of course," Danskin said.

"Well he's up in the house now—Angel saw him. He must have got up there some way."

"We looked," Danskin said. "We can't find it."

"How about these wires. Did you follow them?"

"The wires run down the cliff and into the woods. There's no trail."

Antheil leaned against the rock and peered over at the house for a moment.

"I've been following wires all day. They're strung up and down sheer drops." He sat down on the short grass beside them and took another Geological Survey map from inside his safari jacket. "According to this thing, there are two trails up there. Neither of them exists. The trails I've found aren't on here and none of them goes anywhere."

"So," Smitty said, "they're not so dumb."

"I don't get it," Danskin said. "I thought you had this place doped out. Don't you have any information? Isn't there a file on these people?"

"Look," Antheil said, "every cornpone cop down here knows the way in. All these wetbacks know the

way. Of course there's a file." He put his map away.
"We had to be discreet. We didn't want to make
it official until certain things were taken care of. I
thought we could improvise a little. It seemed reasonable enough."

Smitty looked patiently from Danskin's face to
Antheil's.

"Maybe it's a bummer," he suggested finally.
"Maybe we should just drop it."

Everyone turned to look at Converse.

"No," Antheil said.

"It's getting dark. While we're fucking around looking for a trail, they'll come down here and zap us."

"I'll back you up," Antheil told him.

"Yeah?" He looked at Antheil with something
close to contempt. "You really went for this one,
huh?"

Antheil stared back at him, stony-faced.

"If they can't get to a car, they can't get out. Angel's
got the road covered and he's as good as they come.
They can't leave the house without being seen. If
they try to walk out we'll run them down."

Danskin gnawed his finger in silence.

"You get yourselves where you have a clear shot
at the house. Talk to them. Tell them you'll waste
Asshole here."

"Oh, man," Danskin said, "what do they care?
They'll laugh at us."

"Tell them you've got the little girl."

"They know fucking well we got no little girl."

"Try it, I'm telling you." He turned on Converse
in fury. "You talk, Asshole. Use your influence with
your wife."

Smitty laughed.

"Because goddamn it," Antheil told Converse, "I'm
gonna kill you if you don't produce."

"I think he realizes that," Danskin said.

They watched Antheil climb quickly up the bank

and walk into the woods looking over his shoulder. Danskin's dark eyes were bright with anger.

"He's uncomfortable turning his back, you notice that? He's got a bad conscience."

"He's flipping," Converse told them. "He's obsessed."

"He flips," Smitty said, "and our balls get busted."

Danskin took Converse by the sleeve and pushed him against the bank. "Up," he said. "One thing at a time."

They went back into the woods and wandered among the trees for a while, trying to find where the Mexican had gone. After a few minutes, they gave up and followed a trail that led through the edge of the woods, following the line of the bluff.

"Let's try it here," Danskin said, when they had gone a short way. "It's gonna get dark on us."

They went crouching through the brush; Danskin kept one hand on Converse's arm and carried his air marshal's pistol in the other. Smitty came behind with the rifle.

Just below them was another ledge with a rise of dark rock behind which they could shelter. The stone house was directly across the way and from their new point of vantage they could see the top of its bell tower and a corral against its wall in which a white horse stood.

"Now we play the game," Danskin said when they were lying in the rocks' shelter. "Now we play The Lady or the Tiger." He still held Converse by the arm; he tightened his grip. "What do you think, Converse? You think she'll come through for you?"

"I don't know," Converse said.

Smitty watched the opposite mesa with his binoculars for a while and broke into laughter.

"Hey, man," he said. "I'm gonna shoot that horse." He turned to Danskin, excited and pleading. "Can I?"

Danskin chuckled tolerantly. "What an idiot," he said to Converse.

"Sure," he told Smitty, "go ahead."

There were three shots, one following another, dogged, obsessive. After the second they heard a grunt and after the third a deep bellow, loud and explosive as the shot itself. Kjell screamed in the bell tower.

Marge jumped to her feet.

Hicks was already on the ladder when Kjell came stumbling down. His eyes were wild and he was so pale that Hicks thought at first that he had been shot. He pressed past Hicks and started for the front door. Marge and Galindez intercepted him.

Peering through the slot, Hicks saw the dappled horse on its side in the corral, striking the ground before it with a forehoof like a circus horse counting to music. The horse's teeth were bared and its nostrils bloody, its flank was awash with bright arterial blood.

"For shit's sake," Hicks said.

He had a look through the glasses and noted that the pickup had moved out of sight. There were no signs of life on the opposite hillside but it was plain that the shots had come from that direction. The sun was almost gone behind the pinnacle to the west, shadows moved up the higher slopes. He set the glasses on the rail and went below.

"Would you believe they shot the horse?"

"I believe it," Kjell shouted at him. "I saw it."

"They're crazy," Hicks said disgustedly. "They'll be shooting out the windows next. We ought to put mattresses up."

"Are we going to stay here?" Marge asked. "Won't they come up?"

"If they knew how," Dieter said, "they'd be here."

"How'd you lose them?" Hicks asked Galindez.

Galindez answered him in Spanish, something about a *galería*.

"Through the Indian shelter," Dieter said. "It's right under them."

"I was thinking," Kjell said, "we could hide out in there. That's what it's for."

"Might be the place for you, K-jell. I don't care for holes much myself."

"Look," Dieter said, "it isn't necessary. We can get to Elpidio's place without even crossing the road. There are other people there."

"Maybe we're better off up here, Dieter. Down in the valley they got us in their pocket. It's kind of our game up here."

"But there are all these people down there," Marge said. "They're your friends, aren't they? Won't they help us?"

"Yes and no," Dieter said. "Their heads are in a curious place. If they see there's trouble they'll go away. They're pacifists. And they have a very detached view of the world."

A man's voice echoed over the valley.

"Hello," the voice wailed. *"Hello."*

"Hello, yourself," Hicks said.

The voice called again.

"Marge! It's John!"

She stared at Hicks in panic.

"It is," she said. "It's him."

Hicks went up the ladder, picked up the glasses, and scanned the opposite hillside. Their heads were visible over a rock ledge—Converse, and beside him a blond man squinting down the sight of a hunting rifle. Hicks looked at the rifle barrel long enough to remember that the corner of sun to the left of the pinnacle was strong enough to reflect the lenses of his binoculars. He ducked before the shot and the bullet hit the rail and ricocheted dreadfully against the bell.

"It tolls for thee, motherfucker," someone cried, and there was echoing, half-hysterical laughter.

Hicks ducked back through the trap and went below.

"Yes, it is," he told Marge. "They got him."

"Oh my God," Marge said. She started toward the ladder.

"Stay off there," Hicks told her. "Listen through the door, they don't have a shot at it."

He opened the front door and stood by it.

"Marge!" Converse called to them. *"Let them have it!"*

"I can't stand it," she said.

"Marge! They have Janey!"

She put her hands to her ears.

"That's a lie, Marge," Hicks said. He took her by the wrists. "If they had they'd have her in sight."

"They have Janey!" Converse shouted.

"Who's Janey?" Kjell asked.

"How do I know they haven't?" Marge asked desperately. "How?"

Hicks shook his head.

"Tell them to produce her."

"Produce her?" Marge cried. "Produce her? They'll burn her with cigarettes."

"For Christ's sake, man, they haven't got her. She's with your father."

"Marge!" Converse called.

Marge knelt on the stone floor.

"How can he do it?"

"You know who they are. I'd do it too, if it was me."

"Marge!"

Galindez asked who the man was that shouted.

"Her husband," Dieter told him.

On the far hill, Converse clung to his rock, shouting into fantasy.

"Give it to them!"

"Clear," Danskin instructed him. "So they understand you."

"Give it to them! They'll let us go. If they don't get it—they'll kill me."

"Us!" Danskin said.

"Kill us!" Converse shouted.

"How's anybody gonna know what he's talkin' about?" Smitty asked irritably.

"Yell it again, shithead. Louder."

"Give it to them," Converse called. *"Or they'll kill me. And you. They'll kill everybody. But if you give it to them . . ."* he stopped and drew breath . . . *"they won't!"*

"You think it's funny?" Danskin asked.

"Not at all," Converse said.

Marge stood in the doorway with her eyes closed.

"What was it? What did he say?"

Hicks shuddered. "He's out of his head. What he says is to give it to them. What else would he say?"

"Suppose we do?"

"What do you think? You think they'll let us walk?"

He went round to the rear door that opened to the stream and looked outside.

"Dieter, let your man take the boy down to his place. You can go too if you like. Keep yourselves at this angle to the building," he told them, making a wedge of his hand and pointing south. "I don't think they'll have a shot at you that way. But go quick."

"I have to think," Dieter said. He nodded to Galindez; Galindez and the boy started out the back door.

"While they're going," Hicks told Marge taking her by the arm and leading her toward the front door, "you tell them O.K. Say, 'O.K. Please let us go. We have to dig it up.' "

Marge went to the front door and leaned against the carved doorway.

"O.K.," she shouted. "Please let us go. We have to dig it up!"

"Get your ass down here," one of the men on the hillside called. *"Make it fast!"*

"I'm sorry about your horse, K-jell," Hicks said. Kjell and Galindez were already running across the stream toward the shadowed woods.

"What are you gonna do, Dieter? You staying?"

"Why are *you* staying, Ray? What is it you're going to do?"

"We could call the cops," Hicks said. "That would fake them out."

"That's all right with me," Marge said. "Letting them have it is all right too." She turned her back to the open door and buttoned her jacket. "It was my goddamn thing. Mine and his. We ought to pay our own way."

"What are you talking about?" Hicks said to her. "Who you gonna pay?"

"I've had it," she told him. "I'm through—it isn't worth it."

"I guess it depends on how you think," Hicks said.

Marge wept.

"As far as I'm concerned," she said softly, "they've earned it. They can have the dope and me with it."

"That's stupid."

"Look," she shouted, "there are a million people down there. They can't kill us all in front of all those people. I can bring it down there and hand it over."

"You'd never make it."

He went into the room in which he had slept. It was a narrow room like a monk's cell; the single window was small and square, set in a brick casement. At one time it had been blue with flowering trees in each corner but Dieter had whitewashed the walls since then.

His seabag and the backpack lay on the bare mattress. From one he took the cellophane bag in which he kept his toothbrush and razor and shook the contents out onto the floor. From the other, he took the packet in which the drug was wrapped and removed its outer covering of newspaper. Then, he went quietly across the corridor and out the back door into fading twilight. It was a clear tranquil evening, squirrels chattered in the pines, sparrows chanted.

"I'm bringing it down," Marge shouted from the front door. "I'm bringing it!"

He could not understand what they shouted back.

Kneeling beside the pool where the stream was dammed, he took fistfuls of the fine dry sand between the stones and flung them into the cellophane bag. Finally, he set the bag down and held its end open and shoveled earth in, sand, small stones and all. He took the bag of sand inside and wrapped the newspaper and oil cloth around it and put it in the backpack where the dope had been. Before he tucked the heroin under his mattress he took a pinch of it and sprinkled it in the layer between the newspaper and the oil cloth on the package of sand. He dragged the backpack and seabag into the front room.

"I'm taking it down," Marge declared. "I told them."

"The minute they get it in their hands, they'll blow your head off."

"Not in front of all those people they won't. I'll give it to them in the village. I can get down the way we came up."

Hicks took the trigger housing and the stock of his M-16 from the seabag and started to assemble it.

"Do we have to have more of this stuff with guns?"

"Talk to them about that."

Dieter came in from the tower and watched Hicks assemble his weapon.

"What are you doing?"

Hicks rummaged through the bag for clips.

"Look at your friend," Dieter said to Marge. "The Furor Americanus."

"She wants to take it to them," Hicks said.

"She can try it," Dieter said.

"That's our buddy John they got over there," Hicks said with a blank smile. "We want to help him out."

"Now it's guns and sacrifices," Dieter told him. "The whole number."

"Well," Hicks said, "it can't all be trout fishing and funny lights. We got some old dues coming up."

"We're already dead," Dieter said. "It's all manifestation."

"Speak for yourself, Dieter. I'm not dead."

"Go ahead and play it out with each other then," Dieter said. He went to the refrigerator for another jar of wine. "You're all one."

Hicks took the jar from him and drank with a grimace.

"Some of us are more one than others."

"I'm taking it down," Marge said. She opened the flap of the backback and looked inside; then snapped it closed, and held it against her body. The denim jacket she wore was slack over her shoulders, damp hair was pasted against her temples. She looked pale and sickly, fatal.

"We did this—John and I. I won't have anybody else fucked up over it."

"Since when do you give junk away? You need it."

She slung the pack over her shoulder and went quickly through the front door. Hicks made no move to stop her.

She took the pack toward the cliff edge. Twenty yards from the house, she set it down in front of her and shouted into the valley.

"Here it is! Meet us in the village and we'll let you have it!"

"*Say again,*" someone called.

"I have it here. Meet us in the village and let him go."

When she turned in the direction of their voices, she saw the horse.

Converse, with Smitty close beside him, stared at the figure of Marge on the opposite hill.

"Look at her," Smitty said to him. "I could put a shell through that stuff."

"Tell her it's agreeable," Antheil said.

"It's agreeable!" Danskin called amiably. He turned back toward Antheil. "It's agreeable?"

"Sure," Antheil said.

Danskin looked at him sullenly.

"Where's Hicks?" He shook his head. "They're getting foxy. It's getting dark and they're getting foxy."

"She's not being foxy," Converse said. "She means it."

"This is one of those times when you have to be optimistic," Antheil told them. He pulled up his transmitter antenna and told Angel to move the truck up.

"Better be careful," Danskin said. "That Hicks'll kill you . . . Hey," he called across to Marge, "where's your buddy?"

"He's hiding."

"Hurry up," Danskin shouted. "Carry a light."

When she went back inside, he was sitting on the altar steps fitting the M-70 attachment to his rifle. Beside him were a few of the little five-inch cartridges.

"You handle it any way you want to," he told her. "I'll cover you."

"I don't want you to cover me," she said. "I need a light," she told Dieter. Dieter turned to Hicks.

"Give her a light," Hicks said.

Dieter took a hurricane lamp from beneath his console and tried it and handed it to Marge.

"Keep it on while you're going down. When you reach even ground turn it out."

Marge was trembling. He avoided her eye.

"Just one bad flash after another," she said. "It has to stop."

"Do what you feel the need of."

"What are you laughing at?" she demanded of him. "What are you always laughing at?"

"I'm not laughing."

"When you get to the dirt road," Dieter told her, "run. Make sure the light's out."

Going out the door, she looked back at Hicks. He was securing the M-70 grenade launcher to his weapon.

Hicks and Dieter moved to the doorway and watched her walk to the top of the trail.

"She didn't even say goodbye," Hicks said. "How about her?"

"It's the right thing to do."

Hicks laughed at him.

"You think so, do you?"

He looked out into the gathering shadows.

"Man, are they ever out there. Their ears were picking up. You can feel the spit on their teeth." He turned to Dieter, smiling bitterly. "You just don't care, do you? You just want her out of here."

"I do care," Dieter said. "What she says is right."

"She's hysterical. She's tired of living."

He went back to the bedroom and carried the new package he had made into the front room. A backpack of Kjell's was slung on a hook over the console wires—Hicks shoved the package inside it.

"We're doing this your style," he said. "Where things aren't what they seem. She's carrying sand down there."

"You're an idiot."

"Did you see her walk out, Dieter? You dig her walking to her fate thataway? Nothing but class."

"You're not going to beat those people, Hicks. They don't care about your games."

"She's the love of my life, no shit," Hicks said. "Beats hell out of Etsuko. Out of all of them."

"Hicks," Dieter said, "be warned. They're smarter than you."

"Now I don't believe that for a minute," Hicks said. He put the pack on his back and set the automatic fire. "The trails still the same as they were?"

Dieter nodded.

"Well, I'm gonna give it a shot. Down through the shelter the way your man came up."

"It's absurd," Dieter said. "You'll get everyone killed for nothing. You can't do it."

"Oh man, don't go and piss me off. Of course I can. Why can't I?"

Dieter shivered.

"Your woods still light up all nice?" Hicks asked him.

"They haven't been lit for a long time. Most of them work, I think."

"When you hear a round, light them up. Get on the mikes—I want a real deluge of weirdness. I want an opera."

"Yes," Dieter said, "I can see that. But in real life, you can't pull it off."

"Well then, fuck real life. Real life don't cut no ice with me." He transferred a couple of clips from the seabag to his pockets.

"Do you think they'd do something like this for you?"

"Come on," Hicks said. "What kind of a question is that." He went around to the rear door and listened for a moment.

"Watch this, Dieter," he said, "this is gonna be the revolution until the revolution comes along."

Sheltered, as he hoped, from the opposite pinnacle, he ran along the dammed stream with the rifle slung over his shoulder. He held the barrel pointing downward with one hand and in the other clutched his dope and a light.

The trail dipped steeply into darkness, a barely visible vein among the rock and root. There was no wind at all in the forest; he was sweating, short of breath. For a minute or two he could see Marge's light below him.

Shapes came out of the darkness at his eyes.

Not that I was ever any good at this, he thought, a lover is what I am. The something in everybody's hole, everybody's shift and stir, everybody's handler. An easy man to walk away from.

A half mile down was the entrance to the Indian shelter. The rocks that concealed it were clear in his recollection, but in the almost total darkness it took him nearly twenty minutes of feeling along packed earth at the bottom of the bluff before he found the right tunnel. The trouble made him angry and despairing. He tossed the bag and his light into the chest-high opening and struggled up into it, lashing out with his foot at the spider webs. He wriggled into it, feet foremost, lying on his back, clutching the slung rifle and shoving the bag and light along with his heels until he heard them fall. Another push and he was able to sit up; the tunnel opened into a chamber. He found the light and turned it on.

The walls were the solid stone of the mountain, rising to a vault forty feet above and covered to an improbable height with a Day-Glo detritus of old highs.

There Are No Metaphors, it said—in violet—on one wall. Everywhere he turned the light there were fossilized acid hits, a riot of shattered cerebration, entombed. The floor was littered with filter tips and aluminum film cans, there were mattresses reverting to the slime, spools of tape and plastic pill bottles. A few light brackets and speakers were strung with rusted copper wire over supporting pegs set in the stone. The unnatural colors had hardly faded at all.

He walked across the chamber and into a smaller area separated from the first by a partial wall of factory brick. The ceiling there was lower, supported by an oak pole that rose, through a brick-lined hole in the dirt floor, from a lower story. He tried the pole, dropped the lighted lamp and the sack into the hole, and eased down along the pole.

The hole was the mouth of a brick chimney which widened to form a buttress for the upper story. The place into which he had descended was the Dick Tracy room; the lamp shone on Dick's neat rep tie and on the base of his mighty chin. Next to him there were portraits of Flyface and Flattop and Vitamin Flintheart. A girl named Lightning Webb had painted them there years before because it was the center of a hollowed-out hill, a Dick Tracy sort of place.

He left the heroin there. The walls of the Dick Tracy room narrowed into a tunnel, through which he had to move in a crouch. As he remembered it, there were tarantulas in the tunnel; he walked heavily, trying not to touch the walls. It was a long way before he got a taste of the outside air. When he did, he turned the light out and went more slowly, trying the invisible ground ahead. When he felt the breeze, he knelt down and felt for the edge of the drop he knew would be ahead.

He lay on his belly, his head and shoulders overhanging the bluff, trying to see into the black woods. It seemed to him that he heard women singing far off. Now and then, a patch of purple glistened in the darkness before him, a little flash from his mushroom.

There were people who claimed to have gone into the line on acid but he had never believed them.

He was not very high, not high at all, it seemed to him—but prone to small marginal hallucinations. He felt at home in the darkness.

After lying still for a while it occurred to him that he was losing time; he felt along the edge of the rock face for the handholds that were carved there and when he felt two of them, swung himself over the edge and started down. He lowered himself very slowly, his feet scurrying over the rock to find the next foothold. It was awkward and he was off balance. With each descending step, his weight more oppressed his grip.

He was three quarters of the way down when he heard the first flutter—a second later a solid weight crashed into his chest, closing off breath and knocking him from his handhold. He landed with his ankles together and rolled over on his shoulder, lying still until his breath came back. When it came, he felt the wounds on his chest—there was blood on his shirt. A black shape whistled close over his head and disappeared into the trees; a bat he thought at first, then realized that it must have been an owl or a nighthawk, panicked bird, a freak, to the Japanese the worst of omens.

There was no trail where he was and he saw no light. He stumbled downward, making an unconscionable amount of noise.

He would be below them now. They would come down the trail to his left, Marge from the right. Acting on instinct, they would be able to intercept her where her trail joined the dirt road at a point he reckoned to be almost directly below him. He struck off through the woods again, wary of the drops and deadfalls he knew were all around him.

The women's voices came to him again—they were faint but real enough. The Brotherhood's women—singing in the village.

A little farther down, he saw a shape below him that made no sense. He slowed and stalked it, bringing his weapon up—when he saw what it was, he ducked and hurried off to the left, easing into steep hollow grown with ferns which he had made out just in time.

It was the pickup truck and through its window he could see the lighted end of a cigarette burning.

Covered in ferns, he sought higher ground, then sat listening as hard as his concentration allowed. His frame arched from the fall but he was beginning to enjoy himself. The folly and complacency of the smoker in the truck were a great comfort to him.

I'm the little man in the boonies now, he thought.

The thing would be to have one of their Sg mortars. He was conceiving a passionate hatred for the truck—its bulk and mass—and for the man who sat inside it.

The right side for a change.

Marge tried to make it like walking into the ocean, picturing herself a swimmer on a beach stepping into the tide. The image of ocean kept her almost calm; she clung to it.

All it could do, she assured herself, was kill—there would be no need to talk to it. At intervals she shifted the package from arm to arm.

Where the grade of the trail eased, she switched off her light. The sky was moonlit but the moon itself invisible, sealed off by close hills. There was light enough for her to make out tree shapes and rocks along the trail. She heard singing but she had forgotten whether the voices were real or imaginary.

A sound in the woods on her right caused her to stop; the sound was like a shod footstep on metal with the creak of a steel hinge. She could smell gasoline. Turning around slowly, she saw against the dark trees the figure of a man in a broad-brimmed hat above on the trail. Oceanic comforts shattered; her body ached with fear.

A little farther on, she was certain she had passed a second man who was standing just beside the trail. The man followed her, moving through the brush, level with her descent.

"Stop," a voice whispered. She stopped.

"I have it," she said softly.

"Shut up," the voice whispered back. A whisper of authority, clearly enunciated.

The three of them stood in the darkness; for what seemed several full minutes neither of the men moved or spoke.

Hands took the package from her.

"Where is he?" she asked.

The figures before her swayed as the package passed between them.

"Right over there," a man said.

"Where?"

"Just right down there," the man's voice told her. "Just ahead. Turn your light on."

She moved away from them and switched on the flashlight; its beam probed among rocks and ferns. There was no one.

One of the men who had intercepted her stepped off the trail and a few moments later headlights flashed out of the darkness into which he had gone. He had set the package on the fender grid of a truck and was unwrapping the tape that bound it. The man in the Stetson was coming behind her, about ten paces back.

Ahead on the trail, in a clearing where it intersected the dirt road on which the truck was parked, she saw someone move out of the shadows. She hurried toward them.

"John?" she called.

In spongy darkness among ferns, they watched her light.

"It could turn out O.K.," Smitty told Converse. His arm was thrown loosely, in a comradely fashion, around Converse's neck; in his other hand he held a large square pistol. He had passed the rifle to Danskin who was waiting in the brush behind him.

"I hope so," Converse said.

The fear of death had come back for him with darkness, a mindless craving for light.

Danskin moved down with them, crouching on one knee.

"Here she comes. They got it."

He stood up and went quickly across the trail.

"She brought it," Converse said. "Don't hurt her."

"No, no," Smitty told him earnestly. "No need, man."

Marge's light grew larger; he could see her bare legs and recognize the Enseñada sandals she wore. Smitty rose slowly, his hand resting on Converse's shoulder. He had released the safety on his pistol and was leveling the weapon in Marge's direction.

Converse heard her call to him.

He leaned back on his heels and prepared to jump. There was no force to uncoil, he would have to go on nerves, as always.

Antheil called up from the truck.

"Whoa now, folks! Just a minute here!"

Smitty paused in what Converse realized was the act of taking aim. Converse dived for where the gun might be seized and the hand that held it.

"Go, Marge," he shouted.

"Go, Marge," a laughing voice called. It was Danskin across the road. There was a rifle shot close by.

Smitty's arm was like iron; he could not bend it. He looped his leg between Smitty's legs, bent his knees, and hung on. The pistol went off twice as he turned his face from Smitty's left-hand blows. As they wrestled, Converse heard to his astonishment a sound which he was certain might be heard in Vietnam and nowhere else—a *pwock,* like a steel cork popping from an empty metal drum, the sound of an M-70 grenade launcher firing its cartridge. In a moment a monstrous ball of fire swelled up under the trees down the hill from them.

He had been used to thinking of Smitty as a weak link and the man's strength surprised him. His own was ground down—Smitty's hand was shortly free. He turned to stare over his shoulder at the fire and then adjusted his grip on the gun while Converse, turtled on the ground, scurried backward in a panicking flail of arms and legs. Clawing at pine needles, trembling in every muscle, he covered up awaiting the shell—when the forest around them burst into pure white light, then darkened and glowed white again. Smitty froze, his eyes wild. Converse turned over, landed a kick below his knee, and lunged for the gun a second time. Desperately, they searched out each other's hands—there was only skin.

They rolled on the floor of the flashing forest and around them erupted what sounded like an artillery barrage. Smitty was struggling for freedom now; Converse clung to him afraid to let go. Marge and her light had disappeared.

Smitty and Converse together rolled down a bank and landed on the packed earth of the trail. The din of battle swelled over them—bazookas, mortars, rockets, tank guns—it was Dienbienphu, Stalingrad. They scrambled to opposite sides of the trail, Converse moving on his elbows toward cover and low ground. As he crawled into the brush it occurred to him that there was something wrong with the artillery noises. Breath. Spit. There were loudspeakers in the trees. It was someone doing it, someone playing games with a microphone.

But the column of white flame down the hill rose higher; at its core was the dark outline of a truck. Danskin stood in the firelight without his rifle, he was searching for something inside his jacket. A few feet from him a burning Stetson hat marked the trail.

The roar of mock battle coming from the trees subsided into drunken laughter—but there was a machine gun firing now, a real one and close by. Converse struggled farther from the trail—shells pounded into the earth around him, peppered the trees, chewing up leaf and branch. He shoved himself farther along, trying to put at least a tree trunk between

297

himself and the automatic fire. The flashing lights blinded him and oppressed his brain.

As he huddled against the roots of a great oak tree, from the dazzle of lights above his head there sounded a great voice, louder than the weaponry.

"Form Is Not Different From Nothingness," the voice declared.

Converse shut his eyes and cringed.

"Nothingness Is Not Different From Form."

"They Are the Same."

Converse was compelled to wonder if nothingness and form were not, in fact, the same. He kept his head down.

When the voice came again, it rose above rifle fire up the trail that was answered by another burst from the machine gun. Converse became aware that the flashing lights above him were revealing his position. As he prepared to crawl again, he saw Smitty run past him along the trail, in the direction of the village. Twenty feet on, Smitty stopped suddenly, sliding on his heels, turned round as though he had forgotten something of importance and charged headlong into a stand of pine saplings; his feet left the ground as though he intended to jump over them.

A network of violet lights flashed from the face of a sheer rock higher up the hill and Converse saw Angel and Antheil crouching back to back at its base. They had hunting rifles like Danskin's. A pistol went off somewhere near the burning truck sounding thin and tinny after the heavier weapons; they turned toward the sound and fired together, composed against their illuminated rock like figures in a sculptured frieze commemorating their own valor. Angel fired and loaded with a speed that baffled vision.

"They Are the Same," the voice said.

The machine gun opened up again, first near Converse, spraying the earth and foliage around him, then dusting the trail, finally finding the rock face. The shells rang a demented steel band's tattoo off its violet surface, and shattered the lights and wires in a phantasmal burst of stinking smoke and electrical flame.

Raising his head Converse caught a glimpse of Antheil's figure rolling across the trail. But he had not been hit, his roll was coordinated and calculated, as different—even at a glance—from the sickening spin of a dying man as anything could be. Two figures crashed though the brush behind him, heading downward; he saw them cross the dirt road and disappear into the darkness of the flat ground at the foot of the hill. The machine gun fired on after them. From the flying twigs and leaf meal, Converse judged its angle to be a few feet above his head. The gunner changed clips and went at it again, setting up a line of constant fire that closed off access to the village.

"They Are the Same," the voice in the trees declared.

When the firing stopped, he looked up and saw that all along the range, empty forest was bursting into light. The flashing illuminations lit rank on rank of motionless pine, on remote silent ridges far above them. On the lower slopes, baubles danced and gleamed. He stared in wonder.

Darkness settled on the place where he hid until the only light close by came from the flames that licked about the hulk of Antheil's pickup truck and the branches nearest it which had taken fire. The air was thick with smoke.

Converse crawled along over holly. The gunner had changed position but he kept firing. The darkness into which Angel and Antheil had retreated flickered with licks of flame as dry leaf caught and sputtered out.

Converse rolled over on his side and urinated sideways into the brush. After a few more rounds, he decided to attempt communication.

"Chieu hoi," he shouted to the gunner.

The firing stopped for a moment, then resumed.

"Where are you?" Hicks called back.

"Out in front of you."

"You're in the way, man."

Converse got to his feet and approached the trail at a crouch. He moved along the edge of it for several yards until he was even with the smoldering truck. A package wrapped in plastic lay on the ground just in front of him; he picked it up.

"I'm coming in," he called ahead of him. He thrust the package under his arm like a football and rolled into the stand of pine saplings on the other side of the trail. A shadowy figure recoiled from his advance.

"Marge?"

She was sitting on the ground at the base of a rock; there were hot M-16 cartridges and broken glass bulbs all around her. Hicks was sprawled across the rock itself, with the smoking weapon under him. His breath sounded far back in his throat, almost a moan.

"He's been shot," Marge said. "He keeps passing out."

Converse reached up and touched Hicks' arm. He felt blood on it.

"What happened?"

Hicks' body stiffened in a sudden spasm. He raised himself on his elbows and brought up the weapon.

"For Christ's sake. Are you alone?"

"At the moment," Converse said. "How are you?"

Instead of answering, he swung the piece around and nudged Converse aside with the barrel and fired a round at the rock wall across the canyon. Marge and Converse bent away from the noise, dodging the cartridges.

"There's two of them," Hicks declared. "I got them boxed. I can keep them out there all night."

Converse lifted himself to the rock on which Hicks was lying; he could see nothing beyond the burned truck but dark trees and the mass of the rock wall.

"That fucking guy," Hicks said. "Who is he?"

"He's some sort of cop. He's not straight."

"No shit," Hicks said.

"There are more of them," Converse told him. "Two others."

Hicks shook his head.

"I got one. I guess he got the other." He leaned his head on the rock and his shoulders trembled. "He was gonna peel everybody's potatoes, that guy."

"Figures," Converse said.

"How are you?" Marge asked Hicks.

He took a deep breath and swallowed.

"This is what you do. You get down there and get my four-wheel drive. Drive it out to the highway while I keep them in here. Then you're gonna pick me up on the other side. I have to go back up and cop."

"And cop?" Converse asked. "Are you crazy?"

Marge took the bag that Converse had carried in and tossed it between them.

"This? This is here. Who needs it now?"

Hicks reached down into it, took a handful of the stuff that was inside and flung it in their laps. Marge and Converse picked up the grains and sniffed at them.

" 'The pellet with the poison's in the chalice from the palace,' " he recited, " 'but the flagon with the dragon has the brew that is true.' "

He rolled over on his shoulder and fired off another whole clip at the trees.

"It's up the hill," he told them. "I'll get it."

"No," Marge said.

"You go in there and get that vehicle. Anything else in there that runs—slash the tires. Don't leave them anything. When you get on the highway you go west until you're crossing flat ground—you're gonna see dry washes and salt. When you come to tracks crossing the road you turn off and you follow the tracks back here toward the mountains. You're gonna see me on those tracks."

"He's bleeding," Marge told her husband.

Hicks reached down and started punching Converse's arm with his fist.

"Go for Christ's sake—while they're still back there. You think you know better than me? Do as you're told."

Converse stood up, pulling Marge with him. When he stepped out on the trail, she followed. She held his sleeve as they went and it gave him an odd feeling. Smitty and Danskin had been holding him by the sleeve for days. From the grove of little pine trees, Hicks continued to fire round after round.

"Are they really back there?" Marge asked.

"They better be," Converse said.

All the lights were on in the village, but the lighted windows were vacant, the tents gone. The field where the rows of trucks had been parked was empty. They went cautiously past car skeletons and the ruined teepee. At the edge of the rubbish pit a woman holding a tartan beverage cooler fled from them.

In the center of the village street a single truck remained. The driver was a young Mexican; he had the hood up and was working grimly on the truck's engine while his family stood by. There were three children who were still staring, rapturously, at the face of the mountain.

Marge and Converse went to the Land-Rover and Converse took a camper's ax from under the back seat and set about slashing the tires of Danskin's station wagon with it. The Mexican family watched him in silence. The young man did not look up from his truck's engine. Hicks' M-16 clattered on.

Converse got behind the wheel of the Land-Rover and stared at it.

"Keys," he said.

Marge threw up her hands and shook her head.

He went through his pockets, found a nail clipper and began working the screws out of the front panel.

"They didn't have Janey," Marge said.

He was shaving down the insulation on the starter wire.

"No, they didn't. She's with Jay."

"Thank God," Marge said. "That at least."

When the engine turned over, the fuel gauge registered a quarter full. Converse exchanged glances with the Mexican truck driver and gunned for the road out. He moved the Land-Rover as fast as it would go until a bad curve frightened him. He had difficulty with the four-wheel drive.

"Could you always do that?" Marge asked.

"Hot-wire it? No, I learned it over there. From a Vietnamese."

"That's a switch."

"Yes," Converse said. "It is."

There was a clear road ahead of them. For nearly a half hour they climbed—for the hump of the ridge, then the road descended in hairpins along the north side of the wall. Marge poked her head out and looked up and down the track.

"We're fucked now," she said. "There'll be cops."

"It hadn't occurred to me," Converse said. "I suppose there will be."

"What do we tell them when they stop us?"

Converse sighed. "I don't know. If they give us back to Antheil we better get a receipt for ourselves. Antheil," he told her, "is that guy back there."

"He must be a pretty corrupt cop."

"Yes," Converse said.

"I suppose," Marge said, "they were waiting for us all the time."

"Yes, they were."

"I knew it would happen."

"I did too," Converse said.

She was leaning over to see his face. He kept his eyes on the road.

"Did they give you a tough time?"

"Pretty tough."

"I knew they must have," Marge said, "when you said they had Janey."

"Sorry about that."

"You couldn't help it."

"You know," Converse explained, "they said . . . or else."

"Right," Marge said.

After the next turn, they saw lights ahead—the tail lights of a line of trucks moving before them out of the valley. They had overtaken the main body of the Brotherhood's retreat. They moved behind the last truck at about fifteen miles an hour. Small brown fingers clung to its tailgate grid, frightened eyes peered from under blankets at their headlights.

"He wants us to pick him up," Marge said.

"I heard him."

She was silent.

"Even if we get that far," Converse told her, "he won't be there. You must realize that."

She had buried her face in her hands.

"I'm sick," she said. She curled herself against the seat.

"Look," she said after a moment, "I have to try. But you don't. Maybe if we get through here you can get up to Janey."

"He won't be there."

"Him," she said, "he might be."

"If he is," Converse told her wearily, "he'll just have the dope and the goddamn thing will start over again. He's not a sane person. And he's not very bright."

She wiped her face with her sleeve.

"He came down for you," she said. "That's why he came down. We could have gotten out."

Fatigue wore him down. He kept himself hunched

forward to see through the dust and gloom ahead and his muscles ached.

"That can't be true."

"He's not a sane person," Marge said. "And he's not very bright. Sometimes," she told him, "people do simple-minded things like that. They take a chance to help their friends. Can't you respond to that?"

"Yes, I can respond to it," Converse said. "I'm responding to it. He won't be there."

"Haven't you ever done anything like that?"

"Yes and no," Converse said. When he turned to her, she moved her back to him pressing her forehead against the hard metal seatback. "Like what?" he demanded. "I don't know what that guy did or why he did it. I don't know what I'm doing or why I do it or what it's like."

"It's something simple," Marge said. She twisted in the seat, bringing her head to rest against the plastic window. "Jesus, I think I'm really sick now."

"Nobody knows," Converse told her confidently. "That's the principle we were defending over there. That's why we fought the war."

WHEN HE WAS PARTWAY UP THE HILL, THE moon rose over the mountains on his left, tracing the ridge line in hard silver light. Moonlight made the wound hurt more. He eased down on one knee and slowly rolled over a shelf of loose rock until his weight was supported by his hip and good shoulder. Tucking his knees up, he rocked slightly on the ground, trying to shake the pain off. It had seemed bearable at first and he had climbed to the place he was by marching to songs and cadences in his mind.

It was like eating morning glory seeds. Not so bad at first, you think you can take more and more of them but after a while they're the worst thing in the world. At first you think, well, I've had these before but presently they get to you.

Part of himself had seemed to come off in his hand; it had taken him some time to realize that the bloody mass he held was a canvas bag, some kind of expanding cartridge that had struck him under the arm and sent him sprawling.

A man with a beard had fired it.

It hurt him very much to stand up. He closed his eyes to the moonlight and began to erect a blue triangle against the base of his skull. The background was deep black and there was some effort involved in delineating the borders of blue. At the heart of the triangle, he introduced a bright red circle and within the circle he concentrated his pain. The circle glowed and lit the triangle from within, making it lighter against the blackness.

Give me a triangle and a song, he thought, and I'll climb this son of a bitch.

For the song you wanted something simple and pleasant because you would be hearing it for hours over and over and it could drive you out of your mind when the pain got to it.

He started up to "Red River Valley." His breathing felt so mechanical and unrewarding that he feared his lungs were not filling, that there was a puncture somewhere—but he convinced himself that his trunk was sound, the vital organs untouched and functioning.

He was glad to be alone. The triangle held and his legs with it.

The most difficult part of the climb was the rain. It was light rain, that grew warmer and warmer, jungle rain that closed off the breeze—it took an act of concentration for him to realize that it was the clearest of moonlit nights, that the ground on which he walked was dry as dry bones, as chalk, as dry as his mouth was dry.

At the entrance to the shelter, he took a few deep breaths and brought the bag out and slung it by its straps across the rifle sling on his good shoulder.

The trees at the top of the hill were full of lights and music; they wrecked his concentration and infuriated him. The mission building was flashing on and off. He made steadily for the carved doorway; when he had climbed the steps and passed through it he was disappointed that the pain did not subside. He would have to take it in with him.

Dieter had turned off the interior lights. The only illumination in the room came from the flashes outside and the tubes of the console in front of him. When he saw Hicks, he stood up in alarm.

"How about some light," Hicks said.

Dieter lit a desk lamp and closed the switches on his forest. Hicks sat down in the stiff Spanish chair and tossed the little bloody bag which had wounded him on the floor. He had carried it all the way up the hill, clenched in his right hand. He flung the dope at the foot of Dieter's altar.

Dieter stared at the things and then at Hicks.

"What's the matter with you, Dieter?"

"You've been shot. You're bleeding."

"Did you think everybody was kidding?" Hicks asked, trying to pull his matted shirt away from the wound. "You been away, man. You been living in the country too long."

"What happened?" Dieter asked breathlessly. "Who's out there now?"

"I got their fucking car with an M-70," Hicks said laughing. "Did you see it?"

"No," Dieter said. "I heard it." He sat down slowly on a chair beside Hicks. "Ray—did you put a rocket in a police car? Did you kill an agent down there?"

"They're killing each other," Hicks said. "They're nuts, the greedy bastards. I got a car, that's all I know. Give me some water."

Dieter brought him a drink of creek water in a ceramic bowl.

"Where's your girl?"

"They split." He stood up, tried to move the arm above his wound and sat down again.

"If they got through they'll meet me. I've got to get to route eight before the heat comes in."

"Ray, that's her husband down there. If they're alive they won't be looking for you."

Dieter searched among the shadows for his glass of wine.

"We'll go," he said. "We'll get out of here for a while." He found his glass atop the refrigerator and drained it. "Maybe for good. Maybe it's time."

"I'm gonna walk that wetback trail out of here. She'll get him to pick me up." Hicks stood with difficulty and walked to the altar where the pack was and sat down beside it.

Dieter looked at the pack, holding his empty glass.

"The first thing we'll do is toss that bad medicine."

Hicks wiped the sweat from his eyes.

"Here's what you do, Dieter. You take my works and cook up and hit me here—" he tapped his limp left arm with his right hand. "Because I got pain there. Then help me strap the fucker on."

When he had the shot he nodded off into rain. Dieter had poured something ice cold over the wound and was taping bedsheeting over it with Band-aids.

"You're bleeding a lot, you know that?"

"You should have seen me last time."

He put a hand on Dieter's shoulder to move him out of the way and vomited explosively across the stone floor.

"It looks awful," Dieter said, when he had finished the bandage. "It's huge."

"Beautiful," Hicks said. "Now strap it on."

Dieter wiped his hands on the extra sheeting.

"We're going down to the village. We'll pick up my boy and ride out with Galindez. Can you walk?"

"I can walk fine," Hicks said. "Give me a hand with the pack."

"Galindez won't carry dope. It's against his religion." Dieter picked up the pack and shook it. "This goes, you hear me? You came here to get rid of it and that's what we'll do."

Hicks reached out and seized the pack by a strap. Dieter pried it from his fingers.

"That's called grasping, remember? Grasping is ignorance." He backed away, holding the backpack beyond Hicks' reach. "There is no payoff in grasping."

"Dieter damnit, don't fuck around."

"We're at a primitive stage in our development," Dieter said. "But we shall learn from our mistakes."

Hicks stared at him, fighting off another nod in the rain.

"No nonsense, no vulgarization. No occultism, no lambs, no dope. Strength!" Dieter cried. "Discipline! Love! Words much debased—nevertheless I dare to speak them."

Hicks turned around in his chair to see whom it was that Dieter was speaking them to.

"You're drunk, Dieter. Hand it over."

"I know how you are," Dieter said. "I understand you better than anyone else in the world. I love you more than anyone else in the world. I know your courage and your obstinacy." He was red-faced and swaying. He kept shaking the bag. Hicks reached out and made a swipe at it but his fingers never came close. "This is not strength, Hicks. It goes."

He marched down the altar. On the last step, he tripped and the pack fell from his hands and into the streaks of Hicks' vomit.

Hicks tried to stand without success.

Dieter scurried after the pack and picked it up.

"Look at it, Hicks. It's full of puke and blood! On the inside it's all illusion and false necessity. It's suffering human ignorance. It's hell!"

"Sounds good," Hicks said.

"The truth is," Dieter said, "that I talk too much." His slack mouth broke into a smile. "This was perhaps the problem all along."

"Einsicht!" he shouted. "Agenbite of inwit! I'm a runner-over at the mouth. If I had kept my mouth shut—who knows?" He extended the bag toward Hicks. "With this goes my wine and my loquacity." His eyes filled with tears. "Oh Hicks—listen to me! We begin again. We begin. Again. First I throw it."

"Sounds good but it's my dope. You bring it back here."

Dieter watched him as slowly and painfully he unslung the M-16 from around his good shoulder. He stood the weapon on its stock and caught it by the trigger housing as it tipped.

"You're wired into grasping," Dieter told him. "You've got to fight."

"Dope got you up this mountain, Dieter, and you figure dope's gonna get you down. Dope is what you're all about, man. You think I don't know the difference between what's real and what's not? You think you're gonna bluff me out of my good shit and con yourself another mountain with it?"

"It appears to be evil," Dieter assured some interested presence, "but it is in fact mere ignorance. The first is actually nonexistent and the second is mistaken for it."

He started for the door. He was afraid and Hicks found his fear enraging.

"Where do you think you're going, Dieter? I'll kill you, man!"

Dieter turned, his mouth quivering with fear and disgust.

"I'll kill you, man!" he shouted mockingly back at Hicks. "That's the slogan of this stupid age! The land of dope and murder! You accuse me of coveting this filth?"

"You're the greatest show on earth," Hicks said. "But you're not conning me out of that pack."

Dieter's legs trembled.

Hicks lowered his good shoulder to cradle the stock under his arm and started down the steps.

"Bring it here, Dieter."

"It goes," Dieter said. "You're stoned, you're delirious." He backed further away, toward the door. "Dope is not what I'm all about," he said. "What I'm all about is much stronger than this." He drew himself up and closed his eyes for a moment, trying for instant serenity. "This is one I have to win."

He turned and walked carefully out the front door and down the steps.

Hicks sauntered after him.

The space outside the mission building was bathed in light from the spotlights on the tower. Dieter was striding purposefully across the plaza toward the cliff. Darkness commenced about thirty feet ahead of him, and the paths down began in that darkness. Hicks smiled at Dieter's cleverness.

"Hey, Dieter. You're not gonna make it, man."

He released the safety and brought the clip up into Fire position.

Well, they just kept coming, he thought, one of them after another. Pieces and bayonets, lies and cunning and deviousness but none of them were worth a shit. None of them could take him off.

"You're not gonna make it, Dieter."

Dieter stopped and turned toward him.

Hicks sighed and sat down on the top step.

"Please," Dieter said. His own spotlights dazzled his eyes. He raised a hand to shield them.

Hicks laughed.

"No, Dieter. No, Dieter. You just bring that on back here, man."

Dieter performed a fat man's shuffle and began running for darkness.

Hicks spread his legs out behind him on the top

step and crouched over his weapon. He brought the barrel up.

All right—

Dieter made for the darkness, for a moment he was out of sight. A moment later his running figure was visible against trees, totally available against the moonlit sky.

You dumb—

A little man running against the trees, Hicks thought, I've hit that one before. And Dieter wasn't so little, he was paunchy and slow.

Son of a bitch.

Look at his dumb ass up against that pretty sky.

All right you dumb son of a bitch.

An automatic round—it sprayed him with shells and splintered the fence he was trying to climb. Hicks walked down the steps through the smoke and over the still clattering cartridges. He went across the plaza toward the cliff. In Nam, he would have fired another two clips into the darkness as he came.

Dieter was lying on his belly under the remnants of his fence. His wrist jerked. Hicks walked up and kicked him. The pack was not beneath his body.

After a while, Hicks found it, quite near the cliff edge.

So he threw it, Hicks thought. He was running for the edge and he threw it.

"For Christ's sake," Hicks said.

Dieter had not been taking him off. Of course not. Not Dieter.

It was a gesture. A gesture—he was going to throw it over because there was no fire for him to throw it in.

Throw it over was what he had said. A gesture.

"What the hell, Dieter," Hicks said. "I thought you were taking me off."

It was one he had to win. He was trying to get it on again. He was being stronger.

Damn it, if you're going to make a gesture you

have to have some grace, some style, some force. You have to have some Zen. If you act like a drunken thief, and people haven't seen you in a while, they're likely to think that's what you are.

He had certainly fucked his gesture.

"Semper fi," Hicks said. The pain came up again, he sat on a standing part of the fence in the rain.

Lousy stupid thing. Like the Battle of Bob Hope. Like everything else.

During the long and painful time it took to get the pack on his back, he put it out of his mind.

Walk.

The first part of the walk was through happy forest; Dieter's knickknacks flickered in the moonlight and the earth was soft and mossy under his feet. He fell several times, experiencing with gratitude the tenderness of the ground and its reluctance to injure. Disneyland. Each time he had to stand up again, he felt the throb and although it was diffused, its fangs drawn by the drug, he was sorry that it had happened.

Another sort of light was creeping up on him; it seemed at first to come from the trees. Morning. In spite of what it meant, he was innocently glad to see it.

His satisfaction in the coming light made him feel like an ordinary man with a child at his core, out walking one morning for pleasure. He was tempted by anger and self-pity.

The light was not good news and the sentiments were the stuff that killed, the warrior's enemy.

Hungry bluejays chattered. He touched his side and felt blood flowing. When the pie was opened, his child's voice prattled, the birds began to sing. He wondered if in their hunger and ferocity the screeching jays might not be tempted by the blood and the mauled flesh. There were things that lived in wounds.

At the edge of the trees was a cattle gate strung with wire. He unhooked the wire loop and stepped carefully over a rusted grid and into a high meadow where the tall dew-covered grass soaked his trouser legs. The sun was rising over purple hills behind him; the track ahead led downward into a canyon that was crowned with tortured rock spires like the towers of the pagodas along the Cambodian Mekong.

He walked down on his heels, arching his back to support the weight of the pack, gripping the stock of his slung M-70 to keep it from knocking against his thigh.

Down had a rhythm of its own, bad for discipline because the lowered foot on striking sloping ground caused the body to lurch and lose cadence, broke up concentration. The temptation was to coast, let the feet find their own quick way down—an ankle buster. To hold back and descend deliberately was work. He detached, thought of the water that would be at the bottom, watched for rattlesnakes, and imagined the wild pigs whose tusks had tested the trail for buried oak balls. By the time the rising sun touched the tops of the pagoda spires over the canyon, he was into shade. The canyon bottom was cool, but windless and rank smelling. It filled him with suspicion and he walked tensely, ready to crouch and unsling his weapon.

The canyon opening was a hole in the wall, so narrow that he had to turn sideways to advance through it. When he was out, he saw the flat before him. The near edge of it was still in shade; across its yellow stony surface, balls of tumbleweed ran before a wind he could not feel in his protected place. At the end of it were round brown mountains; they were an insupportable distance away, but he would not have to walk that far to reach the road. Miles out, the dun color of the ground gave way to something unearthly, a glowing twinkling substance without color that grew brighter as the sun strengthened and sent off waves of heat that made the mountains shimmer. A line of rusted tracks, supported by mummified crossties, shot dead straight across the barren.

Between the desert and himself were shaded grass and a small stream that ran down from red boulders to nourish three cottonwoods and a lone stunted oak. He followed the stream and rested among the trees, ran the cold water over his face and filled his canteen. In trying to drink from it, he did a foolish thing. As he lowered his face to the water, the backpack slid forward over his neck and the strap tightened on his torn underarm; the pain made him straighten up and increased the pressure. He let himself slip into the water and got the pack so that he had it hanging from one strap balanced on his right shoulder. The water hurt at first, but in a few moments it felt very good indeed. When he climbed out, he noticed for the first time how swollen his left arm was and that he could not move it, not at all. Spot of bother.

He threw away the captured pistols and most of his M-16 clips. In spite of its weight, he could not bring himself to leave the rifle. Conditioning, something—he could not imagine such a walk without it. He kept two clips, one in the weapon, an extra in the pack.

The edge of shade had narrowed when he started out. The farther he went from the canyon wall, the more the wind rose and it was against him. That shaded part was a stroll. The moment he stepped out under the sun, the wound began to bother him.

A triangle and a song. First to keep the brilliant sunlight from the base of his skull, then to assemble the figure—black background, blue triangle, red circle. The pain in the circle looked like it might catch fire in the heat. It wasn't easy to get it all in there, it took a while. The song wasn't easy either because there were so many things to think about.

Gate, gate, paragate, parasamgate bodhi swaha. That was cool all right, that was lovely but you might disappear into it, pass out and bake.

Form is not different from nothingness. Nothingness is not different from form. They are the same.

Try a little nothingness.

Nothingness was cool too but you couldn't count cadence to it. It helped with the triangle but it certainly didn't make you feel like walking.

Well, he thought, the old songs are good songs, they used to say.

He sang as he walked beside the tracks. He had tried walking over the ties and of course that was murder. Walking beside them was the only way.

"I don't know," he sang.

> "But I been told
> Eskimo pussy
> Is Mighty Cold
> Your left."

P.I. without sandfleas and hotter. P.I. reminded him of salt. He took the shaker bag from his pocket and had a lick. Your left. The pain was contained, he was covering ground.

Can pussy be cold? Yes. No.

Philosophical discussion at the Little Tun, Yokasuka, F.P.O. San Francisco.

Converse, can pussy be cold? How would he know?

Eskimo pussy might be funky from wintering fur pants but it wouldn't be cold in any weather. An eskimo granny—put her out on the ice to starve, by and by her pussy will be cold.

That's not what the song's about. The song's about walking—picking them up and putting them down, that's what the song's about.

Etsuko was a clean girl. And smart. Full of surprises, always something happening with her. Very straight head, many laughs.

Look at me Etsukee, I'm out here with my weapon in this terrible place, how you like them apples?

I don't worry 'cause it makes no difference now.

No Hank Williams songs, please, it bothers the triangle.

It seemed to him that he could still hear the birds in Dieter's forest. He resisted the impulse to run and gauge the distance he had covered. It wasn't possible. It was too far, there were no birds where he was, there was no place for them to light, nothing for them out there. We hope.

More blood, and we don't really know how bad it is. Nothing to do but walk however.

There was one really subversive thought, one sorry piece of negative thinking: You'll never do it twice. Walking away from the Battle of Bob Hope was one thing and this was something else. This was twice.

Negativity.

He took a deep breath and gathered up the pain. It was hard to gather. Stack it like hay? Draw it up with a siphon? Put it in something.

Where's that triangle?

But maybe it's a mistake to separate it like that. Maybe it's ignorant to keep it off by itself where it just gets angrier and angrier, festers in there waiting to creep out and cripple you. If you set it in there locked up like that you might be keeping it going.

Experiment. Get with it, and for all you know it'll disappear. It's part of you—you've always got something sore on you, burned lips, hangnails, blisters, toothaches. It's just you, there's always some pain around.

Merge, it's you, you're it. The triangle dissolved and he embraced the pain.

No, he decided immediately! Indeed not!

The experiment had gone so badly he had to stop walking. It was unmanageable.

He stood staring down at the tracks. The hot metal glowed right through its coat of dust and oxidation, blinding him.

Get back in there, you fucker, you ain't no friend of mine.

Those All Is One numbers were very difficult to employ in practice.

I'll try it again, he thought, when I'm a hundred and ten years old and the birds bring me flowers.

It broke down between what hurt and what didn't and the difference seemed very important. That was as it should be. If you couldn't tell the difference between what hurt and what didn't, you had no business being alive. You can't have any good times if you can't tell. If you don't know the difference between busting your toe and a glass of beer, where are you? That was Converse's trouble.

List of things that don't hurt: Birds. Mountains. Water.

It really is all one though, he thought. Contrary to sense as it might seem.

He took a drink of water to balance the pain and it became apparent to him that what hurt and what didn't could come together in a hurry and that throwing up was a fine example. He leaned forward clutching the rifle butt and retched over the tracks.

Fine mixture of sensations but you lose all your water that way.

Expedite. The triangle will assemble to the rear and to the left of the right ear under the direction of the duty NCO . . .

Dress it up. Bracing the back in the specified position, bring up the weight with a smart twist.

He opened his mouth in surprise at the sudden wrenching. Pain within pain.

Do not twist too hard. Do not twist suddenly. Proceed resolutely in a military manner.

It turned out there were birds, but he could never have heard them. Hawks, three of them, way up there, gliding on the wind. There was a jet trail over them.

"Some of you birds think I'm down here to play fiddle fuck around," Hicks told them. "Let me be the first to inform you that I'm not. Any bird that makes that mistake will encounter the meanest cruelest son of a bitch they could conceive of. If I catch a bird grabassing, that bird can give his soul to Jesus because his ass belongs to me."

Belay that. Give Jesus the ass, I'll take the soul.

I'll trade these one-after-another railroad tracks for the soul and fly out of here.

What I need railroad tracks for I got no railroad.

Whatcha doin down there on those tracks, little speck?

Playing I'm a train, sir.

Water. Hold it down because it's so nice. It's the real thing.

Without the weapon, without the pack, things would be so much easier. He recalled that the pack was what he wanted so he would have to carry it. Serious people existed in order to want things, and to carry them.

As for the weapon, he thought, I didn't abandon the creature at the Battle of Bob Hope, I won't give them the satisfaction now.

The Battle of Bob Hope was in the rain. Like Austerlitz.

Slipping and sliding around the Rockpile, the warm rain that never dried out. AKA-47s, the Big Sound of Charles.

The fuck it isn't, that's them!

There they are and there they are and now I fall on my ass. Yes they are, they're all over the place. Don't follow them, they're being wasted down there.

NVAs I think it is, pith helmets.

He fired the rockets where they figured he'd come out—ka-thop ka-thop. Whee it's football, fake with rockets and then, clever, I'm off like a fucker through the bad smelling green and oh boy they're gonna get me but they don't and then, oh my goodness, they do.

Blind through the asparagus to the land where

the friendlies are. Hello, friendlies, you no shoot. Me U S Maline. LBJ number one!

Worse time I ever had, worse than now.

He turned round and looked behind him; there was a heartening distance between himself and the canyon. But the land around him was not heartening at all. It was dirty white, lifeless.

He crouched down, put his finger on the earth and tasted it. Salt. How about that!

As he prepared to rise, he noticed that his left arm was hanging limp and his left hand was touching the salty ground, bent at the wrist and without sensation.

Well, something hurts, he thought.

As he looked out over the salt, it began to glow. For a moment he was filled with terror.

Oh mama. What kind of place is this?

He took a deep breath.

Never mind your mama, never mind the questions. This is home, we walk here. It's built for speed not for comfort.

If you don't like it here, then walk away. Nobody gonna do it for you.

He stopped by the tracks and tried to throw up again but there was nothing to throw. When he finished retching he had trouble drawing breath.

What is this, rain, for Christ's sake? The trouble with the rain, hot as it was, was that it made you cold eventually. It made everything slippery and rotted your feet.

I got no dry socks, he thought. Stowed my handgun, my M&M's and forgot my dry socks. Or somebody swiped them. One of you bastards misappropriated my socks, I'll burn your ass.

Absolutely no rain. He took the thermos and poured a bit of water over his face.

It's so dry, he thought, it feels like rain.

When he found the triangle again, the stuff in it was congealed and festering. He might construct a new triangle. Or else secure the old one and wash it out.

Turn to on that triangle. Hot weather you have to hose it down.

Negative, doc says to leave it alone if it's not actually hurting him.

It's not actually hurting, it's more of an attitude.

He had to laugh at that.

He had scraped the knuckles of his right hand and for a while the pain concentrated there. He let go the lower part of the rifle and shook it.

A while before, his knuckles had been rapped with the edge of a deck of cards. The Adjutant had taken his cards and slapped his knuckles with them. The Salvation Army didn't go for cards and he was teaching the other kids in the Booth Shelter to play Go Fish. That was the Booth Women's Shelter in Chicago, North Side, Wisconsin Avenue.

Satan's Game.

His mother was washing pots in the kitchen. She said they put saltpeter in the food.

The salt burned his eyes and the sky was even brighter. Nowhere to look.

There was a child around somewhere, the same child he'd almost met that morning in the forest, the one who'd had his knuckles rapped. He knew immediately that the child would be the most dangerous thing he had to face, the hardest thing to get by.

A turned-around kid who made up stories—wise guy, card player. They all made up stories in the Booth Shelter, they all told lies about themselves. The boys and the girls both.

The kid walked beside him, making him feel bad, making him feel like a kid himself.

"Whaddaya doin'?"

"Walking across this here."

"My father's got a rifle like that."

"You got no father and if you had he wouldn't have no rifle like that."

"He bought me a twenty-two and showed me how to shoot it. The first time I did, the concussion almost knocked me over."

"There's no concussion to a twenty-two. You like guns?"

"I love 'em. I love the way they look. I'm from out west. From Texas. I'm part Comanche."

"You're from Bloomington, Indiana, and then Milwaukee and then Omaha and then Chicago. You never saw an Indian but on a nickel. You can't shit me. How come you tell lies like that?"

"Nobody calls me a liar."

"Yes, they do. All the time they do. You wait till you grow up, you'll have all the guns you want, all the dope and all the women."

"I could go for that, I guess. I'm gonna join the Marines."

"You better believe it. That's the Training School tradition, you join the fucking Marines whether you want to or not. The social worker'll shame you into it. When you get down to Parris Island you'll recognize the other kids from the Training School because they steal."

"I'm a good stealer."

"No, no," Hicks said, "you cut that out, that's for punks. You'll wash the punk off you when you're out in the fleet. Just keep your mouth shut and watch how people do. Watch how the Japs do, they're the coolest people in the world."

Just as he had feared, he began to feel cold. His side began to hurt as though for the first time.

"I know you," Hicks said. "I wish I didn't but I do. You better do something about the way you cringe and whine. I don't want to see you do it. That's why I don't want you around here now."

He stared down at the tracks as he walked, the crossties one after another kept him going.

"For one thing it makes you weaker. For another

nobody gives a shit. Who are you whining *to?* People? They don't care.

"Look where we are kid, we're walking on salt, nobody gets us out of here but me. The people are over on the other side of those goofy and we don't need a single one of the son of a bitches."

He stopped and watched the mountains vibrate.

"You know what's out there? Every goddamn race of shit jerking each other off. Mom and Dad and Buddy and Sis, two hundred million rat-hearted cocksuckers in enormous cars. Rabbits and fish. They're mean and stupid and greedy, they'll fuck you for laughs, they want you dead. If you're no better than them you might as well take gas. If you can't get your own off them then don't stand there and let them spit on you, don't give them the satisfaction."

Careless of the pain, he unslung the rifle and propped the stock against his hip.

"Knuckle me, you fucking pig, I'll kill you. Go up on a bridge and let them have it, watch the motherfuckers die."

"I'll kill you," Hicks screamed.

"Ray," the old lady said, "don't get so mad. You'll just throw up on the tracks again."

"It wasn't me that did, Ma Ma. It was another kid I seen him."

Oh man, don't cringe. It's a terrible thing to cringe.

At the Training School, he was still pissing his pants at thirteen. He'd carry the underwear around with him, hidden, afraid to put it in the laundry bag because it was labeled. Hid it under the bed and then did the same with the next pair. Oh my God, two pairs of them all pissed on, they'll beat shit out of me.

Terrible thing.

Like the nigger who shined shoes in the basement of the enormous roadhouse they had near the Jacksonville stock-car track. Old man who went back to oughty ought. Whenever a drunk staggered down the stairs, he'd grin. Grin for all he was worth. The meaner the old boy who came in down to piss, the wider that grin got, big horse teeth straining under the lip meat.

Smiling through. Shit, maybe he was amused.

What's funny, boy?

No—there's no forgiveness for that, nobody can forgive anybody for making them *that* scared. No man forgives another man for scaring him like that.

There was a bullet-head priest in the German Catholic church on the Northside and one day he and his mother went there to beg. The squarehead slammed a fifty-cent piece down on a table so they went to North Avenue and had sundaes and saw *The Crusades*. Taking Jerusalem.

Thanks for the flick, you Kraut bastard, I wish I had your fat ass out here now.

God, Hicks thought, it just makes it hurt.

Dieter. Got him back on the mountain. Friendly fire. You couldn't hear him, you could only watch the way he was acting. He was asking for it. Cringing.

All those people. Marge.

Remember what this is for. Remember what it is you want or it won't make any difference. Sometimes it's work remembering.

Indifference to the ends of action—that's Zen. That's for old men.

It's worse. It's getting away.

Triangle.

It's distorted in the heat, it can't hold its shape.

Get up there you devil.

Gate gate paragate parasam gate bodhi swaha.

Again.

Gate gate paragate parasam gate bodhi swaha.

No not that one. You'll go out on that one.

Absolutely nothing out here, he thought, but me and the mountains and the salt. Nothing to manipulate, nothing to work with but the tracks. What a waste of awareness and coordination.

He worked on the triangle, honing its edges, cleansing it of salt, blotting out the image of the tracks. It was hard, but for a while the pain was contained. When it stopped him again, he took a drink of water and looked at his arm. His arm was enormous, so swollen within his sleeve that he could not take hold of the cloth between his fingers. It occurred to him that he might try making the triangle larger.

It worked. With what seemed to him extraordinary ease, the triangle's dimensions expanded, the red circle within it swelled and vibrated to the beating of his heart. He could make it as large as he chose, there was no limit.

The containment of pain, he realized suddenly, was the most marvelous and subtle of the martial arts, a spiritual discipline of the highest refinement. As his own pain eased, he came to understand that now he might carry within his mind and soul immense amounts of it. A master of the discipline, such as he was now becoming, might carry infinite amounts of pain. Far more than his own.

A lesser man, he thought, might consider making money out of this. He grew excited and his excitement almost caused him to fall and upset the infinite triangle.

He could do it for other people, for those not acquainted with the martial arts. If there was a way for all the people on the far side of the goofy mountains to let him have their pain, he could take it up and bear it across the salt.

Happy as he was, he began to cry because Dieter had not lived to hear of it.

All that cringing, all those crying women, whining kids—I don't want to see that, I don't like it. Give it here.

I don't want to see all you people so scared, it drives me nuts, it makes me mad. I'll take it.

That kid—some joker shot him off his water buffalo—I'll take care of that for you, junior.

Napalm burns, no problem—just put it on here.

Straighten up, pops. That's O.K., brother. Well I can't explain it to you but it's easy for me.

"All you people," Hicks shouted, "let it go! Let it go, you hear! I'm out here now. I got it."

They must know I'm out here now, he thought, they must be feeling it.

"Everybody! Everywhere! Close your eyes and let it go. You can't take it—you don't have to take it anymore. I'll do it all.

"You see me walking? You see me stepping out here? No—it doesn't bother me a bit."

No I don't require any assistance, beautiful, I do it all myself. That's what I'm here for.

Got it. Got it all now.

So there was always a reason, he thought. There had always been a reason. You never know until the moment comes and there it is.

He walked along and the triangle dissolved. There was no need for it.

In the course of things Marge would be there; he was pleased that he had not forgotten her. He wanted Converse too, Converse had always sold him short, always put him down a little. But he would understand it.

He loved them both—they would understand it and as lonely a business as it had to be, you wanted people sometimes, people who would understand it.

I don't know how it works, he told them, I do it because I can do it—it's as simple as that.

What are you carrying? someone asked.

"Pain, man. Everybody's. Yours too, if you only knew it."

What's the weapon for? What's in the bag?

The bag.

"It's mine," Hicks said. "I carry that too."

It's not necessary now.

It's not necessary but it's mine.

All right then. Maybe it's not so simple.

He reached behind his right shoulder and felt for the strap.

Can't get it off. Doesn't matter. Let's just say I carry what I carry and leave it at that.

It's not so simple because there are as many illusions as there are grains of sand in the goofy mountains and every one of them is lovable. The mind is a monkey.

The bastards, he thought, now they'll take it back.

Let them take it back then. Let them have all the illusion back. Strip it down, we'll have it whole. The answer is the thing itself.

So much for the pain carrier.

So much for the lover, the samurai, the Zen walker. The Nietzschean.

Take it all back.

Look, he told them, I can love those birds up there as much as anything in life. I don't need your charity.

After a while, he could no longer see the birds and he began to be frightened again.

I am not my five senses, he thought.

I am not this thought.

Though I walk through the valley of the shadow . . . Belay that.

In the end, there was only the tracks. That's enough, he said, to himself, I can dig tracks.

Out of spite, out of pride, he counted the crossties aloud. He counted hundreds and hundreds of them. When he had to stop, he leaned his head on his rifle and held to the blazing rail with his strong right hand.

T HE ROAD SOUTH AND WEST RAN BETWEEN YELLOW
hills, dappled with stands of live oak like fairy forts.

An hour after sunrise, they came to a diner with
drawn black shades across its windows and three
dusty pumps out front. Converse pulled in and sounded
the horn. After a minute or so, an old man wearing
a holstered pistol on his belt came out and filled their
tank, and watched Converse spark the wires.

"It's all different over here," Converse said, when
they were riding again. "You'd never guess that place
was back there."

Marge wiped her nose on a corner of the quilt
she had gathered around her.

"Are you badly?" Converse asked her.

"I don't know."

"Well," he said, "it can't be all that bad then."

He was so tired that he could barely keep his hands
on the wheel. He talked to keep himself awake.

"We might try going south," he said, "we're so
close to the border."

But the border was not the way. They would get lost
in the desert going overland, and if they drove south
of the frontier zone the Mexicans would demand all
manner of automobile registration and put stickers
everywhere.

"Maybe east," he said. But east was desolation,
a day and a half of dry barrens to be chased across.

"Do we know anyone in San Diego?" he asked
Marge.

"I don't."

"I like the idea of San Diego. If we get that far."

"He wants us to pick him up."

Converse was certain there would be no flats, no
place where tracks crossed the road. The clarity of

freshness of the dawn had encouraged him to aspire toward a reality in which there was no place for such corners.

"Why does this shit happen to me?" he asked Marge. "Do I like it?"

"You manage to handle it," she said.

"Handle it?" He was outraged.

"One thing I hate," he told her, "is tough-mindedness. It repels me."

"Sorry," she said.

"When the bomb fell on Hiroshima, my father was working in Twenty-One." Marge stirred in pain and turned her face toward the window. She had heard about it before.

"He kept the papers away from me when he came home. He never told me about it. He thought it would upset me."

"He was a nice guy," Marge said.

"Yes, he was. He was a very sensitive man. He never saw a light-up hidden valley, or an Elephant Bomb. Neither did his father. He would never have imagined such things."

"He's lucky he's dead," Marge said.

"They say the world is coming to an end. They say that's why it's so fucked up."

"Wishful thinking," Marge said. "The world will go on for a million years."

At the mention of a million years, Converse nearly fell asleep at the wheel. He caught himself in time and kept them on the road.

As they drove farther, the hills were lower and dryer—before long there were no more oaks to be seen and no more yellow grass. At last, the land was flat on both sides of the road, and they came to a grassless plain of mesquite and creosote bushes that stretched northward to the brown rims of the mountains. The outer ridges were steep and spired, capped with wind-worn fantasies that gave jagged edge to the horizon line. After several miles, they came to narrow tracks crossing the paved road. The tracks led northward into the emptiness, toward the ridge.

Converse stopped the car and climbed out. There was no one in sight, no other cars on the road in either direction. He leaned his folded arms on the square hood and put his head down.

"Listen to it," he said, when he had raised his head again, "it's incredible."

Marge shook her head impatiently.

"What?" she asked, almost pleadingly.

"The silence of it," he said. "It comes out of nothing to nowhere."

Marge got out and looked down the line of tracks.

"He's walking out there."

"I don't believe it, do you?"

"Yes," she said.

Converse got back in the Land-Rover.

"O.K. then. Let's get him."

She walked back to the vehicle and looked down at him in pity.

"Look," she said. "You could have gotten out. You were driving—you could have gone to a bus stop. You could have stayed back at that filling station."

"Don't trifle with me," Converse said. "We'll see if he's out there. We've got nothing better to do."

She got in.

"He'll have the dope."

"I daresay he will. And you'll like that, won't you? Because you can use some."

"I don't know."

"That's ridiculous," Converse said. "You must know whether you need to get straight or not. Everybody knows that."

"I want to get straight."

"Just give me a little reinforcement," he told her, "that's all I require."

He held the Land-Rover as close as possible to the tracks. Ruts and sinks that were insignificant to look at sent them off the seat. The road behind them became invisible; they dodged black ore-bearing rocks and ocotillo shrubs with whiplike branches.

"You want to get straight and you want to pick him up."

"I have to," she said.

"Don't you want to?"

"It's not a matter of what I want. I have to."

"So we've reached the level of inchoate need," Converse said. "That's the level we'll work on. That's where it's at."

Marge looked at him impatiently.

"I told you, you didn't have to come. What's the matter with you?"

"I'm tired."

It had become very hot inside the Land-Rover. Converse opened his shirt.

"Jesus, you're a drag," she said. "The way you are now."

Converse was not offended. He increased his speed as his familiarity with the nature of the ground increased. He wondered what the way he was now was like.

A short time later, Marge covered her face with her hands.

"It's insane. They'll get us for sure out here."

"There's nothing out here," Converse said. He was not certain what he meant by it. There was sand, and wind whipping the creosote and the shrouds of the jeep. There was the risk of cracking up. All real. He felt as though he had awakened from sleep to find himself driving within his own mind.

"It's a lousy place," he told Marge. "It's no place to be."

"I haven't been this scared ever," she told him.

"Probably physical. The mind-body problem extended."

"Please stop talking shit," she begged him.

The grim brown wall of the ridge grew larger before them.

"I see something," Marge said.

Because of the dips, Converse kept his gaze on the ground immediately ahead. At length he caught a glimpse of something blue beside the track. It had metal parts that the sun glinted on. He slowed as they came up to it.

When they got out, Marge started to run. Converse left the engine turning. Following her, he saw that it was Hicks beside the tracks. There was a rifle slung across his shoulder and a pack on his back. One side of his body was covered in dried blood; one of his hands rested on the rail. Some bluebottle flies had gathered over the wound under his arm.

Marge stood looking at him and then ran back to the jeep. She came back carrying a canteen full of water.

"He's in shock," she said softly.

"No," Converse said, "he's dead."

He walked over, looked down at Hicks, and at the mountains beyond. They were miles and miles away. It was incredible to Converse that he had carried so much weight so far. Lifting the flap of the pack, he saw that the dope was inside.

Marge started to sit down on the rail, but it was hot and she rose from it quickly. She sprawled on the white dust, brushed the bluebottles from Hicks' side, and cried.

Converse watched her. For all her wastedness she looked quite beautiful in her tears. He might, he thought, if things were different, have fallen in love with her again right there. He was not without emotions and it was very moving. Real. Maybe even worth coming out for.

He looked around him at the blanched and empty land to see what it was he felt. Fear. Sparkling on the gun metal, twinkling in the mesquite. A permanent condition.

Marge swayed in her grief; the wind that stirred the dust blew her hair and molded her skirt to her body. When she stopped crying, she lifted the flap of the backpack and scooped some of the dope from it with the sleeve of her jacket. She picked up the canteen she had brought and went back to the Land-Rover.

Converse came and stood over Hicks—in a moment he found himself trying to brush the flies away. He had seen so much more blood, he thought, than he had ever thought to see.

Marge's teared eye measured the liquor in her needle. Converse watched the throb of blood rise in the tube.

"We lost him," he told Marge.

She was bent at the waist; she rested the top of her head on the seat next to her.

"He wasn't the only one. Sauve qui peut."

When she did not straighten up, he became concerned.

"Marge?"

She came out of it.

"Marge, can you see me? Can you hear me?"

"Yes, of course," she said.

"We have to go, baby. We can't stay and grieve or we'll be just as dead as he is."

She seemed less pale, her eyes less dull. She made a sound in her throat.

"Marge?"

"Does it matter?" she asked him with a smile.

Converse considered her question.

"I don't know. But nobody's replaceable."

"John," she said, "you are so full of shit. Honestly—you're a bad guy."

He had begun to pace beside the sputtering jeep, turning on his heel.

"We came after him, for Christ's sake. I'm really going to try not to regret it.

"In the worst of times," he began to tell her, "there's something."

"Ha," Marge said. "There's smack." She watched

him pace in bewilderment. "In the worst of times there's something? What?"

"There's us."

Marge laughed.

"Us? You and me? That's something?"

"Everybody," Converse said. "You know."

"Sure," Marge said, "that's why it's so shitty."

Converse shook his head and walked back to where Hicks lay. It was a difficult point to make in the circumstances. He hunkered down beside Hicks and wondered if he would have understood what it was that he sought to say.

The thought came to him that if, years before, in the Yokasuka geedunk, they had been able to see how everything would end, they would probably have done it all anyway. Fun and games, amor fati. Semper fi.

"Peace," he said to Hicks.

Turning away, he looked toward the mountains and saw a column of dust rising from the valley floor along the edge of the tracks. It rose at the wake of something that moved; the wind carried it upward and whirled it.

He stood for a moment fighting panic; then it occurred to him that one thing to do would be to button down the pack flap so that the dope would not blow away—so that it would be there for them. When he had buttoned it, he took a folded Kleenex from his pocket and tied it on the strap of the pack. Then he sprinted for the jeep and threw it in gear.

"We're running, baby," he told her. "The bastards are behind us again."

He could not see what it was at the core of the cloud, but it moved slowly; in a few minutes he had put a comfortable piece of barrenness between themselves and the thing that came.

"If they come up," Marge said, "if they have guns—if they say stop—we won't stop. We'll just keep going."

334

"Right," Converse said. He watched the cloud approach in the rearview mirror.

"Who is it?" Marge asked.

Watching it, Converse began to laugh as he pressed down harder on the gas. The column rose, a whirling white tower with a dark core, spewing gauzy eddies from its spout, its funnel curving to the shiftings of the wind—the gross and innocent measure of some drugged, freakish process. In the mirror it seemed to fill the sky.

"Look at it," he said to Marge. "Look at it in the mirror."

Marge leaned over to where she could see the mirror, turned to look behind them, then turned back to the mirror again. Her face flushed, her eyes grew wide.

"Oh God," she cried. A burst of spitty laughter broke over her lips. "Oh my God, look at it."

She leaned out of the window and screamed back at the column.

"Fuck you," she shouted. "Fuck you—fuck you."

When they reached the road again, the column had settled, the thing had stopped. There were still no cars in sight.

"Let it be," Converse said.

ANTHEIL AND HIS COLLEAGUE ANGEL RODE ACROSS the flats on a Michigan articulated loader. It belonged to Galindez and it had dug several of Dieter's trails.

The loader was a reliable vehicle for rough country and very expensive but it had a speed of less than twenty miles an hour. It was no good for chasing anyone unless he was on foot.

Antheil swept the plain with his binoculars, perched,

like Rommel, on the wing of the machine. When he saw the parked Land-Rover, he picked up his Mossberg and cocked the hammer but he did not fire—in the hope that its occupants might be asleep or stoned.

"As I said," Angel told him.

It was Angel who had suggested that Hicks might walk out and who had found the loader.

As Antheil watched, the Land-Rover started up and sped southward toward the road, in a trail of white dust. It was not even worth a shot at the distance. Antheil became extremely upset, but he kept his temper in bounds because he did not want to seem undignified before Angel. There had been far too many lapses already.

He let his binoculars dangle and turned his gaze upward to see if there were any aircraft in view—but the morning sky was untroubled. When he scanned the flats again, he saw Hicks' body beside the track.

He jumped down from the loader's cab before Angel had parked it and ran to where Hicks lay. There was a pack on the corpse's back with a little pennant of white tissue tied to it. He lifted the flap and saw that the heroin was inside.

He stood up with a tense smile.

The sight of Angel sitting above him on the loader's seat made him a bit uncomfortable.

"It's there?" Angel asked.

"Yes," he said after a moment.

"Well, you bastard," he said to Hicks, "you led us a merry goddamn chase." He kicked the corpse's shoulder. Angel nodded in sympathy.

He stood for a moment, staring after the Land-Rover's dust, and then looked down at the pack again. Reaching down, he tore the rag of Kleenex from the strap.

"What the hell's this?"

"Surrender," Angel said.

Antheil wiped the sweat from his eyes.

"Is that what it is?" He crumpled the tissue and threw it away.

"These people are so fucked up, it devastates the mind. They're utterly unpredictable—absolute mental basket cases. You have no idea what associating with them can do to you."

He did not trouble to translate for Angel.

It was a bedlam, a Chinese fire drill. He would have to draw strongly on his reputation for efficiency and rectitude, and then leave the country at the very first practical opportunity. It was a bit untidy, but there was no compromising evidence and even if some entertained doubts, the agency might be content to let him withdraw gracefully. Others had left the service in circumstances as potentially compromising. In the place to which he planned to repair with Charmian, he might do them some service from time to time, should they discover him. He had many friends there, and no one would trouble him. It was a country where everybody did it.

In many ways, he thought, the adventure had been instructive. His heart filled with native optimism.

If you stuck with something, the adventure demonstrated, faced down every kind of pressure, refused to fold when the going got tough, outplayed all adversaries, and relied on your own determination and fortitude, then the bag of beans at the end of the rainbow might be yours after all.

The Converses were a sore, an itch—but he would have to live with them. It was not likely, being who they were, that they would undertake to spoil things.

He took the parcel of dope from the pack, showed it to Angel, and put it in the loader's toolbox.

"The bag of beans," he said.

"Beans?" Angel asked.

Angel was causing him some anxiety. It was a lonely place, and the dope was very valuable; he would have to be on his toes. With Mexicans, he reminded himself, and with people like them, it was command voice and assured presence that counted.

"We'll bury him," he told Angel.

"We can dump him over the line," Angel said.

Antheil grimaced at the indolence and fecklessness such a proposal indicated. The *mañana* spirit.

"No, *hombre*. We can bury him in the hills. We have the very machine." He looked at his watch. "Then we call for assistance."

He leaned an arm against the loader's tire and looked skyward.

"We have been holding the property under surveillance," he informed Angel. "You and I—old friends from neighboring countries, working on our own time. A hunch. During our surveillance a ripoff ensued, a dispute among smugglers of dope. Some were killed, others escaped."

"With the dope," Angel said.

"Precisely," Antheil said. *"Precisamente."*

They got Hicks aboard the loader, and Angel looked over the horizon for a suitable wash. The wind played hell with tracks, and in a day or so even the traces of a substantial displacement would be obliterated. They could put thirty tons of desert over him.

Riding toward the hills, Antheil's uneasiness about Angel began to dissipate. He slapped him on the back and Angel smiled in gratitude.

Angel, Antheil thought, was the sort of officer who was bent out of principle, so as not to be thought of as a fool. It was not venality that made him a crook, merely tradition. Antheil reflected that his service had brought him in contact with many peoples and cultures other than his own.

An anecdote occurred to him, and he thought it was one that Angel might particularly appreciate.

"Someone told me once," he said, "something that I've always remembered. This fellow said to me—if you think someone's doing you wrong, it's not for you to judge. Kill them first and then God can do the judging."

He began to translate for Angel, but then thought better of it.